Praise for
THE HISTORY KEEPERS series

'Move over Harry Potter, it is time for Jake Djones
to take the limelight' – *Telegraph*

'There are desperate chases and hair-raising escapes and
Errol Flynn-style swordfights, complicated traps . . .
a complete 16th-century Venetian travelogue and
more comical or eccentric secondary characters
than you could shake a wand at' – *Guardian*

'A great read' – *The Bookseller*

'If you've got *Harry Potter* withdrawal, *The History Keepers*
is just the thing. A cocktail of time travel, secret societies,
double agents and edge-of-your-seat excitement, it's sure
to fill that fantasy void. The only problem? You won't
be able to put it down' – *Glamour*

'A rollicking rollercoaster of a tale that barely pauses
for breath . . . It's pure entertainment' – *INIS*

'Today's answer to *Harry Potter* crossed with
The Hunger Games' – *Tatler*

'The plot is superfast, and is just the kind of story that
could suck in even the most reluctant of
readers' – *bookzone4boys*

www.**randomhousechildrens**.co.uk

Also available in *The History Keepers* sequence:

The History Keepers: The Storm Begins

THE
HISTORY
KEEPERS
CIRCUS MAXIMUS

DAMIAN DIBBEN

CORGI BOOKS

THE HISTORY KEEPERS: CIRCUS MAXIMUS
A CORGI BOOK 978 0552 56429 8

First published in Great Britain by Doubleday,
an imprint of Random House Children's Publishers UK
A Random House Group Company

Doubleday edition published 2012
Corgi edition published 2013

1 3 5 7 9 10 8 6 4 2

The Random House Group Limited supports the Forest Stewardship Council® (FSC®),
the leading international forest-certification organisation. Our books carrying the FSC label are
printed on FSC®-certified paper. FSC is the only forest-certification scheme supported by the
leading environmental organisations, including Greenpeace. Our paper procurement
policy can be found at www.randomhouse.co.uk/environment

Corgi Books are published by Random House Children's Publishers UK,
61–63 Uxbridge Road, London W5 5SA

www.**randomhousechildrens**.co.uk
www.**totallyrandombooks**.co.uk
www.**randomhouse**.co.uk

Addresses for companies within The Random House Group Limited
can be found at: www.randomhouse.co.uk/offices.htm

THE RANDOM HOUSE GROUP Limited Reg. No. 954009

A CIP catalogue record for this book is available from the British Library.

Printed and bound in the UK by CPI Group (UK) Ltd, Croydon, CR0 4YY

For the mad and marvellous
Morrisons of Derw Mill

1 THE QUEEN OF THE NIGHT

The night Jake Djones brought total disgrace upon himself and jeopardized the very survival of the History Keepers' Secret Service was so unnaturally, bitterly cold that the Baltic Sea almost froze over.

From the rocky, windswept shores of Denmark in the west to the frozen remoteness of Finland in the north, an endless expanse of ice – as thin as gossamer and a ghostly silver in the moonlight – curved across the horizon. A continual dusting of soft snow seemed to silence this far corner of the Earth in an otherworldly hush.

A ship with blue sails broke through the veneer of ice even as it was forming, heading for the twinkling lights of Stockholm – a fairytale archipelago of bays, promontories and islets.

The ship was called the *Tulip*, and at the creaking wheel stood a tall figure in a long fur coat. He reached out an elegant gloved hand and rang the bell. 'It's time, gentlemen,' he announced in a soft Charleston drawl.

Immediately two more silhouettes, both well wrapped up, came out of the snowy darkness and joined him at the helm, followed by a brightly coloured bird – a parrot – who nestled, shivering, on his master's shoulders. They gazed out eagerly through the snow as the ship sailed on towards the port. Their faces were slowly illuminated . . .

The figure in fur was strikingly handsome, a smile playing across his chiselled face. Next to him stood the owner of the parrot – a shorter boy with spectacles, his brows raised in a studious frown. The last person had olive skin, curly dark hair and big brown eyes that blinked with excitement. Three intrepid adolescents, young agents of the History Keepers' Secret Service: Nathan Wylder, Charlie Chieverley . . . and Jake Djones.

Charlie was the first to speak. 'Head for that central island there,' he said, pointing towards a group of spires and towers. 'That's Stadsholmen, Stockholm's old town – the grand jewel of these islands, centre of the Swedish Empire. Though sadly, of course, we're not arriving in the city's heyday. In 1710 our old friend the plague came here, taking out nearly a third of the population.'

'Not arriving in its heyday?' drawled Nathan, pulling his coat tighter against the snow. 'That's putting it mildly. Sweden in the winter of 1782 has got to be the most inhospitable place in history.' He produced a tiny box from his pocket and applied lip salve. 'If my lips get any drier, they'll fall off.'

'Hell's bells, Nathan, '92!' Charlie exclaimed, closing his eyes and clenching his teeth in annoyance. 'We're in 1792. Honestly, I sometimes wonder how you made it this far.' Mr Drake – that was the name of his pet parrot – squawked in agreement, puffing up his feathers indignantly at the American.

'I'm pulling your leg.' Nathan smirked. 'Do you really think I'd be wearing this ankle-length sable coat in 1782? Not to mention these buckle-less riding boots – so austere they're practically Napoleonic.' He turned to Jake. 'The 1790s are all about dressing down.' Nathan loved clothes almost as much as he loved an adventure.

'Buckle-less riding boots, my aunt,' Charlie

muttered to himself. 'And don't even get me started on your sable coat. It's a work of barbaric savagery. Those poor animals had the right to a life as well, you know.'

As Jake listened to their banter, he felt a great swelling of pride at the thought that he belonged to the greatest and most mysterious organization of all time: the History Keepers' Secret Service.

Just a month had passed since his life had changed for ever. He had been kidnapped, taken to the London bureau and informed that his parents had been secretly working for the service for decades – and indeed had gone missing in sixteenth-century Italy!

From then on it had been a nonstop roller-coaster ride. He had travelled through time, first to Point Zero – the History Keepers' headquarters on the Mont St Michel in Normandy, 1820 – and then to Venice in 1506, as part of the mission to find his mum and dad, and to stop the diabolical Prince Zeldt from destroying Europe with bubonic plague.

He had been reunited with his folks – but they had left behind Topaz, the mysterious and beautiful young agent to whom he had become devoted.

Most extraordinary of all, he had discovered that his beloved brother Philip, who had apparently died in an accident abroad three years ago, had also been a History Keeper; there was a chance – a very slim chance – that he was actually alive somewhere in the past.

And now Jake was already on his second mission. Admittedly he had been selected more through luck than anything else (nearly everyone at Point Zero had come down with an appalling tummy bug after eating mussel soup, and agents were thin on the ground), and it was not a dangerous assignment – otherwise he would definitely not have been included, as he was still a novice. But nonetheless here he was, travelling to the Baltic in the 1790s to collect a consignment of atomium, the precious liquid that made travelling through history possible.

'So, tell me something about the person we're meeting,' he said, trying to hide the tremor in his voice.

'Caspar Isaksen the Third?' Charlie shrugged. 'Not personally acquainted, but he's our age, I believe. I cooked a pumpkin tagine for his father once. He said it would live with him for ever.' Charlie loved food with a passion and was an expert cook – although an experience in the kitchens of Imperial Paris had left him a staunch vegetarian.

'*I've* been personally acquainted with Caspar Isaksen the Third. Twice,' drawled Nathan with a roll of his eyes. 'You can't really miss him – he eats cakes like they're going out of fashion, and never stops sneezing.'

'So what is the Isaksens' connection with atomium?' Jake persisted. He had learned all about this substance on his first voyage. To travel to a particular point in the past, agents had to drink a dilution of it, mixed with exact precision. Generally it worked only out at sea, in the magnetic maelstrom of a *horizon point*; and then only on the few humans with *valour* – an innate ability to travel through the ages. The History Keepers needed this precious liquid in order to watch over history, protecting the past from dark forces that sought to destroy it and plunge the world into darkness.

'The Isaksens *are* atomium,' replied Charlie. 'The family have been in charge of its production for more than two hundred years. As you know, it's notoriously tricky to make. To produce an effective batch, its ingredients – which themselves are kept a secret from all but a handful of keepers – have to be refined over a period of years . . .'

'Decades, I'd say,' Nathan added.

'Quite,' Charlie continued, 'and it must be created in freezing conditions. That's why Sejanus Poppoloe, the founder of the History Keepers, set up the laboratory in northern Sweden. After he had done so, back in the 1790s, he handed duties over to Frederick Isaksen, the first of the line. To this very day, *all* atomium – as used by every bureau in the world – has been created in the Isaksens' laboratory.'

'So, why are we meeting in Stockholm and not at the actual laboratory?' Jake asked.

'Dear me,' Charlie sighed, 'you *have* got a lot to learn. No one goes to the laboratory. *No one* has the slightest idea where it is, not even Commander Goethe.'

Jake stared back in surprise. Surely if anyone knew where the laboratory was based, it would be Galliana Goethe – the commander of the History Keepers for the past three years.

'Only the Isaksens keep the secret and pass it on,' Charlie continued. 'Can you imagine the disaster if its location got into the wrong hands? Catastrophe times infinity!'

'There's a myth,' Nathan said, 'that it's set within

a mountain, accessed through a secret limestone cave.'

'In any case,' Charlie concluded, 'when the atomium is ready, a member of the family delivers it to a prearranged location. As Caspar Isaksen is a fan of the opera, like me, the opera house was the venue chosen on this occasion. And not a moment too soon,' he added sombrely. 'Atomium stocks at Point Zero are at an all-time low. This consignment is vital.'

'So no slip-ups from the new boy,' Nathan said mischievously, thumping Jake on the back.

Jake looked around at the port. There were ships everywhere, an intricate forest of masts and rigging. Along the shore, depots and warehouses teemed with activity as sailors and tradesmen, their breath visible in the freezing air, worked into the evening, loading and unloading their cargoes: iron, copper and tin; crates of wax, resin and amber; sacks of rye and wheat; consignments of animal furs; and end-less boxes of shining fish. Mr Drake surveyed the bustle with a keen eye, always intrigued – and just a touch nervous – when arriving at a new destina-tion.

The *Tulip* docked in a narrow berth next to

a huge warship. Jake and Nathan gawped up at her great rounded hull punctuated by two cannon decks. High up on her starboard side a cluster of sailors, thick-necked and shaven-headed, stood talking in gruff voices.

Nathan caught their eye and lifted his fur hat in a flamboyant gesture. 'Lovely evening for the opera, wouldn't you say?' The sailors ignored him completely.

'You be a good boy and stay here.' Charlie stroked Mr Drake and gave him some peanuts. 'We shan't be long.' The parrot watched the three young agents jump down onto the quay.

They pulled their coats tight and, stepping carefully across the icy cobbles, made their way through the bustle of people streaming along the dock. Jake glanced at the stalls selling cooked meats, salted fish and wooden cups of steaming cider. His attention was caught by a fortune-teller shrouded in a lace shawl, her wizened hand clutching tarot cards. She held them up to Jake, imploring him to listen to his destiny. He stopped briefly, his eye drawn by the card at the top of the pack: a smiling skeleton in front of a moonlit sea. The fortune-teller's eyes opened ominously, swimming in cloudy grey.

'Let's not get involved,' said Nathan, firmly taking Jake's arm and guiding him on. 'She probably works for the tourist office.'

The three of them skirted round the royal palace, then crossed a wide timber bridge into the formal square in front of the opera house – a graceful three-tiered building capped by a giant stone crown. A steady stream of carriages was arriving, from which the cream of Stockholm's society – all wrapped in furs – disembarked and entered the building.

'Opera?' Nathan complained. 'Is there anything more ridiculous? Overweight people warbling on about nothing! Couldn't that rogue Isaksen have arranged a rendezvous somewhere more appropriate?'

'How dare you, Nathan Wylder! How dare you!' Charlie fumed. 'This is a wonderful performance of Mozart's *The Magic Flute*. It was written only a year ago. The ink is barely dry on the manuscript and the great man is already dead – God rest his soul. It's a once-in-a-lifetime opportunity.'

Nathan pulled a guilty face at Jake and the three of them forged on through the crowds to the entrance.

Meanwhile two figures on horseback emerged

from the shadows on the other side of the square, their gaze fixed on the three agents. They dismounted, and the first, dressed in a high-collared coat, stepped into the half-light of a street lantern. He was tall, upright, and had straight shoulder-length fair hair. His accomplice wore a dark cloak and a distinctive wide-brimmed hat. The blond man whispered something in his companion's ear, gave him charge of his horse, then hurried across the square in pursuit.

Jake's eyes lit up at the sight of the foyer. In contrast to the wintry gloom outside, it was an immense space of white marble and gilded mirrors, lit by constellations of chandeliers. Its inhabitants were as magnificent as the surroundings: poised, elegant people, the polished black boots of the men and the long silk dresses of the ladies reflected in the gleaming floor. Many were arranged in chattering clusters; others were ascending a grand staircase, their eyes eagerly scanning the crowds for the latest source of scandal.

Nathan was in his element. 'I genuinely think this might be one of fashion's all-time greatest moments,' he announced, sweeping off his fur coat to reveal a splendid ultramarine jacket and breeches. 'Look at the silhouettes, look at the detailing, the sheer pizzazz. Their buttons alone could win prizes.'

An attendant wearing a coiffed wig, white gloves and an expression of loathing helped Jake and Charlie out of their coats. Jake's hand caught in his sleeve, and an undignified tussle was followed by the sound of ripping.

'Ooops.' He blushed and tried to stifle a giggle as he passed it to the man. The attendant merely sighed, collected all three overcoats and exchanged them for ivory counters with golden numbers before he withdrew.

'And be careful with my coat,' Nathan called after him. 'It was worn by the Duke of Marlborough at the Battle of Blenheim.' He then confided to Jake, 'Not really, but you can never be too careful with vintage fur.'

A bell sounded and the opera-goers started making their way into the auditorium.

'Well, we might as well get it over with,' Nathan sighed. 'The opera is not going to bore itself. Where are our seats?'

'Royal circle, box M,' Charlie replied curtly, indicating the next tier.

The three of them headed up the stairs, oblivious to the figure with long blond hair, who watched them keenly from behind a pillar.

Another white-gloved attendant led them along a candle-lit corridor and through a door into their private box. It was a small room lined in dark red, with four gilt chairs and a spectacular view of the auditorium. Jake felt another surge of excitement – it was like being inside a giant jewellery case. Five tiers rose up from the stalls in a sweeping oval shape, each containing a succession of private boxes with a batch of gossiping aristocrats. It was like some crazy human zoo – everyone was looking around and whispering slyly to their neighbours.

'Well, where *is* Caspar Isaksen?' asked Nathan with a wry look at the empty chair. 'He's late.' He picked up a pair of silver opera glasses laid out on a side table. 'I suppose, while I am here, I may as well study some Swedish architecture . . .' He started to scan the space with the binoculars – and then stopped. 'Intriguing . . .'

Charlie turned to see that the object of Nathan's attention was a box containing three young ladies, coyly blushing at him from behind their fans.

'Oh, please concentrate,' he sighed. 'This is

work, remember.' He snatched the glasses and passed them to Jake. 'I'm sure *you'll* find something more interesting to look at.'

Jake examined the audience more closely. He half fancied inspecting Nathan's three beauties for himself, but felt it would be rude, so he started at the other end of the tier. He had never seen so much wealth, so many expensive clothes and glittering jewels. Suddenly his binoculars picked out a young girl in a white dress sitting on her own. There was something about her that reminded him of Topaz. He felt a pang as he remembered that dreadful night aboard the *Lindwurm* when she had disappeared, probably for ever, into the vortex of time. To take his mind off the memory, he swiftly continued along the row. Two boxes on, his gaze alighted upon a fair-haired man pointing a silver pistol directly towards him.

Jake gasped, dropped the binoculars, picked them up, looked through them again, shook his head, turned them the right way round and quickly searched for the box once more.

It was empty. The man was nowhere to be seen.

'What on earth is wrong with you?' Nathan asked.

'The box over there! There was a man pointing a gun.'

Nathan and Charlie examined the offending box. An elderly gentleman and his wife were now taking their seats.

'He's gone now, but I promise you I saw him.'

Nathan and Charlie gave each other a look.

'You're new to this' – Nathan meant to be reassuring, but of course it came out as condescending – 'so you're jumpy, that's all. It's the opera; everyone is spying on everyone else. That's the name of the game.'

'He wasn't spying. He was pointing a gun, a silver gun,' Jake insisted.

'Silver?' Nathan noted. 'You're quite sure they weren't opera glasses?'

In truth, Jake wasn't one hundred per cent certain. The moment had been so fleeting.

'Besides, not a soul knows we're here. Only Commander Goethe has our exact time location, so let's not panic.' Nathan leaned over and whispered in Jake's ear, 'If I were you, I'd be more frightened of what's about to happen out there.' He pointed at the stage.

Jake nodded and tried to calm his thumping heart.

An excited hush descended around the theatre as the lights started to fade. A moment later, the orchestra suddenly struck up in a great fanfare of horns and bass drums. Jake once again scanned the tiers of people in search of the blond man, but there were just too many people. Everyone was leaning forward, eyeglasses poised. Another blast of trumpets, and then the violins began.

Jake felt a chill go down his spine as the curtains slowly rose, revealing a dark landscape. At first this was difficult to make out, but a series of lighting effects, each one drawing sighs of admiration from the crowd, gradually illuminated the stage: in the background, a huge moon hung above mountains and pyramids; in the foreground stood palm trees and giant flowers.

'We're in Egypt,' Charlie whispered in awed tones, 'in the realm of the Queen of the Night. In a moment Tamino is going to enter, pursued by a giant serpent.'

'It's a roller coaster,' added Nathan, stifling a yawn.

There was a soft ripple of applause as the young hero materialized out of the desert mist, then fearful sighs as a giant snake curled down from above. At the sight of this, Jake froze. He knew the reptile was nothing but a piece of stage machinery – albeit a very convincing one – but memories quickly came flooding back. It was only a short time ago that he had been thrown into a hideous chamber of snakes and ladders. At the last minute he had been saved by two other History Keepers' agents – his mum and dad, actually – but the incident had left a scar.

Gradually the stage filled with curious characters: three mysterious ladies in veils, a man dressed as a bird – 'Mr Drake would have hooted with laughter,' Charlie commented – then, heralded by ominous claps of thunder, a majestic, fantastical figure took shape out of the stars.

'*That's* the Queen of the Night,' Charlie murmured as she emerged high above the others. 'She's going to ask Tamino to save her daughter from the clutches of the evil sorcerer Sarastro. It seems like she's this frightened mother,' he carried on breathlessly, 'but actually she's the villain and wants to steal the sun and plunge the world into darkness.'

'Don't they all? Mothers-in-law?' Nathan said

with a mischievous smile.

Jake was so hypnotized by this figure, so lost in her spine-tingling voice, so focused on her evil eyes, that when a knock came at the door behind him, he jumped in shock.

He and his companions turned round.

Another knock came, but this time it was followed by three sneezes and then a high voice: 'It's me, Caspar.'

All three of them gave sighs of relief. Nathan opened up and Caspar Isaksen squeezed himself into the box. Jake stared. Caspar was his age, but as wide as he was short, with ruddy cheeks, a runny nose and crazy fair hair going off in all directions. He had a worried smile and glistened with a layer of perspiration. He wore a bright turquoise jacket and breeches that were far too small for him, and Jake noticed that he had done up his buttons wrong.

'Sorry – so sorry I'm late,' Caspar puffed, madly wiping his nose and dabbing his forehead with a handkerchief. 'Hello. Caspar Isaksen . . .' He shook Jake's hand, then Charlie's. 'Ah, Nathan! We've met, of course. As you can see, I didn't forget your advice – you said turquoise would do wonders for my figure. I *never* wear anything else,' he added with great pride, then turned to show off his outfit from all sides and caught sight of the stage for the first time. 'Good heavens! The Queen of the Night is already on! Has she sent Tamino on his mission? She's a sly one, isn't she?'

Nathan was already losing patience. 'Yes, yes – but business first. I take it the atomium's in there?' he asked with a nod towards the holdall in Caspar's hand.

'The atomium is—' Caspar froze mid-sentence, holding up his finger. Jake was just wondering what was going to happen next when suddenly the other boy sneezed. Then again; and a third time for luck.

'Sorry, sorry,' Caspar sighed, wiping his face with his damp handkerchief. 'You're quite right – business first.' He knelt down, opened his case and started to remove the contents. Jake, Nathan and Charlie watched, bewildered, as he unloaded cake after cake after cake. 'I couldn't come to Stockholm without paying a visit to Sundbergs Konditori. Strawberry custard, cinnamon bun, Christmas knäck – yummy yummy,' he muttered as he laid them out one by one.

Finally, from the bottom of the bag, he retrieved a small veneered box. He wiped off a layer of icing sugar and a dollop of cream, and passed it to Nathan. A concentrated stillness descended on the agents. Jake could see that the top of the box was inscribed with an elaborate I – for Isaksen. Nathan opened it, and a golden light shimmered across their faces.

Inside, in a midnight-blue casing, lay two crystal vials, each full to the brim of the infinitely precious liquid.

'That's one consignment for Point Zero,' said Caspar in a more business-like tone, 'and one for the Chinese bureau.'

Nathan was just closing the case when Jake caught sight of a face in the crowd and his stomach churned. Down in the stalls, everyone was looking in the same direction, their faces bathed in light from the stage – except for one person: the blond man seated in the far corner, who was staring fixedly up at them.

'There!' Jake shouted out, pointing at him.

Nathan, Charlie and Caspar turned at once and saw the figure quickly rise from his seat, a silver pistol in his hand. Nathan snatched the opera glasses from Jake and used them to follow the man as he ran up the aisle and stormed through the double doors.

'We've been compromised!' he exclaimed. 'Back to the ship immediately!' He chucked the binoculars back at Jake and carefully took hold of the box of atomium. He adjusted something – Jake couldn't see what – inside, then flung open the door and looked both ways along the curving corridor: nothing but flickering candelabra. 'Charlie, you go that way. Whoever gets to the *Tulip* first, prepare to set sail straight away.'

In a heartbeat, Charlie was racing along the corridor and disappearing down the stairs at the end.

'Jake, Caspar, come with me!' Nathan barked. Caspar was hurriedly picking up his cakes and putting them back in his bag. 'Now!'

Nathan led the way, heading in the opposite direction to Charlie. Jake followed, with Caspar wheezing behind. Footsteps approached from the other end of the passage and a figure appeared.

The three agents froze. Time seemed to stand still as Jake saw their adversary clearly for the first time. He was the same age as Nathan – sixteen or there-abouts – and in many ways a crueller, fair-haired version of him. He had striking features, a superior look in his eye and, judging by his tailored clothes, the same pride in his appearance. His hair, in particular, was a work of art: long, blond and perfectly straight.

Jake could see that Nathan had gone pale.

'Who in God's name is that—' the American started to say as the man raised his pistol – and fired.

2 THE WIDE-BRIMMED HAT

The bullet whistled over their heads and struck one of the crystal chandeliers. It came down on the floor behind them with a crash.

'That was a warning shot,' the boy announced silkily in a slight foreign accent. 'You will give me the box,' he said, holding out his hand as he advanced. 'Resistance is pointless. Your sword is no match for my Chaumette flintlock,' he added with a shake of his beautifully crafted gun.

There was a pause, then Nathan spoke calmly. 'All right,' he said, lifting his hands, with the box in clear view. 'I'm not prepared to die over a couple of bottles of *the undrinkable*. You win.'

'Nathan?' Jake exclaimed in disbelief.

'No, I don't think that's such a good idea...' Caspar whimpered. He was peering over Jake's shoulder and mopping his brow with his handkerchief.

Nathan ignored them, keeping his attention on the stranger. 'What's your name?' he asked politely. 'I don't believe we've met.'

The blond boy sniggered. 'Impertinent question.' But after a pause, he shrugged and replied, 'You can call me the Leopard.'

'Leopard? Great moniker.'

'*The* Leopard,' the boy snarled with a shake of his perfect fair hair. 'I'm one of a kind.'

'That I can see,' Nathan concurred. 'Your double-breasted waistcoat is *way* ahead of its time, and the Chinese button detailing on your breeches is, frankly, sublime.'

The smile on the Leopard's face faded. 'Just hand over the box.' He levelled his pistol with one hand while holding out the other.

Nathan clenched his jaw, took a deep breath and gave it to him.

Just for a second as he opened the box, the boy took his eye off Nathan – and saw that it was empty. Then everything happened at once. Nathan snatched Caspar's sodden handkerchief and threw it into the Leopard's face, where it stuck, blinding him completely. The gun went off, but the bullet went through the ceiling. Nathan kicked high and smashed his boot into his opponent's jaw. The boy teetered backwards, lost his balance completely and landed in a tangle on the floor, his head giving a *crack* as it hit the wall.

'I lied – those Chinese buttons are the height of vulgarity,' Nathan said as he and the others escaped down the corridor. At the far end, he threw open the door to another box and quickly pushed Jake and Caspar inside. He bolted the entrance behind them and turned to face the occupants. It was the three pretty ladies he had spied earlier.

They stood in shock, clutching the jewels around their necks, but clearly relishing the intrusion. 'Under different circumstances' – Nathan tossed his auburn locks and showed his glinting teeth – 'this might have been hello and not goodbye . . . Quickly, you two,' he said, throwing his legs over the balcony and jumping down into the stalls, provoking murmurs of annoyance amongst the audience. As he hit the carpet, the bottles of atomium slipped out of his pocket. He quickly scooped them up.

Jake nodded politely at the girls, while Caspar

froze, turning crimson and clutching his bag of cakes to his chest. As Jake helped him to clamber over the balustrade, the unfortunate girls were treated to the sight of his bright turquoise trousers ripping – revealing a half-moon of large pink backside. They tore even more as Caspar awkwardly scrambled his way to the floor – giving the whole audience a glimpse of his derrière. Jake followed with a single athletic vault. As he landed, Nathan pressed the two bottles of atomium into Jake's hand. 'Holes in my pockets,' he said, patting his jacket. 'You hold onto them.'

Jake felt a sudden flutter of panic, of daunting responsibility, but he slipped them into the deep pouches inside his jacket.

'This way,' Nathan commanded, skirting round the auditorium to the exit at the back. He stopped dead when he saw the Leopard swing through the doors, then turned on his heel and cut straight along a row of seats. The others followed, apologizing as they pushed their way past the acres of fine silk and crinoline. Caspar yanked up his trousers, tripping over their priceless shoes and shedding chunks of Christmas knäck as he did so, provoking jeers of outrage; one ancient lady was so furious, she bashed him over the head with her fan.

'Quickly, quickly.' Jake pushed him into the aisle. The Leopard was now bearing swiftly down on them and they had no choice but to run up the steps at the front of the auditorium. A great swathe of opera-goers half stood in astonishment as the three of them shuffled over the bridge spanning the orchestra pit and onto the stage itself. The Queen of the Night did not falter in her aria; rather she focused her falsetto fury on the invaders, hurling notes at them like barbed daggers.

The Leopard quickened his pace and was on the point of firing his pistol again when a number of guards – they'd evidently been alerted to an incident – quickly filed in through the side doors, muskets at the ready. The Leopard froze and slowly replaced his weapon in its holster. Realizing that it would be madness to try anything now, he reluctantly slunk back up the aisle.

Nathan watched him retreat before turning roguishly towards the Queen of the Night. 'Love your work – simply spine-tingling . . .' He saluted her with a theatrical air-kiss. 'Mortified to be missing the denouement.' The rest of the cast watched, slack-jawed, as the three agents steered their way around the set – with Caspar bumping into a pyramid and toppling a palm tree – and exited into the wings.

They flew along the backstage passageways, weaving their way through clusters of performers, set-movers, candle men and wig-makers. They tore down stairs into a strange underworld of old props and painted backdrops; slithers of history piled up against each other. Jake noticed one in particular: a vast rendition of the Colosseum of ancient Rome – a gigantic crumbling arena beneath a bold blue sky. For a second he lost himself in it before Nathan pushed him on along the network of passages.

By the time the three of them reached a side exit – one of many leading out of the opera house – Caspar looked half dead, his chest heaving like a bellows. Nathan carefully edged open the door and checked that the coast was clear. There was a line of carriages parked along the side of the building and a huddle of drivers playing cards, rubbing their hands together to keep warm.

Nathan signalled to the others, and they crept out and ducked down in the shadows behind the coaches. From here they could see the main entrance. At length, the Leopard marched out –

darting his head this way and that in search of his prey. He quickly strode over to his accomplice, a man in a wide-brimmed hat, and spoke to him. The latter then mounted his horse and disappeared round the far side of the building.

Nathan motioned for Caspar and Jake to climb into one of the carriages. Jake carefully opened the gilt-framed door and let himself into the silky interior. When Caspar stepped up, the whole vehicle creaked under his weight, sinking down on one side. As the card players looked round to see what the noise was Nathan jumped up onto the driver's seat and flicked the reins.

The horses didn't move.

The drivers started shouting and ran towards him – immediately alerting the Leopard to what was going on – and he flicked the reins again. 'Come on, come on!' Nathan begged. When he finally stood up and delivered a sharp kick to each rump, they suddenly whinnied and took off, careering across the square.

In a flash the Leopard mounted his steed and whistled for his companion. The man in the wide-brimmed hat came charging back and they tore off in pursuit of the carriage. Two of the other carriage drivers, outraged at the theft, leaped up onto their own vehicles and joined the chase. The convoy hurtled across the bridge, with Nathan at its head.

Jake and Caspar were shaken violently as the wheels juddered over the wooden planks. Then they were hurled to one side as the coach swerved round a corner, Jake crushed under Caspar's huge belly. Once they had righted themselves again, the Swede, his hands trembling, fished some broken pieces of knäck out of his bag and starting shovelling them into his mouth.

'What are you doing?' Jake shook his head in disbelief.

'Sugar calms me down in an emergency,' Caspar spluttered, scooping up another handful.

Suddenly a gunshot rang out and a bullet smashed through the window behind them. Jake glanced back – a biting wind now blowing in his face – and saw the Leopard tearing up the hill, a smoking pistol in his hand, with his partner galloping swiftly behind.

Suddenly the carriage veered to one side again as Nathan swung round another bend, the wheels skidding on the ice. He shook the reins again, weaving skilfully through the narrow cobbled streets of the old town – up, down, left and right – as their pursuers tried to catch them.

The two vehicles at the back did not make it: the leading one tried to navigate a sharp bend but it met a patch of black ice and skidded across the road, smashing, in a shower of sparks, into the steps of a church, completely blocking the path of the second.

Nathan plunged down the hill towards the harbour. Between the narrow buildings, far below on the dockside, he could see the hulking silhouette of the warship, next to which the *Tulip* was berthed. Then disaster struck. A cart laden with coal came tottering over a crossroads ahead, blocking his way. The horses reared up, whinnying, their hooves slipping on the ice. Suddenly the whole carriage swung round and took charge of its own destiny. With an ear-splitting screech, it crashed into the window of a cake shop, plunging into an elaborate display of baked goods.

Nathan dismounted in a flash and pulled open the door for the others. 'Quickly! Quickly!' he yelled, helping them out.

'Sundbergs Konditori!' Caspar suddenly gasped on seeing the name of shop they had just crashed into. He quivered at the sight of a thousand buns and cakes ready for the taking; but Nathan and Jake took an arm each and dragged him down a steep flight of steps to the port. Within seconds they were lost in a labyrinth of narrow passageways and winding steps which the others, on their horses, could not negotiate.

They came to a wide portico that led, through a series of arches, into the customs house – a great high-windowed chamber still full of activity and chattering people even though it was well into the evening. Throngs of richly dressed merchants haggled with dour, bespectacled officials as goods were weighed, and gold and silver coins counted and reluctantly handed over. Nathan, Jake and Caspar weaved their way through the busy crowd (amongst the exotic-looking people here – seafarers from all over the world – even Caspar in his ripped turquoise suit didn't look out of place) to the main door on the other side, which led directly onto the harbour.

'There – look.' Jake pointed at the *Tulip*, further along the dock in the shadow of the warship. He remembered he still had the opera glasses in his trouser pocket. He took them out, surveyed the ship and spotted a figure hoisting the mainsail. 'It's Charlie – he made it.'

But Nathan had seen something else: two riders coming onto the quayside, one fair-haired, the other in a wide-brimmed hat. 'In here – quickly!' he said, darting across the flagstones and up into the fish market.

They were hit immediately by the salty stench of fresh fish. Like the customs house, the market – lit by wax lanterns hanging from the rafters – was bustling with activity. Dock workers were delivering and taking away boxes of fish, while fishermen bartered noisily, their mouths firing gusts of vapour. The agents threaded their way through and hid in the shadows behind three vast stacks of boxes. Caspar pulled a face when he caught sight of their contents: live eels, thrashing and writhing about. Jake and Nathan peered out. Through the throng they saw the Leopard and his sidekick dismount and cautiously approach the other side of the market.

As they came into the light beside the building, the accomplice nudged up his hat to wipe his brow and his face became visible for the first time. Jake started. It was hard to see through the clouds of icy vapour, but he recognized something about him.

He squinted to get a better view and could see that he was young – seventeen or so – handsome, broad shouldered, with olive skin.

Then it dawned on him: his eyes widened and his heart stopped. His hands shook. His face went pale.

'Philip . . .?' he said softly to himself. The man, he was certain, was his lost brother.

Three years ago, tragedy had come to the Djones family when Philip, Jake's older brother, disappeared, presumed dead. Jake had always been led to believe that the disaster happened on a school trip, and had learned only recently that Philip had actually been on a History Keepers' mission at the time – an assignment to Vienna in 1689. They hadn't heard from him since – but neither had a body been found, and Jake, who had loved his brother deeply, now clung to the belief that he was still alive somewhere.

The phantom said something to the Leopard and they both turned away from the market and headed back to remount their horses. They trotted off along the quay in the other direction, eyes searching for their prey.

'Right, let's go,' Nathan whispered, stepping carefully out from their hiding place. Caspar followed, but Jake paid no attention; he was spellbound, rooted to the spot, watching the two figures retreat. His heart was pumping at double speed, his breaths short and quick, his brain teeming with questions: was that really his brother? It was three years since he had seen him. He had only caught a fleeting glance – but is that what he would look like now? And if it *was* his brother, why was he here with the enemy? Jake wanted to cry out '*Philip?*' at the top of his voice and see if he turned round.

'What in God's name are you doing!' Nathan hissed, coming back and taking Jake's arm. 'Let's go!' He dragged him through the market and onto the quayside towards the *Tulip*. Half in a dream, Jake turned again. The two riders were almost out of sight. He stared at the figure in the wide-brimmed hat.

'Nathan, I know you're going to think I'm crazy,' he said, finally stopping and turning, 'but I cannot leave here until I know something.' He started wandering, as if in a trance, towards the riders.

Jake was right: Nathan *did* think he was mad. 'Come back here!' he thundered. 'Come back at once!'

The horsemen, hearing the voices, stopped and

turned. They peered into the half-light and made out the silhouettes behind them on the quay – and started heading back.

'We have precisely a minute to get out of here.' Nathan yanked Jake on across the icy cobbles towards the *Tulip*, Caspar panting at his side.

'Here!' Charlie identified himself from the prow. 'Furnace lit, ready to set sail.' All the History Keepers' vessels, whatever age they originally came from, were modified for speed, and the *Tulip*'s propeller was turning slowly in the water.

They were just ten yards away when Jake, unable to contain his curiosity any longer, twisted free of Nathan and turned towards the two riders, who were now fast approaching along the quay.

'Philip?' he shouted at the top of his voice. 'Is it you?'

'Stop it!' Nathan yelled, once again taking hold of Jake.

'Let go of me!' Jake snarled, swinging his arm savagely and cracking his fist into Nathan's jaw. Charlie, who was not prone to dramatic gestures, held up his hands and gasped in horror.

'He has the atomium!' Nathan said as Jake ran back along the quay towards the horsemen. He froze, unable to process what he should do next.

'Philip, is it you?' Jake called again, half demented. He stopped as the Leopard's horse drew up at his side, its rider cocking his pistol and pointing it at him. Jake paid no heed to it. He wasn't scared; all he cared about was the identity of the other man.

This figure now approached and, in an instant, jumped down from his horse. He advanced slowly towards Jake, his face still in shadow. Jake could feel tears welling up. 'Philip . . .?' he asked in a desperate, quavering voice.

For the first time, the man removed his hat.

Immediately the hope drained from Jake. Close up, he could see, with terrible clarity, that this was *not* his brother: wrong nose, wrong mouth, wrong eyes. It was a complete stranger. Now the impostor also drew his weapon and, with a sly smile, aimed it at Jake.

'We'll take those vials now,' the Leopard said in his silky voice. 'Henrik, would you oblige?'

Henrik jabbed his gun closer towards Jake's chest.

Nathan, Charlie and Caspar could only watch powerlessly as Jake retrieved the two bottles from inside his jacket and passed them over. Henrik in turn handed them to the Leopard, who slotted them back into their original box. 'Such a pleasure doing business.' He bowed to the forlorn agents of the History Keepers as Henrik replaced his hat and mounted his horse.

Suddenly a cry came out of nowhere: 'Nooooooooo!' Caspar screamed as he rushed towards the Leopard. 'It doesn't belong to you!' Then there was an explosion – a gun was discharged so close it made Jake's ears pop. Smoke was coming from the Leopard's pistol. For a moment no one moved, then Caspar gasped in agony, his eyes swimming in shock. Blood seeped through his fingers as he clutched his abdomen. He slipped on the ice, lost his balance and fell into the sea.

'Caspar!' Jake shouted. He was about to launch himself into the harbour when he noticed Henrik's gun trained on him once again.

'Do we kill them?' Henrik asked.

But the Leopard had noticed activity on the deck of the warship docked next to the *Tulip*. A group of soldiers had spotted the fight and were disembarking, heading towards them.

'Too late,' he said decisively. 'We have what we

need.' The two of them turned their horses round and charged off.

'Caspar!' Jake shouted again, now tearing over to the quayside. He was about to throw himself into the water when Nathan yanked him back.

'Stay there!' he said furiously. 'You've caused enough damage!'

Jake watched, his lips quivering, his face ashen, as Nathan dived into the freezing sea, yelling at the shock that immediately made his lungs seize up. When he reached Caspar, the boy was wheezing and trying to move his arms, but his body was stiff, motionless, already frozen. On the other side of the harbour Jake could see the Leopard and his sidekick – the man who might have been his brother – heading up a narrow alley and out of sight.

Charlie ran to Jake's side, ready to help the others out of the water. 'I'd say they have about a minute before their vital organs start closing down,' he murmured.

Nathan managed to drag Caspar back to the quayside, where Jake and Charlie started to haul him up. This was an almost impossible task: he was unconscious and seemed to weigh more than the two of them put together. They made four unsuccessful attempts before a group of Swedish soldiers from the warship came to help. Finally they were laying him out on the stones. For a second Jake, Nathan and Charlie stood over his prone body, chests heaving, teeth chattering. The soldiers stood wide-eyed at their side.

Nathan sank to his knees, put his hands on Caspar's chest and started to push down repeatedly, stopping every so often to blow air into his mouth. For a while the boy remained motionless. Jake bit his lip in anxiety. Finally Caspar vomited seawater, gasped and opened his eyes. He was conscious, but only barely so.

Nathan immediately turned his attention to the gunshot wound. He could see the entry point to the left of Caspar's abdomen, and could feel an exit hole round the back. The blood that had congealed in the freezing water was now starting to seep out again. He turned to the soldiers. 'On board?' he asked. 'Do you have a hospital? *Har ni ett sjukhus?*'

The soldiers nodded, then picked up Caspar and carried him towards the warship.

The unfortunate Swede was laid out on an operating table in the cramped, low-ceilinged cabin that was the ship's sickbay. His face was white, his jaw shaking, and he was mumbling to himself feverishly. A masked surgeon, eyes red from tiredness, was threading a needle by the light of an oil lantern. Nathan and Charlie stood watching; Jake waited sheepishly by the doorway. On the wall behind the operating table he eyed up a collection of instruments – ancient medical tools, blades and eye-watering saws, some black with dried blood.

The doctor uttered something in Swedish.

'This is going to sting a bit,' Charlie translated quietly. He nodded at Nathan and they each held one of the patient's arms, while a soldier grabbed his legs.

Caspar yelled out loud and thrashed about as the surgeon inserted the needle. Jake winced and had to clench his jaw. Eight gruelling minutes passed (it seemed more like an hour) before the thread was finally tied and the wound cleaned and dressed.

Eventually Caspar's delirium passed and his breathing steadied. As he came to his senses, he realized he was angry. His eyes sought out Jake's; they seemed to burn like embers as they stared savagely at him. 'You . . .' he spat. 'I wish to say something to you.'

Jake nodded and stepped forward. 'I'm so, so sorry,' he sighed softly. 'It's my fault that you were shot.'

'Shot?' Caspar spat. 'Do you think I care about that? It's nothing compared to the damage *you* have done.'

Jake could only hang his head and take his punishment. Caspar was no longer merely the clumsy, amusing boy who liked cakes and opera. He continued through gritted teeth: 'I don't know who you are, or where you've come from, or what you have to do with the History Keepers' Secret Service, but you need to know that you have ruined everything. *Everything.* It is not just that it took ten years to distil that atomium; or that it will take another ten to replace it; or that vital, life-saving missions may now have to be aborted because of your folly. No, worse than all this, you have armed our enemies – armed them with the power to take control of history like never before. So, whatever your name is – I neither remember nor care – feel bad . . . *feel like a traitor – because that's what you are.*'

Jake gulped and a tear rolled down his cheek.

3 JOSEPHINE OF NANTES

'Where on earth did she get them?' Miriam asked under her breath.

'From a circus ringmaster in Nantes, she told me,' Alan whispered back. 'He'd fallen on hard times and had to sell off his animals to pay his debts. Apparently Oceane only wanted one of them – she'd fallen in love *à première vue* – but was forced to take the whole lot as part of the deal.'

It was an exceptionally blustery day on the Mont St Michel. Alan and Miriam, Jake's mum and dad, were standing on the pier, along with a collection of similarly intrigued History Keepers, as Oceane Noire, bossing everyone around in her usual haughty manner, oversaw the arrival of her 'menagerie' of circus animals. Everyone was dressed, Miriam and Alan included, in clothes of the 1820s, the women in long gowns and the men in tailcoats, breeches and top hats. There was a sudden gust of wind and the ladies' dresses flapped violently, while the men clung onto their top hats.

A barge had docked and the crew were guiding various bemused-looking beasts down the gangplank onto the quay: a pair of ponies and a couple of horses were followed – quite dramatically – by a lumbering elephant. All the animals were a little past their prime, but the elephant looked very ancient and tired, its back sagging, its head drooping, its skin rough and worn.

'Poor thing,' Miriam sighed. There was such a sad look in its eye, it brought a tear to her own. Alan put his arm round her and gave her a cuddle.

Needless to say, Oceane was not moved; in fact, she could barely hide her disgust. She sprinkled a few drops of perfume onto a silk handkerchief and held it to her nose as the beast shambled past. When it stopped, turned and swung its trunk in her direction, she shrieked out loud and threw herself into the arms of Jupitus Cole, who was also staring, with typically icy blankness, at the bizarre scene.

To the bafflement of everyone at Point Zero – the tiny Mont St Michel in Normandy – Jupitus and

Oceane had recently announced their engagement. He was the dour Victorian second-in-command, she a tricky heiress from the court of Louis XV. And though they were in every way as haughty as each other, no one had ever guessed at romance between them.

'Where on earth is she going to put them?' Miriam asked her husband.

'Galliana has said they can go in the old stable block for the time being,' Alan replied, 'but she is not impressed!'

Miriam looked at the commander. On the surface she seemed as calm as ever, but she was clearly displeased.

'We're supposed to be a secret service,' Galliana muttered, 'not drawing attention to ourselves with circus animals . . . though they do look like a friendly lot.'

'Just as well,' said Miriam with a mischievous smile, 'as you'll probably be cleaning up after them. Somehow I can't quite see Oceane Noire sweeping up elephant dung.'

At this moment, as if to demonstrate her point, the elephant lifted its tail and posted a package from its behind. Two great lumps of grassy brown compost landed on the ground with a thud.

'*Oh, mon dieu, mon dieu!*' Oceane gasped, clutching the pearls around her neck as if the animal had delivered a couple of live bombs.

'Told you,' Miriam commented. 'She's never seen one of those before. Of course, she doesn't produce any herself.'

She and Alan looked at each other; in unison their eyes flashed, their lips trembled and they started giggling.

The final animal to emerge from the cargo hold, the chains around her neck held very firmly and warily by two members of the crew, was a young lioness. There was a collective intake of breath as she padded onto the quayside. She was little more than a cub, not yet grown into her giant paws, but already had a sly look in her eye.

'There she is!' Oceane exclaimed, running towards the creature. '*Ma petite.*' There were more gasps as she knelt down and actually threw her arms around the lioness. 'We don't need these silly shackles,' she said, unfastening the chains and tossing them at the two crewmen. 'Josephine is quite tame; she was reared by humans – by French blue bloods, no less . . . the ringmaster was a distant relation of Eleanor of Aquitaine. Look, she even eats rocket.' Oceane snapped her fingers at one of her browbeaten attendants, who duly handed her an embroidered bag. From this she produced a handful of leaves and held them out. The lioness sniffed them a couple of times, then consumed them without a great deal of interest.

'Isn't she the cleverest thing?' Oceane trilled, clapping her hands together in excitement. '*Adorable, tout simplement!* And don't you love the name? Just like Madame Bonaparte herself.'

There was another gust of wind – this one strong enough to sweep up Alan's hat and carry it off, first in a swirling eddy around the mount, and then out to sea. He and Miriam watched as it dropped into the rolling waves.

'Wasn't keen on it anyway,' Alan announced with a shrug. 'Signor Gondolfino said it would "set off" my face, but it just made my head itch.' Miriam started giggling again, and he joined in.

'Take all the other beasts to the stables,' Oceane ordered her flunky, then turned to her young lioness. 'Come on, my darling, let's get you inside, *il fait trop de vent.*' She led the beast by the scruff towards the main doors of the castle. 'I'm going to find you something clever to wear around your neck. I'm feeling diamonds – how about you?'

The lioness stopped and gazed with narrowed eyes at the assembled company, then they both went inside.

As Oceane's attendant guided the elephant and the other animals to the stables, Miriam looked out towards the horizon. 'Jake should be back soon. I do hope everything went all right.'

Since they had set sail from Stockholm across the thawing sea, the mood aboard the *Tulip* had been solemn.

Before they left, Nathan and Charlie had transported Caspar to the house of a family friend (Jake had not been allowed to accompany them, but instructed to wait alone below deck), and had sent word to the Isaksens to collect him. They had bought some provisions for the return journey and set off as the sun started to rise over the sea. It had turned out to be the first warm day in weeks and the ice had begun to melt instantly.

For hours Jake had skulked in the background, offering to assist wherever he could – to help Nathan unfurl the sails or lend Charlie a hand in the galley. Both had declined his offers with a terse shake of the head, barely looking at him. Mr Drake had also seemed to pick up on the atmosphere. Jake had offered him some of the fruitcake that his mum had pressed into his hand on his departure. Though the parrot usually loved cake (even Miriam's disastrously tipsy concoction), he had declined it with a toss of his head and had flown off to perch on the yardarm. That was when Jake had retreated to his cabin.

As it started to get dark again, Jake was still picking over the awful events in Stockholm. *Feel like a traitor – because that's what you are*, Caspar Isaksen had told him bluntly. The knowledge that he had let people down – not just his new friends, but *all* the History Keepers – was bad enough; but the notion that his actions might lead directly to the suffering of innocent people was so dreadful it turned his stomach to liquid.

Charlie knocked on the cabin door and asked if he would like some polenta and porcini fricassee. Although Jake didn't have a clue what it was, he accepted with exaggerated enthusiasm.

Over dinner he kept respectfully silent as Nathan and Charlie discussed who the Leopard might be working for and how he'd come by the precise details of the keepers' rendezvous with Caspar Isaksen at the Stockholm opera house.

'I hate to be the voice of doom,' Nathan said, putting his empty plate to one side and retrieving a small veneered box, 'but what other explanation can there be?' He opened the box and took out its contents: the silver Horizon Cup and two small vials of liquid – the remaining atomium for their return journey to Point Zero. He set the destination dial on the silver device and muttered grimly, 'There must be another double agent amongst us.' It had been a matter of weeks since Norland, the seemingly amiable chauffeur, had been uncovered as a spy at Point Zero.

The three agents drank their doses of vile liquid, Charlie sharing a few drops with a reluctant Mr Drake, and an hour later they hit the horizon point. Here Jake experienced the usual out-of-body sensations, accompanied by the same flashing snapshots of history in his mind's eye; but partly because of the short distance they were travelling – just twenty-eight years – and partly because of his lingering feeling of guilt, the ride wasn't as thrilling as it had been before.

Soon after arriving in the less chilly waters of 1820, the *Tulip*'s engines suddenly stalled. Nathan stripped off his shirt ('Oil and Japanese silk are a match made in hell,' he explained) and tried to repair a ruptured gasket. In the end, however, he and Charlie were worried about the risk of fire and decided to continue using wind power alone. It was past one in the morning when Charlie finally spied the distinctive conical silhouette of the Mont St Michel in the distance, and almost two by the time they drifted across the bay.

'It looks like Galliana's waited up for us,' said Charlie, nodding towards the light in a casement window high up in the castle.

Jake's heart thumped a little harder as the island, its flanks covered in building upon building, loomed up ahead of him: he had been hoping, as they were arriving so late, that the news of his 'treachery' might wait until morning. That was evidently not to be. He searched the black façade for more lights, particularly in the tower where his mum and dad slept. It saddened him a little to discover that this part of the building was pitch-black; they must have already gone to bed.

'Jake,' Charlie called across to him. 'Nathan and

I have discussed everything: when we arrive, let *us* do the talking. There's no point in you getting into unnecessary trouble.'

'I don't think I would feel right about that,' Jake replied in a quiet voice. 'I'm to blame.'

'Blame is pointless,' Charlie persisted. 'It doesn't get anyone anywhere. We'll sort it out, all right?'

Jake still felt unsure about this but he reluctantly agreed. 'Thank you.'

Charlie shrugged. 'That's what friends are for. We all make mistakes. It's how you learn from them that's important.'

Jake appreciated Charlie saying this, but as he watched Nathan, sullenly coiling ropes at the prow of the ship, he wondered whether the American's forgiveness would be a little harder to earn.

'There he is! There's our boy,' a familiar voice called out from the shadows as they drew in to the quayside.

Jake searched the darkness to find two figures reclining on sun loungers, wrapped up in blankets.

'Mum? Dad?' he exclaimed joyfully, temporarily forgetting his troubles. He leaped down onto the pier. 'What are you doing here?'

'What are we doing here, Miriam?' Alan turned to his wife. 'Taking the pleasant night air, aren't we?' he said, referring to the blustery wind. 'We're waiting for you, you daft plank.'

Miriam stood up and threw her arms around her son. 'How are you, darling? Good trip?'

Jake tried to nod, but it came out more like a shrug.

'Fancy a nice cup of tea?' Alan asked, giving his son a great bear hug. Jake tried to keep hold of his emotions.

There was a clattering sound, and a shape bounded across the cobbles.

'Felson!' Jake cried as the dog leaped up at him, panting with delight. 'I missed you too,' he said, kneeling so that Felson could give his face a good licking. This was the sturdy, battle-scarred mastiff that had once belonged to his enemy, Captain Von Bliecke. Jake had befriended him when they had both been abandoned at sea.

'He had a nice time with us,' Miriam commented. 'Though of course your father overfed him and let him sleep on the bed – but he never stopped staring at the horizon, waiting for you to come back.'

'So how did our son get on, Mr Chieverley?' Alan asked Charlie as he jumped down from the *Tulip*. 'Did he do us proud?'

'He acquitted himself quite professionally, yes,' Charlie replied in a very business-like voice.

'Blimey,' Alan chuckled. 'That bad, eh?' and he and Miriam started laughing. 'Come on – let's get you all inside.'

The six of them, Jake and his parents, Nathan and Charlie – along with Felson, glued to his master's side – made their way up the steps and through the large double doors into the castle. The wind whistled round the great staircase, making the tapers flicker.

Jake could bear the suspense no longer. 'Mum, Dad, I've got something to tell you—'

'There's Commander Goethe and Jupitus Cole!' Charlie interrupted, and gave Jake a sidelong glance to remind him that *he* was doing the talking.

Galliana and Jupitus were coming down the stairs to meet them. The commander, smiling serenely, was in her dressing gown, and her long silver hair was swept right back. Jupitus, dressed impeccably in a tight-fitting jacket with a starched collar, stepped down in her wake.

As they met halfway, the whole company came to a standstill. Felson looked eagerly from one face to another.

Nathan nodded at Charlie, who spoke first. 'Commander Goethe, Mr Cole, I'm afraid we have bad news.' Jupitus looked up. 'We have failed in our mission. We were intercepted and the entire atomium consignment has been lost.'

'What?' Jupitus gasped in disbelief. 'Lost?'

'Regrettably, yes,' Charlie replied stoically.

'*Regrettably?!* Have you any idea what this means?' Jupitus was livid. 'Who intercepted you?'

'There was a young gentleman who called himself the Leopard,' Charlie went on. 'I intend to start research immediately to find out where he has come from and who he may be working for.'

'But how did this happen?' Jupitus persisted.

'It happened because I mucked everything up,' Jake blurted out. 'I disobeyed orders, completely. Everything was my fault.' Galliana listened carefully while Jupitus's mouth gaped open. 'And I'm afraid that is not all,' Jake continued grimly. 'As a result of my error, Caspar Isaksen was shot.'

'*Shot?*' Jupitus repeated.

Charlie quickly butted in, 'Though it seems he'll make a full recovery.'

Miriam, aware of her son's deep remorse, held him firmly by the shoulders. 'You poor thing . . .' she whispered in his ear.

'Poor thing?' Jupitus scoffed, using the wall to support him in his shock. 'This is a disaster, an unmitigated disaster.'

'Mr Cole, Commander . . .' Nathan finally spoke. 'It was very honourable of Jake to own up, but I can assure you the fault lies with myself more than anyone else. Jake tried to warn me that he had seen a man with a gun, and I did not pay attention. I am the one who was culpable.'

'How civil of you. Such a martyr.' Jupitus shook his head, not believing a word of it.

Despite his distress, Jake felt a warm pulse of happiness: Nathan was his friend after all. There was a degree of truth in what he had said, but Jake knew that he alone was responsible.

Suddenly, at the foot of the stairs, the double doors flew open and the wind gusted in, blowing out the tapers and leaving everyone in almost complete darkness. Alan went down, closed the door and bolted it.

Galliana glanced at Jake, taking the measure of him with her calm grey eyes, before ordering the group, 'Sleep now. We can discuss this further in the morning.'

With heavy hearts everyone made their way up to their beds.

Jake lingered behind for a moment. On the walls, the life-size portraits of famous History Keepers of the past stared at him silently. He turned and looked at one in particular: Sejanus Poppoloe, the founder of the secret service, dressed in his characteristic cloak and turban. His gaze was stern, as if he too understood the magnitude of Jake's treachery.

4 MESLITH FROM DEEP HISTORY

Jake was woken by a commotion in the corridor – people rushing by, speaking in urgent whispers. Felson, who was stretched out diagonally across the bed, also stirred, lifting his head and pricking up his ears. Jake looked at his clock: it was six thirty in the morning. Early morning light was peeking through the curtains. He had been given a room in one of the oldest parts of the castle. It had ancient casement windows, a small four-poster bed and a fireplace, where embers still glowed from the night before.

He got out of bed and put his head round the door. Jupitus Cole flew by, followed by Truman Wylder, Nathan's father, buttoning up his shirt as he hurried down the stairs. Then Signor Gondolfino, impeccably dressed even at this time of day, limped by as quickly as his old legs and ivory cane would allow him.

'Has something happened?' Jake asked. He dreaded the answer – maybe some calamity had already taken place as a result of the disaster in Stockholm. But Gondolfino had an entirely new revelation, a piece of news that made Jake's heart beat even faster.

'They think a Meslith has arrived . . . from Topaz St Honoré. Commander Goethe has called an emergency meeting.' A Meslith – Jake was now familiar with the term – was a message that was transmitted through time, sent and received on a Meslith machine, an intriguing typewriter-like instrument with crystalline rods that fizzed with electricity.

Jake dressed at breakneck speed, throwing on his trousers, shirt and jacket. He couldn't find any socks, so he pulled on his boots without them and stuffed the laces inside. 'I'll come back for you in a minute,' he told Felson, and ran out of the room. He tore through the maze of corridors and staircases – sometimes jumping down entire flights – until he arrived at the double doors to the stateroom. He ran his hand through his hair, pulled his collar straight and stepped inside.

Fifteen or so people, mostly older History Keepers, were chatting seriously, some seated around the large table, some gathered in clusters about the room. Light was streaming through the four giant windows that looked out across the sea. Jake immediately felt the hostile gaze of Jupitus Cole, who was seated at the far end of the table with a bundle of maps laid out in front of him. Jake nodded at him and tried to smile. Jupitus merely stared icily back as Jake edged round the room towards Charlie, who was standing next to a buffet table laden with French pastries.

'Do we know anything yet?' asked Jake breathlessly. 'Where did this message come from?'

Charlie held up his hand to indicate that his mouth was full. He carried on munching for a while. 'I always thought brioches were overrated,' he said after he had swallowed the last mouthful, 'but this one has a subtle hint of lemon, which really lifts it. If you're referring to Topaz, I'm as much in the dark as you.' He changed the subject. 'I don't think you've met Dr Chatterju?' he said, indicating a distinctive-looking man in a turban and round spectacles. 'He's in charge of our inventions division. He arrived back from Bombay yesterday . . .'

'A necessary but exhausting trip to see my relations,' Chatterju explained, his voice as elegant as his appearance, 'who are spread, disobligingly, not only throughout India, but throughout the centuries!' He smiled broadly and held out his hand to Jake. 'Zal Chatterju – it's such an honour to meet you. I knew your brother. A wonderful young man. And I sense that you are gifted like him . . .?'

Jake smiled shyly. He was immediately taken by Chatterju, aware of an eccentric, mischievous mind. The man wore a thickly embroidered kaftan fastened with an ornate golden belt. The face above the perfectly groomed grey beard was distinguished, aristocratic. His turban was secured with a brilliant sapphire that matched his eyes.

'What exactly is the inventions division?' asked Jake.

'Oh, you'll find out soon enough,' Chatterju chuckled. 'I'm just a lowly scientist with a few crackpot ideas.' Suddenly he looked agitated. 'Where has that boy got to? Has he disappeared off again? He's always disappearing!'

'I'm here, Uncle, right behind you.' A young boy stepped out.

'Right behind me? Don't be so impudent. Come here where I can see you.'

The boy did as he was told. He was about eleven, Jake guessed, with a face as warm as dark honey that looked as if it never stopped smiling.

'I'm Amrit,' he introduced himself cheerfully to Jake. 'Dr Chatterju's nephew.'

'My assistant!' Chatterju corrected him. 'That's what you are. And you're very much on trial.' With a roll of the eyes he confided to Jake, 'He's little more than a child but thinks he knows *everything*.'

There was a final influx of people into the room, including Jake's mum, his dad – who was still half asleep and couldn't stop yawning – and his aunt Rose. Behind them trotted Galliana's greyhound, Olive, who immediately padded over to her place at the top of the table. A hush then descended as Galliana herself swept in and took her seat. Jake noticed that she was wearing her long navy cloak embroidered with motifs of clocks and phoenixes, and was holding a bundle of papers.

'Is everyone present?' she asked Jupitus.

'All except Nathan Wylder and Oceane Noire. The former,' Jupitus sighed, 'is apparently working off his frustration with some deep-sea fishing. Mademoiselle Noire is still dressing.'

'So we won't see her until the end of the century,' Miriam chuckled to her husband.

'We'll have to start without them.' Galliana spoke in a quick, business-like voice, looking around at all the faces. 'We have two matters on the agenda: firstly, for those of you who are not up to speed, the mission to Stockholm was unsuccessful. The agents were intercepted by an enemy faction and the atomium consignment was lost.'

There was immediate uproar amongst those gathered, with shouts of:

'*The whole consignment?*'

'*How can that be?*'

'*Who was responsible?*'

Jake shifted uncomfortably, aware of Jupitus's narrowed eyes settling on him once again.

Galliana held up her hand. 'The whys and wherefores of how this happened are irrelevant.' She read from her notes: '*The perpetrator was in his late teens, five feet ten, blond Caucasian. He went by the name of the Leopard. Assisted by a dark-haired youth of a similar age.*' Jake looked down. 'Does this ring any bells?' Galliana asked the group.

Nothing but blank faces. 'Miss Wunderbar . . . ?'

The stately woman in charge of the Library of Faces, beautifully dressed in the fashion of the 1690s, shook her head. 'Nothing, I'm afraid,' she announced in her curt Bavarian accent. 'I'm in the process of a more detailed search of faces. Agent Chieverley is helping me.'

'It goes without saying,' Galliana continued, 'that *anyone* who can shed any light on the matter should come forward immediately. This is of paramount importance. Now, to the second matter . . .' She withdrew a piece of parchment from her bundle. 'I received this message an hour ago, apparently sent from deep history.'

Jake craned his neck to see: he could just make out a very long series of symbols.

'Obviously it was encoded in Hypoteca, which has been translated as follows.' Galliana held up another scroll for all to see. This one contained more numbers, in larger, bolder type.

'What's Hypoteca?' Jake whispered to Charlie.

'It's a cipher, a secret code, invented by Magnesia Hypoteca, the wife of one of the first commanders.'

Jake looked at the translated message: there were twenty-eight digits, nearly all numerals, divided into four groups of eight – the order of which didn't make any sense to him – followed by a single phrase of English: *Follow the shadow's hand.*

'Well, the numbers are obvious,' Jupitus purred. 'The first set refer to Topaz's date of birth: the nineteenth of September 1356.'

'Correct.' Galliana nodded.

Jake remembered Topaz telling him that she had been born in a campaign tent during the Battle of Poitiers in the Hundred Years War. History Keepers could be born in all sorts of eras, depending where their parents were stationed – or travelling to – at the time.

'The middle section,' Jupitus continued, 'presumably refers to geographical coordinates.'

'Indeed,' replied Galliana. 'In this case, an island in the Tyrrhenian Sea called Vulcano. And the final set presumably indicate the historical date the message came from.'

'Sorry – I haven't got my glasses on,' Rose piped up. 'What *is* the historical date?'

Jake was also dying to know – he could not read it from his end of the room, either.

'The tenth of May,' Galliana said, then added in a sombre voice, 'AD 27.' Some of the agents glanced anxiously at each other as she continued, 'The date would make sense as we have recently picked up a quantity of Meslith chatter linking those coordinates with Agata Zeldt – a figure who has been silent for years.'

Now there were gasps around the table. Alan accidentally dropped his coffee cup into his saucer with a clatter.

Jake felt his stomach flip. He had heard all about the diabolical Agata on his mission to Venice. She was, in Charlie's words, *The most evil woman in history*; the monster who, as a child, had tried to drown her elder brother in a freezing lake; who had taught her maid a lesson by forcing her to sit naked on a throne of red-hot iron until she burned to death. She was also – and this was the most disturbing fact of all – Topaz's *real* mother. Of course, Topaz had disowned her completely – at the age of five she'd had the strength of mind to defect to Point Zero – but they were related by blood.

Rose put up her hand. 'Does anyone know what *follow the shadow's hand* means?'

It was clear from the blank faces that no one had a clue.

'And, more to the point,' said Jupitus, 'how do

we know it has actually come from Topaz? Perhaps Agata sent it herself—'

The double doors flew open. 'Sorry – I came as soon as I heard!' Nathan strode into the room. The sight of him brought an amazed smile to Jake's face: his clothes and hair were dripping wet, a rope and a harpoon hung from his shoulder and he carried a dead swordfish in one hand and a conger eel in the other, the latter trailing across the floor behind him. 'I hope I haven't missed too much; the conger was particularly tricky to land.'

'He has no shame,' Charlie muttered in horror, looking at the dead fish. 'No shame at all.'

'These may look grisly,' Nathan announced, chuckling at all the squeamish faces, 'but they'll make a change from roast chicken.'

Galliana groaned wearily. 'Thank you, Agent Wylder. Most thoughtful . . . Now, if you would put them down and take a seat . . .'

Nathan deposited his catch on a side table. 'By the way,' he said, ignoring the invitation and going over to the window, 'is there any reason why there's an elephant wandering around on the pier? For a while I thought I was imagining things, that it couldn't possibly be real, until it – how can I put this politely? – until it dispensed a particularly noxious parcel, which I can assure you was very real – *way* too real for early Tuesday morning.'

'It belongs to Oceane Noire,' Galliana snapped. 'If you had read the daily communiqué, you would know. Now sit down!'

Nathan looked shame-faced and took a seat next to Jupitus. 'So, news from Topaz, I hear.' He flashed his smile as he looked at the list of numbers, understanding their relevance immediately. 'Good gracious, she *is* a long way away. Are we sure it came from her?'

Galliana took a calming deep breath and addressed everyone. 'The fact of the matter is, though the use of the Hypoteca code would suggest that it is authentic, we have no *absolute* guarantee that this was written by Topaz. But that said, given that she would contact us only when she had *absolutely vital* information concerning the enemy – that was her original brief – I have decided to send a team to these coordinates to investigate. It goes without saying that travelling back one thousand, seven hundred and ninety-three years to AD 27 is an extremely gruelling undertaking so I can send only those of first-rate valour.' Galliana took a deep breath. 'I assign Nathan Wylder—'

'*Qui est le champion?!*' Nathan punched the air. His French accent was truly appalling.

'– and Charlie Chieverley.' Charlie just nodded soberly. 'Group leader—'

'I assume will be myself?' Nathan interrupted.

'– will be Jupitus Cole,' Galliana finished her sentence.

There was another round of murmurs. Jupitus coolly took a sip of coffee. Some of the older agents around the table – Dr Chatterju, and Signor Gondolfino, the head costumier, in particular – glanced at him with a hint of envy: once a keeper's valour had matured, he or she was rarely invited on the type of exciting mission they had taken part in when they were young.

Nathan put his hand up. 'Commander . . . is it not somewhat unusual to send an agent of Mr Cole's' – he chose the word carefully – '*experience* on a mission so far back in time?'

'If you're referring to his age,' Galliana replied, 'Mr Cole tested his valour only yesterday and his scores were off the chart – even better than yours.'

At this point Jupitus couldn't hide his sly smile. Try as she might, Rose was unable to conceal her admiration. Nathan was silenced: even he wouldn't dare put up a fight against the venerable keeper.

'You will sail tonight on the *Hippocampus*, a Roman merchant ship—'

'The *Hippocampus* . . .' Jake repeated the name to himself; it sounded intriguing, familiar.

'Tonight?' Nathan interrupted. 'Any reason we can't get going immediately?'

'A compelling reason, yes,' Galliana answered drily. 'The *Hippocampus* will not be delivered from the Calais workshop until late afternoon.'

'I get you,' Nathan said. 'They're souping it up – good to hear!'

Galliana looked down, indicating points on the map. 'You will take the Brest horizon point, vault to Sardinia East, and from there make your way to the Aeolian Islands. Your final destination is the islet of Vulcano. Is that clear?'

'Crystal,' Nathan replied.

Everyone else murmured their agreement – everyone except Jake, who stared solemnly at the floor. The first time he had attended a meeting, he had put up his hand and volunteered to join the mission to Venice. His offer had been flatly rejected, humiliatingly so. He knew that if he suggested joining *this* expedition, the rebuff – given the importance of the mission, the huge time span to be crossed, not to mention his failure in Stockholm – would be more resounding still. Despite this, his thirst for adventure, his need to be – at the very least – part of the mission to save Topaz was too strong. He tentatively raised his arm and spoke in the deepest voice he could muster. 'May I say something, Commander?'

There was an uncomfortable shifting amongst the History Keepers. Miriam looked at her son apprehensively. Charlie occupied himself by reaching for another brioche. Jupitus went so far as to roll his eyes heavenward.

'Commander, I am aware that I have brought dishonour to this service.' Jake turned to the rest of the room. 'I should tell you all now that it was I, and no one else, who was responsible for losing the atomium in Stockholm.'

There were more murmurs.

'I disobeyed orders and made a mistake for which I will never forgive myself – not until I have somehow, someday, put the situation right again.' He took a deep breath and saw that his mother was becoming increasingly anxious. 'I am aware also that this is a very hazardous and crucial assignment for which I am sure you consider me unworthy, but I beg you to offer me one last chance to prove myself. If you send me on this mission, I promise I will not let you down—'

'This is ridiculous!' interjected Jupitus, getting to his feet to make his point. 'Not just ridiculous – insulting! It shows a total lack of respect for the work that we do here.'

'Calm down, Jupitus – don't get your knickers in a twist,' Rose retorted, protective of her nephew.

'I am perfectly calm!' Jupitus hissed, then carried on, 'This secret service has operated for decades, for *centuries*, with strict tried-and-tested systems. No agent ever goes out in the field until he has had the most intense and thorough training. Then this *boy* appears and thinks he can do everything by his own rules. He already contravened orders by stowing away on the Venetian mission—'

'And as a result' – Alan was now ready to join the fray – 'did more to stop Zeldt than anyone else!'

'He then pushes his way onto the Stockholm operation' – Jupitus continued his diatribe – 'turns it into a farce, threatens our very existence, and now has the gall to stand here and volunteer again. If he was working for Zeldt himself, he couldn't make a better job of destroying us.'

Now nearly everyone in the room got caught up in the argument, all voicing their opinions loudly. Galliana did not interrupt, but listened judiciously.

Nathan leaned over towards her. 'Commander, would you allow me to say something? I may be able to resolve this.' Galliana nodded her consent.

'Listen . . .' He stood up. 'Listen to me, everyone.' When he wanted to be serious, Nathan – with a charm and authority beyond his years – was able to command respect. The keepers quietened down. 'Maybe Mr Cole is right, maybe Jake has disobeyed orders in the past, but I can tell you that he acted impeccably in Italy and Germany – even in Sweden. As I have already informed the commander, he warned us of an impending threat, and tragically I paid no heed. I envy his natural flair for what we do.'

'Hear, hear,' Charlie added.

'And maybe this *is* the wrong mission for Jake – in truth, I do think it is too far back for him – but it is still *incredibly* brave of him to volunteer.'

'Hear, hear.' Alan and Rose now joined Charlie in their agreement.

'And let's not forget, Mr Cole . . .' said Nathan, drawing to his conclusion. 'You yourself brought Jake into this dangerous world of ours, and I believe you owe him a little more guidance.'

It was clear from the silence that now descended that everyone agreed with Nathan. Even Jupitus looked remorseful. He sat down and sighed deeply.

Jake looked over at Nathan with a warm smile. Nathan winked back.

Galliana took charge again. 'Jake, Nathan Wylder is right: you have shown great courage. However, I must also agree that this assignment is not right for you.' Jake reddened as she looked at him before turning to the others. 'Agents Cole, Wylder and Chieverley – Signor Gondolfino will take you up for your fittings in the costumiery.'

'There's the rub.' Nathan turned to his neighbour. 'Roman fashion – it's a minefield.'

'Usually this would go without saying,' Galliana concluded, 'but I must ask you to treat your atomium consignment with the utmost care. We have only enough stock for a handful of journeys. You set sail at seven tonight.' And she stood to indicate that the meeting was over.

Just as everyone was bustling out, Oceane Noire

swanned in, the vast panniers of her dress sticking out on either side, her hair in a towering beehive. '*Qu'est-ce que s'est passé?* What's happened? Have I missed anything?' she asked the tide of chattering people coming the other way.

Rose, upset by recent matters, couldn't resist a dig at her old adversary. 'Yes, Jupitus is off to a beautiful island in the Tyrrhenian Sea – without you!'

She smiled curtly and exited as Oceane's expression turned to vinegar.

Jake went back to his room and threw himself down on his bed. Felson nestled in close, propped his head on the boy's knee and licked his hand.

When Jake was allocated this room after his return from Cologne, he had been told it was the one his brother had used whenever he visited Point Zero. Jake had searched through the drawers and cupboards for any sign of Philip. Of course, after three years, all his things had been removed or sent back to London, but Jake did find one item: wedged under the drawer of the little desk below the window was a photograph of the whole family at Christmas time – Jake, Philip, their mum and dad all smiling happily in the Djones kitchen in Greenwich.

Jake had not shown the photograph to his parents for fear of reviving sad memories, and kept it under his mattress. Now he pulled it out and examined it once again.

Philip was taller and broader than his brother. He was only fourteen in the photo, but already looked handsome and confident, with an adventurer's spark in his eye. He had his arm protectively round Jake, while Jake looked proudly up at him.

There was a soft knock on the door. 'It's Mum,' Miriam announced quietly. 'Can I come in?'

Jake slipped the photograph under the blanket as the door creaked open and she came in.

'How are you feeling, darling?'

Jake smiled and nodded. His mum came and sat on the bed. 'You're not too upset about Jupitus Cole, are you?'

Jake shrugged. 'He's entitled to an opinion.'

'Well, he's got a lot of those,' agreed Miriam. 'Dad and I never paid too much attention.' She took a deep breath. 'Listen, darling, I have some more bad news – we're going to have to go back to London.'

'What?' Jake felt his stomach flip again.

'We can stay a couple more days, then we need to pack up – the three of us and Rose too. Captain Macintyre has agreed to take us on the *Escape*.'

'Wh-why?' Jake stammered.

'Why? Because you need to get back to school, to your friends. We need to get back to work. People are waiting for their bathrooms. Dolores Devises' overflow pipes were supposed to be fitted three weeks ago.'

Jake's face was thunderous. 'When I first met Jupitus Cole, he said that school was pointless, that *the world was the place to learn*.'

'Well, you see, just another of his opinions—'

'And your bathroom shop's a disaster. Only your friends order things there – out of pity – and most of them have to get it all fixed again after you've installed it.' Jake bit his tongue, immediately feeling awful, but unable to take back the words.

Miriam sighed. She reached out and took his hand. 'I know all this seems very exciting to you. And it *is* exciting, it's a roller coaster, but it's also dangerous – so very, very dangerous. I couldn't bear it if anything happened to you.'

'All because of what happened in Stockholm?'

'No! We decided this before you even went there. We wanted to tell you last night, but it didn't seem the right time. Jake, you can't stay here. None of us can.'

He looked steadfastly down at his hands, his face crimson. 'It's not fair – you had *your* chance, you travelled all round history, you went everywhere . . .'

Miriam saw something sticking out from under the blanket. She picked up the photograph. The moment she set eyes on it, her face froze with both joy and unbearable pain. She stared down at her elder son, who was arm in arm with Jake, smiling so happily. It was a while before she said anything.

'Look at the state of that Christmas tree,' she murmured finally, deliberately making light of the situation. 'Your dad's tinsel obsession is verging on the criminal.'

At length she gave the photo back to Jake and wiped the tears from her eyes. She kissed him on the cheek and stood up. 'I'm sorry, darling, we have to leave by Friday,' she said, then left the room and closed the door behind her.

5 THE *HIPPOCAMPUS*

As the sun was setting over the mount, a bell rang to announce the departure of the agents. Jake was in the stables, where he had spent most of the afternoon with Oceane's elephant – now christened Dora – and the other circus animals. In return for apple treats, Dora had shown Jake some of her tricks – in particular, balancing a ball on her trunk and standing on her hind legs. They had developed an immediate rapport.

Before that, Jake had spent most of the day alone, shunning company. He felt desperately sad, as if he didn't belong there any more. Earlier that morning, after their fitting in the costumiery, Charlie and Nathan had come to find him, asking whether he wanted to join them for sword practice in the armoury. Jake had told them that he wasn't really up to it – he had to take Felson for a walk anyway.

As the bell tolled, he wondered if he even had the courage to go down and say goodbye to the others. 'You have no choice in the matter,' he finally told himself, and set off along the path that led to the quayside.

As he came down the steps, he saw that a small group of people had already gathered there. Some were carrying lanterns and there was an atmosphere of excitement. The ship they were looking at was very simple – quite different from the rest of the keepers' fleet. Her hull was fashioned from light, sun-bleached timbers; her prow was steep, like that of a Viking longship, and she had two square sails in cream and blue stripes. One was very large and attached to the mainmast (along with the triangular topsail); the other was much smaller and hung over the prow. A neat, square timber structure stood at the stern.

As Jake stared at her, a peculiar feeling came over him: his mind was filled with curious images – brilliant sunlight shining down on a palm-fringed bay, stacks of old amphorae, a cloud of sweet incense wafting on the warm wind. 'Incense?' he said to himself. 'When have I ever smelled incense?'

The ship seemed familiar, as if he had seen it somewhere in a dream.

'There he is,' Rose exclaimed, holding out her arms to him. 'We were about to come and find you.' She was standing with Miriam, Alan, Galliana and Signor Gondolfino – who was wrapped in an elegant cape against the chilly evening air. Oceane Noire stood haughtily apart from the rest, her lion cub at her side in its new diamond collar.

'All right, darling?' Miriam asked Jake hopefully.

He nodded and continued to study the ship. Her name was inscribed in faded letters on the stern. '*Hippocampus*?' he said softly to himself. She still seemed familiar to him. 'What *is* a hippocampus?' he asked his dad.

'Interesting fact.' Alan clapped his hands. '*Hippocampus* is Latin for seahorse, but *also* the name of the part of the brain to do with memory.'

Jake started to work his way along to the prow; as he did so, vivid images came into his head – scales carved in wood and shining rubies. No sooner had this vision formed than he saw the figurehead curving up from the front of the ship – a creature with a long scaly neck and glinting red eyes. It was uncanny: he had imagined it precisely.

'Why do I recognize this ship?' he asked his parents.

Out of sight, behind his back, Miriam clutched her husband's hand. 'What's that, darling?' she trilled.

'This ship wasn't here when I came to Point Zero the first time – Galliana said it was in the workshop in Calais – so why does it seem familiar?'

Three faces – Rose's, Alan's and Miriam's – had frozen in perplexed smiles. 'I know!' Miriam said finally. 'The maritime museum in Greenwich – remember we went last year? They've got a model of one just like this.'

'That's right,' Alan agreed, nodding enthusiastically.

Jake could usually tell when his parents were lying. This, he felt instinctively, was one of those occasions. However, there was no time to pursue the matter as the three departing agents were now coming down the steps.

'Oh, good gracious me,' gasped Rose. 'Just look at those legs!'

She was referring to Jupitus, who led the group. He was wearing a tunic, belted at the waist, that came down to his knobbly knees, revealing long, ghostly pale limbs. On his feet were sandals and slung across his back was a leather holdall. Rose couldn't stop giggling: Jupitus looked so stiff and awkward in his informal garb.

For very different reasons, Oceane was also struggling to come to terms with the vision. She smiled as bravely as she could, and even clapped a little, but she was clearly embarrassed. If she had her way, Jupitus would never take off his trademark tailcoat and breeches, even to go to bed.

Behind him, Charlie looked much more at ease in a similar outfit, Mr Drake bouncing happily on his shoulder. Nathan brought up the rear in a typically ostentatious get-up. Over his tunic he wore a golden breastplate and a skirt of thick leather strips. On his head was a helmet – also in gold – with a feathery red plume. The sight of Nathan in such an amazing costume made Jake feel very jealous. His comrades were going off on an adventure to the ancient Roman world, a thrilling place of gladiators and charioteers; of conquerors, emperors and armies; of Roman baths and theatres; a place that Jake could only dream of – while he was headed for London, which would doubtless be damp and drizzly, and school.

'In case you were worried,' drawled Nathan as he

spotted Jake, 'this is just my goodbye outfit. None of it really goes.' Jake hadn't been worried about his outfit at all, but Nathan carried on regardless. 'You see, the leather lappets are actually Thracian' – he indicated the skirt – 'and the breastplate is pre-Empire. But what the heck?'

'Exactly,' Jake found himself agreeing. 'It's a great ensemble.'

'So, I hear you're leaving us?' Nathan blurted out. 'Charlie and I are not happy about that at all.' He leaned closer and whispered, 'We tried to persuade your parents otherwise, but they seem to have made up their minds.'

'Well, you know,' Jake mumbled, 'I'm three weeks behind in history.'

'Very funny . . .' Nathan replied, then, as Charlie came to join them, 'I wanted to give you this . . .' He presented Jake with a sword in a scabbard. Jake's eyes lit up: it was the same gleaming weapon, its hilt shaped like a dragon, that Jake had asked to borrow on his first keeper's voyage to Venice, 1506. Then, Nathan had refused point blank. Now he was giving it to him to keep.

'Are you sure?' Jake gasped, taking it carefully and admiring the fine craftsmanship.

'But you can only have it if you promise to come back.'

Jake nodded enthusiastically and thought he might burst into tears again.

'And this is a little something from me and Mr Drake . . .' Charlie handed Jake a leather pouch. He opened it to find a collection of beards and moustaches. 'That's my spare set – thought it might as well go to a good home.'

Jake threw his arms around Charlie to thank him, making Mr Drake squawk and puff up his feathers. He then turned to Nathan, giving him a great bear hug. 'Find Topaz, won't you?' he whispered in his ear. 'And wherever you go, keep a lookout for Philip.'

'We'll do our best,' Nathan promised, resisting the urge to straighten his clothes.

With a serious look in her eye, Galliana handed Jupitus the box that contained the atomium and the Horizon Cup. 'Be safe, be careful,' she said, her hand still clutching the case. He nodded and she let him take it.

'All aboard!' Jupitus called out as he made his way towards the gangplank.

Oceane rushed after him dramatically, dragging

Josephine along with her. 'You'll write, won't you? Just a little Meslith from time to time?' Jupitus responded with a curt nod. 'And I'll start preparations for the wedding! I was thinking *un thème classique*, with lots of nymphs and satyrs and acres of silk tulle?' He nodded again. 'Good luck, *mon amour*!' Oceane leaned forward and pecked him on the cheek.

Jupitus looked coolly down at the lioness. 'Be careful with that thing, won't you?' Before jumping aboard the *Hippocampus*, he turned and searched the quay for Rose. His eyes lingered on her for a minute, making her freeze in shock – then he shouted again, 'All aboard!'

Charlie and Nathan headed up the gangplank, Nathan gave a short 'impromptu' speech, and they cast off. Jake felt miserable. He longed to charge across the cobbles and leap onto the ship, but he knew it was pointless. He clenched both fists until he had his emotions under control again.

Rose was secretly battling a similar impulse to jump aboard. Ever since Jupitus had announced his engagement to Oceane, she had put any romantic thoughts about him firmly to the back of her mind. The look that he had just given her brought them surging back. She furiously twisted the bangles around her wrist as the ship moved away. Before long, the blue and white sails were already far out to sea.

Jake watched the *Hippocampus* until it was just a hazy shape on the horizon. Then a mist came in and it was gone – along with his hopes and dreams. 'The *Hippocampus* . . .' he repeated to himself. 'I know I've seen that ship before.'

The bell in the clock tower struck two. With Felson at his side and a lantern in his hand, Jake tiptoed down the corridor to the communications room. He checked that no one was watching, then slipped inside. The desks where the decoders usually sat were empty; the main Meslith machine – the *Meslith nucleus*, as it was known – stood in its glass case in the centre of the room, two inked quills poised over blank rolls of parchment in anticipation of the next message from history.

'This way,' he whispered to the dog as he headed for another door on the far side, carefully opened it and went in. He shone his lantern around the long vaulted room, lined from floor to ceiling with shelf after shelf of ancient leather-bound tomes. It was reminiscent of the London bureau below the Monument, with its succession of study tables adorned with globes, but these ones were lit by the pale moonlight shining through the skylights.

After his mission to Venice and Germany, and before the Stockholm debacle, Jake had spent two weeks at Point Zero, getting to know the island and all its secrets a little better. He had been shown the testing chamber – a room with tapestry-covered walls and a mass of scientific equipment, where an agent's valour could be analysed and assessed – and the assault vault, a labyrinth of spiral staircases and stone passageways where training exercises were carried out. This vault, accessed through the armoury, had reminded Jake of a ghost train at a fair, with its flying arrows, slicing swords and life-size 'enemy' puppets jumping out or shooting up from the floor.

Jake had also discovered the archives, where records were kept – not only log books of every mission and journey undertaken, but also precise accounts of the weather throughout time, as well as tide tables, moon tables, sunrises, population statistics and a host of other information. Here you could find out, for example, how many people lived in Cadiz in 1740, how warm their summer was and what they were eating for lunch.

This was the room into which Jake and Felson, having waited for everyone to retire, had now crept. If Jake was to be denied an assignment, he had decided he would set himself one: he wanted to find out more about the *Hippocampus* – why it seemed so familiar and why his parents were so evasive about it.

At the far end was the section that detailed all the sea voyages – which ships had been used and to which destinations. The volumes – the spines imprinted with the History Keepers' symbol of planets whizzing around an hourglass – were arranged alphabetically: a series of twelve belonged to the *Barco Dorado*, another fifteen to the *Campana*, twenty or so to the *Conqueror*, and so on. Jake noticed one book standing slightly proud of the others: it was the last in the series dedicated to the *Escape*, the ship on which he had first sailed from London – that fateful journey during which he had learned that he could travel through time. He took it down and flicked through its pages, each one densely inscribed with beautifully curling letters. The last entry brought a smile to his face:

at the end of the list of passenger names – *Jupitus Cole, Charlie Chieverley, Topaz St Honoré*, etc., etc., was his own: *Jake Djones, 14. So I'm leaving Point Zero*, Jake thought to himself, *but here's the proof, in black and white, that I'm a History Keeper.*

He put it back and found the records of the *Hippocampus* – only six volumes. Jake took down the first and started scanning its contents. There was nothing but a succession of unfamiliar names. The second had no more to offer. In the third, Galliana Goethe's name appeared a number of times. In the fourth he saw Jupitus Cole's, and then, to Jake's amazement, the name Djones started making an appearance. Alan, Miriam and Rose were all there, either travelling alone or together, on trips to Macedonia, Persia, Numidia, Ostia – even a trip to Londinium, as London was called during Roman times. Next to each entry was the agent's age at the time. It was odd for Jake to imagine his parents when they were only seventeen and eighteen. How different they must have been.

The fifth volume revealed further unfamiliar names, but on the second page of the sixth, Jake got a shock: listed amongst the passengers on a mission to Cagliari in Sardinia in AD 121 was *Philip Djones,*

14. Jake ran his finger over the inscription as if it could somehow connect him with his lost brother. He carefully scanned the remaining records, but that was the only mention of him.

Jake was just returning the tome to the shelf when Felson started growling quietly, eyes fixed on the far end of the room. 'What is it?' Jake asked. The dog's growl deepened and he started to curl his lip and bare his teeth. A table scraped on the floor in the communications room. Just as Jake started looking around for a place to hide, the door began to creak open. At first it seemed as if the visitor was a ghost. Then Jake realized that it was an animal – he glimpsed dark golden fur. The creature padded into view – a lioness cub with a menacing look in her eye. Josephine stopped dead when she caught sight of Jake and his companion. There was a moment of frozen silence; then she gave a low snarl and began to advance towards them. Felson also pressed forward, protective of his master, eyes narrowed, teeth bared.

'Stay there – that's a good boy,' Jake commanded quietly, quickly scanning the room for another exit; there was nothing but book shelves on all sides. Then everything happened at once: Josephine shot forward, Felson intercepted her, the lioness's giant paws came down on him; and they tumbled to the floor in a tangle of limbs, both snarling savagely.

'Felson!' Jake shouted in terror, rushing to intercept them as the dog gave a yelp.

Then another voice boomed out: 'Josephine, *arrête*!' Oceane Noire swept into the room. '*Arrête tout de suite!*' she shouted. She was carrying an old book, which she hurled at the lioness, who reluctantly let go of Felson. Oceane was holding a lantern in front of her face and didn't notice Jake at first. 'What's going on?' she demanded of her pet. 'Why is this stupid dog here?' It wasn't until she had pulled Josephine away by her diamond collar that she became aware of another figure, half hidden behind a globe. 'You?' she said, stiffening.

'You should keep your animal under control,' Jake replied firmly, putting his arm around Felson, who was trembling with fear.

'That mutt of yours must have frightened her. She's sensitive, you know – just a little baby.' Oceane ran her hand along the creature's back. 'What are you doing here anyway?'

'I could ask you the same question,' Jake replied, kneeling down to pick up the book that she had thrown. It was a small, thick, leather-bound tome with an engraving of a palm tree on the front.

'Give that to me,' Oceane snapped, stepping forward and snatching it back. She stuffed it into her bag, then smiled sourly. 'As far as I know, the archives are for everyone,' she said sarcastically. 'When I can't sleep, I find it very calming to come here and peruse ancient records.'

Jake found this hard to believe but did not comment. 'Well, we'll leave you to it.' He edged round her, Felson glued to his side, and headed back towards the door.

'I hear you and your *family*' – Oceane managed to make the word sound insulting – 'are to return to London . . . Good luck with that,' she hissed.

'*Bonne nuit, mademoiselle.*' Jake nodded politely and left.

'*Good luck with that?*' he repeated to himself as he crossed the communications room. The whole encounter had been unnerving, but Oceane's parting comment had sent a chill down his spine. 'She's up to something – I can feel it.'

6 CATASTROPHE SICILIANO

From the moment Jupitus, Nathan and Charlie entered the horizon point in the calm seas of the 1820s, they had realized they had a problem. When the Constantor rings were aligned, they had all felt as if a bomb had detonated inside them; as if their bodies – their skin and bones – had been torn asunder and sent flying in every direction. Usually the feeling was dramatic but exhilarating; on this occasion it had been sickening and violent. One second they had been drifting in a vacuum of pitch-blackness, the next spiralling towards the ocean like a crashing jet, or shooting towards each other at breakneck speed.

By the time it was over and they had returned to consciousness on the deck of the *Hippocampus*, they realized that their problems had only just begun.

Now all three looked around in terror. They had arrived in the seas of AD 27 . . . in the middle of a cyclone.

The Mediterranean was a seething mass of black hills and roiling foam; the sky was dark and heavy as lead. It seemed for all the world like night, but Charlie spied, far in the distance, a tiny patch of hazy light where the sun was descending towards the horizon.

'Watch out!' Jupitus cried out over the maelstrom, his eyes widening in terror. Charlie and Nathan turned to see a vast chasm open up beneath them. The great mast tilted, creaking, and the whole ship plunged down into the trough. The agents clung to the rail as a colossal wave broke over their heads and spewed down upon the deck, drenching them instantly.

'Which course?' Nathan shouted over the tempest. He was at the helm, legs apart to steady him. Of the three of them, he looked most at ease, but there was fear in his eyes.

Jupitus tried to balance long enough to unfurl the map he clenched in his hand. Suddenly the ship lurched again, the mast swinging from side to side like a giant metronome. Jupitus lost his footing and tumbled across the deck. As he picked himself up, there was another sickening lurch, accompanied by a screech of howling wind. The map was ripped out of his hand and swept upwards. Nathan's reactions were lightning quick: he vaulted up onto the wheel and plucked it out of the air.

Jupitus, his eyes bloodshot, his face pale green, clawed his way to the helm. He was suffering not only from nausea, but also from guilt. As group leader, it had been his duty to check the weather records before they set off. These were not always a hundred per cent accurate, especially as far back as AD 27, but they would certainly have mentioned a storm of this magnitude. But the truth was, he had been so preoccupied with the prospect of embarking on such a mission, so far back in history, after all these years, that he had completely forgotten to do the checks. He was painfully aware that Nathan and Charlie would know exactly who was at fault.

'May I suggest, sir,' Nathan shouted over the wind, 'lowering the mainsail? The engine will do us more good than the wind.' Jupitus nodded. 'Charlie . . .' Nathan gestured to demonstrate his point. Charlie set about unfastening sodden ropes and lowering the billowing sail. Mr Drake, who had gone below deck the moment they hit the stormy seas, watched him from under a hatch, looking miserable.

Nathan spread the map out across the wheel. Although it was soaking wet, it had a thin waxy coating and the shapes of landmasses were just discernible. 'We're here . . .' He pointed to a star in the middle of the sea, the symbol of the horizon point they had just travelled through. 'Vulcano is here' – he indicated a small island, first on the map, then with a vague gesture out to sea – 'in that direction. Unfortunately that's also where the worst of the storm seems to be.' He was right: the towering black clouds were streaked with pulses of lightning. 'I suggest we head south and make for Messina on the north coast of Sicily. There's a lighthouse that can guide us.'

'Yes,' Jupitus agreed grimly, 'make for Messina.'

'Changing coordinates to south, south-east,' Nathan bawled out to Charlie as he turned the wheel. The ship veered round with it.

Jupitus hung his head and murmured, 'I'm sorry, it's my fault.'

Nathan heard him clearly enough, even through the wind and rain, but he decided to have a bit of fun. 'What's that? What did you say?'

'I said I'm sorry,' the other repeated, cast down with the shame of it.

Nathan smiled and kept his eyes ahead. Just then the *Hippocampus* crested another huge wave and plunged down into an abyss. Jupitus held on for dear life, but by the time the ship had righted herself, he looked like a dead man. He could control his sickness no longer, his stomach mutinied, and the remains of fettuccini Alfredo – prepared an hour ago by Charlie to get them *into the Italian spirit* – surged back out of his mouth. Nathan ducked and watched aghast as it was swirled away by the wind.

The *Hippocampus* and her crew forged on, pursued by the storm. The sun sank below the horizon, and the darkness seemed to amplify the deafening roar. After fifty gruelling, nail-biting minutes (at one point the ship took on a mass of water that threatened to sink her altogether) they finally spotted a pulse of light in the distance.

'There – the lighthouse,' said Jupitus weakly, lifting his head from the rail. He was still chucking up – though now only bile and mucus. 'I think the worst is over,' he murmured, speaking of both the tempest and his own state of health.

But he was wrong: the worst hadn't even *begun*.

They were halfway towards the port of Messina, whose twinkling lights were now just visible, along with intermittent flashes from the lighthouse, when the wind suddenly dropped and the waves abated. Jupitus looked up hopefully, certain that his prophecy had come true. He was able to stand without support for the first time.

Charlie, at the stern, noticed everything going quiet; not a *still* quietness, but a taut, dense one that filled his ears. Mr Drake seemed to be experiencing the same sensation as he kept shaking his head to restore his hearing. Then Charlie saw an unusual shape rising up from the sea far behind them. He took out his telescope and examined it, squinting into the gloom.

'Hell's bells and Bathsheba!' he cried. He had seen something similar two years previously, on a trip to old New Orleans with Nathan and Truman Wylder (most memorable for the number of earplugs he had got through, with both Americans booming at each other all day long). This was the same twisting tube, the same rotating column of water and debris. 'Cyclone!' he shouted to the others, but the word stuck in his throat. 'Cyclone!' he tried again. 'Approaching due north.'

Nathan and Jupitus turned in unison to behold the spectre. It was gaining on them; its tight spout of water, like a giant luminous rope, advanced, retreated and advanced again.

'It's coming straight for us,' Nathan gasped. He looked ahead again, applied full throttle and forged on.

The waves started to build up once more, rolling and breaking in all directions. The calm was replaced first by an eerie whistling, then a low hum, followed by a sound like galloping hooves, and finally an unearthly rumble as the monster suddenly accelerated towards them. Charlie and Jupitus held their hands over their ears, unable to bear the pressure. They looked up in terror and saw a colossal vortex of water shooting up from the raging sea and spinning at three hundred miles an hour.

'Hold on, everyone!' Nathan called, clinging to the helm, his hair now almost standing on end. As Charlie clutched the rail with all his might, Jupitus tottered across the deck and down the steps below.

'I wouldn't advise that, sir. If the ship sinks, you'll go down with her,' the American yelled.

'The atomium is below, and the Meslith machine! We're doomed without them,' Jupitus shouted back, tumbling down the stairs into the main cabin. He spotted the Meslith machine, took Nathan's cloak from the back of a chair, and wrapped the machine in it. He looked around for the box that contained the atomium – it was nowhere to be seen. The ship tilted at a crazy angle and Jupitus flew across the room, his knees smashing against the door frame. As he picked himself up, the *Hippocampus* lurched again. He tried to make his way back, falling through another doorway into the second cabin and hitting his head on the far wall.

As the ship started to right herself once more, he saw the open box lying on the floor, a tiny bottle of atomium and the silver Horizon Cup visible in its velvet interior. Still clutching the Meslith machine, he grabbed the little box and stumbled up the steps onto the deck.

At this same moment the eye of the cyclone slid tipsily across the sea, finally focusing its might on the stricken *Hippocampus*. The suction started: a tarpaulin lying on the deck was whisked up into the funnel; a wooden bucket followed. Then the whole structure started to judder as it was lifted out of the water. Jupitus threw his arms around the mast.

Suddenly there was an ungodly creaking, a splintering of wood, and the mast broke in two. The top half took off, lurching up into the raging sky, yanking the mainsail with it. As it flapped away, the mass of ropes suddenly became entangled around Jupitus's legs, pulling him upwards. He was flipped upside down as the top half of the mast fought to rise into the air, stretched in a tug-of-war between cyclone and sea.

Neither Nathan nor Charlie had ever seen such a sight: it was a battle of the elements, weather versus gravity, with Jupitus at the epicentre.

He screamed out loud – a long, defiant curse – as the box of atomium was plucked out of his hands and went spinning into the vortex. Then it was gone, eaten up by the storm. He clung onto the tangle of ropes, his cheeks juddering, his eyes bulging. Then, as suddenly as it had appeared, the cyclone was gone, and Jupitus was deposited on the deck. Charlie looked up in horror as the broken mast thundered down on top of him.

Nathan stared, ashen-faced. One of Jupitus's legs was bent right back and his eyes were closed. He didn't appear to be breathing.

* * *

Jake was forcing down an almond croissant when the shocking news came from AD 27. He was sitting in the corner of Galliana's living room, dressed in his school uniform. It was horrible to be wearing those itchy trousers again – he had got used to the luxurious feel of the breeches he'd been wearing at Point Zero. He was almost beginning to understand Nathan's passion for clothes.

They were due to set sail for London in thirty minutes' time, and Rose had hurriedly organized a 'sending-off breakfast' in the commander's quarters. It was a genteel affair, with everyone making polite conversation and handing round plates of pastries. Rose, Alan and Miriam – the three of them squeezed together on an ottoman – were now dressed in their modern clothes, Jake's father in his trademark corduroy trousers and his mother in an old woolly jumper. Sitting beside them was a familiar item: their red suitcase, which Jake had discovered when he first arrived here. Truman and Betty Wylder, Nathan's parents, had also joined the party, along with Signor Gondolfino and a smattering of others. Oceane Noire had declined to attend, pleading a phantom migraine, but this gave everyone an opportunity to gossip about her and her *ridiculous lioness.* Jake hadn't told anyone of his encounter with the pair two nights previously, and now that he was leaving the Mont St Michel, there didn't seem any point.

He glanced around the room. He had been here once before, for tea with Rose, shortly after returning from Cologne. He had been entranced by its glass cabinets crammed with objects from different corners of history – everything from old clocks to jade figures to dinosaur bones. On that occasion, at Rose's insistence, Galliana had taken a violin from a case – an ancient, gleaming Stradivarius – and played a suite by Bach. Although she was an exceptional violinist, the sound had filled Jake with sadness: Philip had also played the violin – it was just one of his many skills, learned, it seemed, without really trying.

Jake saw the violin lying on Galliana's dining table. He turned away and looked out of the window. Down below on the pier, the *Escape* was being prepared for the journey.

Miriam had told Jake that they would be getting home exactly two weeks after he had first left London, in late February, just after half term. The thought of school horrified him. He couldn't help remembering Jupitus Cole's opinion on the subject: *Perhaps you would like to stay at that dull, insipid school of yours?* he had sneered. *Day after day of tedious study. Dates and equations . . . For what? To pass some pointless exams? To be rewarded with a tiresome, bland employment followed by a slow, meaningless death.*

Jake had never forgotten those words, and now they haunted him more than ever. As he was wondering if he would dare tell any of his classmates of his adventures, the double doors flew open and a decoder rushed in, sought out Galliana, and breathlessly presented her with a scroll.

Galliana put on her spectacles and examined it.

'What is it?' Rose asked. Galliana passed her the message, and she read it out loud: 'Hippocampus *down; atomium lost . . .*' There were worried glances. 'Dear me, that doesn't sound good . . . *Send reinforcements, port of Messina, urgent!*' Her face fell again as she came to the last phrase. *'Jupitus critical . . .* Critical?'

Alan took the message and put on his glasses to look at it. Miriam peered over his shoulder. 'Messina?' she asked. 'What happened to Vulcano?' There were puzzled faces.

Jake had nearly choked on his croissant. *Send reinforcements* – he had heard the phrase clearly. He wanted to put up his hand and volunteer straight away, but thought it would be better to keep quiet for the moment. Instead he sat up straight and looked attentively from one person to the next.

'What would you like me to do, Commander?' the decoder asked. 'Shall I call all agents to the stateroom?'

Galliana's brow furrowed as she thought through all the options. 'The problem is the distance,' she mused. 'AD 27 would be a stretch for any of us, without a young diamond to carry us.'

Jake didn't say it out loud, but thought: *I'm a young diamond! Send me – I'll carry you*. But no one was even looking at him.

At length the commander turned back to the decoder. 'Ask Dr Chatterju to set up the testing chamber and assemble all eligible agents there in half an hour. We'll see whose valour reads the strongest.'

Valour, Jake now knew, referred to an agent's ability to travel through time, those with the strongest being able to voyage the furthest (as well as support – or *carry* – the weaker-valoured agents with them). The general rule was that valour was stronger in the young, particularly when they were diamonds. (Each keeper could see a shape in the darkness when they closed their eyes. Jake, along with the rest of his family, saw diamonds, though many agents saw only squares or irregular shapes.)

Galliana turned to Miriam, Alan and Rose. 'I hate to do this, but I may have to ask you to postpone your journey.' Immediately Jake felt a surge of excitement at the possibilities that had opened up. 'I hesitate to send you on any dangerous mission,' Galliana continued, 'but I may ask you to consider a routine assignment to deliver atomium. Would you mind testing along with everyone else?'

Alan and Miriam looked at each other uncertainly and shrugged. 'Well, we can't leave them stranded, can we?' Miriam said without a great deal of conviction, casting a worried glance in Jake's direction.

'If I'm up to it,' Rose stated with much more enthusiasm, 'you can count me in!'

'Good,' said Galliana, taking off her glasses and making to leave. 'I shall see you all presently. I must go down to the communications room.'

Jake stood up in the hope that she might realize that *he* was their best bet. But she didn't even notice him. She left, along with the decoder, under a cloud of worry.

'*Che dramma!*' Signor Gondolfino shook his head as he struggled up with the aid of his cane. He bestowed a crinkling smile on Rose. 'Your delicious breakfast is ruined.'

'Mum? Dad?' Jake felt compelled to speak. 'Shouldn't I be testing? I'm the only young diamond here.'

Miriam's face darkened immediately. 'No, Jake, absolutely not!' she said firmly. 'Tell him, Alan.'

Alan agreed sheepishly. 'Your mother's right – not a good idea.'

Although there was clearly no chance of Jake being considered for the mission, his parents finally agreed to let him accompany them to the testing chamber to witness the procedure. He persuaded them by making them feel guilty about possibly leaving him alone again, as they had in London. Jake needn't have bothered: Miriam and Alan were quietly hoping that someone else would be picked over them.

When they arrived, several people were already waiting, dressed in the clothes of the period of history from which they came. Jake recognized one – a dandyish man in a wide-brimmed hat and lacy cuffs who looked like one of the Three Musketeers – as the man he had sat next to at his first ever meeting in the stateroom. All of them were at least a decade older than Jake. Some, such as Truman Wylder, who came *to try his ancient hand*, were four times his age. They all looked very serious, and a handful were stretching as if preparing for a race.

The chamber – Jake had only seen it once, and then in semi-darkness – was a high-ceilinged, square room decorated with large tapestry panels depicting moments in history: battles, voyages and processions. The centre was dominated by a large machine that looked a little like a giant Constantor: at its core was a solid, semi-spherical compartment with a red-cushioned seat – large enough to accommodate one person. In orbit around it were three metallic rings, each of a different thickness and circumference. Beside this were a number of levers and control panels, and a shelf full of bottles of coloured liquid and measuring devices. Here, Dr Chatterju, wearing a white laboratory coat over his kaftan, was carefully mixing a solution in a glass vial. His assistant – his young nephew Amrit – was checking the metal rings.

At length Galliana swept in, along with Olive, her greyhound. 'Pay attention, everyone. I have selected an extremely distant destination for the test, even more so than AD 27. It will be the same for everyone. Dr Chatterju, is the atomium replica blended and ready?'

Chatterju nodded. 'The participants will need to brace themselves.' He held up the vial and inspected it. Jake could see that it contained a quantity of luminous purple liquid that emitted violet steam. The scientist cast his twinkling eyes around the room. 'Who is to volunteer first?'

The dandyish musketeer stepped forward and doffed his wide-brimmed hat.

Galliana nodded. 'Thank you, Monsieur Belverre. When you're ready . . .'

Jake watched carefully as Belverre drank his dose of liquid. Amrit helped him up into the seat of the spherical compartment, carefully secured his arms and legs with velvet straps and placed a pair of large, dark, horn-rimmed glasses in front of his eyes.

'Enjoy the journey.' Dr Chatterju smiled as he

pulled a golden lever next to the machine.

The three rings started to rotate, each at a different angle, slowly at first, but quickly picking up speed. Within seconds they were travelling so fast they were merely a blurry haze around the central core. Within this, Jake could see Belverre, his hands twitching and his head gently nodding as if he were dreaming.

'What's happening now?' Jake whispered to Rose, who was standing next to him.

'Well, it's all very technical, darling,' she told him, 'but somehow it tests our valour; our ability to travel to history.'

Dr Chatterju was on hand to clarify more scientifically. 'The purple liquid is replica atomium,' he explained (Jake loved the way he made every word sound interesting). 'An exact quantity has been mixed to take the subject to a precise destination – in this case, far, *far* back into deep time. The machine simulates the effects of a horizon point. The subject then simply observes the scene and describes his experience afterwards. It is from the clarity of this description that *valour* is then graded.'

'The clarity?' Jake repeated, not fully understanding.

'Some people see it as clear as crystal; some don't see anything at all.'

'And some people disappear altogether.' Rose hooted with laughter. 'Do you remember when Oceane Noire's aunt was given *real* atomium by mistake and ended up in the year 606, when the Mont St Michel was occupied by marauding Franks?'

'I was doing Amrit's job then,' Chatterju commented with a mischievous twinkle, 'so I wasn't entirely to blame. But I will *never* forget her face when we finally managed to track her down.'

After a few moments the rings slowed and then stopped. Amrit unstrapped Belverre and helped him down. The musketeer looked as if he was half drunk – bleary-eyed and unsteady on his feet. Chatterju took him to one side and sat him down, then started asking him a series of questions, while carefully noting down his answers.

Amrit was just about to help Miriam Djones into the seat when the door flew open and Oceane Noire stormed in. She nearly knocked Jake for six with her wide skirts as she swept over to Galliana, '*Je viens de recevoir des nouvelles tragiques* – I've just heard the tragic news.' She sighed dramatically, clutching her neck. 'My poor, poor Jupitus – I must go to him *tout de suite*!' She didn't wait for permission; simply pushed past Miriam and jumped up into the seat. She had to squeeze her huge panniers flat against her hips to fit in.

Galliana shook her head, unimpressed, but nodded at Amrit to continue.

As the rings on the machine started turning once again, Rose whispered mischievously to Jake, 'With any luck, she'll disappear like her aunt.'

After Oceane and Miriam had been tested (needless to say, Miriam got the giggles the moment she was strapped in and had to do some deep breathing exercises to calm down), the others took their turn. After each interview, Chatterju passed the scores to Galliana, who looked at them with increasing concern.

It was past midday by the time they had finished. Galliana talked to Chatterju in a low voice, then solemnly announced, 'I am sorry to say that only one person has succeeded in the test. Miriam, you were very close, but not quite strong enough for this distance – which leaves only Rose. As she is also trained in ship navigation for that era, I will certainly be sending her to the Tyrrhenian Sea.'

'*C'est ridicule!*' cried Oceane. 'There must be some mistake – my vision was as clear as crystal.'

Galliana was tired and worried – otherwise she might not have answered so curtly. 'Mademoiselle, your score was quite the worst of the lot.'

'Out of interest, how did I do?' Alan asked with a nervous smile.

Reluctantly the commander answered, 'Perhaps you were worn down by your time in the sixteenth century – but your reading was low.'

His smile froze. Jake hadn't often seen his father look humiliated and it hurt more deeply than if the shame had fallen on himself. Miriam squeezed her husband's hands.

Galliana carried on, 'As you all know, we never allow agents to travel alone, however routine the journey, so we will need to spread our net wider. I will contact a number of overseas agents. Hopefully we can find someone in the next twenty-four hours.'

Jake could hold back no longer. 'Commander, could I say something?' He didn't wait for an answer, but pushed through the crowd, deliberately avoiding eye contact with his parents. 'Given that the mission is – in your own words – a routine delivery, and that our agents are obviously in urgent need of atomium, would you at least consider testing me for the assignment? It would save a lot of time.'

Alan Djones sometimes said things without really thinking, as if his voice were independent of his mind. This was one of those occasions. 'Go on, Commander – give him another chance,' he blurted out.

'Alan!' Miriam clapped him on the shoulder. 'We discussed this, remember?'

'Mum, please just let me try.' Jake turned to her, beseeching. 'I understand that you're frightened and I know I have a lot to learn – *everything* to learn – to be a real History Keeper. But I've never been particularly good at anything else—'

'Not good at anything else?' she interrupted. 'What about science and art and basketball? And your geography thesis was the best in the class.'

'And even you couldn't read it, it was so boring. Mum, working for the History Keepers, being part of this amazing organization – it's something I think I can do . . . I want to do it . . .' He made his voice deeper and squared his shoulders. 'I *will* do it, one way or another.'

There was silence, then Miriam heaved a deep sigh. 'I'm just your mother – what do I matter?'

Jake knew this was the closest he was going to get to her consent. He kissed her on the cheek and turned hopefully to Galliana.

She scrutinized him, then nodded. 'No promises. We'll test you, that is all. Dr Chatterju, one last measure, please.'

'Thank you, Commander, thank you!' Jake exclaimed excitedly, stepping forward to take his dose.

As Chatterju passed him the small vial of steaming purple liquid, he whispered roguishly in Jake's ear, 'Actually I had a dose standing by – just in case.'

Jake smiled conspiratorially and drank it down quickly. He had braced himself, assuming that it would taste as repulsive as genuine atomium, but actually it had a sweet citrus flavour.

Without waiting for assistance from Amrit, he leaped up into the cushioned seat. His legs and arms were duly fastened and the glasses positioned in front of his eyes. These were mirrored on the inside, and Jake could dimly make out his own honey-brown pupils staring back at him. Then he heard the soft whirr of the three spinning rings as they began to accelerate. Suddenly he felt a cool breeze in his face. He was overcome with a drowsy numbness and his eyes grew heavier and heavier. Just as it seemed as if he would fall into a deep sleep, brightness suddenly filled his vision and he jolted upright. He found himself in an extraordinary place . . .

7 A NEW BEGINNING

He was moving under a canopy of palm trees towards brilliant sunlight. Soft sand muffled his footsteps. The air was no longer cool but scorchingly hot – or certainly it felt hot; Jake wasn't sure if it was just an illusion. He came to the edge of the palms, stopped and surveyed the scene.

Ahead of him lay a palace compound – a low, sprawling group of buildings connected by shady colonnades. It was surrounded by clusters of tall palm trees, and its vibrant red walls stood out against the intense turquoise sky. Beyond it and on either side there was desert – an endless succession of softly undulating dunes shimmering far into the distance.

Suddenly there was a squawking sound that made Jake start. A bird took off from the palms behind him and soared over his head and out over the desert. It was a beautiful creature, glistening like a jewel in the sunlight, wings of emerald green stretched wide. As it glided into the distance, Jake saw a series of shapes on the horizon. They were hard to distinguish at first, as the air danced in the heat; but as he looked closer he made out three triangles, similarly proportioned, one smaller than the other two.

'The pyramids . . .?' Jake murmured in wonder. 'The pyramids of Egypt . . .' As he gazed at the ancient structures, serene and alone in the vast land-scape, utterly untouched by the modern world, he felt a sudden surge of emotion. His heart swelled and a tear came to his eye. 'History is amazing . . .' he whispered solemnly. 'Just amazing!'

The sun was burning into him like a blowtorch. His throat was parched and he needed water, so he started to make his way across the sand towards the palace – a fourteen-year-old boy in his school uniform, with just his shadow for company in this vast landscape.

He approached the striking entrance – triple-height wooden doors riveted with silver straps. These were flanked on either side by a towering statue: two giant golden figures with human bodies and animal heads. Each held its forearm imperiously across its chest, clutching a sceptre in its hand. Jake squinted up at their heads, with their long snouts and pointed ears; he was completely dwarfed by them – his head only came up to their knees.

He pushed open the doors, stepped into the echoey coolness of the interior and followed a wide marble passageway into a large atrium. He had visited ancient buildings before (just last year, on a dismally wet Tuesday, his class had gone to look at some dusty Roman mosaics), but he always found it hard to imagine what they would have *actually* looked like when they were first built: ruins, by definition, are worn and drab. The first thing that Jake noticed here was that it was full of colour.

On all sides were rows of stone columns, painted every colour of the rainbow: carmine, indigo, cerulean blue, dark lavender, lapis green and cadmium red. Beyond the columns, the walls were covered in intricate hieroglyphics, a million vivid symbols: birds, beetles, moons and countless other images. Cats dozed in the shadows. One got up, arched its back, stretched its legs, then curled up to sleep some more.

In the centre of the room, open to the sky, there

was a square pond, around which incense burners gave off a scent of jasmine. Jake went to examine it, kneeling down and sinking his hands into the water. His throat was now as dry as paper and he wanted to scoop some up to drink; but the water, like everything else, was just a vivid illusion.

The only piece of furniture was a spindly-legged table bearing a number of parchment scrolls. Jake went over to examine one that had been unfurled and weighed down at the corners with stones. It was a map – certainly the oldest he had ever seen – showing the twisting Nile and the little towns that lay along it. He was just bending down to study it more closely when he heard the sound of quick footsteps coming along one of the passageways.

Jake turned round as a number of guards filed into the chamber. They were dark-skinned, lithe and strong, and carried swords with distinctive curved blades; they wore leather breastplates, thick sandals and bronze helmets. Jake edged back behind a pillar as they started to check around, but it seemed that he was invisible to them. In fact, one walked straight through him. Their search complete, the guards stood to attention as soft pattering footsteps approached: five young ladies appeared, in pleated white dresses, with belts and neckpieces as colourful and elaborate as the painted columns.

The last figure to enter clearly commanded respect – everyone bowed as she came in. She was shorter and slighter than the rest, but she seemed to fill the space with an aura of power. In her bare feet she stepped over to the table and looked at the map, then, without turning round, addressed her retinue. To Jake's ears her voice sounded as foreign and musical as birdsong.

He stepped forward to examine her more closely. He knew he was invisible – he knew he was actually sitting inside a piece of apparatus in a room in Normandy – but he was frightened of this tiny woman who radiated such authority. She wore a headdress fashioned in the shape of a bird, just like the emerald-winged one he had seen before entering the palace. Her skin was as pale as marble, her lips as red as strawberries, her eyes as dark and dazzling as jet.

As Jake gazed into them, he felt a cool rush of air. All at once he was aware of golden rings rotating around him, and the woman's eyes started to fade – until all that remained were two shining black pupils; then, with a pop, those also disappeared.

Jake found himself once more in the testing room, with his parents and all the other agents peering at him.

'All right, darling?' Miriam asked hesitantly. 'You were certainly shaking around a lot.'

Jake nodded blearily, stunned by the sudden transition from a bright palace in Egypt to this dimly lit chamber with its dark tapestries. Amrit untied the straps and helped Jake down. Then Dr Chatterju stepped forward with his notepad, smiling warmly. He looked down through his round spectacles and started asking all sorts of questions about the journey Jake had just taken.

Jake needed no coaxing; he described everything in detail, from the palm trees to the palace, the bird, the pyramids ('You actually *saw* them?' Alan exclaimed out loud. 'No one ever *sees* them!'), the courtyard, the pond, the map and the women. With each additional piece of information, the group around him grew more and more astonished, some shaking their heads in disbelief.

'*C'est impossible!*' Oceane snorted when Jake gave the exact colour and form of the imperious lady's headdress.

After a while Chatterju, who had been scribbling

furiously, trying to keep up with Jake, shook his head and put down his notepad. When the boy finished, the other agents were all looking at him in amazement.

'So?' he asked them. 'Did I pass?'

Galliana took a deep breath and looked at Miriam with a questioning eye. It was Alan, however, who spoke first. 'Did you pass?!' He stepped forward and threw an arm round his son. 'Did you ever! I've never heard the like! Not even Nathan Wylder can see so much detail in a test that far back.'

Jake rewarded himself with the glimmer of a smile as his dad pinched his cheek proudly. 'He's an adventurer, Miriam,' he said with a tear in his eye. 'Our boy's an adventurer – nothing we can do about it!'

Miriam just stared back at him, stony-faced.

Galliana nodded at Jake. 'Congratulations. You just travelled to 1350 BC. The test proves that you could travel there in real time – although, of course, the actual journey would not be so pleasant. You have an uncommon talent, Jake.'

At this point Oceane Noire had heard enough. 'I must go and feed Josephine, she'll be starving,' she announced, and flounced out of the room, bumping into Jake with her panniers again. No one paid her any attention.

'1350 BC?' Jake murmured. 'That's . . . over two thousand years ago.'

'Three thousand, one hundred and seventy to be precise. Apart from Rose, all anyone else could make out was vague shapes.'

'And who was the lady at the end?' Jake asked. 'Was she real?'

'She was real once. I had the dubious pleasure of meeting her. She was charming, but as dangerous as a pit of vipers.'

'Cleopatra?' Jake asked excitedly. In truth she was the only famous Egyptian he knew.

'Dear me, no, not that troublemaker.' Galliana shook her head. 'And way before her time. It was Nefertiti.'

Jake took a deep breath. He drew himself up as tall as possible and affected his deepest, most grown-up voice. 'So does this mean I can go on the assignment with Rose?'

Galliana looked round at Miriam. For a moment there was silence, then Jake's mum shrugged and resigned herself to fate. She knew that, try as she might, she could not prevent her son becoming a History Keeper. 'It was the same with Philip,' she said quietly. 'The power was simply too strong.'

In less than an hour Jake and Rose were being fitted for their Roman outfits in the costumiery – Jake by Signor Gondolfino himself. He'd already been given a white tunic and sandals similar to the ones Charlie had worn, and now the tailor was carefully adjusting his brilliant-white toga.

Gondolfino was chatting to him: 'I'm dressing you as a young nobleman, the handsome son of a senator or some such. I've said it before, I will say it again' – his old eyes twinkled – '*bel viso*, such a face for history.' He fastened the toga in place with a gold pin and smoothed it down. 'Now, you'll need a sword of some description.' He was about to step over to a table where an assortment of Roman arms were laid out when Jake stopped him.

'Can I wear this one?' he asked hopefully, holding up the weapon Nathan had given him.

Gondolfino adjusted his eyeglass and examined the silver hilt in the shape of a dragon. 'Well, it's not strictly speaking the right period' – he shook his head – 'but it has some of the characteristics of the *gladius hispanus* . . . perhaps we could just about get away with it.'

Jake excitedly fixed it to his belt.

'*Molto galante* – very gallant!' Gondolfino nodded, motioning for Jake to admire himself in the mirror. He looked at his reflection: a proud young Roman stood staring back at him.

On the next level up, Rose was being fitted with a dress, a Roman *stola*, by one of the other costumiers – a tall, haughty man in a checked jacket and breeches. Her hair had already been piled high up onto her head and studded with jewels. Once the costumier had secured a band around her waist he stood back to admire his creation. The dress made the most of Rose's curvaceous figure.

'Somewhat on the voluptuous side, wouldn't you say?' she chuckled as she mischievously slipped a leg through the split at the front of the dress and adopted an alluring pose.

'I think it's pleated perfection,' the costumier swooned, clasping his neck dramatically.

When they were finished, Jake and Rose quickly went down to the armoury. Dr Chatterju had asked them to pass by on their way to the harbour; he and Amrit were waiting next to the shooting gallery.

The doctor called them over to look at something in his hand. 'I have this for you to take to Sicily. It's the prototype hoisting device designed by Agent Nathan Wylder. He's been nagging me about it for months, so I dare say you had better give it to him now that it is finally operational.'

'Hoisting device?' Jake asked. He was perplexed: the object looked like a belt. It had a large golden buckle, fashioned in the shape of a lion's head, its eyes marked with jewels, one green and one blue and each minutely engraved with the History Keepers' logo of planets around an hourglass.

Chatterju demonstrated how it worked. He moved Jake to one side, aimed the buckle – like a gun – towards a wooden beam in the ceiling and pressed the blue eye. There was a sudden whistling sound as a small dart flew out of the mouth of the golden lion, trailing a thin wire. The dart struck the beam.

'Amrit, if you would be so kind . . . ?' The boy stepped forward and Chatterju tied the belt around his waist and fastened it tight. He then pressed the green eye. To Jake and Rose's amazement, Amrit – grin still firmly in place – started to ascend towards the beam, ratcheted up by the ingenious device until his head bumped into the ceiling. Even then, he carried on smiling.

'It's a feat of deceptively simple engineering.' Chatterju chuckled proudly. 'It could take the weight of Henry the Eighth – even in his heavy period.'

Amrit was lowered down and the wire wound back. Then the device was reset and handed to Rose.

On their way out of the armoury, Jake spotted something out of the corner of his eye. He looked straight ahead, pretending he hadn't seen it; but, hidden in the shadows behind a rack of weapons, a figure was watching them. The silhouette, with its huge panniers, was unmistakable: Oceane Noire.

'As soon as you arrive, you'll let us know, won't you?' Miriam asked Jake the moment he appeared on the quay. It was a sunny afternoon and a handful of well-wishers had gathered, including Dora the elephant and Felson, his ears pinned back anxiously at Jake's leaving.

'Yes, Mum.'

'And when you reach the horizon point, hold onto Rose *tightly* – do you understand? It's one thing going back millennia in the testing chamber;

the reality is a lot more terrifying. The first time I travelled that distance, I practically went into a coma.'

'She's right.' Alan nodded. 'Had to give her mouth-to-mouth resuscitation.' He patted his wife on the back. 'There are *some* benefits to the job.'

'I got it,' said Jake, tossing his bag onto the deck of the small ship that was waiting for them. He read her name – the *Conqueror* – written in faded gold letters. He remembered that Topaz had pointed her out to him when he first arrived on the mount, describing her as a Byzantine dhow. She was similar in shape to the *Hippocampus*, but much smaller, the size of a large fishing boat. Her square brown mainsail was decorated – also in faded gold – with the motif of a trident.

'I made you both some food for the journey,' Miriam continued brightly, handing her son a holdall containing various covered dishes. 'They just need heating up. I think I may have surpassed myself,' she added with a proud twinkle, before a tear came to her eye. 'You look ever so handsome, darling. Doesn't he, Alan?'

Alan gave his son a hug. 'We're proud of you,' he whispered in his ear.

'Mum, Dad, before I go, I need to tell you something.' Jake was suddenly very serious; he looked from one to the other, then lowered his voice. 'Will you keep an eye on Oceane Noire? I don't trust her. Someone passed on information about the Stockholm mission. Maybe *she's* the double agent?'

At this moment he and his parents spied her on the battlements above them. They watched as she leancd over the parapet, her back to them, and flicked open her fan.

'A double agent?' Miriam chuckled. 'That would actually mean doing some work.'

Jake leaned in closer. 'A couple of nights ago,' he whispered, 'I found her going into the archives in the middle of the night.'

'The archives?' Miriam frowned. 'What were *you* doing there in the middle of the night?'

Jake shrugged. 'It's a long story. We should talk about it another time. But Oceane was behaving really oddly. She was holding a book with a picturc of a palm tree on it.'

'I don't think it's a crime to carry a book with a picture of a palm tree on it,' Miriam pointed out.

'She got into a terrible panic when I picked it up,' Jake persisted. 'As if she was hiding something.

And just now, in the armoury, she was watching us.' He put his hand on his mother's shoulder. 'Please, will you promise me – just look into it?'

'Of course we will, darling' – Miriam smiled – 'if you think it's important.'

Galliana gave a little speech, at the end of which she handed Rose the atomium for their journey. 'Guard it with your life,' she whispered to her old friend. 'Our situation is perilous.'

She watched as Rose carefully placed the consignment in her bulging carpetbag. Galliana knew that the luggage was completely wrong for ancient Rome, but said nothing, knowing that – like a talisman – Rose's carpetbag went everywhere with her, even to AD 27.

They all said their goodbyes. Jake was just heading up the gangplank when Felson padded forward hopefully. Jake knelt down and ran his hand across the great scarred head. 'I'll be back soon. Mum and Dad are going to look after you, along with Dora here.' The elephant showed willing by reaching out her trunk and playfully hooting in his ear.

Jake and Rose climbed aboard the *Conqueror* – as Rose was trained in navigation, they would sail her between the two of them – and cast off.

Rose felt a shiver of excitement. 'This is just the sort of boat I loved to take out back in the old days – sturdy and fast.'

Jake watched the party of people and animals on the shore as they became smaller and smaller. Even when Miriam had vanished to the size of a dot, he could see that she was still waving. Then she was gone, lost in the haze.

The wind filled the sails and buffeted Jake's hair. Once again he was overcome with the sheer thrill of the adventures that lay ahead. 'It feels amazing, doesn't it?' he shouted over to Rose, who was at the helm. 'Like a new beginning?'

Rose nodded, smiling determinedly, hiding from Jake her deep dread of the approaching horizon point. However many times she had done it in the past, however much she assured herself it would be all right, travelling into deep time filled her with terror.

On this occasion it turned out that her fears were justified.

8 OCEAN TO THE ANCIENT WORLD

The hour between taking the atomium and arriving at the horizon point was one of the most peculiar and sickening in Jake's life. As she handed him his dose with a shaking hand, Rose had warned him that no two journeys through the time flux were ever the same. 'There are so many variables,' she had said in ominous tones, 'and the further back in time, the more variables there are.' So, even though this was the sixth time Jake had taken the vile-tasting liquid, this episode was unique.

As usual, minutes afterwards, his head started to throb and he felt dizzy and disorientated; the sound of the sea became distant, and everything around him – the ship, the cabin, even Rose herself – seemed unreal. Uncomfortable as these sensations were, he was familiar with them from previous journeys. Far more unsettling were the disturbing visions. Before, usually at the horizon point itself, Jake had glimpsed snapshots from history – the glimmer of a castle in the moonlight or a half-built cathedral. Those images were fleeting and strangely uplifting; the ones he experienced now were both diabolical and prolonged.

To begin with he heard a series of sounds: snorting horses, the clash of swords, bells tolling, distant cries – first of single people, then of multitudes. Then the noise grew, like bacteria, into *solid images*; suddenly Jake saw gory vignettes of war, of collapsing palaces, raging fires and thunderous earthquakes. He saw bloodthirsty horsemen storming a citadel; a group of wailing women escaping a massacre across a moonlit river; a procession of masked men being led to a scaffold in a snow-covered city; two vast armies charging towards each other across a valley. The sounds of battle were so loud that Jake had to cover his ears. And still the visions haunted him: skies cracking with thunder, fleets of ships sinking and graves filling with bodies.

After what seemed like a lifetime, the nightmares began to dissolve and Jake was once again aware of the ship, the wind and the sea. He felt normal enough to sit up – he was leaning against the balustrade at the prow – and check that Rose was all right. To his horror, he found that she was no longer on deck. The ship's helm was unmanned, the wheel turning this way and that. The rings of the Constantor were almost aligned, signifying that they were fast approaching the horizon point.

'Rose?!' he shouted out as he leaped to his feet. 'Rose, are you there?' He tore along to the stern and scanned the ocean. If the unthinkable had happened and she had somehow fallen overboard, he would need to know immediately – before he took off into the past. He couldn't see her, but he had no idea how long he had been in a trance. He looked again at the Constantor – the axes were closer still.

'Rose?' he yelled desperately as he jumped down the steps and into the main cabin; but it too was deserted. A lurch of panic was added to all Jake's other symptoms – his nausea, dizziness and thumping head. He threw open the door into the second cabin. There was no one in there either; the bunk beds were empty. Just as Jake felt himself dropping into a vortex of despair, he heard a moan and saw a sandaled foot sticking out from behind the bed.

'Rose, are you all right?' he said, rushing to her side.

At first she didn't notice Jake; she was in her own world, rocking deliriously from side to side, clutching her carpetbag.

'Rose, you have to get up. We're close to the horizon point.'

She became aware of a figure leaning over her and smiled. 'He loves me, you know . . . Jupitus Cole loves me.' Then her face darkened. 'But he's marrying Oceane Noire.'

'Rose, we don't have much time,' Jake insisted, trying to pull her to her feet.

'I thought I didn't love him,' she murmured, 'but now I'm not so sure . . .'

Jake thought she must be drunk and even looked around for an empty bottle. Then he remembered the time he had gone to Venice in 1506: he had started doing an Irish jig and ended up embracing Topaz on the prow of the *Campana*. *He* must have seemed drunk then.

Jake had another idea: he ran along to the galley and grabbed a glass of water, went back and – apologizing before he did so – tossed it in Rose's face. Charlie had done the same to him, and it had revived him immediately. Now the opposite was true: Rose's smile froze momentarily, then she passed out.

'Rose?' He shook her again, but she was unconscious. *All right, take the initiative*, Jake said to himself. *How hard can it be to enter a horizon point? I've seen them do it . . .*

He charged back up the steps, flew over to the helm and grabbed the wheel. It was heavy and seemed to have a will of its own; he had to use all his strength to turn it right, left and right again, until finally the golden rings were aligned.

The ship started to judder.

'Ten, nine, eight . . .' Jake counted down, holding onto the wheel with all his might. A whirlwind encircled him; colours flashed. He had only reached three when suddenly everything became silent, diamond shapes exploded outwards, and he took off like a missile into the sky.

Everything he had experienced in the last hour might have been horrific – the sickness, the appalling visions, the panic – but this moment was sheer magic; one of the most mysterious and breathtaking of Jake's life. He shot (or, at any rate, his alter ego did) noiselessly into the sky, as graceful and swift as an arrow, searing through the troposphere, the stratosphere and into the deep, deep blue of the thermosphere. The Earth shot away from him and, for the first time in his life, Jake saw the planet as a whole. As he gazed down at it – a shimmering blue ball in a never-ending firmament of twinkling stars – he felt calm. In that moment it struck him that on this little sphere below him, *all* of history had taken place – from modern-day London where he'd grown up, to the nineteenth-century Mont St Michel, to sixteenth-century Italy and Germany, to the Roman times to which he was now travelling. All this – and all the hundreds of civilizations beyond: the Greeks, the Phoenicians, the Assyrians, the ancient Chinese and Egyptians. That blue planet had been home to all those epochs and their glories – their art and learning, their progress and invention; their kings, conquerors, explorers and despots. It was a moment of profound wonder that Jake knew he would never forget.

Within seconds he was flying back to Earth. As he shot through the sky, the continents took shape once again: Africa and Europe formed beneath him. A moment later he was careering towards the Mediterranean. Finally he saw the *Conqueror*, all alone in a sparkling sea. He saw himself standing at the helm in his white toga, and Rose stumbling up the steps onto the deck. With a final rush, he returned to himself.

Jake looked around, squinting in the sunlight. The sky was completely different here – a brilliant cobalt blue – and the air was fresh and warm. Rose, still a little bleary-eyed, came and put her arms around her nephew.

'We made it!' she murmured. 'AD 27.' They looked at each other and she burst out laughing.

They set their course and sailed through the warm afternoon, serenely cutting across the sparkling sea. Rose felt groggy (travelling to history, she explained, was far more gruelling for adults than it was for youngsters), and Jake suggested that she lie down while he took the helm. She insisted that she was too excited to sleep but would give it a go. She settled down on some cushions, and within seconds she was snoring like a foghorn.

As the sun started to set and the sky turned from pink to maroon to indigo, Jake – while keeping an eye on the wheel – brought a table and two stools from the galley and set them up on deck. He laid the table with a white cloth, knives, forks, napkins, and a lantern that he found in a dusty cupboard. He heated up the dishes of food his mum had given him, lit the candles and finally woke Rose.

It took her a while to surface, but when she saw what Jake had done, she burst into tears. 'Sorry,' she sobbed, searching in her carpetbag for a tissue. 'A touch emotional this evening . . .'

Jake showed her to her seat like a professional waiter. 'Mum said she surpassed herself,' he said as he whipped off the dish covers. There was a moment of stunned silence as Jake and his aunt studied their contents, then they both burst out laughing. Each dish was burned to an unidentifiable cinder.

'All right, presentation may need some work,' Rose conceded, plunging a serving spoon through the outer crust of charcoal on one of them, 'but I'm sure it tastes delicious.' She served up two portions and they both ate with trepidation. Just one mouthful produced more uncertain giggles, followed by a discussion as to what the dish might or might not contain – 'Nuts? Bacon . . . ? Toenails?' – which brought fits of such uncontrollable guffaws that Rose had to leave the table, shaking her bangles, to take some calming air at the prow.

Feeling guilty about laughing at Miriam's expense, after dessert ('dread and butter pudding', Rose christened it) Jake and his aunt drank a heart-felt toast to her: 'To absent friends!' they exclaimed and clinked glasses.

As the stars began to light up all around, like some boundless celestial theatre, Rose closed her eyes and let the warm wind caress her face. She began to tell Jake about some of the missions she had undertaken in her youth – in particular an expedition to the mountains of Tibet in the ancient time of Kanishka, and another to Incan Peru, where she'd fallen in love with a handsome farmer in the emerald-green plains below Machu Picchu. 'Of course, it's hopeless falling for a civilian,' she sighed, misty eyed, 'because they can't go back with you. It's hard enough explaining you live on the other side of the world, let alone the other end of history.'

The word 'love' reminded Jake of what Rose had said earlier about Jupitus – *I thought I didn't love him, but now I'm not so sure.* He decided he didn't want to embarrass her by prying further, but he was desperate to know whether it was down to the effects of the atomium or was actually true. As he gazed up at the north star, pulsing gently in the heavens above him, he pondered his own feelings on the subject.

Up until a month ago, when Topaz St Honoré had come into his life, with her mysterious smile and her indigo eyes, love – *romantic* love, at any rate – was something he didn't understand at all. It had always seemed to require the unnecessary expenditure of such a lot of energy. He couldn't put it into words, but Jake felt differently now. Somehow the sheer existence of Topaz made him want to do things better; be braver and more daring. She didn't ask anything of him, but Jake felt nonetheless compelled to make the world a better and safer place. 'A better and safer place?' he said to himself, shaking his head. 'Where do I get these phrases from?'

At dawn the next morning Jake spied land on the horizon and called over to Rose, who was fast asleep under a blanket, her head cushioned by her carpetbag.

'Here already?' she cooed. 'I must have dozed off again.'

Jake couldn't help but smile: she had slept solidly through the night. The journey back in time really had knocked it out of her. She sat up, her corkscrew hair going off in every direction, and squinted into the distance.

Despite the sunrise the distant lighthouse still glimmered with fire, but he could see a big landmass ahead. The faint outline of a town was just discernible, beyond that rose a volcano in hues of shimmering purple. 'Mount Etna, looking majestic,' Rose sighed dreamily. She took a compact from her bag, opened it and examined her puffy eyes. 'Rose Djones, looking majestic too,' she added with a giggle.

As Jake steered the *Conqueror* on towards the harbour of Messina (he was increasingly enjoying navigating), he noticed another ship approaching from the other direction, her two dozen oars moving swiftly and perfectly in time. He gaped in awe as she sped past them, decks teeming with activity. There were several men – personal guards – many of them bearded, and each wearing a golden breastplate that glinted in the morning sun. At the stern, under an awning, an imperious-looking couple reclined on a large velvet divan. An attendant was fanning them with peacock feathers. The man, dressed in a brilliant white toga, had narrow eyes and dark walnut skin. His companion was thin-lipped and pale and clutched her neck as she gazed out across the seas.

'*Salvete, amici!*' Rose called out mischievously. One of the guards, a particularly burly and handsome man, smiled and winked back at her, but the haughty couple ignored her completely. 'If you thought Oceane Noire was bad,' she confided to Jake, 'Romans – some of them, anyway – take snobbery to a whole new level. But who can blame them? They're the first civilization in history to rule the world, practically from one end to the other.'

Once they had rounded the island on which the lighthouse stood (Jake noticed that its light was produced by *real* fire; dark smoke was rising up into the blue sky), the port started to take shape: a jumble of square white buildings with terracotta roofs, interspersed with clusters of cypresses and palms, spread up into the surrounding hills. The harbour itself was teeming with ships of all shapes and sizes, docking or setting sail, delivering or loading up amidst a cacophony of shouting people and squawking animals.

'If all has gone according to plan,' Rose said, coming over to Jake at the helm, 'the others should be waiting here. See if you can spot them while I try and bring this thing in safely – I need the practice. Parking has always been my downfall!'

As Rose took charge of the wheel, Jake stood at the prow and scanned the quayside for his friends. He was thrilled at the prospect of seeing them again. Jake had only known Nathan and Charlie for a matter of months, but he already felt that they were his best friends. When people of your own age are prepared to actually risk their lives for you – and you're prepared to do the same for them – it gives a different meaning to friendship.

Jake trembled with excitement as he surveyed the busy Messinians – an attractive people, robust and glowing from the Mediterranean sun – going about their morning business, all dressed in tunics, togas and sandals. He searched amongst them for Nathan's tall figure, for Charlie's crazy brown hair, even for Jupitus's thin and haughty silhouette. He gasped when he caught sight of a multicoloured parrot, but then realized he was sitting on the arm of an old fishmonger with a crinkled face, and was a totally different colour to Mr Drake, anyway.

As Rose drew closer, she crashed into nearly everything heading in the other direction. It took four increasingly embarrassing attempts for her to dock, each time mumbling profuse apologies to an assortment of angry Sicilians, until finally the ship bumped against the quayside. Now familiar with the routine, Jake jumped out and fastened the moorings.

'Any sign of them?' Rose asked.

Jake shook his head. 'Shall I go and have a proper look round?' he asked hopefully. As well as being keen to find the others, he was desperate to explore this new and exciting world.

'All right, but don't go too far.'

Jake headed along the dock, gazing in wonder at all the activity, taking in the myriad smells and sounds. Everywhere tradesmen and merchants were buying and selling – amphorae of wine, sacks of grain, vats of golden honey and crates of fresh olives. There were stalls selling pottery and glass, animal hides piled high, cloth and parchment. There were pyramids of powdered dye in brilliant colours – crimson, burnt umber, ultramarine and cadmium yellow. Traders sold marble, mosaic tesserae, ivory, gold and chunks of amber. Meat was being roasted over coals, and there were pens of *live* animals – sheep, goats and chickens.

Jake took it all in. Only one sight wiped the smile

off his face: a cage containing several terrified-looking humans. They were chained together, dressed in rags, their hair matted and their skin filthy. A pot-bellied man with black teeth and lank grey hair held a girl by the arm as he auctioned her off. She was even younger than Jake.

He was overcome – first with pity and then with anger. 'Slaves?' he murmured to himself, and stopped and stared, jaw clenched, at the pot-bellied man. When a prospective buyer – a man with a white beard – went to examine the girl's teeth, as if he were buying a horse, Jake found himself stepping forward in outrage.

It was at this moment that he saw the parrot staring at him. It was perched on a windowsill, and this time Jake was in no doubt about its plumage. 'Mr Drake?' he whispered.

The bird suddenly took off, flew over Jake's head and landed on the shoulder of someone in the crowd. At first Jake couldn't see who it was, but then his heart soared as Charlie appeared. Nathan was at his side, looking magnificent in his brilliant-white toga. They were both tanned from their week in the sun. Jake wanted to shout out to them at the top of his voice, but decided it would be wrong to attract attention, especially as he was still on trial as an agent for the History Keepers. So he waited patiently, assuming the most serious expression he could muster, his heart pounding beneath his tunic.

As it turned out, Jake needn't have worried about showing his emotions: the moment the three of them were face to face Nathan dropped his bag, stepped forward, took Jake in his arms and hugged him hard. Then Charlie did the same.

'How are you, Jake?' Nathan beamed. 'It's great to have you here.'

'Is it?' he asked with a tremulous smile.

'Of course it is – we missed you. You're looking very dashing in the tunic department.' Nathan reached out to get a feel of the fabric. 'I thought so . . . Egyptian cotton – light, durable and positively zinging on the eye. I can tell Gondolfino likes you. We saw you arrive from the villa. Shall we . . .?' He turned towards the quay, where the *Conqueror* was moored. 'We're on a tight schedule.'

Jake looked back towards the slaves' enclosure. The young girl was being unchained and handed over to the man with the white beard in exchange for a number of gold coins.

'Unpleasant, I know,' said Charlie quietly, ushering

him forward, 'but these times are different. You'll need to get used to that. Besides' – he indicated the buyer – 'he looks kind. Her life might even take a turn for the better.'

Jake reluctantly tore his gaze away and followed Nathan back to the ship. Rose jumped down onto the pier when she saw them coming. 'Thank God you're safe!' she said, kissing them in the continental way with a peck on either cheek. Mr Drake, on Charlie's shoulder, edged away distastefully. 'So where's old misery?' she asked, looking expectantly around for Jupitus.

'Mr Cole is at the villa,' Nathan muttered through gritted teeth, 'mining every last drop of sympathy from his dreadful state.'

'And what exactly is his dreadful state?' Rose asked nervously.

'You'll see when you get there. I'm afraid he has selected you to look after him while the three of us continue on to Vulcano.'

Jake felt an immediate thrill at the notion of *the three of us*: whatever the mission was going to be, he was now part of it. 'So what happened to the *Hippocampus*?' he asked.

Charlie briefly recounted the terrible events of

the storm and how they were nearly drowned. When he had finished, Rose shook her head and took a deep breath. 'Dear me, did no one check the storm records?'

Nathan couldn't resist smirking. 'Good question.'

Charlie was, as always, diplomatic. 'Mr Cole, I gather, was rather preoccupied before he left, so the oversight was understandable.'

'I love it!' Rose trilled. '*Not* that you had such a terrible time,' she added quickly, 'but that the infallible Jupitus Cole actually messed up.'

'Anyway,' Charlie continued, 'it took three days and *all* my ingenuity to fix the Meslith machine, which is why you didn't hear from us for so long. And, most amazing of all, the *Hippocampus* will sail again.'

Nathan pointed along the docks towards a warehouse. 'They're rebuilding her down there as we speak. That's your other job, Miss Djones: to keep an eye on progress. They should be finished by the end of the week.'

'It sounds like I'm on holiday,' Rose announced happily. 'So where is this famous villa?'

'Follow that path all the way to the top . . .' Nathan pointed to a flight of steps. 'It's the double

doors surrounded by bougainvillea. And good luck.'
He turned to Jake. 'So, you ready to set sail again?'

'Absolutely!' Jake found himself replying with a
salute, much to Charlie's consternation.

'Please don't encourage him,' he said, casting his
bag onto the deck of the *Conqueror*. 'He already
thinks he's God.'

Before the agents went their separate ways, Rose
produced the hoisting device that Dr Chatterju had
given her – the belt with the lion-shaped buckle –
and handed it to Nathan.

'My invention!' he exclaimed when he realized
what it was. 'Chatterju is a genius!' he added,
immediately substituting it for his current belt and
attaching his scabbard.

The three young agents all said their goodbyes to
Rose, boarded the *Conqueror*, and cast off. Nathan
confidently weaved his way through to open water.
As Charlie unfurled the new map of the Tyrrhenian
Sea, Jake watched his aunt head up the steps until
she had disappeared from sight.

Rose followed the path all the way up, along narrow,
sun-baked passageways that cut between the jigsaw
of houses, until the air freshened and the bustle of

the town was left behind. From within the houses she could now hear the sounds of lunch being prepared.

'Ah, the bougainvillea.' She smiled as a shock of flaming pink came into view. The flowers tumbled around an old doorway. Rose turned the bronze handle, opened the door (it was ancient, even for AD 27, and creaked tantalizingly) and went inside. She sighed with delight as she found herself in the spacious, untamed gardens of a handsome villa. On all sides, a series of crumbling terraces, each lined with pots of sweet-smelling flowers, teetered down the side of the hill. The sound of trickling water came from a number of little fountains and ponds. There was also the most spectacular view of the harbour, the bay beyond and the perfect blue sea.

Rose looked around for any sign of life. 'Jupitus? Are you there?' she asked quietly, more to herself than anyone else. Then she spied a figure seated in the shade of a loggia. As she approached, she saw that the person's right leg was entirely encased in plaster and rested on a stool. The remaining flesh on show was a ghostly shade of alabaster – unmistakably belonging to Jupitus Cole. Assuming that he was fast asleep, Rose approached on tiptoe.

'I can hear you, Rosalind,' Jupitus murmured, without turning his head. 'A herd of bison galumphing towards me couldn't be less subtle.'

Momentarily Rose bristled with anger, but when she realized what a sorry state he was in, she softened. 'You'll have to be nice to me,' she said with a twinkle in her eye, 'otherwise I won't make you lunch.'

He shrugged without removing his gaze from the ocean. 'Already had lunch.'

'Well, you'll have to be nice to me anyway,' she replied in a firmer, steadier tone.

Now he did look up at her, with eyes that were proud and sad at the same time, and with the tiniest glimmer of a smile. 'It suits you, your hair like that, Rosalind,' he said quietly. 'Quite romantic.'

And he turned his gaze back to the sea.

9 THE SHADOW'S HAND

'So, AD 27 – how much do you know about it?' Charlie asked.

Jake shrugged. 'Well, the usual amount, I suppose . . .'

'I see – basically not a lot?'

They were standing at the prow in the shadow of the sail. Nathan was still at the helm, his head tilted towards the sun and a makeshift collar of shiny metal around his neck to maximize his tan.

'How much do you know about ancient Rome in general?' Charlie continued.

'I know about Julius Caesar,' Jake began excitedly. 'He was murdered.'

'Yes, in the Theatre of Pompey, by his fellow senators – though that was over seventy years ago now. Do you know *why* he was murdered?'

Jake replied with a gesture somewhere between a nod and a shake. He quite liked it when Charlie acted like an eccentric schoolteacher, but was also a little scared.

'Because he wanted to rule Rome all by himself. In short, he wanted to be *king*,' Charlie explained.

'I see,' Jake murmured wisely.

'But Rome hated the idea of a king, a single ruler. For hundreds of years it had been what they called a *republic*, with a new government elected every year. So they killed Julius Caesar.' Charlie demonstrated with a little mime of being stabbed a number of times. It was disconcerting enough for Mr Drake to go flying off in a huff and resettle on the yardarm. 'The trouble was, Julius Caesar had convinced so many people that a king – or rather an *emperor*, as they called it – would be good idea that it was too late to go back to the old ways. Anyway, to cut a long story short, there were seventeen years of exceedingly bloody civil war, some very gory decapitations and so on and so forth – until eventually Caesar's son, Augustus, became the first true emperor of Rome.'

'Quite a man, Augustus,' Nathan chipped in as he rearranged his sun reflector.

'Very accomplished indeed,' Charlie concurred. 'He expanded the Roman Empire dramatically, to Egypt and North Africa and east to Macedonia, connecting it all with hundreds of roads, as well as completely rebuilding Rome itself, transforming it – in his own words – *from a city of bricks to a city of marble.*'

'So is he still the emperor?' Jake asked.

'Died thirteen years ago,' Charlie replied. 'His stepson, Tiberius, is now in charge.'

'Bit of a tricky one, Tiberius,' Nathan put in.

'Nathan's right. He was once a good general, but he never really wanted the job of emperor, which explains why he now lives as a recluse on the island of Capri, governing at a remove through his right-hand man Lucius Sejanus, another gruff army type.'

'At a remove?' queried Jake.

'By post,' Charlie clarified. 'He rules the entire Roman Empire by letter.'

'But make no mistake' – Nathan left the helm and approached the others, holding out his arms dramatically and speaking in his most theatrical tones – 'Rome is in its heyday, rich beyond belief, huge armies everywhere; the greatest, most powerful civilization the world has ever known.'

'I'm sorry . . .' Charlie shook his head. 'I can't take you seriously in that ridiculous collar.'

'What?' Nathan shrugged. 'You'd prefer an untanned neck? Like some barbarian? Romans are very judgemental, very body conscious. You get things even slightly wrong and you're a laughing stock. Besides, I have standards, Charlie Chieverley.' He stuck out his chin and retreated back to the helm.

'You? A laughing stock?' Charlie shook his head at Jake. 'Surely not possible?'

Jake smiled to himself: he'd missed the friendly banter between the two of them. As he stared out to sea, he found himself standing straighter, his shoulders back, proud to be on a mission with his friends again. Then his mind turned to their assignment: to find Topaz St Honoré. Out of the blue she had sent that Meslith to Point Zero with her time and place coordinates – the island of Vulcano in May, AD 27 – along with the coded phrase: *Follow the shadow's hand.*

Topaz had haunted Jake's thoughts every day since she disappeared into the foaming waters of the North Sea. Her image sometimes appeared to him smiling or laughing – like on the day they first met in London, or at the village dance by the Rhine in

Germany. At other times she lurked in shadows, lost, full of sadness, a prisoner of her own dreadful history. Although she had been brought up – since the age of five – by Nathan's family on the Mont St Michel, she was actually related by blood to one of the History Keepers' greatest enemies, the diabolical Zeldt family. Daughter of Agata, she was also the niece of Xander, the prince who had plotted in vain to destroy the Renaissance.

By early afternoon an island had come into view ahead. 'That'll be it,' Charlie commented. 'Vulcano, the most southern of the Aeolian Islands.' He raised his telescope to examine it, then passed it over. Jake surveyed Vulcano with keen interest: it was maybe eight miles across, with sheer cliffs, and so thickly wooded it appeared like a giant emerald rising up out of the sea.

'Quite an odd destination – it's barely populated, with just one little port,' Charlie said, pointing towards a cluster of houses at the base of a steep slope, 'servicing various mining outfits. Even the volcano is dormant. Of course, like everywhere in the Roman world, there are all sorts of local stories: some say the island is the chimney from Vulcan's workshop, others that it's the entrance to the underworld.'

At the word 'underworld', Jake noticed Nathan giving Charlie a nervous glance.

As the *Conqueror* glided into the bay, Jake noticed a smell – a pungent, sour stench – which grew stronger as they approached. He looked round at Nathan, whose face was screwed up with distaste.

'Dear me, Charlie,' the American drawled. 'Have you been at the lentils again? I thought we discussed that.'

'It's sulphur, you idiot,' Charlie retorted. 'It's obviously one of the minerals they excavate here. Look . . .' He pointed to crates full of yellowish stone. 'Along with charcoal by the look of it,' he added with a nod towards a mound of black rocks.

The sulphur was a little too much for Nathan, who took out a silk handkerchief and held it to his nose.

As they docked at the makeshift wooden quay, various sullen-looking locals, their faces dirty from the mines, watched them through narrow, suspicious eyes.

'Friendly looking bunch,' Nathan commented under his breath.

Charlie, who was never one to take hostility personally, disembarked and cheerily approached a particularly grim-faced group; they looked like they might tear him in two and eat him for tea, but he simply bade them good morning, showed them his map and questioned them at length – needless to say, he was the only one of the agents who could speak and understand Latin with real fluency. The miners replied with a lot of grunting and ominous shaking of heads. Once he had found out what he wanted to know, Charlie returned to the others.

'Right, I think I have deciphered everything. Apparently Topaz's coordinates refer to a small temple, an hour's walk up the mountain. It's been deserted for decades, but was originally dedicated to Proserpina, the Roman goddess of the underworld.' Once again Nathan shot Charlie that look of trepidation. 'Sometimes known as the "Queen of Shades", which is very interesting, given Topaz's message: *Follow the shadow's hands*. According to the legend,' Charlie explained, 'Proserpina was abducted by Pluto against her will, and her goodness turned to evil, causing her mother, Ceres, to heap all sorts of revenge on mankind.'

'Yes, fascinating,' Nathan interrupted impatiently.

'Why were they all shaking their heads?'

'Oh, just some silly local story about the temple being haunted by the ghosts of her victims.'

'No!' Nathan suddenly exclaimed in a high-pitched voice that took Jake by surprise. 'Absolutely not! You know full well that I don't do ghosts in *any* form.' He shivered with horror. 'You two go alone. I'll wait here and keep my eye on the ship. Besides, the whole business is suspect – why would Topaz lead us to some derelict temple in the middle of nowhere? It makes no sense.'

'Which is precisely why we need to investigate,' insisted Charlie, fastening his cape. '*All* of us! Non-negotiable.'

A short while later, having left Mr Drake happily eating his lunch, Charlie led the way up the steep path towards the old temple. Jake noticed that Nathan was looking nervously from side to side. It was cool in the forest, out of the sun, and a scent of pine filled their nostrils. It was quiet apart from the occasional caw of a bird, but sometimes a twig would snap and Nathan would stop dead, staring into the dark canopy of trees, certain that some phantom was about to strike.

'If it was a ghost,' Charlie pointed out, pulling him on, 'you probably wouldn't hear it coming.'

'Thanks,' Nathan snorted. 'You really know how to put a man at his ease.'

Finally they emerged from under the trees and rounded a rocky peak. Gradually the terrain flattened out. It was an even more unsettling place than the forest. An otherworldly stillness hung in the air; the soil was black and dry, and giant boulders of pumice lay strewn about amongst gnarled, dead trees. Nathan became even more jittery, and when the temple finally loomed up ahead – two crumbling, lopsided columns framing a dark opening – the blood drained from his face entirely.

'This has got to be some kind of mistake . . .' He shook his head. 'Why don't we check Topaz's coordinates again?'

Charlie ignored him and headed for the doorway. A flight of cracked stone steps descended into darkness.

Nathan kept his distance. 'Well, what can you see?' he asked nervously.

'*Ssh*,' Charlie ordered. 'I can hear something . . .' He listened intently. 'Something . . . or *someone*.'

'Who?' Nathan gulped. 'What can you hear?'

Charlie continued in a low whisper, 'Lost souls . . . I can hear them calling. They're saying . . .'

'What are they saying?'

'*A man approaches who poses danger to all; a man of strong physique, of limitless vanity.*'

Nathan screwed up his face, listening for the voices, but heard nothing but the wind swirling out of the dark opening.

'*A man who thinks that ultramarine makes his eyes really pop. Bring us the head of Nathan Wylder—*'

'Shut up, Charlie, just shut up! That's an order. We all have our little foibles. You don't like goat's cheese or unpunctuality, so please respect my one tiny little phobia.'

'Look, why don't we all go in together?' Jake suggested, trying to suppress a smile. 'I'll take your arm if you like.' If he was honest, Jake was frightened too – the whistling of that wind did sound ghostly – but he felt that they would get on quicker if he appeared as unbothered as Charlie. Under any other circumstance Nathan would never have accepted Jake's offer, but now he took his hand and squeezed it tight.

Charlie grabbed a fire torch from his holdall, lit it and set off.

'I'll take that, thank you very much.' Nathan swiped the light and followed closely behind, with Jake at his side.

Grit crunched underfoot as they went down the steps. The air became colder as they proceeded further into the mountainside, and the faint breeze continued to whistle eerily. Finally they found themselves in a chamber and looked around. It was not a sight to put Nathan at his ease. Even Charlie found his heart beating fast.

It was unexpectedly large – like a crypt under a big church – paved with great slabs of ancient black stone, with a ceiling that disappeared into the gloom above. At the far end, dominating the space and ominously watching any intruder, was a great statue on a pedestal.

'Our friend Proserpina, I take it,' Charlie said, adjusting his spectacles.

She was much larger than life size – a scowling warrior goddess, seated, but with clawed hands outstretched as if she were about to tear her enemies apart.

Nathan was standing like a statue himself, clutching Jake's hand in a painful grip. Jake loosened his fingers a little before examining the rest of the room: set in recesses in the walls stood four much smaller statues, looking frail compared to the menacing goddess. Two lamps hung, unlit, from the ceiling, but otherwise the chamber was bare. There was a scurrying sound, and it was Jake's turn to freeze as a rat darted along the wall.

'I hate those creatures,' he muttered under his breath as he joined Charlie in front of the statue.

'This must be an antechamber,' Charlie said, watching the rat disappear through a hole in the corner. *'Follow the shadow's hands . . .'* he mused, peering at the goddess. 'Here – give me a leg up.'

Jake obliged, cupping his palms together and helping Charlie up onto the pedestal so that he was on a level with the statue's eyes. Carefully he examined Proserpina's fearsome hands to see if there was any movement in them. 'The hands must be the key – to let us in somewhere.'

Nathan tentatively advanced towards one of the smaller statues. He held up the torch and examined it in detail, his face wrinkling in disgust. Finely carved from stone, it looked like an emaciated corpse in a ghostly gown, with its head hanging down at an angle and stone worms crawling out of its eye sockets. As he looked closer, the head suddenly shot up and glared back at him. Nathan screamed, the torch went flying, and the whole room was plunged in darkness.

'Hell's bells! Nathan, what are you doing?' Charlie's voice shouted out.

'It moved! The statue moved – it looked right at me!' Nathan cried.

Jake had heard the torch drop and felt along the floor until he found it. He produced his flint lighter (ever since Nathan had given it to him on that dark night in sixteenth-century Venice he had never been without it) and re-lit it.

Nathan was cowering on the floor. 'You see?' he said, pointing at the statue. 'It was looking down before.'

As much as Charlie wanted to scoff at Nathan's silliness, he had to agree. 'Unbelievably, you're right . . .' He looked around at the other effigies. 'A moment ago all four of them were looking down; now only that one is.' As they turned to look, there was a grinding of stone and this last figure also lifted its grisly head.

'That's it, we're leaving,' said Nathan emphatically. 'There must be another way in to wherever we're going.'

'Just calm down!' Charlie told him. 'They're obviously *intended* to scare people and stop them coming down here. That's why it's said to be haunted.' To demonstrate his lack of concern, he went over and tapped one on its bony thigh. 'You see, just stone. Far more importantly, we need to find out how we get beyond this chamber – so please, could everyone put their heads together and work out what is meant by *follow the shadow's hand*.'

At this moment a long-lost memory surfaced in Jake's mind: one evening, when there was a power cut in his house (his dad, in a doomed attempt to create a built-in wardrobe in the hall, had accidentally drilled into the main fuse box), they had lit candles in the kitchen and Jake and his brother had made shadow puppets on the wall.

He looked over to the statue of Proserpina with her hands outstretched, and then at the two bronze lamps hanging from the ceiling. He went over to one of these and raised the torch as if to light it. To everyone's surprise, it ignited immediately. He went over and lit the other; this also lit up with a satisfying *whoomph*. Intrigued and perplexed, Charlie and Nathan stood watching as Jake went behind the statue and examined the back wall. 'There,' he said. '*The shadow's hand.*'

Nathan picked himself up, and he and Charlie went to look. They were astonished: the light from the lamps cast two sets of overlapping shadows, creating the image of a single large hand, its forefinger pointing at one brick in particular – one out of thousands that made up the back wall.

It seemed obvious now. Jake put his finger to the brick – it was spongy to the touch – and pressed hard. A moment later there was a deep rasping sound, and the entire middle section of wall rose up, gradually revealing a secret space beyond.

'He'll be putting us out of a job soon,' said Charlie, giving Jake a clap on the back. Nathan was so impressed that for a moment he forgot all about his fear of ghosts.

Jake led the way in as Charlie wedged a stone in the opening so they wouldn't be trapped inside. All three squinted into the gloom. It was roughly the width of a London Underground tunnel, and crisscrossed by a network of gossamer cobwebs. At the far end, standing in an indistinct pool of light, they saw a hunched figure.

'That's either another statue . . . or someone standing very still,' Charlie whispered.

'So kind of you to put me out of my misery,' Nathan replied drily.

'Come on – let's go,' said Jake, forging on. He felt he was tantalizingly close to Topaz and there was not a moment to lose.

'Stop!' Charlie suddenly shouted and pulled him back. 'Look!' He pointed to a shape protruding from the wall: a stone carving of a dog's head with its mouth wide open for the kill.

'There's another one there,' said Jake, making out an identical form on the opposite wall. 'And there!' He nodded at a third one jutting down from the ceiling.

Charlie understood immediately. 'Of course – Cerberus, the three-headed dog who guards the entrance to the underworld. And like the real thing, I have a feeling that this one is not exactly amiable. Look in its mouth there.'

Jake and Nathan peered up into the inky black cavity between the jaws of the dog on the left-hand wall, and could just make out, in the place of its tongue, the faint glint of an arrowhead.

Charlie removed his cape, bundled it up and carefully pitched it forward to a point directly between the three heads. There was a collective *twang* and a sudden rush of air. Three glints of light converged, and the balled-up cloak dropped to the ground – with three arrows sticking out of it. Charlie picked it up, removed the darts, tossed them to one side and shook it out: it had several holes in it now. 'What do you reckon, Nathan? Fashionably distressed?'

Nathan rolled his eyes. 'I hate that look. I have not an iota of respect for it. I mean, honestly – randomly torn material? Where's the craftsmanship?'

Once again Jake was forging on, his eyes fixed on the stooped, still figure at the end of the tunnel. He stopped just short of it. Charlie's first guess was right: it was indeed a statue, but carved from wood, not stone. It reminded Jake of some ancient relic you might find in a cathedral – an old man with a haggard face just visible under his hood and cloak and a wizened hand reaching out, palm up. It stood – like a mast – in the centre of a small wooden boat, set across a channel that disappeared, at either end, into the mountain. In the shadows underneath lay pools of water.

'That will be Charon then,' said Charlie, increasingly impressed by the set-up. 'The ferryman to the underworld. Our hosts, whoever they may be, are certainly doing things thoroughly – although the River Styx has seen better days,' he added with a nod towards the damp channel. 'That's perfect . . .' He had spotted something else. 'There's a slot in the palm of his hand. You know how the legend goes, of course?' he said, turning to Jake. 'You have to pay the ferryman to take you across the Styx; otherwise you must wander in limbo for eternity.'

'Limbo for eternity . . .' mused Nathan. 'Sounds a bit like that trip you once forced me to go on – the cuckoo clocks of Switzerland.' Charlie ignored him, produced a single golden coin from his pocket and inserted it into the slot. 'Wait!' Nathan shouted. 'Discussion first, please.'

'Oops.' Charlie shrugged as he opened his fingers and let go. The three of them heard the coin roll down inside the arm and land with a clink.

Nothing happened for a moment; then, gradually, they became aware of a distant rumble of water. It reverberated from deep within the mountain, quickly getting closer and louder. Finally it started to flow along the channel – just a trickle at first, then a stream, and soon a foaming torrent. Charon's boat straightened and rose up from the bottom of the channel.

'Quickly – all aboard!' Charlie cried, jumping in. Jake followed excitedly, holding onto the rigid ferryman.

Nathan stood his ground, shaking his head. 'It seems to have slipped your minds that I'm in charge here and we haven't discussed this yet – who knows where that river might lead?' But it was pointless putting up a fight – their course was inevitable. 'Totally unprofessional . . .' he grunted, running after them and leaping aboard as the boat took off down the tunnel.

The three of them yelled, half with fear and half with delight, as it careered this way and that, plunging down through the mountain, under the unflinching eye of the wooden ferryman. At one point the tunnel levelled out and they slowed, almost coming to a halt; then it fell away again, and they went plummeting down.

They held onto Charon, mouths open in a non-stop howl as they tore along the final stretch before emerging into the light, at which point they slowed down and stopped. They stepped off and climbed a small flight of steps to see where they were.

They had found themselves in paradise.

10 THE HYDRA GUARD

The sun cast a golden light over a steep, verdant valley that led to a cliff high above the sea. In the middle stood a group of fine-looking buildings, all connected by magnificent gardens filled with brightly coloured flowers, lawns, terraces, colonnaded walkways and fountains. Occupying the prime position, looking out over the sparkling ocean, was a striking villa of white marble, surrounded by tall palm trees.

The whole place swarmed with activity. A small army of youngsters – tanned, healthy-looking and as fit as Olympians – were training in different areas of the camp. In a circular sandpit, two young men were engaged in a swordfight. Even from a distance, Jake could see that this was no casual sparring contest: they looked and sounded as if they were fighting to the death. In other areas, youths practised boxing, archery and Roman martial arts. Those who weren't training sat on benches, watching attentively as they awaited their turn.

Further groups of attendants, workmen and gardeners – all wearing identical brown livery – busied themselves around the estate.

Jake, Nathan and Charlie, who had retreated into the shade between a cluster of trees and a small outbuilding, surveyed all this in silence. In vain, Jake had scanned the girls to see if Topaz was amongst them.

'A holiday camp?' Nathan drawled sarcastically as the vanquished gladiator was dragged limp and bloody from the sandpit.

'Nathan – look,' said Charlie, pointing to a towering structure – a giant domed cage, constructed from an intricate lattice of stone joists. Inside, several huge, vicious-looking birds glided around or sat on high perches. The dome itself was topped by a fearsome statue of a giant bird of prey, wings outstretched for flight. 'Vultures,' he said. 'Or, if I'm not mistaken, a particular type of vulture. Interbred with *Polemaetus bellicosus*, the martial eagle – one of the deadliest birds of prey on the planet – to make them extra bloodthirsty. Nathan and I have heard about these before, haven't we?'

'We certainly have.' Nathan scowled at the vast aviary. 'They're Agata Zeldt's pet of choice. The commander was right: this must be her hideaway.'

Once again, at the sound of Agata's name – *the most evil woman in history* – Jake felt his stomach flip over. She was the sister of Xander Zeldt, the dark prince from whom he had narrowly escaped in Germany. She was also Topaz's mother – although Topaz had disowned her entirely.

The Zeldt dynasty was the oldest enemy of the History Keepers. The mere mention of their name could terrify even the bravest agents. In the beginning, Rasmus Zeldt had been a friend and contemporary of Sejanus Poppoloe, the founder of the secret service; but he had descended into madness, disavowed the organization and pronounced himself king – not just of the world, but of time itself.

Many generations had come and gone before the monstrous King Sigvard had then appeared and declared war on all history, vowing to ruin the world and steep it in evil. He had taken a grand tour of the greatest atrocities of the past, from the Spanish

Inquisition to the witch hunts of Salem, learning his craft, before starting his own campaign of horror – attempting to destroy the past, to pick away at it and make the world unravel into a savage, ungodly place.

When he'd died unexpectedly on a campaign in ancient Mesopotamia, his children, Xander and Agata (Alric, his second son, had been missing for decades), had carried on his work with even greater zeal. For a whole generation, the History Keepers had fought them tirelessly, thwarting plot after plot. Three years ago, around the time that Jake's brother Philip had gone missing, they had disappeared from the scene; but recently Xander had resurfaced with a nightmarish scheme to destroy the Renaissance. He'd been vanquished and left, horribly burned, on his warship, the *Lindwurm*.

But now it seemed that his sister Agata might be up to no good.

'So, do we think that's her personal residence?' Nathan pointed to the white villa.

'That's where Topaz must be,' said Jake, scrutinizing its colonnades. 'What do we do next?'

'Men approaching, twelve o'clock.' Charlie nodded towards two attendants hurrying up the steps in their direction.

They quickly retreated to the other side of the outbuilding. Looking through a window, they realized that it was a laundry – there were vats of washing, as well as sheets and clothes hung up to dry. The two slaves went in, took some tunics from a pile – brown ones like their own – and left.

'Thinking what I'm thinking?' Nathan asked, leaping up onto the window ledge. He double-checked that the room was empty, reached in, grabbed three more uniforms and jumped back down. 'Look,' he said, showing them the stitching on the front of each. 'In case we needed more proof – *A* for Agata.' The letter was inscribed over the symbol of a swooping vulture, talons extended.

The three of them swiftly removed their own light tunics and slipped on the brown uniforms.

'The slave look isn't my bag at all,' Nathan complained, adjusting the cheap material to conceal his scabbard. 'Charlie Chieverley, what on earth have you got on?' he exclaimed. 'I do believe you have surpassed yourself.'

He was referring to the underwear that Charlie was trying but failing to keep hidden as he dressed – half-pantaloons embroidered with Roman figures.

'They're educational!' Charlie reddened as he yanked the new tunic down. 'They're my favourite characters from the ancient world: Aristotle, Archimedes, Cicero – to name but a few.'

He had only just sorted himself out when a stout man with a pockmarked face came round the building towards them, shouting something in Latin. At first Jake's heart stopped, thinking they had been rumbled, but it became clear that the man's annoyance was work-related: he wore the same brown tunic as the others, but seemed to be in charge. Charlie bowed and replied politely. Finally, the tirade over, the man strode off down the steps towards another unfortunate group of slaves.

'We have to take those baskets down to the laboratory immediately,' Charlie translated, once the man was out of earshot; he pointed to a stack of wicker baskets loaded with chunks of rock – the same pungent-smelling sulphur they had seen in the harbour. 'And he also let slip that the *magistra* – that's Agata Zeldt, I presume – is not presently in residence. That may be good or bad news. Quickly, we'd better move those rocks; we don't want to attract attention.'

They set to immediately, grabbing two baskets

apiece. As Jake lifted his, the cloying stench caught in the back of his throat, making him gag.

'Which do you think is the laboratory?' Nathan asked, trying not to breathe as he scanned the various buildings.

'There.' Jake nodded towards a low octagonal building, to which two workers were carrying similar loads.

They headed down the path towards it, passing close to the aviary. It was feeding time, and a man was shovelling great chunks of raw meat into a shoot that dropped down into the cage. The birds, which were almost as big as humans, flew down in a frenzy, cawing and scrapping as they tore off ribbons of flesh with their razor-sharp beaks.

'So what's the deal with sulphur?' Nathan asked. 'Any ideas, Charlie?'

Charlie shrugged. 'It could be used to make hundreds of things – medicines, pesticides, paper, vulcanizing rubber, sulphuric acid . . .'

Presently a gang of young warriors, pumped up after a bloody bout, came swaggering along the path towards them. They reminded Jake of a gang of hot-headed bullies at his school, only these were tough, muscular fighting machines. Close up, Jake could see their uniform more clearly: each wore a pale-grey moulded leather breastplate, with feathers sprouting from the shoulders. More feathers deco-rated the backs of their thick gladiator's boots. To complete the bird-of-prey theme, two of the guards were wearing glinting bronze masks with slit-like eyeholes and an armoured nose, hooked like a vulture's; the others were carrying theirs.

The three young agents kept their heads down as they passed by, but Jake noticed that one of the guards – he had a chiselled face and a dimple in his chin – was watching them through narrowed eyes.

As they carried on down the series of steps and paths towards the hexagonal building, Jake, heart thumping, continued to scan all the female faces in the hope of glimpsing Topaz; but she was nowhere to be seen.

They went in and found themselves in a large room. It was dim and cool – and empty. The air was thick with the most dreadful odour – not just the sulphur, but something even more acrid. There were several work benches covered in gleaming bronze instruments, scales and measuring cups as well as jars of specimens, liquids and powders.

'I assume the revolting whiff comes from those

dreadful things over there,' said Nathan, pointing to an array of curious plants along one wall. Each bore a huge flower shaped like a colourless, giant tongue protruding from deep indigo petals.

'*Amorphophallus titanium.*' Charlie nodded in agreement. 'Corpse flowers, as they are charmingly known. As well as smelling like putrefying flesh, they actually contain a stomach that can eat a small rodent. More and more, I'm endeared to our hostess.'

A man appeared through another door; he headed for a work bench and started pounding something with a pestle and mortar. He was tall and thin, with an angular face and a long plaited beard. Barely glancing at the boys, he indicated that they should deposit their baskets in the corner. They set them carefully down next to a stack of crates filled with crumbling pieces of rock. Jake caught sight of some unusual glass containers, hexagonal in shape – like the building – and filled to the brim with a blackish powder.

However, the bearded man now dismissed them with a brusque clap of his hands and they were forced to turn round and leave the building. On the other side of a stone courtyard was the main villa. A group of uniformed slaves were filing in through a side door.

'That's where we're heading next,' said Nathan. 'The key is to look like we know what we're doing.' With that, he took a deep breath and set off across the courtyard, the others following close behind. They checked that no one was watching and slipped through the side door into a dark passageway that ran the length of the house. At the other end, the slaves were just turning the corner, their feet softly echoing on the stone floor, and were soon out of sight.

The boys passed a doorway that led to a central atrium and peered in. It was as wide, high and bright as the service areas were cramped and dark, with a grand staircase and floors paved in white marble.

Nathan signalled for them to continue along the passage. 'This way for the private suites, I would say,' he whispered, and they headed up the staircase. As they did so, they failed to notice two heavy-set figures watching from the end of the corridor.

Coming to a door, Nathan signalled for silence and carefully unsheathed his sword. He opened it and peered inside, then motioned for the others to follow.

They found themselves in a lady's dressing room. Jake wondered if he might finally set eyes on Topaz, until Charlie announced, 'Agata's quarters – look.' He pointed to a dressing table, its base resembling another monstrous bird of prey. The bird motif was everywhere: on the handle of a vanity mirror, in a ceiling fresco, pictured on the lids of coloured glass jars of perfumes and make-up.

A short passageway led to the bedroom. Again Nathan, weapon at the ready, gingerly advanced and, finding it empty, signalled for Jake and Charlie to follow.

The room was dominated by a throne-like bed illuminated by rays of late-afternoon sun streaming through two huge windows – glassless frames with a single horizontal bar – that looked out across the ocean. The room was empty, but there were signs of recent occupancy: the bed had been stripped, but the bedclothes still lay in a heap on the floor; a chest had been emptied and its drawers left open.

Nathan clicked his fingers at Jake. 'Stand over there – make sure no one's coming,' he ordered. Jake went over to the main door. It was slightly ajar and he had a view of the landing and the top of the staircase.

Meanwhile Nathan headed over to the window and looked down at the vertiginous drop. 'Ouch,' he whistled. 'Quite a plummet.'

Charlie examined some large scrolls that had been unrolled on a desk and held down with weights. On top was an ancient map of Europe, Asia and Africa; the continents were oddly shaped but distinguishable. A great swathe, from the Atlantic, across the Mediterranean and North Africa, and all the way to the Persian Gulf, was coloured red.

'The extent of the Roman Empire?' Nathan asked.

'In theory,' sighed Charlie. 'Though our friend Agata seems to be staking a claim.' He referred to her symbol of a vulture emblazoned with an A that was printed on every country pictured.

From where Jake was standing, he could see only a mass of red spread across the page. As he craned his head round to get a better view, he noticed something lying on the floor – a single sheet of parchment that had got caught under his foot. He picked it up and examined it. It looked like the title page of a manuscript: there was a single heading, scrawled in ink – *Counters* – and below this, a motif of seven golden eggs. Jake wondered if it was important.

'Guys,' he whispered over to the others, 'what do you think about this?' There was no reply. 'Guys . . .?' he called again.

Neither Nathan nor Charlie was listening. They had seen something shocking.

'Is that who I think it is?' Nathan asked. He was referring to a painting set into an alcove: it depicted a young man – arrogant, haughty, with a mane of perfectly straight blond hair.

'The Leopard!' Charlie gasped in astonishment.

11 Exit Paradise

Jake's breath stopped at the sound of the name. *The Leopard* – the vile, silky-voiced spy who had intercepted them at the Stockholm opera house; the man whose accomplice Jake had woefully mistaken for Philip; the enemy agent who had made off with their entire consignment of atomium.

From the doorway, Jake turned round to look at it. Even from the other end of the room, the sneer was unmistakable.

'No, that really is too much,' Nathan declared as he set eyes on a companion portrait in an adjacent alcove. 'Why is Topaz next to that idiot?'

At the sound of her name, Jake abandoned his post, unaware of the two shadows moving up the stairs towards the landing, and was drawn irresistibly to the second picture. It was unmistakably her – the sphinx-like face, the indigo eyes, the tumbling tresses of golden hair. He could see that it had been painted recently; she still had the desperate look of a trapped animal that he had seen on the *Lindwurm*. This was bad enough, but there was an even greater shock: the two subjects were unmistakably similar. The Leopard (or rather *Leopardo*, as his name was given below the portrait) had the same mouth, the same cheekbones, the same eyes as Topaz.

Jake found himself asking a question to which he didn't really want to know the answer: 'Are they related, do you think?'

Charlie looked round at Nathan. 'What do you think? Could she have a brother we didn't know about?'

Nathan said nothing – just stared grimly at the portraits, his jaw clenched.

The discovery had set Charlie's mind racing. 'I hate to be the one to suggest it, but do you think she told him something about the Isaksens? Obviously she wouldn't have known about the rendezvous in Sweden, but it's an odd coincidence: *she* disappears and suddenly *he's* in Sweden.'

'Charlie, you're not thinking straight,' Nathan

pointed out. 'The Zeldts already knew about the Isaksens – they've known about them for centuries. Besides,' he added, almost angrily, 'there are no circumstances under which Topaz would talk, not even under duress.'

'*Omittite arma!*' shouted a voice from the doorway.

All three turned to see two muscular guards – gladiators from the training camp, both armed with swords. In an instant, the History Keepers had drawn their own weapons, though Jake got his caught up in his tunic.

'*Omittite arma!*' the first guard repeated.

'You want us to drop our weapons?' Nathan drawled as the men advanced. 'You're going to have to ask more politely than that.'

Suddenly two doors concealed behind the portraits crashed open and six more soldiers swept in. Jake froze, not knowing which way to turn, his sword still tangled up. Charlie swung round, but was caught off guard and was disarmed immediately. Nathan put up a brave fight, parrying the swords of his attackers – but the numbers were against him and within seconds four blades had converged on his head simultaneously. They hovered, glinting, in front of his eyes.

'I suppose that's as polite as it's going to get.' He shrugged, still refusing to surrender his weapon. With a sharp rap to his knuckles, one of the guards smashed it out of his hand. Jake finally freed his own weapon and, though the battle was surely lost, pointed it defiantly at each soldier in turn, edging towards the door.

He stopped when his back came into contact with something sharp. He turned slowly to see a *ninth* soldier. Jake recognized him as the youth with the dimpled chin who had watched them so intently when they passed by earlier. On impulse he lunged, but the boy quickly caught Jake's hand in his own huge paw, eyeballing him with a strange intensity as he removed the weapon from his grasp.

The History Keepers were herded together and led out of the room, the new arrival guarding their rear. Jake was horrified at himself: once again he had let his friends down. If he had stayed guarding the entrance, they might have had time to escape.

As they crossed the landing and started down the stairs, the ninth soldier shouted out to his comrades. They turned round, clearly perplexed; then, out of the blue, the dimpled youth shunted Jake and the others out of the way, pulled back his fist and punched the first guard with full force on the jaw. The man's neck cracked; disbelief flashed in his eyes as he teetered and fell, toppling the entire platoon like a set of skittles. Like a giant snowball rolling out of control, they somersaulted down the steps in a confusion of flying limbs, ankles twisting, skulls cracking, flecks of blood spattering over the white marble.

'Topaz friends?' the mutineer asked in a thick accent as he picked up the weapons dropped by one of his comrades. The boys were struck dumb, but Charlie managed to hold up a shaking hand. 'Lucius Titus,' the youth announced, flashing his perfect white teeth and firmly shaking each of them by the hand. 'I have waiting for you.' He returned their swords to them. 'Follow me. We have little time.' And he was off down the passageway.

'Where is Topaz?' Jake called after him.

'Quickly!' the soldier hissed as he disappeared round a corner.

'Who did he say he was?' Nathan asked. 'He looks rather pleased with himself.'

Charlie shrugged. 'Lucius Titus?'

In the hall below, Jake saw one of the fallen guards lift his bleeding head, fumble for a whistle and blow hard into it. He needn't have bothered: the front door was already flying open and another group of soldiers marched in.

'We should probably follow the man,' Charlie decided, and they hurried off along the passageway.

Lucius was waiting for them. 'Quickly now!' he ordered, herding them through a door, slamming it behind them and bolting it top and bottom. They found themselves in another bedroom like Agata's, but smaller. Lucius opened a chest, produced two long lengths of rope and started tying the end of one to the iron bar across the window.

'Is Topaz here?' Jake asked.

Nathan added airily, 'We'd love to have a word with her.'

'Gone, with the magistra.'

'The magistra?' Nathan repeated. 'I take it he means the delightful Agata?' he enquired of Charlie. 'The Zeldts do love their vulgar titles.'

'Gone where?' Jake enquired, a slight desperation creeping into his voice.

Lucius tightened the knot, threw the rope out of the window and began fastening the end of the second.

'Excuse me,' Nathan enquired. 'Might I ask what's going on?'

'Only way out . . .' Lucius pointed down. The soldiers had reached the bedroom door and were thumping on it, trying to force it open. 'Or maybe you like to stay and fight?' Charlie examined the escape route: there was a sheer drop right down to the ocean. 'Even if you fall, you be safe,' Lucius reassured him. 'Water very deep.'

But Jake's attention had been caught by something else: a pale blue dress with gold embroidery around its hem and neckline lay over a chair. It belonged to a different era entirely. 'I – I know that,' he stammered. 'Topaz was wearing it when I last saw her. Is this her room?' he asked the soldier, now looking around with keen interest. He noticed a long thick chain: one end was fastened to the wall; the other had a brace with a lock fitted on it. 'Was she tied up here?' asked Jake, going pale. He gritted his teeth. 'Where is she? We demand to know.'

'She has gone!' Lucius insisted firmly, throwing out the second rope. 'To Herculaneum.'

'Herculaneum?' asked Jake.

'It's on the mainland,' Charlie explained. 'Just north of Pompeii. There's a wonderful library there.'

'What's she doing in a library?' Jake continued his cross-examination, but the bangs on the door were becoming more urgent: the casing of the top bolt had almost come loose and the bottom was on its way.

'Questions later, perhaps . . . ?' Charlie leaped up onto the windowsill. 'Jake, shall we?' he asked, taking hold of the first rope.

Jake followed his lead, but then looked down and saw the drop. 'You're joking!' he gasped: they were higher than any cliff he had ever dared to peer over.

'Any time you like,' Nathan remarked sarcastically, one eye on the rattling door.

Jake grabbed hold of the second rope, took a deep breath and started to climb down. As soon as he was below the window – the top floor hung out over the sea – it swung sideways and he nearly lost his grip. When Nathan took hold of the same rope above him, it swung back the other way. Jake clung on for his life, and continued to inch his way down.

The four of them abseiled down the sheer cliff face, Charlie and Lucius on one rope, Jake and Nathan on the other. Suddenly there was a great splintering of wood from above and the sound of a door crashing open. A moment later, ten war-like faces – each protected by a bronze, slit-eyed mask – appeared through the aperture above, and within seconds, the soldiers were aiming bows and arrows.

'I see you at the bottom,' Lucius announced. 'Hurry!'

Jake watched in amazement as he kicked away from the cliff and let go of the rope. He threw his arms into the air and dived, yelling as he plummeted earthwards. Halfway down – simply to show off, it appeared – he tucked into a somersault before finally entering the water, his body faultlessly straight, creating a perfect concentric ripple far, far below.

'No way – I'm not doing that,' Jake stammered, picking up speed down the rope, burning his hands as an arrow from above whistled past.

Nathan was also appalled, but for different reasons. 'Just *one* somersault?' he sneered. 'No twist or pike? What an amateur.' And now he also let go and threw himself out with a flourish, attempting two revolutions *and* a twist on the way down. In truth, despite his bravado, he was not as elegant as Lucius, and hit the water at an awkward angle. Charlie grimaced.

Now, whole swarms of arrows were flying

through the air and, to make matters worse, the enemy were starting to hack through the ropes. Jake and Charlie knew that jumping was their only option.

'I'll count to three,' Charlie shouted over to Jake, ducking his head as a missile sailed past, 'and we'll go together.' Jake nodded grimly. He could feel goose-bumps tightening the skin around his neck. 'Keep as straight as you can. One, two' – Jake closed his eyes in prayer – 'three.'

He opened his eyes again, pushed away from the cliff, and let go. An exquisite chill shot up his spine; colour and light flashed all around him. He heard an arrow pass by in slow motion, then gravity took over as he plunged down, accelerating towards certain death. The ocean shot towards him and he hit the surface. His first thought was that it wasn't water at all: it felt like solid ground, sending an agonizing jolt up his back. But then he lost his hearing, and everything was cold, dark and blue. Within seconds he was swimming up towards the glinting surface. The moment he popped up into the sunshine again, another clutch of arrows whistled past into the water.

'Here!' Nathan was shouting. 'Soldier boy wants

us to go this way.' He pointed towards the mouth of a cave leading under the cliff. 'Apparently it goes through to the harbour.'

Lucius was holding onto a rock, grinning his dazzling smile. 'Let's go!' he urged them.

Nathan, Jake and Charlie – who was not at home in the water, and had swallowed a good deal of it – swam after him into a cavern, dripping with stalactites, that twisted its way into the mountain.

'Topaz told me you come,' Lucius explained, 'and that I help you. I wait three days.'

'The pleasure is all ours,' said Nathan with an insincere smile.

'How is it you speak English?' Charlie asked, holding his head above the water with difficulty.

'We all learn English,' Lucius stated. 'The magistra commands it. Also' – he smiled – 'I had extra lessons from Topaz.'

Jake looked across at him; he wasn't sure if he'd heard correctly in the echoey tunnel, but there was a distinct warmth in the soldier's voice.

'And the magistra is your commander?' Charlie wondered.

'Not any more.' Lucius laughed heartily.

'And what's your connection with Topaz?' Nathan asked tersely.

Lucius didn't answer the question, but instead asked him, 'You swim all right?'

'I swim just fine, thank you,' the American replied firmly. 'In fact I've won a load of prizes for my skill in the water.' He demonstrated by switching to his best front crawl and taking off at speed.

'Your friend is very proud!' Lucius laughed again, the sound echoing around the chamber. As it died away, they became aware of other voices behind them. Charlie looked back and saw a sharp-prowed boat carrying five or six soldiers, their strange hooked-nose masks catching the light.

'The Hydra never give up!' Lucius replied. 'We are trained to fight to the death.'

They all turned and swam quickly along the channel.

'I take it the Hydra are your amiable friends from the villa upstairs?' Charlie spluttered. 'Good name,' he commented to Jake. 'From Greek mythology: the evil serpent with many heads.'

'Not friends any more!' Lucius shouted as more missiles, this time identified by Charlie as *pila* –

javelins – and *spincula* – iron darts – started to fly through the air.

Finally the four swimmers made it through to the harbour. They hauled themselves up out of the water and picked their way quickly across the rocks and onto the rickety wooden pier where the *Conqueror* was waiting. Mr Drake, who was sitting anxiously on the yardarm, squawked – first with delight, when he saw them coming, then with terror when he realized what was going on.

'That is your ship?' Lucius asked, pulling a face. '*Exigua est*. It's small.'

'What does he want?' Nathan shook his head at the others. 'An Atlantic clipper? A Norse longship? Who is this strange person and what is his problem? All aboard – I'll cast off.'

Jake and Charlie climbed the gangplank, while Lucius, in a ridiculous manoeuvre, crouched and vaulted up, twisting in a salto and landing with a flourish on the prow.

Their pursuers emerged from the cave, firing another volley of missiles. Then, to make matters worse, they saw three more vessels, each with its own complement of soldiers, rounding the headland.

'I hate to make the bad news' – Lucius nodded towards the soldiers – 'but we now surrounded.'

Nathan jumped aboard, drew up the gangplank and took the helm. 'You might look the part – the tough physique, the dimple in the chin and the teeth that I can see my reflection in – but we've been doing this for years. And this ship may be small, but it's certainly not *exigua*!' To prove his point, Nathan fired up the engine, set the gear and took off, sending Lucius tottering along the deck. A group of locals, mending nets, watched in amazement. The *Conqueror* smashed into the three boatloads of muscle and careered off across the bay.

As the ship sped on, Lucius clung to the rail, amazed and terrified in equal measure, muttering about *magicus*.

'What's he saying?' Jake asked.

'He is wondering if this is magic,' Charlie translated.

'*Or if it is Neptune's craft,*' Nathan added with a roll of his eyes, before turning to the soldier with a shrug. 'Neptune, that's right – friends in *low* places.'

Once the ship had reached the open sea and Vulcano was just a hazy shape on the horizon behind them, Nathan throttled back and – in his most serious voice – called a meeting.

'So Topaz has gone to Herculaneum?' he asked. 'You're absolutely sure of that?'

Lucius nodded. 'Two days ago, with the magistra and Leopardo.'

'And *who* is Leopardo exactly?' Nathan enquired. 'Apart from someone who needs a good hiding.'

Jake braced himself for the answer.

'Brother of Topaz.' Lucius uttered the unthinkable, but then corrected himself slightly: 'Half-brother. They hate each other.'

'They've gone to Herculaneum for what reason?'

'The magistra—'

'Could we just call her Agata?' Nathan interjected testily. 'That name is starting to grate. And seeing as you're not working for her any more . . .'

Lucius eyeballed him defiantly, before continuing, 'The magistra was picking up a – *quid dico? – sarcina* . . . a package.'

'A package?' Nathan jumped in. 'What package?' Lucius shrugged, so he turned to Charlie. 'Do you think it's atomium?' It was Charlie's turn to shrug. Nathan continued the cross-examination: 'Where exactly was she picking up this package?'

'From the *theatrum*. The theatre.'

'The theatre?' Nathan snorted. 'This is all getting a little far-fetched.'

'Believe me. Don't believe me.' Lucius held up his hands. 'No difference.'

'Actually there *is* a theatre in Herculaneum,' Charlie chipped in. 'It's as famous as the library.' He turned to Lucius. 'I have to ask – why are you helping us?'

'I help you – you help Topaz.'

At this admission, Jake felt another twinge of uncertainty, a premonition of something. He found himself asking the question but didn't really want to know the answer. 'And why do you want to help Topaz?'

Lucius showed his gleaming teeth. 'Because I love her.'

This was bad enough for Jake, but his second declaration was worse:

'And she loves me.'

Nathan was also appalled at the notion. 'Now hold on a minute,' he said, pulling himself up to his full height and pushing his chin out. 'That's my sister you're talking about. I don't know the first thing about you. How old are you?'

'Seventeen,' Lucius replied proudly. He was older than all of them.

Nathan didn't like that at all. 'Well, that's *too* old for her,' he retorted.

Lucius squared up to him: they were of equal height, each as striking as the other, though Lucius was the bulkier of the two. 'I not care you do not like,' he smouldered. 'I risk my life on Vulcano,' he said, jerking his thumb back at the island behind them. 'Everything I had, gone. Now, I am *reus* . . . a criminal . . . *me quaerent* – I will be hunted down.' With a scowl, he put his face close up to Nathan's.

'Let's not be overdramatic!' Nathan grimaced, refusing to back away. 'You made choices – nothing to do with Topaz.'

'All right, you two,' said Charlie, prising them apart. 'Let's cool down a little.' He whispered in Nathan's ear, 'He's obviously just an ordinary chap that Topaz roped in to help. Go a little easier on him.' Charlie turned back to Lucius. 'It was very kind of you to assist us, whatever the reason. Is there anything else you can tell us about Topaz?'

Lucius reluctantly took a step back, loosened his breastplate, reached his hand inside and produced a small package from a secret pocket. 'This is from her,' he announced, placing it in Charlie's hand.

All three History Keepers looked at each other in disbelief. 'You've had that all this time?' Nathan grunted with irritation. 'Why didn't you give it to us sooner?'

'I give it to you now!' Lucius retreated, shaking his head and muttering to himself.

As the other two crowded round, Charlie quickly unwrapped the package. It contained a small wax tablet inscribed with two lines that had obviously been written in a hurry.

Charlie read it aloud: '*Meet me nine a.m., the ides of May, Pons Fabricius . . .*' He took a deep breath. '*Code purple.*'

The three agents exchanged glances. Nathan reached over and took the tablet. 'It's her writing, all right,' he commented. '*The ides of May* – that's the fifteenth, two days away. Is the Pons Fabricius in Herculaneum?'

'Negative,' said Charlie, pushing his glasses up his nose. 'The Pons Fabricius is one of the oldest and most famous bridges in the world: it crosses over to the Tiber Island. It's in Rome.'

'Rome?' Nathan threw up his hands and turned on Lucius accusingly. 'You said she'd gone to Herculaneum?'

'She tell me that!' Lucius replied, and once again they squared up to each other like a couple of stags.

'Just calm down, you two,' Charlie interceded a second time. 'It's quite possible that she has gone to Herculaneum and *then* to Rome. It's on the way there, halfway up the coast. Nathan, I suggest we continue north in any case. We can discuss our destination at dinner. I'll go down and rustle something up. All that excitement has made me famished.'

At length, everyone nodded in agreement. Charlie disappeared below deck, whistling happily. Mr Drake followed quickly, not wishing to be left with the warring factions. Nathan returned to the helm, and Jake and Lucius went to opposite ends of the ship to stew over their various misfortunes. After staring out at the sun setting over the Tyrrhenian Sea for a while, Jake glanced back at his rival.

Lucius was tall, impossibly good-looking, a soldier and, most crucially, nearly three years older than him. For all Jake knew, he was probably kind-hearted too (Jake couldn't imagine why Topaz would be interested in him if he wasn't). In Jake's eyes, this man – it pained him deeply to admit it – was the whole package.

*

Charlie returned from the galley fifteen minutes later, carrying a tray of delicious food. 'Simple Mediterranean fare.' He sighed blissfully as he set it down on the table. 'It's the best!' He indicated each bowl in turn: 'Olive tapenade, yoghurt and fresh figs, sorrel and chicory salad, home-made chickpea falafels and this delicious rye bread I bought this morning in Messina.'

In truth, Jake had lost his appetite a little; but Charlie's meal was, as always, incredibly tasty, and soon every last morsel was being fought over by the four of them.

When the plates were empty, Charlie fetched the pudding. 'I may have surpassed myself here – date soufflé with poppy seeds,' he announced proudly as he set down the dish. Out of earshot of Lucius he whispered, 'It's basically cheesecake.'

They tucked in – Lucius was particularly impressed – and hostilities began to thaw, though not for long.

'Which one of you is' – Lucius spat out a seed as he tried to recall the name – 'Yake?'

'*Jake* – that's me. Did Topaz have a message for me?' Jake asked excitedly.

'No.' Lucius shook his head and took another mouthful. The other three had to wait for him to chew and swallow before he carried on, 'You enemy number one, they say. I am surprised . . . I expect someone more' – he turned to examine Jake and even went so far as to feel his biceps, which were by no means bulging – 'more *infigo*, more *athletico*.'

Jake ignored the slur, focusing instead on the bombshell. For the second time that day he felt as if someone had delivered him a body blow. 'Enemy number one?' he stammered. 'What do you mean?'

'You make the magistra's brother, Prince Xander Zeldt, blind. There is money on your head. Now is money on *my* head too. Maybe I enemy number one now,' he declared with a laugh. No one joined in.

'Zeldt was blinded?' Jake found himself asking, as if in a dream.

'They say he never sees again.' Lucius shrugged as he helped himself to the last spoonful of pudding. 'Though he gone to see a special doctor.'

Jake took in the news. He had last seen Prince Zeldt, Topaz's infinitely evil uncle and scourge of the History Keepers' Secret Service, on board the *Lindwurm*, during his mission to try and save her. It was because of his calamitously misguided intervention that Topaz had had no choice but to set fire to Zeldt's cabinet of embalmed heads – which had exploded in his face. Jake did not know he had been blinded – and though he certainly deserved to be punished (after all, he did try and destroy Renaissance Europe with deadly bubonic plague), Jake was appalled to discover that he himself was now a wanted man.

'I wouldn't worry about it, Jake,' Charlie jumped in quickly. 'We've all had prices on our head. They're two a penny these days. If anything, it's a compliment.' He turned to Lucius. 'Any idea where Zeldt went to see this doctor?'

'A place called . . .' He had trouble recalling the name. 'Vindobona?'

Charlie whispered to the others, 'That's the old name for Vienna. No doubt he's gone to the nine-teenth century, when ocular surgery took off. At least he is out of the way.'

'And did he have that she-devil Mina Schlitz with him?' Nathan butted in.

At the mention of her name, Jake felt another jolt of anxiety. She was Zeldt's right-hand woman, an ice-blooded assassin. Her one concession to humanity was her love for her pet snake – though that had perished in the fire on the *Lindwurm*. Lucius knew immediately who they were talking about and told them that she had gone with her master. 'She and the magistra did not like each other . . .'

'Can you imagine those two together?' Nathan drawled. 'Conviviality soup.'

As evening fell, the three agents discussed where they should head first: Herculaneum or Rome. Jake wanted to go straight to the latter and start looking for Topaz, but Charlie reasoned – successfully – that as their proposed rendezvous with her wasn't for another day and a half, and as they would sail by Herculaneum anyway, they might as well go there first and try and find out more about this mysterious *package* that Agata Zeldt was picking up at the theatre.

When their course was agreed, Charlie took the helm (he loved being at the wheel at night). Mr Drake tried to stay awake on his shoulder, while Nathan and Jake sat down to enjoy the balmy evening and the celestial lightshow. Jake never tired of the magic of the star-rise.

Lucius had fallen asleep on deck. His bulky frame and handsome face were twitching as he took on some invisible foe in his dreams. Jake and Nathan examined him in silence.

'I don't believe Topaz is in love with him,' Nathan said finally. 'She doesn't fall in love – it's not her style.' Another few minutes passed before he spoke again. He turned to Jake very seriously and announced, 'I love my sister, but she's as complicated as a box of frogs, you know.'

Jake nodded and half smiled. He was in no doubt that Nathan meant this as a warning. He didn't reply.

The *Conqueror* sailed on into the night.

12 THE FLAME-HAIRED SIBYL

A convoy of three dark carriages rattled across the countryside. Each was pulled by a team of four black stallions – savage beasts with wild eyes and flaring nostrils, their coats shining in the moonlight. At the gates of a farm a night watchman stared – first bleary-eyed, then with growing alarm – as they charged towards him. The earth rumbled; he heard the vicious cries of the drivers, the crack of whips, and the vehicles thundered past, spattering him with gravel and leaving a cloud of choking dust in their wake. They tore over the brow of the hill and rattled down towards the flickering lights of a sprawling city.

The carriages flew down dark and narrow city streets, careless of both people and animals that got in their way; two wheels lifted off the ground as they veered round corners. They ascended a steep hill and at last clattered through an archway into the large courtyard of a huge villa and came to a halt. Two colossal gates, each decorated with the motif of a giant bird, were closed behind them with a resounding clang.

For just a second there was no sound but the panting and snorting of horses; then, with lightning efficiency, a platoon of guards filed out into the courtyard, standing to attention. The driver of the first carriage and his companion, both with the distinctive grey breastplates and feathered shoulders of the Hydra, jumped out, opened the carriage door and set down the step, before bowing and stepping back respectfully.

First to emerge from the silky blackness of the vehicle's interior was a tall youth, long-limbed and athletic. He too wore the uniform of the Hydra, but each element – breastplate, shoulder pads, boots and helmet – had been finely wrought in gold and ebony. He had a mane of perfectly straight blond hair and a cruel smile. A cloak hung down his back – a luxurious fur with the spots of a leopard.

He descended in one lithe movement, took off his gloves, then inclined his head as another figure appeared, ghost-like. It was a lady, tall and imperious, in a dress of shimmering darkness and a black veil that covered her head and shoulders. Through this, only the faintest glimpse of a pale face could be seen, framed by flame-coloured hair. Her whole being instilled a feeling of dread. It even chilled the blood of her loyal soldiers. As she stepped down, their backs seemed to stiffen in unison and their faces set in expressions of terror.

She placed a languid hand on her companion's shoulder – Leopardo was both her son *and* her lieutenant – and whispered something to him, then turned and swept towards the villa.

Leopardo strode over to the second carriage, opened the door and spoke to its occupant, who now descended – a portly middle-aged man swaddled in a cloak. He cast his tired, puffy eyes around the courtyard as Leopardo went on to the third carriage. This one was locked with chains. With a sadistic smile he peered through its latticed sides and snarled something to the figure inside.

Like a bride of darkness, Agata Zeldt glided down a wide, torch-lit passageway into the heart of the villa, her heels clicking on the marble floor. As she passed, slaves froze, trembling, their heads bowed low.

Ahead of her, huge double doors of ivory and gold swung open.

Beyond them, a vast ballroom was lit by low braziers of flickering flames. It housed a giant cage – an indoor aviary divided into two compartments. The left-hand section was inhabited by a solitary prisoner chained to a post, dressed in the uniform of the Hydra. He was stocky and muscular but now bruised and unkempt after days of incarceration. He lifted his head as Agata entered, but she did not return his gaze; instead she strode over to the right-hand compartment, where three massive birds – the finest and deadliest of all her flock – were squawking excitedly.

A smile lit up her face behind her silken shroud, and she put her pale hands between the bars and waited for the birds to come to her. They swooped down, flapping their wings in delight, nipping her with their beaks and fighting for her attention. Entranced by their devotion, Agata sighed, making her veil billow out in front of her.

She withdrew her hands and clapped to summon the birdkeeper. A moment later, a paunchy man wearing a blood-splattered leather apron lumbered out of the darkness. In his chubby hands he carried a basket, which he held up to his mistress.

Agata examined the contents: it was crawling with living things – rats, mice, thin snakes and monster-sized beetles – all slithering, scratching and scrambling on top of each other in a diabolical soup. Undaunted, she reached in and took hold of a fat rodent with a thick, hairless tail and passed it through the bars. The birds pounced immediately, squawking with pleasure, one snapping off its head, another tearing at its body, pulling it to pieces, their necks bobbing as the lumps of flesh went down.

'You poor things are starving,' she said. 'But not to worry – dinner's coming.' Now she went over to the other compartment. She stopped in front of the prisoner and removed her veil. As it slipped off, it made a soft hiss. Seeing her face, the unfortunate soldier did a double-take, as if he were looking at the Gorgon herself.

At first glance, Agata's face was handsome – proud, with a high forehead. But further scrutiny revealed something more unsettling: the features – nose, eyes, mouth, chin – all striking individually, did not *quite* fit together. It appeared as if they had been taken apart and carefully reassembled like Frankenstein's bride, leaving the faintest reminders of surgery.

Her age was incalculable; like her brother, she could have been forty or sixty, or even older. Her skin – which was pulled tight, erasing all her lines – was pale and translucent like marble, and showed a faint network of blue veins. One of her eyes was blue; the other was slate grey, and slightly duller than its twin. Most striking of all was her red hair, which was as rich and dry as burnt copper.

'Do you know why you are here?' she asked.

'No, Magistra,' the prisoner replied, his voice cracking.

The door opened and Leopardo strode in and came to stand by his mother.

Agata reached into her cloak and produced a small bundle of scrolls, speaking once more to the prisoner. 'This was the last batch of letters you delivered to me – three Imperial missives sent from Capri to Rome – along with a further two from the Senate back to Capri. Five dispatches in all.'

'That's correct, Magistra. As usual, I intercepted them at the port of Surrentum and made the necessary substitutions.'

'So would you like to explain to me about the remaining communiqués?'

'No, Magistra. I got them all.'

Agata stared at the soldier as beads of sweat formed on his brow. She held out her hand and Leopardo deposited into it another bundle of scrolls. The sight of them made the prisoner shudder.

'My son retrieved these from a messenger already halfway to the city. If these letters, from Tiberius himself, had arrived at their destination, all our work would have been in vain.'

'I . . . I don't understand how it could happen,' the soldier stammered. 'I had ten men watching the port.'

The birds peered through the bars of their compartment with mounting excitement, knowing that some treat was in the offing. Their bloodthirsty caws become noisier and shriller as they poked their heads through, flapping their wings in anticipation.

'History is about to be rewritten,' Agata rasped through the bars, 'but your incompetence has caused you to miss the show.' She nodded at Leopardo, who stepped over and slid out the grille that separated the two compartments. At once the vultures took off towards the soldier. He cried out desperately, pulling at his shackles as they circled above his head, savouring the exquisite moment. Then, as one, they swooped down.

Leopardo clutched his mother's shoulders in delight. Agata's mouth fell open as she watched the spectacle, clasping her hands together as the screams of man and birds mingled in one satanic cacophony. A tiny fleck of blood flew across the chamber and landed on Agata's white cheek. She shivered as it struck her, but she did not wipe it off. Within a minute, the man's cries had died away; only the vultures could be heard, and soon their piercing cries were replaced by the sounds of tearing flesh.

Agata's expression returned to normal as the moment of ecstasy passed. She looked melancholy; Leopardo sensed it and kissed her on the back of the head.

'Don't be sad, Mother,' he whispered. 'Less than two days to go now.'

Even though he was used to the goriest sights imaginable, the birdkeeper did not dare look at what had become of the man tied to the post.

Jake was woken by a gentle nudge. He had fallen asleep, as was his wont, amongst the ropes on deck, snugly wrapped in a blanket. Charlie was leaning over him, with Mr Drake peering down from his shoulder.

'I thought you might be interested in something . . .' Charlie whispered (Nathan and Lucius were still sleeping, but Charlie was not so much being polite as enjoying the peace a while longer).

Jake sat up and squinted at the dawn: a band of pink light was emerging above a landmass to their right.

'It's a rather unsettling sight,' Charlie continued, pointing towards a cone-shaped mountain. 'That's Mount Vesuvius there.' His voice became more serious. 'And below it is the town of Pompeii.'

Jake had heard of Pompeii: he knew that it had been destroyed and buried when a huge volcano erupted. He started to make out the shape of a town, high walled and sloping down the hillside between the mountain and the sea. He wasn't sure when exactly Pompeii had met its terrible fate, so he half expected to find it in ruins, but its streets were already busy with early morning activity.

Charlie continued gravely, 'The town has another fifty-two years before calamity strikes. Everything will be wiped out: the forum, the theatres, stadia, temples, shops and palaces, gone in a flash.'

'What happened exactly?' Jake asked, then

corrected himself: 'I mean, what *will* happen?'

'In August AD 79, after eight hundred years of being entirely dormant, that volcano will blow like a volcano has never blown before. A fountain of ash and stone will spew up thousands of metres into the air; it will go on doing so through the day and night. Incredibly, most will survive this, but they'll wish they hadn't. For then will come the pyroclastic event' – Mr Drake edged away from Charlie in distaste; it wasn't so much the words he objected to, rather the florid actions that accompanied them – 'a surge of boiling, choking gas, travelling at two hundred miles an hour, instantly turning everything it touches' – Charlie paused for effect, and snapped his fingers – 'to black carbon.'

Once again Jake scanned the town – the tops of the high city walls were now catching the light of the rising sun – and sadly pondered its fate, taking some comfort from the fact that the people still faced fifty-two years of peace.

'In the other direction' – Charlie pointed far along the coast – 'on that peninsula right at the end of the Bay of Naples, is Misenum, where the Roman fleet is stationed. The Roman navy took a while to get going, but now it is the greatest fleet the world has ever known. It's quite a sight – have a look.' He retrieved his little telescope, opened it out and handed it to Jake, who trained it on the spur of land far in the distance. At first he couldn't make sense of the puzzle of shapes, but then he saw a succession of wharves, each with a flotilla of vast warships: it looked like a city in its own right.

The quiet of the early morning was broken by Lucius shouting in his sleep: '*Bellum parate! Ferte milites!*' He was lying on his back, his hands twitching as he arrested some imaginary foe. After a couple of minutes of role-play, which included Lucius banging his fists on the deck, Nathan emerged from below in a silk dressing gown, pushing his eye mask up onto his forehead.

'I was hoping *I* was having a bad dream,' he drawled, 'but he's still here.' He went over and prodded Lucius awake with a slippered foot. 'Good morning, Lucy,' he offered with a poisonous smile. 'I'm afraid there are chores to be done. We've drawn lots: you've got latrine cleaning.'

Lucius stared up at him in bemusement.

'For goodness' sake, Nathan,' Charlie grunted with irritation, 'leave him alone. He's done nothing to hurt you.'

But Nathan's expression had changed: he had seen the town of Pompeii across the water. He bowed his head respectfully. 'Poor old place,' he murmured.

A short while later they arrived in the small, neat port of Herculaneum, just up the coast from Pompeii. As Charlie steered the *Conqueror* into the harbour, he explained to Jake that this town would also be destroyed by the volcano, though the damage would not be as bad. Lucius overheard them as he was polishing his sword and asked what they were talking about. Charlie, although he was clearly bending History Keepers' rules about not tampering with the future, told him he didn't think it would be the best place for Lucius to settle down – he was an expert on volcanoes, he explained, and had a bad feeling about this one. Lucius looked at Charlie a little oddly, but Jake got the feeling the Roman would heed the advice nonetheless.

Nathan emerged from below deck and threw a bundle of clothes at Lucius. 'You'd better change,' he told him.

Lucius was still wearing his Hydra uniform. He inspected the offering with a look of contempt.

'And you can take that look off your face. Those are quality garments,' Nathan said, adding under his breath, 'Better than those preposterous outfits *she* makes you wear. Agata's Zeldt's obsession with feathers is lamentable.'

For his own part, Nathan had, rather self-consciously, donned a pair of gladiator's boots and a fitted leather jerkin over his tunic. He collared Jake. 'Now tell me the truth,' he said, striking a pose, 'does this jacket make my arms look bigger?'

'Yes . . .' Jake nodded uncertainly. 'I think so, but it looks a little . . . restricting.' He was right: it was so tight around the tops of his arms, it was impeding the blood flow.

'It's fine.' Nathan gave it a sharp tug. 'What about the boots? They're quite masculine, aren't they?'

'Very manly,' Jake agreed – it seemed the best thing to do.

'Because *he* hasn't got a monopoly on looking like a Roman god.' Nathan gave a jealous nod at Lucius, whose muscles rippled as he changed into his new clothes.

The ship docked and the four of them made their way up the main street towards the theatre, which Charlie had already located on the map.

Jake saw that this was a town with money – it was more prosperous than Messina. The streets here were wide and clean; there was white marble everywhere, and well-dressed groups of people window-shopped, sat by fountains or strolled along the harbour.

'It's really just a holiday town,' Charlie commented. 'Rome on sea, if you like.'

Lucius, for one, was impressed, almost overawed, by the displays of wealth. He blushed when three well-bred young ladies floated by in long silk gowns, fluttering their eyelashes at him.

Nathan watched, agog, but they completely ignored him. 'They obviously didn't see me,' he muttered to Jake. As another two beauties approached, he flexed his muscles and fixed them with his most smouldering stare. But they too only had eyes for Lucius.

'I seem to be invisible!' Nathan complained, tugging again at his jerkin, 'Not even the flicker of a glance in my direction. I mean, really, he's just a meathead, whereas I am brains *and* brawn – all wrapped up in a luxury cloak of sensitivity and *savoir-faire*. What's not to adore?'

At length they came to the theatre, a handsome building with arches around it.

'Obviously it's only nine in the morning,' Charlie pointed out, 'so it's unlikely there'll be anything going on.'

Jake and his companions went through one of the arches into a gloomy atrium that curved around the theatre. From there they followed a winding staircase, emerging into the sunlight of the amphitheatre itself. Jake, Nathan and Charlie took in the scene, entranced.

The open-air auditorium was semicircular, consisting of a curving staircase of stone seats that led down to a raised stage. Behind this was a huge marble wall, fronted by high columns, alcoves and statues; three doorways presumably led backstage. Contrary to Charlie's prediction, there *was* a show going on – a performance by some twenty actors, their faces covered by masks, each with a downturned smile of unhappiness. It was being watched by a smattering of people slouched in the front rows.

'It must be a dress rehearsal.' Charlie gasped in wonder as he soaked up the scene.

Two principal characters, a skinny man and a stout woman, were speaking, while the chorus affected theatrical mimes in response, their body language altering from despair to anger to horror, and so on.

'They seem to be covering every emotion under the sun,' Nathan giggled. Lucius – the bluff, straight-talking soldier – was the only one who seemed uneasy here: it was all a little too touchy-feely for him.

Suddenly things on stage hotted up, and the stout lady shouted abuse at her skinny companion. Jake and the others assumed that this was part of the play, until the lady threw off her mask, revealing – to Lucius's horror – that she wasn't a lady at all, but a bearded middle-aged man. The actor stamped on his mask and attacked his co-star. The chorus tried to separate them, but the scuffle grew so violent that even the audience was sucked into it. Finally the cross-dressing actor silenced everyone with a parting curse, before storming off, throwing down his wig in disgust.

Jake and Nathan turned to Charlie. 'My Latin is just passable,' Nathan said, 'but I barely caught a word of that.'

Charlie duly translated, explaining – after putting the pieces together – that the man playing the wife was one of two *histriones primi*, or principal actors. The man who was *supposed* to be playing the husband had left at short notice after some unfortunate business the day before, and the skinny man, the understudy, had taken his place, but was clearly not up to the job. '*Abdico*' was his parting shot: 'I resign.'

'Unfortunate business yesterday?' Jake asked. 'What was that?'

'I don't know exactly,' said Charlie, before adding pointedly, 'But it seems he left with a red-headed woman.' All four of them shared a look. 'Let's go backstage and make further enquiries.'

As the argument onstage continued, Jake and the others crept through one of the doors at the back. They found themselves in a dark passage, full of pieces of scenery, but they could still hear the mutters of the actor. They followed his voice until they reached a dressing room. The man was changing out of his costume, scowling at his reflection in the metal mirror.

Charlie took a deep breath and approached him cautiously, asking in Latin if he might have a word. At first he too received a torrent of abuse, but when he revealed that he and his friends had been watching the dress rehearsal and *totally* sympathized with the actor's plight, his tone softened. He inclined his head condescendingly and introduced himself as Fico Mirabilis – Fico the Fantastic. There followed another rant – Charlie translated bit by bit, mostly for Jake's benefit – about how impossible it was in this day and age to put on drama of quality in the *Greek* tradition (Fico's eyes moistened at this point); how the spoken word was dead; how the gladiators and the vulgar games in Rome had ruined everything; how it was all about cheap thrills and bums on seats.

Charlie nodded in sympathy (in truth, he was probably the better actor of the two) and waited until Fico had run out of steam, then enquired about the events of the day before. This produced a strange medley of reactions: first anger, then resentment, then deep concern. Jake noticed that, at least twice, he contemptuously spat out the name Agata.

Charlie thanked him, said his goodbyes and turned to the others, smiling. 'I've found out everything we need to know.'

As the four of them headed out onto the street and started making their way back towards the *Conqueror*, Charlie gave a full account. 'Well,' he announced with relish, 'the package that Agata

Zeldt was picking up was not a *thing* – it was a person.'

Jake immediately put two and two together. 'It was the missing actor.'

'Affirmative,' Charlie replied. 'According to Fico, the whole nightmare started months ago when a haughty red-head called Agata Zeldt first swanned into town. She watched a performance and then came backstage afterwards and offered Austerio, who should have been playing the husband, a sum of money to do some *private work* for her. If he agreed, she promised to take him to Rome and make him a star. Neither then nor since has Austerio told his old rival what this secret job was to be.

'Anyway, Agata went off and Fico thought that nothing would come of it. But then, yesterday, she suddenly returned to collect him. Fico was furious, jealous; he thought Austerio was the most dreadful ham and totally undeserving of stardom. However, as they set off, Fico – who is Austerio's oldest friend as well as his most deadly rival – had a dreadful premonition about the whole thing, and is now very worried about him.'

'Well, that's certainly as clear as mud,' Nathan commented. 'Maybe I'm missing something, but mentoring second-rate actors is not usually the route to world domination.'

'What about Topaz?' Jake asked Charlie. 'Did Fico say she was here as well?'

Charlie stopped and pushed his glasses up his nose. 'Apparently Agata was accompanied only by a fair-haired boy.'

Jake felt another flutter of fear – as did Lucius, who was trailing behind.

'Well, we'd better get on our way,' Jake said. 'We've less than twenty-four hours until we're supposed to meet her.'

The boys hurried back to the *Conqueror* and set sail again, steaming northwards past Misenum and its vast fleet of hulking warships. (Jake counted at least twenty-five docked there, each with a distinctive curling prow, wide striped sails and three rows of oars punctuating their mountainous hulls.) The sun travelled across the sky as they pushed on up the coast, arriving at Ostia late in the afternoon.

'This is as close as we'll get to Rome by ship. It's a further twenty miles across land – which is quite an epic journey in this day and age. I suggest we head for the local forum and seek out transportation there.'

Nathan disembarked. 'Perhaps we could treat

ourselves to a little snack first,' he said, eyeing up a foodstall on the other side of the quay. 'Is that ice cream? Has it been invented yet? We are on the Italian Riviera, after all.'

'Afraid not,' Charlie sighed, jumping ashore along with the others. 'Unless you're an emperor with an army of skivvies to send to the Apennines to collect snow. That I believe is *Pepones et melones* – cold stewed melon with cornstarch. It's perfectly adequate in a pudding emergency' – he shrugged – 'which I actually agree this is.'

Just as they were crossing over to the stall, a horse-drawn cart, laden with all sorts of amphorae, zigzagged out of control along the quayside, nearly running them over before crashing into a low wall. Lucius started berating the ancient driver in no uncertain terms, and a heated discussion ensued; the man's dog joined in, barking and growling in defence of his master. Jake couldn't help but feel a little sorry for the old man: he was so small and frail, and evidently much loved by his more sprightly canine companion.

'Good gracious, is he blind?' Charlie cried suddenly.

Jake looked more closely and realized that he was

right: the man was addressing Lucius as if he were standing somewhere else entirely.

'Now I've seen it all,' Nathan commented. 'Blind cart drivers. The world has gone mad.'

Eventually the cart clattered off into the town and the boys went to buy their melon and cornstarch snack. As Jake ate his (actually, it was more refreshing than it sounded), he eyed up a pair of warships, much like the ones in Misenum, setting sail further up the harbour, their three strict lines of oars beating in unison. Close up, he could see their decks teaming with soldiers and wondered on what mission, to what part of the huge Roman Empire, they were departing.

'Being so close to Rome,' Charlie explained, 'there's a strong military presence here too.' He thought about it. 'In fact, let's face it, there's a military presence everywhere.'

Suddenly Mr Drake started shaking in panic.

'What's up?' Charlie asked.

'I can see what's up,' Jake gasped, his eyes fixed on a group of figures coming along the harbour towards them, clad in grey leather breastplates with feathered shoulders and beaked bronze masks.

'Hydra!' exclaimed Nathan. 'They must have

followed us here. How did we not see them?'

Just then there was a sharp *thwack!* and a metal dart struck Nathan's *Pepones et melones*, sending it splattering all over him. 'Now that is just rude,' he snapped, then grimaced as he saw four more guards approaching from the other direction. 'Heads!' he shouted as another volley of arrows flew through the air. Some locals ran for cover, while Mr Drake, now in a complete flutter, ducked under Charlie's toga.

'Up here!' Charlie commanded, leading them away from the port, for there was no way to reach their ship without meeting the enemy. As they hurried on, the whole retinue of guards were soon in pursuit.

'Over there! Quickly!' Nathan yelled, rushing towards a large porticoed building on one side of the street. They flew across the marble atrium and through a set of double doors. Nathan caught his leather jerkin on the handle, lost his balance and careered spectacularly across the wet marble floor.

'Damn this thing!' he cursed as he finally straightened up – to see forty pairs of disapproving eyes trained on him. There were men everywhere, mostly old, either swimming or lounging by the giant pool that dominated the room, most of them stark naked. 'Ah, the public baths,' Nathan mumbled with an apologetic bow. 'I'd forgotten how they like to put it all on show.' Quickly and carefully, his eyes trained on the floor, he followed the others out of the chamber.

Behind them, the doors flew open again, and six soldiers rushed in, drawing their swords. The bathers gasped and backed away or sank into the pool as the guards advanced on the History Keepers.

'Swords?' Nathan grinned. 'That's a little more sportsmanlike.' He drew his own, and Charlie and Jake quickly followed suit.

Lucius was shaking his head. 'You not fight close: they have poison on the arm – it puts you to sleep.'

Nathan and Jake didn't have a clue what he was talking about, but Charlie saw that each guard had a silver device strapped to his forearm. 'I think he's saying that those bracelets contain some sort of tranquillizer.'

'How perfectly charming,' Nathan drawled. 'They weren't wearing them before?'

'Not at camp,' Lucius explained, 'but always outside.'

'It's a shame you didn't have time to pick up

yours.' Nathan nodded at Lucius's bare wrist.

They turned and ran through an archway and down a passage. The soldiers dashed after them, pushing a group of cowering bathers into the pool.

Jake, Lucius, Nathan and Charlie flew into the *palaestra* – the gymnasium – where athletes were training with weights and stretching equipment. 'Excuse us,' said Jake, politely taking a small lead dumb-bell from a man with pumped-up muscles and an attitude to match, and pitching it towards the doorway. The others followed his example, grabbing whatever missiles they could find – leather balls stuffed with sand, iron discuses; even the stone busts from a series of alcoves – and hurling them across the room. Some hit their targets before crashing to the ground, but mostly the barrage of projectiles bounced harmlessly off the marble floor.

Negotiating the maze of corridors, they finally saw another set of doors ahead of them. As they ran towards them, a matronly woman in a white veil tried to stop them. '*Vires interdicti sunt!*' she cried as they swept past her.

'What's she saying?' Jake asked.

'Men forbidden,' replied Charlie with a shrug.

They opened the doors and went in, immediately

aware of streams of incense wafting up from two golden braziers. A young girl strummed a lyre as five women of various ages lay on wooden tables to receive a massage. They turned in alarm as the intruders shattered the peace.

'Ladies – or should I say *goddesses*?' Nathan said roguishly, catching the eye of a pretty masseuse.

Charlie rolled his eyes at Jake as Nathan took the jar from her and sniffed its contents. 'Lavender and neroli – there's nothing better for balanced skin and a radiant glow,' he commented before flinging the oil across the shiny floor in front of the doorway.

It was a masterstroke: as the soldiers burst in, they lost their footing, skidding in all directions. Nathan completed the move by upturning one of the incense braziers and igniting the oil, which set fire to the feathered boots of three of the guards.

'Thank you.' Nathan winked at his goddess, who seemed terrified and intrigued in equal measure. 'I've been suffering from a crisis of confidence – but I can see from your face that I still have what it takes.'

'Where does he get these awful lines?' Charlie asked the others. No one replied as they hurried along more white marble passages until they reached a wide atrium.

'Up there!' shouted Charlie. He was pointing to a large open window, at head height, overlooking the garden. Lucius clasped his hands together and gave him a leg up. Nathan did the same for Jake. Charlie jumped down the other side, but Jake waited as Lucius offered to help Nathan.

'After you,' the latter replied smugly. Lucius, in another of his gravity-defying leaps, was up and over the wall in a flash. Nathan tried to improve on it, but his hand – still drenched in lavender oil – slipped, and he fell back down, hitting his head on the ledge and twisting his ankle as he landed on the floor. Jake could see that the two remaining guards were coming up the corridor, preceded by their long shadows.

'Here!' shouted Jake, leaning down, his hand held out. But Nathan was still dazed from his fall, and looked up blearily at Jake, only half recognizing him. 'Nathan!' Jake shouted again.

The American turned to look around the room, an expression of wonder on his face. 'Have I got a massage booked? Aromatherapy?'

There was nothing for it: 'Wait for us!' Jake shouted at the others as he jumped down and grabbed his friend. 'Nathan!' he shouted again, this time slapping his face. It had the desired effect: Nathan's eyes came back into focus — as did his instinct for survival. There was no time to reach the window, so Jake pulled him down one of the four passageways that led out of the atrium. The two soldiers followed, now hard on their heels.

Ahead of them was a single door; wisps of hot steam escaped from all around it. Jake pulled it open and they found themselves in a large, vaulted chamber that was thick with vapour.

The heat was tremendous and Jake could feel his lungs contract. As they edged forward into the steam, they could see the shapes of bathers.

The door creaked open behind them to let in a wedge of light and two brutish figures; then the light was gone again. Two shadows advanced, swords held out before them.

'Any ideas?' Nathan whispered to Jake as they retreated to the back wall.

Jake looked around. He could just make out three vents in the floor, with hot air billowing out of them. He recalled how once, during the school holidays, he had helped his dad fit a steam room in the house of a film director (Alan had boasted that this was the start of the big time, but of course it had all ended in humiliating disaster and threats of a lawsuit). But Jake remembered how dangerous steam could be if pressurized.

'Move that onto the last vent,' he instructed Nathan, indicating a trough of water. Nathan did as he was told, while Jake did the same with the first vent. 'Now give me your jacket.'

'What?' Nathan replied. 'My gladiator's jerkin?'

'Just give it to me – you hate it anyway.'

Nathan reluctantly took it off and handed it over. Jake placed it on top of the central vent. Now, with all three openings sealed, the chamber started to empty of steam surprisingly quickly, and the two guards were suddenly visible.

'Here!' Jake called over to them, holding up his sword. The soldiers muttered something to each other and came in for the kill. 'When I give the word,' Jake whispered to Nathan, 'pull the jacket out of the way.' He waited, his sword clutched firmly in his hand. The men approached, the sharp edges of their swords glinting in the half-light.

'Now!' he shouted. Nathan quickly drew the jacket aside and a jet of boiling steam surged up into the soldiers' faces, burning and blinding them.

As Jake and Nathan made a dash for the door,

one of the guards fumbled for Jake's arm, but he pulled away, kicking his assailant on the knee and sending him sprawling. However, as he collapsed, the guard managed to twist open the capsule on his silver bracelet. A tiny cloud of noxious vapour was released. It had the stench of putrefying flesh – just like the corpse flowers in the laboratory in Vulcano. It made Jake gag immediately; his nose burned and his throat seized up. Then his vision blurred and darkened; it was as if his brain was shutting down. He felt his strength draining away and fell, before Nathan caught him and dragged him out of the room.

The next few minutes were like a bad dream. Jake was half aware of stumbling along more passageways and finally out into the sunlight again. There was running and shouting. Charlie and Lucius came briefly into focus, along with Mr Drake, and Jake was bundled onto the back of a cart. He was moving – then he heard more shouting; finally the confusion of faces and noises dissolved and he blacked out completely.

13 TO THE ETERNAL CITY

J ake awoke to some exquisite aromas. Although his head throbbed and he could still taste the Hydra's poison (much like the after-effects of being drugged in London when he had first met Jupitus Cole), a fragrance like rose petals revived his spirits immediately.

He opened his bleary eyes to find himself in the back of a cart, rattling across the countryside of Latium as the sun was starting to set. Lucius was snoozing by his side and Nathan was staring at the road ahead. They were surrounded by terracotta jars that looked somehow familiar – and were the source of the delicious scent.

'Feeling all right?' Nathan asked, on seeing him stir.

Jake nodded, though in truth he still felt nauseous and groggy.

'That's quite some soporific they let off,' Nathan commented, passing Jake a beaker of water. 'I almost blacked out too. The guards must be resistant to it.'

Jake took a long cool sip. He was about to ask where they were and how they had got onto the cart when a dog leaped down from the driver's seat and started licking his face. Jake recognized it immediately: it was the faithful hound of the old blind man who had nearly run them over in Ostia. Jake put two and two together. He turned round to find that very same man sitting at the front of the cart, chatting and laughing, Charlie at his side with the reins in his hand. Pulling them along was a sturdy horse who looked every bit as friendly as the dog. Mr Drake sat contentedly on his master's shoulder, inspecting the darkening countryside.

'Charlie did a deal,' Nathan explained. '*We* get a lift to Rome; old Gaius there gets to be driven without crashing into everything coming the other way.' Jake looked over at the man's kind face, crinkled brown by decades in the Italian sun. 'He has a story that even I found quite moving,' Nathan continued, putting his hand to his heart (though, as usual, it was the wrong side). 'He comes from a small town on the coast south of Ostia, and used to be a carpenter – built boats, houses, everything. Then he suffered a string of disasters: first his wife became ill – she's still stuck in bed – and then he went blind. How's that for luck? He couldn't work any more, because he couldn't see, but he could smell. So he took to making perfumes, distilling them from the wild flowers of the region. The idea was to sell them to the baths there in Ostia, but the snooty manager tried to fleece him – which makes me feel less guilty about the state we left it in – so he decided to head for the markets of the Eternal City.' He shook his mane of hair and smiled winningly. 'That's Rome, by the way.'

'What happened to the *Conqueror*?' Jake asked.

'We weren't able to get back to check on it,' Nathan replied. 'It had been commandeered by our pursuers – we seem to have eluded them by the way, but keep an eye out just in case. We'll have to keep our fingers crossed that the ancient Rome bureau is still in one piece and there's a Meslith machine there – otherwise we're completely in the dark. Anyway, make yourself comfortable: we'll be travelling through the night.'

Jake looked at Gaius's dog, who was now lying

with his head on Lucius's chest, blinking happily. He realized how much he missed Felson, even though they had only known each other for a matter of weeks.

Jake's thoughts turned to his parents and he wondered how they were getting on with the unfathomable Oceane Noire.

Finally he wondered about Topaz; he prayed that they would find her. Would she make the appointment on the Pons Fabricius; and if so, what state would she be in . . . ? A host of dark thoughts began to gather in his mind. He decided to stop thinking until they reached Rome.

'Rome . . .' he murmured. 'I'm going to ancient Rome.' Now tantalizingly close, the immensity of the idea dawned on him. To visit the city; to see its great buildings intact; to walk amongst its people; to visit the most famous civilization of all time . . . it was a thing of true wonder.

The cart rattled its way up a slope and down into an immense valley, stretching out for miles and miles ahead of them. The road cut a perfectly straight line across it.

They travelled into the night, Charlie, Nathan and Jake taking it in turns at the reins. The song of a million cicadas, hidden amongst the wild flowers of the roadside, floated on the warm air, and a bright three-quarter moon rose in the sky. At the halfway point they stopped for water and refreshments. They changed horses (Charlie negotiated a deal with a yawning innkeeper: Gaius would pick up his own nag – to which he was much attached – on his return), filled the lanterns with oil and set off again. There was still some distance to go and they couldn't risk missing their rendezvous with Topaz.

Occasionally they met another vehicle travelling in the other direction. The twinkling lights seemed to take an eternity to reach them, but finally the oncoming cart would rattle past. As Jake was dozing off, one of these caught his attention. He heard a distinctive clink well before it drew level with them. The driver was dressed in Moorish clothes, and when Jake gave him a tentative smile, he stared back with dark eyes from under his hood – before saluting him with a warm nod; just a stranger from another time, saying hello. His load consisted of stacks of silver, copper and pewter – plates, cups and trinkets – that glinted in the moonlight. The sight of this ancient treasure trove disappearing off into the night added to the sheer magic of the evening.

* * *

'I bought shellfish!' Rose announced, shutting the door with her sandaled foot and heading into the garden. 'Oh! Good gracious . . .' She did a double-take when she saw the constellation of pretty lights – hundreds of candles and lamps – illuminating the terraces.

She called out, 'I didn't intend to buy crab – not live crab, in any case' – she looked uncertainly down at something twitching in her basket – 'but I'm afraid my Latin is on the rusty side. Jupitus, are you there?'

He identified himself by languorously raising an arm in the twinkling gloom. 'Lovely lights,' Rose cooed, bustling over to his seat overlooking the bay. 'Are we celebrating something?'

'Not at all,' Jupitus replied acidly. 'I just need to see where I'm going. Unless you would like me to break my other leg?'

'And demand twice the amount of sympathy?' Rose giggled. 'I don't think I have it in me. Now,' she said, cautiously reaching into her basket, 'as you know, I'm not frightened of many things, but I find live crustaceans a challenge at the best of times— Ow!' She yanked her arm back as a giant crab shot out and landed on Jupitus's chest.

'Off, off!' he yelled in fury as it fell onto his lap. He swiped it aside with the back of his hand. It quickly righted itself and went scurrying away across the terrace.

'No, no!' Rose went chasing after it as it zigzagged this way and that.

Jupitus watched, at first with deep irritation, then with growing amusement as Rose kept closing in on it, then shrieking as it defended itself with its pincers and took off once more. By the time it had taken refuge in a pool of water below a fountain, Jupitus was laughing so hard that his stomach hurt.

'Let the poor thing be,' he called out to Rose. 'I think it's earned its freedom – if only for cheering me up.'

'Jupitus Cole, you really are infuriating some-times!' Rose retorted, storming back towards him. 'You're a miserable, mean-spirited piece of work. Look!' She held up her hands, which were covered in cuts. 'Anyway, it serves you right – they'll be no dinner now.'

'No dinner?' said Jupitus in distress.

'No. And no bedtime story either!'

'Well, just as well there's a plan B,' Jupitus replied

in his most velvety tones, and pointed towards a table (Rose had not noticed it tucked underneath the vast bougainvillea) that was laid out with the most magnificent banquet: grilled fish, fresh salads and platters of cold meats. Not only did the food look delicious, but the presentation, gleaming cutlery, and flowers and candles, was stunning.

Rose's anger melted away. 'How on earth did you manage to do all that?'

'Not bad for a miserable mean-spirited piece of work?' he said with a twinkle in his eye.

At that moment the Meslith machine, which was sitting on a side table, started to come alive, its crystalline rod fizzing with electricity. The smile left Jupitus's face immediately. 'Not again,' he sighed to himself.

'Who is it?' Rose asked.

'My darling fiancée, no doubt,' he replied through gritted teeth.

'Well, it must be important,' said Rose, advancing to look.

'Leave it!' Jupitus snapped, then softened. 'Please.' He took the blanket from under his leg and chucked it over the machine. Then he turned to

Rose and, smiling again, motioned for her to sit. 'Let's enjoy our dinner . . .'

In another corner of Europe, a thousand miles and many more years away from Messina, Alan was standing guard at the entrance to Oceane Noire's suite. He had one eye on the candlelit corridor and staircase and the other on Miriam, who was snooping around inside with a lamp. 'Can you find anything at all?' he called in a loud whisper.

'Nothing yet . . .' Miriam called back. 'Just lots of rather dramatic paintings of her majesty.' She gave a giggle.

They were following their son's advice and searching Oceane's quarters for any sign of treachery – in particular, a book with a picture of a palm tree; the one she was carrying the night Jake discovered her in the archives.

Miriam gazed around at the large and opulent space, fitted out in the style of Versailles before the French Revolution. There were plush chaise longues, elegant screens and gilt-edged tables. Adorning the silk-lined walls were portraits of Oceane in different 'romantic' costumes: as a Grecian deity, an Egyptian queen, a Turkish flower seller, and so on. Miriam struggled to focus on the job in hand.

One painting, however, she simply could not pass by without greater scrutiny. 'Oceane Noire, you are ridiculous,' she snorted to herself as she held her lamp up to it. Here, Oceane was depicted as a mysterious eastern princess surrounded by palms and palaces, lording it over a handsome gardener – who was clearly a less pale, more virile version of Jupitus Cole.

'Someone's coming!' Alan suddenly called from the doorway.

Miriam swung round and, in her panic, knocked the painting sideways. As she was about to straighten it, she noticed something hidden behind. She carefully slid the picture further to one side, revealing a small door. There was a lock with a little key in it. Miriam turned it, opened the door and saw a tiny secret compartment lined with purple velvet. It was completely empty. She hurriedly shut the door and covered her tracks.

'Too late! She's here!' Alan whimpered in desperation. From the doorway he could see Oceane's shadow quickly ascending the staircase. 'You'll have to hide,' he called over, before retreating quickly down the passageway in the opposite direction. He had just managed to slip into the shadows when Oceane appeared at the top of the stairs, pulling Josephine along behind her. Her skirts flared out on either side as she strode into her suite and slammed the door shut behind her. She was too wrapped up in herself to notice Miriam disappear behind one of the folding screens.

Miriam watched as Oceane went over to the portrait and opened the secret compartment. From a pocket in her dress she produced a book – on which Miriam identified a palm tree – placed it inside, closed the door, locked it and threw the key into a pink china pot (also decorated with her likeness) on the mantelshelf. Finally she carefully repositioned the painting.

Meanwhile Miriam watched, aghast, as Josephine padded straight towards the screen.

There was a soft knock on the door. 'Mademoiselle Noire, might I have a quick word?' It was Alan's voice.

'*Qu'est-ce que vous voulez?*' she spat when she found him outside, a rigid smile on his face.

'There seems to be water leaking downstairs,' he said sheepishly. 'Might I check your bathroom?'

Oceane grimaced in irritation. 'I have the worst headache known to mankind. *Depêchez-vous!*'

'If you could just show me where it is,' Alan replied loudly, for Miriam's benefit.

Oceane grunted and led him across the room. Now Miriam made a dash for the door, only to hear a full-throated roar behind her. 'Just shut up, you imbecile lion,' Oceane cursed, silencing her pet immediately. As she disappeared into the next room, Miriam finally managed to slip out and close the door behind her.

Ten minutes later, safely back in their own cosy room, Alan and Miriam, breathless and excited, started to ponder how and when they might get their hands on the book with the palm tree on it and discover what significance it had.

Just before dawn, the traffic began to increase. Soon other roads converged with theirs, forming a wide thoroughfare. Traders and farmers jostled with private carts and carriages. Nathan had the reins and Charlie was describing all the sights to an enthralled Gaius. Jake sat up, excited at the prospect of seeing the ancient city. Even Lucius awoke from his long sleep and took in the sights while stretching his bulky frame.

But this last section of the journey soon grew frustrating: after a series of hold-ups, the traffic finally stopped completely. A huge load of marble had been shed in an impossibly narrow stretch of road, and it took nearly two hours to shift it – and calm the fight that flared up when, for a moment, swords were drawn. It was well past eight by the time the way was cleared, and Jake feared that they might miss Topaz.

Gradually buildings started to materialize out of the dust and heat – just clusters to begin with, but soon becoming more densely packed.

As they passed a line of stalls selling cheap food and household items, Lucius suddenly stood up. 'Do you have money?' he asked Nathan, pointing to one of the stalls. Nathan suspiciously withdrew his pouch. Lucius snatched a copper coin, jumped down and purchased a jar, before leaping aboard the moving cart again.

'Don't mention it,' said Nathan sarcastically.

As the cart trundled on, Lucius popped the cork and took a slug of the contents, grimacing, then passed it to Nathan. 'You need to drink. All of you.'

'What is it?' the American drawled.

'Vinegar.'

Nathan pushed it away politely. 'Thanks all the same, but I'm not thirsty.' He pulled a face at the others. 'He is actually unsound of mind.'

'Drink,' Lucius insisted. 'It will stop poison from Hydra. You all drink. We soldiers, we drink in case of accident.'

Charlie cottoned on at once. 'I think he means it's a kind of vaccine for that gas. I suppose we'd better do as he says.' He grabbed the flask and took a big sip.

Reluctantly Nathan and Jake did the same. Jake didn't like vinegar at the best of times and struggled to keep the sharp, acrid stuff down.

'It good maybe three hours,' Lucius explained. 'Then you must drink again. This will keep you safe.'

'I love this job sometimes,' said Nathan drily as they rattled on through the suburbs.

As he looked around, Jake couldn't help feeling a little sorry for the people who lived here: the houses were misshapen tenement blocks, four or five tottering storeys high and packed one next to the other with narrow dark passageways between. From a window Jake noticed a thin arm empty a chamber pot onto the grimy street below. There were red-faced drunks sleeping in doorways, thin cats and dogs searching for a meal amongst the waste. Pungent smells – of decaying food, of sweat and urine – floated across the hot air. It was not quite the Rome that Jake had imagined.

Charlie sensed his disappointment. 'Just wait till we've climbed the pass between the Caelian and Aventine hills,' he said, pointing to the slope ahead of them. 'It will be another world.'

He was not exaggerating. Five minutes later the road levelled out and ancient Rome spread out before them.

Jake's eyes widened; his jaw dropped; he gaped in wonder. Lucius did the same. Even Nathan was struck dumb. Charlie smiled with the satisfaction of someone who has just magicked from thin air something truly sensational.

Ahead of them, occupying a huge area between seven undulating hills, was a limitless collection of temples, squares and arenas; mile upon mile of brilliant white marble that shimmered in the morning sun. Grand villas spilled down the sides of the hills, and the elegant streets were teeming with life.

'That, if I am not mistaken,' Charlie declared, a tear coming to his eye, 'is the capital city of a civilization that will change the world for ever. The first truly global metropolis. The Romans did so much for history, it's easy to take them for granted.'

'He's right of course,' Nathan concurred, 'although when I try and remember *what* they invented, I always go slightly blank.' He added mischievously, 'I know they were responsible for some shocking haircuts. And curling tongs.'

Charlie became quite flustered and started counting things off on his hand. 'Well, let's see . . . they were pioneers of education, architecture, sanitation, irrigation and modern government. They revolutionized road building, town planning and law.'

'Yes, but apart from that . . .' Nathan winked at Jake.

'They brought us our language, our alphabet, the police system, the benefit system, the sewage system; water-powered milling, high-rise buildings, the calendar, paved streets, glassed windows, public libraries, cement; even apples and pears!' Charlie had started to go red. 'And yes, eventually the Roman Empire crumbled – but their legacy lives on, Nathan Wylder, in every corner of this planet up to Point Zero and beyond.'

'I'm pulling your leg, Charlie,' Nathan chuckled. 'I love Rome just as much as you. Look at it. It's the opposite of shy and retiring. It's got real guts.'

'What's that?' said Jake, pointing down towards a gigantic structure in the basin below them. He felt he should change the subject before the argument got any more heated. A stadium, almost half a mile long, bordered by banks of stone seats, was set within a rectangular colonnade of mind-blowing proportions.

Now it was Nathan's turn to show excitement. 'I've only ever seen it in books. Or as ruins. That,' he announced, 'is the Circus Maximus.'

'*That's* the Circus Maximus?' Lucius repeated in awe. 'It's beautiful.'

'The biggest stadium ever built,' Nathan exclaimed, 'accommodating a staggering hundred and fifty thousand spectators. Obviously it's most famous for its chariot racing, but all sorts of things go on there: gladiatorial contests, grand processions, athletics tournaments and spectacular hunts. Signor Gondolfino tells a really gory story of how he watched sixty-three leopards and eighty-nine wild bears being brought down before his very eyes.'

'With all due respect,' Charlie interrupted

irritably (he detested cruelty to animals), 'the signore does like to exaggerate. Anyway, we're running out of time. The Pons Fabricius is over there' – he pointed – 'running from the city to the Tiber Island. I suggest we hurry up.'

It was only a few minutes before nine, and the bridge was still some way off. Jake could see it in the distant haze: just north of the Circus Maximus, where the river curved round in a loop, it crossed over to an island in the middle. A second bridge, identical in design, ran from the island to the fields on the west bank. Nathan urged the horse on, and the cart rattled down into the pulsing city.

The noise was overwhelming: the din of hooves, the clatter of wheels and the frantic buzz of a million inhabitants. There were so many sights that Jake didn't know where to turn first. People bustled about in every direction: workmen gathered up their tools and started their jobs; groups of children in neat togas were marched to school; ladies strolled under the shade of parasols; soldiers in chain mail swaggered out of their barracks. Animals of all sorts joined the throng: herds of sheep and cows were driven to market; mules and donkeys carried great baskets of goods; dogs of every shape and size played in the streets, padded along with their masters or watched, yawning, from shady doorways.

Mostly the people were dressed in rough, simple clothes, but occasionally important-looking figures in brilliant white togas would forge their way through the rabble. One of these, Jake observed, had a toga fringed with a band of deep purple. He was surrounded by armoured bodyguards who were roughly pushing people out of his way. Following him was a trail of hangers-on, all competing for his attention.

Some people didn't travel on foot at all, but were carried in cushioned litters, veiled from the hubbub by swags of silk. Jake spotted a pale-faced, thin-lipped woman thrust her head through the curtains and bark orders to her bearers, even giving one a lash of her whip.

The streets were lined with shops of every kind. They were open-fronted, windowless, and most had rough counters and painted signs to show what they were selling. There were blacksmiths, goldsmiths, stone cutters and carpenters; florists, bakers, fruiterers and honey-sellers; there was an apothecary, where a pharmacist was pounding herbs with a pestle and mortar; and a copy shop where three hunched scribes carefully duplicated documents onto scrolls of parchment; there were sandal makers, lamp makers, locksmiths and potters; Jake noticed that there were even barbers and hairdressers.

One such place caught his eye: in a gaudy salon with painted walls and garlands of flowers, a number of ladies were having their hair done and ointments applied to their faces. One was telling a story in dramatic hushed tones while the others hung on her every word. The whole scene made Jake think that very little had changed since AD 27.

Nathan urged the horse through the maze of streets. But as their way became increasingly narrow and densely packed, Jake suggested that it would be quicker to continue on foot. Nine a.m. had already come and gone, and he was feeling quite frantic. The others agreed. To say thank you to old Gaius, Charlie offered to help him set up his stall in the Forum Boarium; he would meet the others on the bridge presently.

Jake, Nathan and Lucius quickly said their good-byes, hugging the old man, then set off, weaving their way purposefully through the teeming crowd. Jake's heart was thumping again: if all went according to plan, he would be face to face with

Topaz in a matter of minutes. The sense of anticipation was both joyful and painful. Faster and faster
they ran, until eventually they emerged through the
old city gates and found themselves on the banks of
the Tiber.

'There!' Jake shouted, pointing towards the
bridge that crossed over to the island. He took
the lead, breaking into a run again.

'Slow down, Jake,' Nathan ordered. 'We need to
keep our wits about us. There's always the chance
we're walking into a trap.'

Jake reluctantly obeyed. At length they were
striding onto the Pons Fabricius, heads swivelling,
alert for danger. People were walking briskly to and
fro, or milling about chatting, or watching the
jugglers, fire eaters and fortune tellers. Jake eagerly
scanned the figures and finally spied a young
woman: she was leaning over the parapet, her back
to them, gazing down at the river. She wore a
hooded gown, as delicate as gossamer, from which
strayed locks of honey-coloured hair. Jake could
contain himself no longer: he rushed over, eyes
wide, breath fast, mouth dry.

'Topaz?'

The girl turned round and Jake's heart sank: it

was not her. She was about the same age but her features were plain and she had none of Topaz's mystery. Jake smiled, embarrassed, and turned away. Catching up, Nathan shot him a reproachful look, but Jake was too preoccupied to notice, turning to examine the other people on the bridge.

He soon realized that there was no one else even remotely like Topaz St Honoré.

The three of them waited, leaning against the balustrade, eagerly straightening up whenever they spotted a female figure. After an hour their spirits began to sink. Jake maintained a forced smile, but his eyes were sad.

There was a brief respite when Charlie arrived bearing drinks, snacks and a cheerful account of how Gaius's perfumes were already creating a stir in the marketplace. He then clapped eyes on Tiber Island and became very excited. He told them the legend of how it was formed. 'Five hundred years ago, the body of the last king of Rome, Tarquinius Superbus, a terrible despot, was thrown into the river. Gradually all the mud and silt built up around him until it formed an island. And have you noticed,' he asked, 'that it is now shaped like a boat?'

Lucius looked at Charlie as if he was mad, but

Jake immediately saw the resemblance. The front of the island narrowed sharply like a prow, at its centre a great obelisk shot up like a mast, and a temple set amongst the trees at the rear was the high stern.

'Of course, that is no coincidence,' Charlie went on.

'Goes without saying – that would be idiotic,' Nathan muttered under his breath.

'No indeed – the rulers of Rome wanted it to look like a ship in honour of Aesculapius, the Greek god of healing. You see, three hundred-odd years ago, in 293 BC, there was a dreadful plague, and an envoy was sent to Greece, to the god's spiritual home. As was the custom, a special snake was brought back from there. It spent the return journey wrapped tightly around the mast of the ship. However, when they sailed up the Tiber, it suddenly leaped overboard and slithered across to the island, showing that this was where the temple should be built. And there it stands to this day – Rome's very own shrine to Aesculapius' – he trembled at the sheer poetry of the story – 'on a ship-shaped island!'

'Fascinating!' Nathan murmured through slightly gritted teeth. 'Sometimes I think your talents are wasted on us. Perhaps you should give tours to the locals?'

Charlie just rolled his eyes and shoved his glasses up his nose, muttering something about philistines.

As the sun reached its zenith and the heat became unbearable, Nathan decided he no longer cared what he looked like and bought a parasol – a pink lady's one with tassels, which was the only one left. He put it up and twirled it with such panache, he managed to get away with it.

By mid-afternoon there was still no sign of Topaz. Jake sat morosely, barely moving a muscle, his hopeful smile long gone. The others became fidgety. Lucius went to have his fortune told and objected when the clairvoyant insisted he was destined to be a sheep farmer in Germania. Meanwhile Nathan, to take his mind off things, decided to get his portrait painted by a local artist with a face like a squeezed lemon, who clearly felt that such work was beneath him. Needless to say, Nathan was the customer from hell, insisting in his pigeon Latin that the man had failed to catch his *true manly mystique*. A hushed row ensued, with the artist finally tossing the picture into the Tiber. 'Romans are just *so* touchy,' Nathan complained as Charlie came to calm things down.

The afternoon turned to evening. One by one

the entertainers packed up and left, and the traffic across the bridge slowed to a trickle. As darkness fell about them, and the city dissolved into a myriad of twinkling lights, Charlie took a deep breath and finally voiced the fears of all.

'She's obviously not coming. I suggest we make our way to the bureau. She might contact us there, or we may get word from Point Zero. At least we can find Agata Zeldt's location in Rome. Does everyone agree?'

Nathan and Lucius reluctantly pulled themselves to their feet, but Jake did not move. 'I'll stay here,' he muttered.

'Probably not such a good idea,' Nathan said quietly. 'This place is dangerous at night. The whole city is. The bandits come out like vampires.'

Jake shrugged. 'I think you should go and find the bureau, but I want to stay here.'

Nathan and Charlie exchanged a look.

'I stay with him,' said Lucius, puffing out his chest. 'I am not frightened of bandits. I eat them for breakfast. Go! Yake and I stay together.'

For a moment Jake thought he would rather take his chances with bandits than with Lucius, but then he smiled up at him. Nathan and Charlie took some convincing, but in the end it seemed sensible to split up. Nathan even grudgingly agreed that Lucius, for all his faults, was the strongest of the four and most suited to the job. They agreed to meet again the following morning, and Nathan and Charlie set off for the bureau.

To begin with Jake and Lucius sat quietly, only occasionally smiling at each other or commenting on the weather (a chill wind had drifted up the river, banishing the day's heat). Then Lucius offered to show off his repertoire of bird songs. Jake listened to them one by one, and although he thought they all sounded the same, his nods of appreciation encouraged Lucius to continue for an hour. Occasionally they heard hurried footsteps approaching in the darkness. They would both look up, reaching for their swords, but there was no sign of Topaz. Silence would fall again, punctuated only by dogs howling from nearby streets or distant bells tolling.

By the middle of the night, both were feeling cold and miserable. To take his mind off things, Jake decided to find out some more about his companion: 'So, did you always want to be a soldier?' He knew it was a silly question.

There was a long pause and Lucius's eyes narrowed. 'No,' he replied brusquely. There was another lengthy silence, then he added, 'My father was a shipbuilder in Apulia. I thought I would do the same.'

'Ships – really? That's amazing.' Jake was certain he had found a good subject.

'Amazing?' his companion grunted sarcastically. 'Really? You know nothing.'

Jake was taken aback – even in the gloom, he could see the sudden murderous look on Lucius's face. There was another hiatus before he continued delicately, 'And your father? Is he still . . .?'

'Not seen my father in seven years,' Lucius snapped. 'Or my mother.' He didn't look at Jake, but seemed fascinated by something on the back of his hand.

It was clearly a sore point. 'Sorry, I didn't mean to . . .' Jake's voice trailed off, but then he went on quietly, 'I know how you feel. I lost my—'

Lucius interrupted Jake with even more venom: 'We change subject – yes?' To show that the matter was closed, he stood up, tugged at his tunic and strode over to the other side of the bridge, his lips pursed.

Jake yearned to talk to him; to tell him how he too had lost his parents for a while. The story of how he found them again might reassure Lucius. Jake also longed to share his own heartache for his lost brother. On the other hand, he was hurt by Lucius's reaction; it was as if he were the only person in the world who had ever suffered.

Conversation stalled after that. They were both exhausted and tetchy. Jake pulled his cloak around him and settled down beside the stone balustrade; and just as he was thinking it would be impossible even to doze in such a place, he drifted off.

14 Dawn Encounter

Jake woke to the sound of footsteps. He sat up. His neck was stiff and his throat parched. Dawn was breaking across the city, and shafts of searing light extended between the buildings. They burned into his eyes, making it almost impossible to see the lone armour-clad figure heading from the city gates towards the bridge – a slight figure, walking with a determined stride.

'Lucius,' Jake called over to his companion.

In a flash the soldier's eyes were open, and he fixed them on the approaching form. A moment later, he was on his feet, his sword drawn.

When Jake realized that the figure wore the feathered epaulets and helmet of the Hydra, he too hurriedly unsheathed his weapon. 'What do we do? Do we run?' he asked, looking around for the best escape route.

'Two of us, one of him,' Lucius grunted, clutching his sword tightly while grabbing the jar of vinegar, pulling the cork out with his teeth and taking a swig. He passed it to Jake, who followed suit. He could see something bulging on the forearm of the advancing man – presumably a metal bracelet. Jake wasn't sure about Lucius's plan of action – more soldiers could well be approaching from different directions. He peered over the parapet to see if they could escape by water, but below them – a long way down – surged a foamy torrent.

The man did not break stride, his boots echoing on the stone bridge, his helmet glinting in the morning sun.

'Hold your ground,' Lucius growled at Jake, feet planted, ready to rebuff an attack. The man continued to advance. Jake stood beside Lucius, narrowed his eyes, and assumed a warlike stance.

The man stopped just short of them. For a moment he did not move. All three of them stood there like statues at the midpoint of the bridge. There was silence, broken only by a flock of lapwings taking flight over the island.

Jake realized that the metal bulge around the

stranger's forearm was not a device, but a tightly wrapped length of thick chain. The man removed his helmet. Immediately long honey-coloured tresses tumbled down. There was a moment of astonished silence, then Jake's face lit up.

'Topaz!' he exclaimed, his heart soaring.

'*Je savais que tu attendrais*. I knew you would wait,' she replied breathlessly, rushing towards him and hugging him tight. 'It's so good to see you. I didn't know who to expect. Sorry I am so late. I could not get away.' As she clung onto him, Topaz and Lucius shared a lingering look.

Jake blushed. 'Yes, well,' he said in the deepest voice he could muster, 'Nathan and Charlie are here too. They went to find the bureau.' He could hardly get the words out; he was so overwhelmed by the warmth of Topaz's welcome, especially after the coolness of their last meeting aboard the *Lindwurm*. He noted that she had come straight to him, not Lucius, and suddenly felt thrilled.

However, now Topaz broke away and turned to the soldier. 'You know, the last time I saw Jake,' she said, 'he sailed all the way up the Rhine just to save me; fought his way onto the enemy's ship. *C'est le garçon le plus courageux que je connais*. He's the bravest boy I know,' she said, tickling him under the chin, 'and he's even more adorable when he blushes like that.'

Jake went a deeper shade of crimson as Lucius took Topaz's hand, gathered her to him and lifted her off her feet.

'*Arrête*,' she said, half laughing. '*Lâche-moi*.' As he carefully put her down, Jake heard her whisper in Lucius's ear, 'Thank God you're safe!'

Jake's dream evaporated in an instant. He was embarrassed for even thinking it. Topaz and Lucius were clearly besotted with each other. With Jake, she behaved more like an older sister.

At last she untwined herself from the soldier and suddenly became serious. She swung round and checked that no one was watching. 'Quickly! We don't have much time and nowhere is safe. Follow me,' she said, setting off across the bridge towards Tiber Island. 'We can talk in the temple of Aesculapius. Then I have to get back before they notice I am gone. As you can see' – she indicated her armour – 'I had to go to some lengths to escape from the villa.' She knocked on her epaulettes to show that they were hollow. 'I don't know how you men carry great shoulders around with you all day long. We females are far neater.'

The comment made Lucius smirk and flex his muscles. He caught up with her and took her hand, while Jake followed behind.

Topaz led them onto the island, through a dense copse of trees, across a small courtyard where the obelisk was situated (Jake noticed that it was inscribed with Egyptian hieroglyphics) to the temple. It was an impressive building: high, square and colonnaded on all sides. As she went up the steps, Topaz took one last look around, then the three of them slipped inside.

They found themselves in a large, dim chamber, lit only by the embers of two braziers and soft shafts of light filtering in through the high windows.

As Jake grew accustomed to the gloom, he noticed that there were people inside: most were lying on the floor, but some were moving amongst them with the quiet, careful tread of nurses.

'The sick come here for comfort and protection,' Topaz explained in a whisper. 'It is one of the most civilized places in the city.' As she passed one of the helpers, who looked angelic in flowing white robes, Topaz smiled warmly and received a serene nod in response. Jake scanned the row of patients, some trembling, some hunched in pain. One in particular drew his attention: a youth – barely more than a boy, one-legged and painfully thin – who shook with fever.

Topaz led Jake and Lucius into the shadows in the far corner of the room. She stopped and leaned in close. '*Écoutez* – listen carefully, I am going to tell you what you must do.' She started to uncoil the chain from around her forearm. 'As I said, I have barely any time. Agata Zeldt, my "mother", has begun, little by little, to trust me, and it is imperative, *absolument imperatif*, for the safety of everyone – for the safety of the world, of history – that I retain that trust. Do you understand?'

Jake and Lucius nodded, the latter clenching his jaw with determination.

Topaz continued: 'She has been preparing for an event that she calls *the end of dominions*. You should know that she does not exaggerate. If her plan is to end dominions, that is what she will do – and on an unimaginable scale.'

'Topaz . . . your wrist!' Jake interrupted. He could now see that the chain was attached to a manacle that was so tight, it cut into her skin, leaving painful sores. He remembered a similar device in her room on Vulcano and immediately put two and two together. 'They chain you up?' he asked in horror. 'You said she trusted you!'

'I said she has *begun* to trust me,' Topaz replied. 'Which, believe me, is more than I could ever have hoped for.' She spoke simply so as not to confuse Lucius. 'Jake, you know my mother and I were separated for many years? You know where I grew up, living with her greatest enemies? I have convinced her that I have changed, turned against all that. *Que je cherche la puissance noire.* That I am now seeking dark power.' She took a calming breath and gave the glimmer of a smile as she held up the end of the chain. 'Besides, as you can see, I found a way to undo the links. So, right now, I'm not chained up. I'm here with you.'

Jake said nothing. He nodded, but was secretly frightened by Topaz's manner: despite her warm welcome on the bridge, she seemed far steelier than when he first met her. Her face looked harder, more cunning. He couldn't help wondering if, in her attempts to convince her family, she really *had* changed, really *had* been tinged with some of her mother's malevolence.

'So listen,' she continued. 'I have only one key

piece of intelligence of my mother's plans: the first strike will take place tomorrow.' She looked at them both very seriously. 'It will all begin with what is called a *caedes publica* – a public murder.'

'A public murder?' repeated Jake, the notion sending a shiver of dread down the back of his neck.

'I don't know who or where – or indeed *how* this will lead to *the end of dominions*, but I have heard the phrase repeatedly.'

Jake nodded seriously.

'And you need to find out more.' Topaz took a deep breath. 'So, your instructions. My mother has a campaign room in the compound of her villa. Needless to say, it is heavily guarded and almost impossible to infiltrate. I have tried on two occasions; both times I nearly broke my neck – it is not a solo job. Tonight she is holding a masked ball. You must all attend. Cover yourselves well – especially you, Lucius. My mother will not recognize you – soldiers' faces mean nothing to her – but there could be guards from Vulcano. Try to gain access to this building and discover her plans.'

She unrolled three pieces of parchment and gave the first to Jake. He saw a list of names. 'Use those aliases when you arrive. They are entirely credible and will match those on the guest register.' She passed him the next roll, which was covered in roughly drawn maps. 'This is the location of the villa, on the southwestern corner of the Palatine. And this' – she handed him the third – 'is a plan of the building. The party will take place in the arena in the centre of the compound. My mother's campaign room is on the far side in this domed structure . . .' She indicated it on the map. 'The only possible access is over the roofs. Understand?'

Jake and Lucius nodded.

'Tonight, there will be dinner followed by what my mother calls *ludi sanguinei* – blood games. I cannot say when is the best moment to make your move, but when the time is right, find the concealed door at the north end of the arena, next to a statue of Saturn. This key will unlock it . . .' She handed Jake a small bronze key. 'Inside there is a staircase that will take you to the top of the building, onto a private terrace. From here you can climb across the roofs to the campaign room. You will enter through the open skylight at the apex of the central dome here. It is high, so you will need to be lowered on ropes – that is why you must all go.'

'And what are we looking for?' Lucius asked. He was clearly a little out of his depth.

'Anything – find anything! For we are completely in the dark. We need to know about this public murder, and why Agata went to so much trouble to pick up the actor from Herculaneum – Austerio, I believe he is called – and if there is any connection between the two.'

Trying to sound as knowledgeable as possible, Jake chipped in, 'I saw a film once where spies used an actor to memorize secret information; maybe that's why they have him.'

'Who knows? I caught sight of him only briefly from my carriage window, when he was collected in Herculaneum. After we arrived in Rome he was taken to another part of the villa and I have not seen him since.' Topaz looked up at the high windows. Light was now streaming through them, illuminating a swirling constellation of particles. 'Morning is upon us and I must return.' Having given her lacerated wrist a chance to breathe, she started to wrap the chain around it once again. 'One last thing: tonight, *on no account* should any of you acknowledge me. You will not speak to me or even look at me. Is that understood?'

Jake nodded.

'If I cannot look at you tonight,' Lucius added with studied charm, 'I will ask a kiss of you now.'

At first Topaz shook her head, but when he pulled her to him and embraced her, she did not resist, melting into his arms. It went on for so long that Jake had to pretend to be interested in the mosaic floors.

Finally he coughed nervously. 'Just one last question,' he asked, still unable to look up. 'Who else will be at this party?'

At last Topaz was released. Her cheeks flushed, she took a moment to compose herself and straighten her clothes. 'What I call the *milliardaires affamés* – the hungry billionaires,' she replied. 'Dignitaries from all over the empire: merchants, lawyers, generals; people with one thing in common apart from their wealth – a desire to be *more* wealthy, by any possible means. It's incredible – Agata's lived here for just three years, but in a city famous for its snobbery, not a single person has questioned where she came from or who she is. She just appeared one day, with a load of gold. She headed for a vast villa on the Palatine, next to the emperor's. An old aristocrat had lived there for decades, but she just kept increasing her offers of money until he finally moved out.'

'And *why* did no one question her?' Jake asked. He couldn't help but be intrigued by Agata Zeldt.

'Because she is the richest of them all; richer than the devil, they say.' Topaz looked stern, her mouth a tight line. 'Not just richer; crueller too.'

She turned and saw that the white-robed attendants had started handing out bread and water to their patients. 'Now, I must return.' She started to lead Jake and Lucius back towards the exit. Suddenly she stopped, unclasped a gold necklace from around her neck, and approached the poor one-legged youth Jake had seen before. With a kindly word, she dropped it into his trembling hand and closed his thin fingers around it.

She returned to Jake and Lucius, and they left the temple. Topaz hurriedly said her goodbyes.

'And remember,' she called back, 'you don't know me.' She replaced her helmet and hurried back over the Pons Fabricius into the city.

It was another half-hour before Charlie appeared for their agreed rendezvous. Jake quickly filled him in on their meeting with Topaz – explaining about the public murder and showing him the papers she'd given him.

'I know this building from my research – it's one of the grandest in the city,' Charlie commented, studying the map. 'It even has its own miniature stadium. Let's go back to the bureau now and make plans. The place hasn't been used for a while and it was overrun with creepy-crawlies. Nathan is still cleaning up.'

He led them through the gates and along a series of streets until they came at last to a large open square bordered by striking buildings. 'The Roman Forum,' Charlie announced. 'The epicentre of the Empire. This is the seat of law and government.'

Jake and Lucius looked around. Some of the buildings were low and sprawling, others stood high over the square; but all were built from the same everlasting white marble that was Rome's trademark. They saw many finely dressed people: nearly everyone wore togas as white and pristine as the buildings around them.

'That's the Palatine hill,' said Charlie, pointing to a steep slope at one end; tier after tier of grand villas rose up its flanks. 'That's where Agata Zeldt lives. Fascinating fact: the word *palace* actually comes from *Palatine*,' he added. 'At the other end is the Senate House – the *Curia Julia*, built by Julius Caesar in 44 BC, when he was at the height of his powers. All the senators meet there to pass their acts and laws. Quite incredible to think that it's the model of all parliaments to come.'

Jake looked up, surprised to see that the building was one of the plainest – just a simple box-like structure with a series of high windows. A meeting had just finished, and a mass of white-robed senators poured out through the doors, chatting as they filed down the steps.

Beside the Senate House stood a long, two-storey structure of distinctive red stone, fronted by a succession of *tabernae* – small shops mostly dealing in silver, gold and tin. 'This is the Basilica Aemilia,' Charlie informed them as he led them through a narrow doorway. Jake noticed a man with a hunched back and pinched face weighing small chunks of gold on a set of scales.

Inside, it was as cool and spacious as a cathedral. 'It's like a miniature forum . . .' Charlie gestured at the people dotted around the central nave. 'All sorts come here,' he said, indicating each group in turn. 'Moneylenders, lawyers, bankers, estate agents, politicians – all plying their trade. It's a madhouse. In fact that's precisely why the bureau is located here.'

He led Jake and Lucius over to a dark recess between two pillars. He checked that no one was watching; then, with his foot, delicately depressed a brick in the base of one of the columns. Jake squinted down at the stone and could just make out a faint symbol that he recognized immediately: an hourglass with three atoms whizzing around it – the History Keepers' symbol. A second later, there was a click and a section of the wall opened. Charlie waved the others on into the dark chamber beyond, took one last look and followed, shutting the opening behind him. No one in the Basilica Aemilia was any the wiser.

Jake looked around. This entrance reminded him of his very first foray into the extraordinary world of the History Keepers – via a secret staircase below the Monument in the city of London. *These* stairs also spiralled down into the earth and were decorated with a series of murals depicting emperors, armies and processions (though rendered in mosaics rather than paint) that made Jake's spine tingle in anticipation.

'You said the bureau had not been in use for a while?' he asked Charlie, out of earshot of Lucius. 'No one works here?'

'You'll find that the further you go back in time,' Charlie whispered, 'the fewer local agents there are – these places are more *safe houses* than bureaux per se. It's to do with the limited number of people being able to travel to deep history.'

At the foot of the staircase there was another door concealed in the wall. Charlie knocked on it, using a special code.

'Charlie?' a voice asked from the other side.

'It is I.'

A key was turned in the lock and the door opened. 'Did you find her? Did she come?' Nathan asked immediately, seeing Jake and Lucius. He was wearing an apron and brandishing a feather duster.

'She's alive and well,' Charlie answered. 'We have an appointment tonight.'

'Good work, boys – brilliant work,' Nathan replied.

Jake stepped into a spacious vaulted chamber. It seemed welcoming and familiar, its dark wood panelling, and tables covered in maps, charts and globes completely at odds with the austere marble of the city above them. The room was lined with shelves full of books from all ages, and there were two sets of bunk beds.

Nathan listened with keen interest as Jake repeated the story of his encounter with Topaz, asking questions and looking carefully at the maps she had given him.

When Jake was finished, Charlie pointed him towards the bunk in the far corner of the room. 'You can take that one there, next to that statue of Oceanus taming the waters.'

Jake happily obliged, slinging his bag down. He examined Oceanus, a hulking bearded figure carved in brilliant alabaster – as beautiful a piece of sculpture as Jake had ever seen, set casually in a corner of a History Keepers' bureau.

On the floor, sticking out below the bunk, was a large metal grille with a padlock. Beneath this, Jake could hear the rush of flowing water. 'Where does this lead to?' he asked, tapping the grille with his foot.

'It's an underground branch of the Aqua Virgo,' Charlie explained. 'One of the aqueducts supplying Rome with fresh water. It was built by Agrippa in AD 19, and comes eight miles from near Collartina, east of the city, mostly underground, ending up at the baths of Agrippa half a mile down the road. Of course, we use it for our personal water supply.' He indicated a bucket on a chain next to the opening. 'Saves us having to go all the way upstairs when we fancy a drink.'

Jake peered down into the cavity and could just make out a wide, echoey tunnel.

Lucius was also inspecting the room apprehensively. There were many objects with which he was completely unfamiliar. 'What is this?' he asked, pointing to a globe that came from a more modern era.

'That is the world, but not as you know it,' said Charlie dismissively. It was best not to open the can of worms that was time travel, so he led Lucius over to a table of freshly prepared food. 'There's homemade muesli and a breakfast soufflé – prepared in an oven older than the ark – which has even me reaching for superlatives.'

After breakfast, as Lucius had a snooze, Charlie, Nathan and Jake sat down, first studying Topaz's map in greater detail, then poring over volumes of leather-bound annals that described all the key events of the previous decade. Amongst many things, they learned in detail about the Emperor Tiberius and his eccentricities.

In his twenties he had shown himself to be a brave general, conquering swathes of land in Germania, as well as Dalmatia and Pannonia in south-eastern Europe. But he never enjoyed his position of supreme commander or grew accustomed to life in the largest city in the world. Soon he was regularly disappearing off to the island of Rhodes – much to the frustration of his senators. As he grew older, his paranoia had worsened, and a year ago he had left Rome for good in order to rule via Sejanus, his prefect, from a secret hideaway on the isle of Capri.

'What worries me,' Charlie murmured, 'is that, at the moment, Sejanus is not in the city either. He's on a state visit to the eastern frontier and is not due back for weeks. Certainly there are six hundred senators – but Rome is essentially leaderless. Which is interesting timing . . .'

In the afternoon, with their plans made, Nathan asked if anyone would mind if he went on a small shopping expedition. 'I feel the need to get under the skin of early Imperial fashion,' he announced. 'It's always been such a grey area.'

No one had any objections, so Nathan sloped off.

An hour later, he bustled in with armfuls of bulging linen sacks, his eyes shining with excitement. 'Revelatory!' he gasped. 'May I just say: *hemp* – it's just wrong, and usually I wouldn't touch it with a barge pole; but who knew how versatile it could be in the right hands?' He pulled out a couple of items from his bag to demonstrate. 'It's shabby, but *sooo* chic. At the other end of the scale' – he produced a silk tunic from another bag – 'if it's sheer gold you're after, may I introduce you to sea silk? It's startling. A revelation . . .' he added, a tear coming to his eye. 'Actually woven from the filaments of the *Pinna nobilis*, the rarest seashell in the Mediterranean.'

Nathan allowed Jake and Charlie to feel the fabric, then showed off some snakeskin boots and an assortment of chains and bangles that he described as 'very manly jewellery'.

Later, Charlie and Jake also popped out to visit a little shop that sold masks and other party paraphernalia. (Jake had noticed it down a narrow side street on their way from the Pons Fabricius that morning.) They came back with a whole collection, all similar in style to the ones worn by the actors in Herculaneum, with big cut-out mouths in either *happy* or *sad* mode. Needless to say, Nathan and Lucius both wanted the same one – which looked like a ferocious warrior; but just as a heated row was about to erupt, Charlie pointed out that the colour didn't go with Nathan's skin tone and he dropped it like a hot potato.

They got changed into their smartest-looking outfits – togas with capes, as worn by the young noblemen of the city – and armed themselves with swords and daggers, concealed under their togas. Nathan and Jake each volunteered to carry a length of rope, which they hid by winding them around their waists. They all took a hateful swig of vinegar, Charlie left Mr Drake with a handful of nuts, and they lit torches and set off, ascending the spiral staircase. At the top, Nathan checked through a spy-hole that the coast was clear, then pulled a catch to open the door and they filed through. Charlie closed the wall behind them.

The basilica was now half empty. A few clusters of people lingered in the fading afternoon sun. At one end, a handful listened uncertainly to a red-faced man on a podium speaking in rousing tones. He had obviously had too much to drink, for he suddenly staggered and fell down amongst his audience.

Nathan led the others out into the Roman Forum. Dusk was descending and a warm pink light picked out the villas of the Palatine. It was towards these grand and ancient buildings that the intrepid young agents set off, each clutching his mask and silently pondering what lay in store for them that evening.

15 Diabolical Dinner

The villa that Agata Zeldt called home clung to the southwestern side of the Palatine, over-looking the Circus Maximus on one side and the great field of Mars on the other. Jake and his companions approached it, first up a steep slope from the southern end of the Forum, then along a wide, tranquil boulevard that snaked between the grand residences of this most ancient and revered district. The air was much fresher up here, and sweetened by the fragrance of the pines. It was quieter too, away from the bustle of the city below; they heard only the sounds of running water mixed with the muffled conversations of well-to-do people behind the walls of their luxury compounds.

Occasionally, the tranquillity was broken by a carriage rolling up the hill or by the grunts of slaves bearing litters – all evidently transporting illustrious guests to Agata's party – before disappearing down a driveway near the crest.

As they approached the gated entrance, which was lit by a succession of tapers and guarded by all sorts of soldiers and attendants, Nathan stopped in the shadows behind a tree.

'We should go in two groups,' he whispered. 'Draw less attention to ourselves. Lucius and I will enter first. You two follow in fifteen minutes. Good luck.'

Nathan took a deep breath, put on his mask, puffed up his chest, clicked the bones in his hands and set off. Lucius went through the same routine, in a more exaggerated fashion, then followed. Jake and Charlie watched them stride up the narrow drive, give their fake names to an attendant and disappear through the gates.

To kill some time, Jake and Charlie wandered up to the summit and looked down at the Circus Maximus. The sight of it filled Jake with wonder. From above, it looked even more sensational than it had appeared on their way into the city the day before. Illuminated by torches set around its track of white sand, it had an otherworldly quality, as if it were the stadium of the gods themselves.

Some kind of training exercise was taking place there: a couple of chariots, each harnessed to a team of galloping horses, were flying around the track as a coach shouted instructions from the side-lines.

'There's a big race tomorrow,' Charlie explained. 'One of the biggest of the year. By tomorrow morning, the whole of Rome will be here.'

Jake could also hear distant shrieks and roars of animals. He couldn't tell where they were coming from.

'Wild beasts,' said Charlie. He pointed to the great stone island in the centre of the arena that divided the track in two. 'They're caged under the *spina* there. They'll be bears, tigers, perhaps even a rhinoceros – animals from every corner of the world.' He screwed up his face with distaste. 'They parade them before the chariot races or use them for their gory entertainments.'

As Jake looked more carefully, he noticed workmen erecting a wooden balustrade around the edge of the island. 'Do people stand up there too?' he asked.

'Oh yes, the *crème de la crème* watch from the *spina*. Rome's six hundred-odd senators. It's symbolic, you see: *standing on top of the beasts*. To show the people that they are kings – not just of the world – but of all nature. Although actually it's a new tradition; they used to sit beside the *pulvinar* over there.' Charlie pointed towards a stone structure opposite – a temple with columns fronted by a wide terrace. 'That's the imperial box, where the emperor sits.'

Again they heard distant roars from the *spina*, carried up on the warm night air. Charlie's eyes lingered for a moment. 'Anyway, we should go now,' he said at last.

They slipped on their masks – Jake's had a cheerful smile, while Charlie's looked a little confused – and headed up the drive. A doorman stepped forward to take their names. Jake gave his in a steady voice that belied his terror. A thick-set guard opened the gates and they were both ushered inside.

A line of slaves, each standing rigidly to attention, heads bowed, marked the way through a series of wide corridors towards the sounds of the party. At last they emerged into the open air.

They were greeted with such a spine-chilling sight that Jake faltered. A hundred frozen masks turned in unison to scrutinize the new arrivals. Jake felt beads of sweat running down his forehead under his own mask.

'All right?' Charlie whispered, laying a reassuring hand on his shoulder. Jake nodded and took a deep breath. Gradually the masked faces turned back to their own groups and the chatter resumed.

It was an extraordinary space, long and colonnaded, echoing the form of the Circus Maximus below, but in miniature. It was open to the stars and adorned with eye-catching statues. Dinner tables were set up along the sides, with elegant, silk-covered couches. (Jake had learned that Romans – the rich ones at any rate – did not use dining chairs but ate lying down!) In the centre, steps led down to an arena, elliptical in shape, bordered by a low wall and illuminated by lanterns. Here, no doubt, Jake realized with a shiver, Agata's *ludi sanguinei*, or blood games, would later take place.

At the very edges, half in the shadows of the stone columns, musicians played lutes, flutes and lyres, and a small army of slaves waited discreetly to attend to the whims of the guests.

'Monster she may be, but it's undeniable that Agata Zeldt has taste!' a voice said from behind a mask. It was Nathan, excited to find himself at such a lavish event. Behind him, Lucius's hulking frame looked ill at ease. 'She has a sense of theatre, of *grand guignol*, which is quite refreshing after her brother's gloomy Gothicism.' Nathan held up his silver goblet. 'May I recommend the honey and watermelon cocktails? They're chilled perfection, as you might say, Charlie. No doubt as icy as our hostess.'

'And where *is* our hostess?' Charlie asked anxiously. 'Any sign?'

'Not to mention Topaz,' Jake added. He had already scanned all the females in the garden.

'Well, *there* is the statue of Saturn.' Charlie nodded towards a sculpture under the colonnade: a chunky, bearded deity holding a torch in his hand. 'There's a door next to it.'

Just then they heard a loud roll of drums followed by a fanfare of horns, and three figures appeared through the grand archway at the far end of the arena; there were gasps of wonder from the guests, followed by a spontaneous ripple of applause.

Leading the group was their hostess herself, dressed in a fantastically devilish costume inspired by dark birds of paradise. A bodice of feathers clung to her lithe frame and a bustle sprouted magnificently from her behind. A collar of long peacock quills encased her head and set off her flame-coloured hair. She wore a half-mask – in deep ultramarine – exposing her cruel, bloodless lips.

'Well, of course she's playing fast and loose with every fashion under the sun,' whispered Nathan in awe, 'but what a sensational result!'

'Wake-up call!' said Charlie, clicking his fingers in front of Nathan to get his attention. 'She murders for pleasure and she's about to destroy the world as we know it!'

Jake was not looking at Agata; he was staring at the two figures behind her. His lip curled in disgust at the sight of the blond youth on Agata's left, whom he recognized immediately – even behind his spotted mask – as the arrogant Leopardo. But his heart went out to the chained and manacled figure the boy was pulling along as if she were a circus animal: Topaz.

Lucius started snorting and flexing his muscles, and Nathan had to hold him back. 'Remember what you and Jake were told? We don't know her.'

Once again, Jake couldn't help thinking how different she looked from the bright, vivacious

Topaz he had first met in London. Earlier that morning she had been steelier; now she was almost pathetic.

Agata held up her hands majestically and said a few words in Latin, her voice soft and deadly as poison. '*Welcome, all. So happy you could join us in our humble home,*' Charlie translated with a roll of the eyes. Then she clapped her hands together and instructed everyone to recline and enjoy the feast.

'That's our cue,' Nathan said, nodding at the others.

While the guests took their positions on the couches, the slaves brought in chargers of food. In the confusion, the four boys surreptitiously made their way towards the concealed doorway next to the statue of Saturn.

They had nearly reached it when a shadow loomed up ahead of them. Jake's heart stopped when he realized that the figure was wearing a leopard mask and was trailing the unfortunate Topaz behind him.

'*Sedete,*' he said in a silky voice, motioning for them to sit.

There was some space amongst a group of diners reclining around the nearest table. The boys couldn't very well refuse. Charlie thanked Leopardo with a gracious bow and they took their places as calmly as they were able. Jake noticed that Topaz looked terrified, but her half-brother gave no indication that he suspected anything, and lay down with his back to them.

As she took a seat next to the monster, Topaz quickly glanced around. Her eyes made contact with Jake's. She glared at him for a moment – in fear or friendship, he couldn't tell – then turned away.

Jake looked at the other diners; they were an unappealing lot, arrogant and overfed, gossiping and laughing, one eye fixed on the new arrivals. They had half pushed up their masks in anticipation of food and motioned for the boys to do the same. Keeping their faces hidden as much as possible, they followed suit.

Suspended just above the table – and, indeed, Jake noticed, above *every* table – was a little cage containing a small bird with vivid yellow plumage singing an exquisite song. Charlie was immediately taken with it and tried to reach his fingers in, but the creature was unfriendly, puffing its feathers and shrinking away from him. Suddenly something far more alarming caught Charlie's attention. 'Hell's bells,' he muttered under his breath as a slave approached with a great platter and set it down on the table in front of them, explaining what it was.

'Baked flamingo and swan surprise,' Charlie translated in a horrified whisper.

The guests were all cooing with delight, but Jake could barely believe his eyes: from the roasted bodies of two giant birds (still covered in charred feathers) two necks – one pink and one white – rose up to create the shape of a heart between them, their beaks touching in a delicate kiss of death.

'I wonder what the surprise is?' Nathan asked out of the side of his mouth. Usually he was quite imperturbable, but even he looked a little worried.

The attendant plunged a knife into the side of each bird. From within came a chorus of high-pitched cries, and out flew a handful of live nightingales. Lucius stood up and half drew his sword in fright, much to the amusement of their fellow diners, but Nathan pulled him down again. From every table, amidst applause and cheers, nightingales took off, fluttering in confusion into the sky.

'Barbaric,' Charlie whispered under his breath, shaking his head. 'Absolutely barbaric.'

The culinary horrors did not end there. Dish after dish of macabre recipes were brought out. Mostly they had an avian theme: turtledove ragout with pomegranates, peacock stewed in honey and damsons, and ostrich flambé; but there were other recipes to bring shudders of distaste: jellyfish and eggs, pickled sea urchins, and eels stuffed with sprats.

Lucius ate nearly everything, which meant that Nathan felt obliged to do the same. Jake bravely tried to swallow something, so as not to attract too much attention, but Charlie ate practically nothing, and became more and more upset by what he called 'the dreadful savagery of the rich'.

Towards the end of the meal, a figure appeared at the main door: a tall, strange-looking man with a gaunt, unmasked face and a long plaited beard. Jake recognized him, but couldn't remember where from. Eventually he started to weave his way between the tables until he was at Agata's side. She received him with a nod and he leaned down to whisper in her ear.

Jake suddenly realized: 'It's the man from the laboratory in Vulcano,' he said quietly. They had seen him working in the room with the foul-smelling plants. Nathan and Charlie looked over.

'No doubt he has come to assist her with *the end of dominions*,' the latter commented, his gloom sharpened by hunger.

After the dishes had been cleared away, an unusual-looking man wearing a wig of curling red hair – a master of ceremonies of some kind – stepped into the middle of the arena and made an announcement in a deep, gravelly voice. What he had said soon became clear – for at each table the guests opened their birdcages to let loose the yellow songbirds. They flew up in unison, circled one way, then the other, before finally settling on the man, so that he looked like a giant bird himself. To complete this image, he started to rise up into the air as if he were indeed flying. Jake realized that he was actually being raised up by some underground mechanism, but it was such an eye-catching trick that the amazed audience immediately stood up to get a better look. It was at this moment that Topaz turned and nodded at the others to indicate that now was the time to go.

No one noticed the four boys disappear into the shadows of the colonnade and creep over to the statue of Saturn. In a flash Nathan had produced Topaz's key, unlocked the door, and led the others inside.

Nathan and Jake breathed a sigh of relief as they unwound the lengths of ropes and slung them over their shoulders. They made their way up the narrow steps, flight after flight, their footsteps echoing around the dark stairwell, until finally they came to a door. At first it would not open, and Charlie feared it might also be locked; but Nathan gave it an almighty shove, burst through, and the others followed him out onto the terrace.

They were at one of the highest points in the city and the view – 360 degrees of it – was astounding. Under a perfect evening sky of midnight blue, the white marble of the city extended into the distant purple haze. It seemed much more peaceful at night, especially viewed from this vantage point, and a warm breeze swirled around them with a faint whistle.

'Well I'll be blowed,' said Charlie excitedly, spotting a distinctive shape on one side of the terrace. 'An original Montgolfier, if I'm not mistaken.'

Jake, Nathan and Lucius turned to see a large

basket connected to a mammoth bundle of material in gold and indigo.

'Montgolfier? Montgolfier?' Nathan pondered. 'I know the name . . . Remind me.'

Charlie sighed and shook his head. 'Nathan, sometimes I wonder if you've done any basic research at all. The Montgolfier brothers, inventors of the world's first hot-air balloon?' As Jake and Nathan went to investigate, Charlie carried on, 'Actually, that's not strictly speaking true. The Chinese had a go in the era of the Three Kingdoms, around 200 AD. And I've heard rumours that the Nazca of Peru might have got there even earlier. But October 1783 – four years after the French Revolution – was the official date of the first manned flight. Whatever way you look at it, it's still *totally* out of place here. Agata Zeldt truly has no respect for history. Can you imagine this taking off across the skies of ancient Rome?'

Jake found the idea entrancing: a hot-air balloon from the other end of history wafting over the city, to the amazement of all.

With Nathan leading the way, the four of them hauled themselves over the balustrade at the back of the terrace and surveyed the dark geometric rooftop landscape.

'There,' said Jake, identifying, in the furthest corner, the domed building that Topaz had told them housed Agata's campaign room. They set off across the roof tiles, four silhouettes against the ultramarine sky. Occasionally they reached an impasse, a wide gap between the buildings, and would have to double back and find a different route. At one point they passed a skylight. From it emerged a strange fluttering sound that intrigued Jake. He couldn't resist kneeling down and peering through the bars.

A dim light from below illuminated his face as he examined the large, empty chamber. There was a shape on the floor – some kind of creature, tied to a metal post, lying perfectly still on a bed of dark crimson. Then the sickening truth dawned on him: the creature was the half-eaten remains of a man, its bed a pool of dry blood. Suddenly there was an ear-splitting squawk, a rush of air, and a bird almost the size of Jake threw itself at the bars, thrusting its head between them and snapping at him with its razor-sharp beak.

Jake cried out, stumbling back across the tiles and falling heavily. The others stopped and turned as he picked himself up. Now the heads of three savage vultures were straining through the bars, shrieking like banshees.

'Such charming pets our hostess has,' Nathan commented drily. 'They make her brother's snakes look positively cuddly.'

Jake stared at the birds with disgust as he edged his way along the tiles and caught up with the others.

Agata's campaign headquarters were housed in a solid, square, domed structure. Its far walls dropped straight down to join the sheer cliff face of the Palatine; on the near side, it was separated from its neighbours by a gap of nearly two metres. The boys gingerly made their way over to the drop and looked down. Below them stood two hulking men guarding the double entrance doors. Round the side, they saw two high windows, both tiny and barred. Topaz had explained that the only way in was through the skylight at the top of the dome; they could see a soft light shining up through it. But to reach it, they first had to get across the gap.

'I'll go first,' Nathan whispered to the others. He took a few steps back, then ran, vaulting over the divide and landing perfectly, with barely a sound, on the other side. He peered down: the guards were talking to each other, oblivious to what was going on above their heads. Lucius went next, landing in an elaborate somersault and making it look like child's play. Charlie followed, showing no fear at all. Then it was Jake's turn. He didn't like it one bit, but kept his fears to himself. He stepped back, took a deep breath and lunged forward into the air. As the void opened up beneath him, he had a sudden premonition of disaster. His foot came down short, landing on the edge. His eyes widened as he teetered on the brink, then Charlie grabbed him and pulled him forward. The sentries failed to notice the light dusting of stone that fell down into the gap.

They tiptoed across the roof, clambered up the side of the dome and peered inside. Below them was an octagonal room with a black and white floor of shiny marble that reflected the light from a series of low-hanging lanterns. In the centre stood a circular table with a map spread across its tapestry cover. Even from this distance Jake could make out the shapes of continents: Europe, Africa and Asia. It was mostly emerald green, but there were blocks of other colours. Other tables were dotted around the room, many piled up with plans, tables and diagrams.

'Can I go first?' Jake asked the others. He was embarrassed about what had just happened on the roof and wanted to prove himself. 'I'm very good with ropes,' he lied.

For once, Nathan couldn't find a reason to disagree. 'Sure.' He shrugged. 'What's the worst that could happen?'

'Well, the worst that could happen,' said Charlie, pushing his glasses up his nose, 'is that he falls, crashing onto that map, and alerts the whole villa to our whereabouts.'

'It was rhetorical, Charlie.' Nathan gritted his teeth. 'You don't have to answer that question every time I ask it.'

Jake was harnessed to the rope, and Lucius, by far the strongest of them, lowered him down. As he descended, Jake noticed that the inside of the dome was painted dark blue and covered with symbols of the constellations over faint golden grids of latitude and longitude.

His foot edged towards the chart, his toes touching down on Italy – on Rome itself; indeed, on a tiny replica of the Circus Maximus. Only now did Jake realize that the map was not flat, but a three-dimensional relief. He carefully leaped down onto the floor, before turning round to have a closer look. It was a beautifully realized miniature of the western world in AD 27. It illustrated, in breathtaking detail, not only the terrain – the mountains, deserts and forests – but many of the famous landmarks, from the pyramids of Egypt to the ancient stone circles of Britain.

But the map was not only geographical; it was scattered with legions of armies. Battalions of minute soldiers (it was these that had formed the blocks of colour Jake had seen from above) were stationed everywhere – from the white peaks of the Alps to the plains of Persia; from the deserts of the Sahara to the wintry forests of Scandinavia. And each soldier, of the thousands that populated the map, wore the same uniform: the familiar armour of the Hydra.

Charlie was the next to descend, followed shortly by Nathan (Lucius was showing off again, proving he could lower two people simultaneously). Once he was on the ground, Nathan called up to him, 'Maintain that position! We may need to leave at any second.'

'Anything you say, sir,' Lucius replied with a smirk, and sat down with his legs dangling through the skylight.

'I've said it already and I'll say it again,' Nathan said, glancing up at the constellations on the inside of the dome, 'you have to admire Agata's chutzpah. The world is not enough for her – she wants the *universe*.'

'Good gracious, you're right,' Charlie replied, examining it in greater detail. 'She's renamed Scorpio after herself, and Leopardo has been substituted for Ursa Major.'

Jake hadn't noticed before, but now he could clearly see their names inscribed in curling gold letters across the blue sky. He also realized that another section was in the process of being repainted – no doubt to include the new member of the family: Topaz.

Nathan and Charlie turned their attention to Agata's map – in particular to the armies. 'Unless Agata Zeldt plans to produce half a million soldiers out of thin air,' Nathan commented, 'I guess her plan is to somehow take command of the Roman army.'

'I'd say that was about the size of it,' Charlie concurred.

'And how big is the Roman army?' Jake asked. 'I mean, how many men in each of those divisions?'

Charlie shrugged and whistled through his teeth. 'Well, in the last hundred years the army has grown tenfold, from a haphazard collection of forces scattered here and there into a hardened and super-efficient machine, capable of conquering anyone.'

'He's right,' Nathan agreed, picking up one of the miniature soldiers and inspecting it. 'Look at poor old Mithridates and the Persians. One of the most ancient and revered nations in history, wiped out in a decade.'

'Regarding actual number' – Charlie was adding it up in his head – 'there must be at least twenty-five legions with roughly five thousand infantrymen in each, and probably three hundred *auxilia* regiments – including the navy, cavalry, et cetera, as well as the multitude of foreign conscripts. Which all adds up to about 400,000 fighting men.'

'In short,' Nathan concluded, 'enough to enslave the western world and have a good stab at taking over the rest.' Then he added with a theatrical arch of his eyebrows, '*The end of dominions.*'

'But how is she planning to get control of the Roman army?' Jake asked.

'That is the question we must answer,' Charlie replied. 'Buttering up a few corrupt lawyers and generals with flamingo surprise and eels stuffed with sprats is only going to get you so far.'

'And the other question is' – Nathan held up the tiny soldier – '*who* was responsible for these gaudy uniforms? It's a travesty on every level. If you're going to take over the world, get the *look* right first. Wouldn't you agree?'

Charlie snatched the figure, replaced it on the map and suggested they should all stop talking and start looking. He and Jake began to go through the piles of papers to see if they could find any more information on *the end of dominions* or this *public murder* that Topaz had told them about, while Nathan opened all the doors that led off from the chamber to see if there was any sign of the actor Austerio.

Their various searches bore no immediate results: Nathan could find only storerooms, while the charts and papers turned out to be either irrelevant or indecipherable. Only one thing caught Jake's attention: a drawing of seven golden eggs, with the word *Counters* scrawled underneath. He remembered, from Agata's suite in Vulcano, something with an identical illustration.

'Does this mean anything to you?' he said, holding it up to Nathan.

Nathan glanced over, but made no sense of it. He shrugged, suggesting that it was of no importance; before turning his attention to a wall mirror, its reflective properties derived from a layer of mercury behind glass. As he admired his teeth, he claimed it was the most ingenious and charming thing he had seen all year.

After about twenty minutes, Lucius gave an urgent whistle from above. 'Someone's coming.'

A moment later, they heard the sound of a key in the lock and muffled voices. They looked at each other in alarm.

'Raise the ropes now!' Nathan commanded Lucius. 'Everyone else, under here . . .' He went over to the map table, lifted the tapestry cover and pushed Jake and Charlie underneath. The ropes shot up through the skylight and disappeared. Nathan squeezed into the dark space under the table with the other two. In unison, without prompting, all three silently drew their daggers as they heard the door opening and footsteps approaching.

Jake and Nathan could see what was going on through a hole in the tapestry. They breathed sighs of relief when they saw not guards but a couple of slaves, each carrying a tray of food – some familiar items from dinner. The two men headed across the room, one reaching down to pull on a lever. Immediately a section of black and white floor rose up, revealing a set of steps that led down into a room underneath.

The two slaves descended. Moments later the boys heard a voice. It was so deep and fruity – so like the voice of an actor – that they were in no doubt as to its owner. Presently the slaves returned empty handed and, leaving the trapdoor open, walked back across the room, locking the door behind them.

Jake, Nathan and Charlie crawled out of their hiding place as Lucius appeared grinning in the aperture above. 'They've gone,' he said in his version of a whisper.

Nathan put his finger to his mouth to signal for everyone to be silent. He led the others down the small flight of steps and stopped in front of a red velvet curtain. Behind it, the distinctive, almost comical voice had started up again, practising the same phrase over and over using slightly different tones each time: '*Veni, vidi, vici.*'

It was one of the few pieces of Latin that Jake

knew – 'I came, I saw, I conquered' – spoken, he was certain, by Julius Caesar after invading some new country.

With the tip of his dagger, Nathan drew back the curtain to reveal the man in the room beyond. He looked both magnificent and ridiculous. On the one hand he was tall, aristocratic-looking, dressed in a dark purple toga, with a laurel wreath on his head. On the other, he kept pulling peculiar faces at himself in a mirror, doing odd exercises with his mouth, while striking poses and waving around a half-eaten leg of baked flamingo.

Jake and Nathan were trying hard not to laugh, but Charlie's expression was serious. The moment he set eyes on Austerio, he understood what was going on: the facial likeness, the purple toga, the oratory. 'Tiberius,' he murmured. 'He's going to impersonate the Emperor Tiberius.'

'What?' whispered Nathan, his smile suddenly evaporating.

'The emperor is a recluse, remember?' Charlie explained. 'He lives on Capri. He has barely been seen in public for years, but this man is the spitting image of him.'

As Jake craned to get a better look, he knocked

Nathan's dagger from his hand and it dropped with a clang on the floor.

Austerio – for it was surely he – swung round, gasping in horror as the three boys swept in. Perhaps if they had been unarmed he might have reacted differently; but as they came towards him, he waved his arms, moaning and rolling his eyes like some character from a Greek tragedy. Realizing that gestures alone were not going to save him, he flung his flamingo drumstick at them, then his plate of food, along with a couple of candlesticks. Nathan finally managed to clap a hand over his ranting mouth.

'*Ssh!* Listen, we're not here to hurt you,' he told him. 'We're friends. *Amici sumus.* You are Austerio – *tu es Austerio, amicus Ficium* – Fico the Fantastic.'

Austerio had been struggling and trying to yell through Nathan's fingers, but on hearing his name, and then that of his friend (or enemy), he gradually calmed down. Eventually Nathan removed his hand.

Austerio collected himself, rearranging his few strands of hair before replying tersely, 'Fico is not fantastic, it is *I* who is fantastic.' And to demonstrate the point, he struck a dramatic pose, showing his face first front-on and then in profile.

'You speak English?' Charlie asked, bemused.

'Of course.' The actor shrugged. 'I have a thousand talents. Fico has none.'

Nathan picked up a bound book from the table. '*Latin–English dictionary*,' he read from the spine, then opened it and looked inside. 'Published 1590 – somewhat advanced for Roman times?' he commented to the others before turning back to Austerio. 'Did Agata Zeldt tell you to learn English? How long have you known her?'

Austerio carefully examined them all before finally answering with a petulant shrug, 'Who are you and what business have you here?'

Nathan and Charlie looked at each other blankly, but Jake jumped straight in: 'We're writing an epic poem. About you – about all your achievements.'

'An epic poem?' Austerio asked, immediately interested.

'We're your greatest fans,' Jake assured him with a bow. 'Your most loyal supporters. In Herculaneum, we have watched every one of your performances – haven't we?'

Charlie and Nathan nodded eagerly.

The actor was hooked. 'But you're just children,'

he said patronizingly, but couldn't resist adding, 'Really? Every performance?'

'All the classics,' Charlie chipped in. 'Plautus, Terence . . .'

'You saw my Phormio?' he asked, striking another heroic pose. 'My towering Greek commander?'

'It was so moving,' Nathan stated with absolute sincerity, 'I nearly threw myself on my sword.'

'By Jupiter! If that's how you find my comedies, my tragedies must be *unbearable*.'

'You have no idea.' Nathan shook his head and put his hand on his heart – once again choosing the wrong side.

Suddenly Austerio frowned and glanced towards the stairs, then leaned forward to whisper, '*Periculosus est hic* – but it is dangerous here. If you are found, they will think you are spies. How came you in?'

'We followed you all the way to Rome,' said Jake, 'then waited outside the villa for an opportunity to see you.'

Moved by such devotion, Austerio sighed, his eyes welling with tears.

Then, not to be outdone in the acting stakes,

Charlie added, 'For our own sanity, you must tell us what it is you are doing here. Herculaneum is barren without you.'

At first Austerio was reluctant to discuss the matter, but after a good deal of coaxing, his vanity got the better of him and he began to talk – first in snippets, then in ever-increasing torrents. He spoke of how he had first met his *patroness* – as he called Agata – six months ago; of how she had admired his talent and wined and dined him in all the fashionable eateries of the bay of Naples; of her desire for him to learn her peculiar language to make him an even bigger star. He recounted how she had picked him up in Herculaneum and transported him – by ship and then by carriage, in the lap of luxury – to Rome.

'That's all very exciting,' Nathan butted in, 'but what exactly are you doing here?'

Austerio looked down his nose at them. 'I am here to give the performance of my life; to play none other than the Emperor Tiberius – it is a matter of national security.'

Charlie nudged Jake. 'Didn't I say so?'

'That's right. I, the humble Austerio,' he declared, 'just a small-town boy from the wrong side of the Apennines, using my oceanic talent to save my beloved country!'

'*National security?*' Charlie repeated. '*Save your beloved country?* What do you mean?'

Austerio leaned in close and whispered, 'Dear boys, I hate to be the bearer of bad tidings, but an uprising is afoot. A bloody revolution across the Empire, ten times more deadly than that of Spartacus. The world is on the brink of calamity!' He put his hand on his heart – choosing the correct side, unlike Nathan, Jake noticed. 'But I shall be playing my part to bring safety back to the people.'

Needless to say, when questioned about exactly how he would be doing this, he couldn't give a straight answer – mumbling something about *an empire needing its emperor* – and when asked who would be leading this revolt, he also looked blank.

They were about to ask him all sorts of other questions when they heard a bell tolling.

'That's it,' Austerio gasped. 'The fourth hour. They'll be coming for me at any moment. You must go,' he said, pushing them out of the room. 'They will think you are spies, and have no mercy.'

'Coming for you?' asked Nathan.

'I am to make *a regal appearance* at the party,'

Austerio said, 'before the big day tomorrow.'

'*Tomorrow?*' Jake, Nathan and Charlie repeated in unison. 'What's tomorrow?'

'My first *public* show. I am to appear at the games at the Circus Maximus. Now go . . .' He ushered them up the stairs. 'Leopardo will be here any second and I must get ready.'

Hearing this name, the young agents looked at each other. None of them fancied bumping into Leopardo. They quickly said their goodbyes, promised to look out for Austerio the next day, and charged back up the stairs.

'And be careful, boys.' He sighed, putting his hand on his heart again. 'I will do everything in my power to prevent the revolution, but Rome is not a safe place to be.'

Charlie whistled up to Lucius, who lowered the two ropes. Nathan quickly climbed up first, without any help. Charlie took the second rope. Jake was always surprised that Charlie, who spoke twenty languages and understood quantum physics, was so agile as well. He had none of Nathan's style but he had shinned up the rope in no time at all.

In contrast, Jake, even with Lucius's help, struggled to pull himself up. He had nearly made it to the skylight when he heard the sound of a key in the lock below. In a flash, the door flew open and Leopardo strode into the room.

Jake had stopped breathing. He was hanging in midair from a spinning, creaking rope.

16 ANDROMEDA AND THE SEA MONSTER

Nathan, Charlie and Lucius, their faces hovering in the darkness above the skylight, watched in horror as Leopardo strode over to the trapdoor and called out to Austerio. They hoped he would go down the steps so that they could pull Jake to safety. But he simply waited, pouting at himself – just like Nathan – in the mercury wall mirror, until Austerio appeared.

The actor immediately caught sight of Jake, suspended in the dome, and gasped out loud. Jake lost his grip and slipped down towards the table, the coarse rope burning his palms as he did so.

The boys were sure that it would end in disaster, but Austerio acted quickly, pretending that he was simply shocked by the sight of his reflection in the mirror. He muttered something about everything being off centre and asked Leopardo to straighten his crown of laurels. As the latter complied with a curl of his lip, Jake was hauled up towards the skylight.

He was almost there when Leopardo clapped his hands and announced that they must leave immediately. At this moment, disaster struck: Jake's mask, which he had tucked inside his toga, fell out. He tried in vain to grab it with one hand, then with a foot. As it spiralled down towards the floor, Austerio started speaking again, this time complaining loudly about the cut of his tunic.

Losing patience, Leopardo barked that there was nothing wrong with it and headed towards the door. Suddenly he stopped dead, catching sight of the mask on the floor. He picked it up and examined it, looking at Austerio – and then up at the dome. There was nothing there: just a dark patch of sky framed by the skylight. He opened the door and ushered the actor through.

From the rooftop, four silhouettes, all breathing great sighs of relief, watched Leopardo and Austerio cross the courtyard below and enter the villa.

For a short while they stood there in the darkness, mulling everything over.

Charlie was the first to speak. 'He said that the Circus Maximus was to be his first *public* show.'

'Yep.' Nathan nodded seriously. 'I heard that too.' He turned to Jake. 'And what did Topaz say? Everything will begin with a *public* murder?'

Suddenly it dawned on Jake – a shocking and terrible idea. '*He's* going to be murdered? Austerio?'

'Not Austerio,' Nathan corrected him. 'Tiberius.' He raised his eyebrows. 'I know my Roman history is not as good as yours, Charlie, but ever since Spartacus, isn't everyone in the empire paranoid about another rebellion?'

'Spartacus,' Lucius suddenly chipped in. 'I've heard of him.'

Nathan turned to Jake. 'He was this rogue gladiator who got all the slaves to rise up against their masters. What better way to spark *the end of dominions* than by assassinating the emperor and then blaming it on a bunch of "rebels" who probably don't even exist. It would be mayhem. A civil war could erupt within days.'

Charlie was shaking his head. 'It's a good theory but it doesn't make sense. Why would Agata bother to teach Austerio English if she was going to do away with him?'

'Well, we don't have much else to go on' – Nathan shrugged – 'except that *something* is going to happen at the Circus Maximus tomorrow. So I suggest we get back to the bureau and work out what we're going to do about it.'

He led his companions back across the roofs. They jumped down onto Agata's private terrace and descended the dark staircase to the door that went into the arena. The party had become a good deal more raucous and the music much louder.

'Here – you wear this,' Nathan said to Jake, passing him his mask. He turned to the others and whispered, 'Let's get out of here as quickly as we can.'

Charlie agreed, but Jake said nothing. He hated the thought of leaving Topaz again. Just as Nathan was about to open the door, silence suddenly fell on the other side. Then they heard Agata saying something in Latin, ending with the phrase: '*Salutate imperatorem!*'

It was followed by a chorus of respectful cheers and shouts of '*Salve, Caesar!*'

Jake, Charlie and Lucius put on their masks, while Nathan pulled up the hood of his cape. He edged open the door, and the four of them slipped through. The guests were all on their feet (at least, the men were; some of the women were still reclining) as Austerio, 'the Emperor Tiberius', passed regally among them, bestowing nods here and there and occasionally offering his fat, bejewelled hand to be kissed. Jake had half imagined that he might play the part like a pantomime character, so he was surprised by how subtle and convincing he was in the role. The 'emperor' was shown to a throne next to Agata's, and everyone else sat down again. This was when Jake realized that Topaz's place was empty. He searched all around for her, but she was nowhere to be seen.

'Let's go,' Nathan said in his ear, guessing the reason for his delay. 'Topaz knows where we are – she will contact us if she needs to.'

They crept along in the shadow of the colonnade towards the exit. They had almost reached it when the musicians struck up again. The horn players and the drummers started marching, in time to the music, towards the edge of the arena. There was a ripple of excitement, and everyone started whispering in anticipation of what was to come.

The music grew even louder. Then suddenly the stone floor at the centre of the arena began to open;

first there was a strip of darkness, then a gaping cavity. Out of this rose a vast misshapen boulder that looked like it had been torn from a wild seashore. On top of this, in a pose straight from Roman mythology, lay a nymph, manacled to the rock, her face hidden by a mass of soaking hair. She was perfectly still, as if under a spell; and Jake realized, with a lurch of horror, that it was Topaz.

He guessed that they were about to witness Agata Zeldt's *ludi sanguinei* – the blood games that Topaz had mentioned earlier. 'What are they going to do to her?' he asked, the words sticking in his throat.

'Come on . . .' Nathan gently tugged him on. 'Remember what she told you? We must not look at her.'

But Jake was not listening and shook Nathan's hand off. Lucius was rooted to the spot, his eyes fixed on the spectacle. Charlie was also reluctant to leave, and in truth, Nathan felt the same: he knew that his duty lay with the History Keepers, but he was as concerned as the others for his adopted sister.

The floor continued to rise; the boulder was now surrounded by a rocky pool, foaming and churning as if alive with fish. The whole section rose up until it was level with the audience, then stopped.

The guests were now waiting, agog, shifting this way and that to get the best view. Jake saw Agata Zeldt removing her mask to reveal a face twisted into a sadistic smile, while Leopardo, standing behind her, dug his fingers into her shoulders.

The music was deafening now – the horns blared and the drums beat like thunder. Jake felt the hairs stand up on the back of his neck. Suddenly there was a gasp as a terrifying creature slowly rose out of the centre of the pool. It was a sea monster – or at least a fierce warrior dressed as one. He was tall, broad and muscular, and his gleaming helmet was fashioned in the shape of a grotesque shark's head, mouth gaping to reveal his own savage face within. His enormous chest heaved under a breastplate of armoured scales. His forearms, each the size of a tree trunk, were encased in gauntlets studded with sharp razors, and daggers glinted from the backs of his metal boots. In his hands, each the size of Jake's head, he grasped a broadsword and a trident.

Jake's heart was now pumping at double speed. His stomach had turned to liquid. 'What is he going to do to her?' he said through clenched teeth.

'It's just a show,' Nathan tried to reassure him. 'Dreadful as she is, Agata Zeldt wouldn't put her own daughter in any *real* danger.' Even as he spoke the words, he did not entirely believe them. The depravity of the Zeldt family had never ceased to amaze him.

The music reached a thunderous crescendo. The 'sea monster' rose until his feet were level with the surface of the water; then he stepped onto the edge of the pool and pumped his arms above his head. The music stopped dead and he let out a war cry of such ferocity that Jake had to cover his ears. Then he turned to the figure of the nymph and waited, chest heaving, for battle to commence.

All eyes swivelled to the motionless Topaz. Slowly she awoke, moving first an arm, then a leg, then lifting her head. Gradually she rose to her feet. Jake now spotted the sword at her side, which she brandished aloft, with a battle cry to challenge the monster's.

The audience cheered and leaped up in delight. Even the slaves had stopped to steal a glance at the entertainment.

'It's Andromeda and the sea monster,' Charlie said, as if in a dream.

'Who?' Jake asked, both appalled and mesmerized.

'The legend goes that her mother, Cassiopeia,

the queen of Ethiopia, bragged that she was more beautiful than Poseidon's own daughters. In revenge, the sea god let loose a terrible monster, Cetus, to lay waste to the coastline. He would stop only if Andromeda was sacrificed. So she was chained to a rock and abandoned.'

'And what happened to her then?' Jake was clenching his fists so tightly, his knuckles were white.

'Actually' – Charlie's tone brightened – 'she was saved by the warrior Perseus, who was on his way back from finishing off the Gorgon, Medusa.'

'Not that you should get any ideas,' Nathan added quickly, keeping an eye on Jake. 'Perseus was a killing machine, not an innocent schoolboy.'

Suddenly the fighting started. Cetus's massive body lunged forward, swiping at Topaz with the broadsword. Showing lightning reactions, she parried, then kicked out at him. There was a loud crunch as her foot connected with his jaw. The audience erupted as Cetus fell back. For a second his eyes swam in his head; but then fury took hold again. He surged through the water, and a nerve-shredding duel followed – parry, riposte, parry. Steel sliced against steel; sparks flew; water sprayed onto the crowd. Topaz was quick and nimble, her foe slow and brutish. He slashed at her feet, and she jumped nimbly down into the pool – but the chain stopped her from escaping, and yanked her back.

Jake was filled with panic as she lost her footing, tripped and fell into the water. Without hesitation, Cetus's trident came down on her. She tried to dodge it, but it grazed her shoulder. Blood dripped into the foaming pool.

'We have to stop it!' Jake exclaimed, stepping forward.

'No, Jake!' Nathan held him back. 'She's ten times more able than he. It is entertainment, that is all. This is ancient Rome, remember – nothing like the place you come from.'

Topaz and the monster had retreated, panting, gazes fixed on one another. Agata's eyes sparkled and Leopardo licked his lips in anticipation. The crowd started chanting for the battle to resume. This time Topaz lunged first, and the duel became even more desperate. Suddenly she swiped her sword at her opponent's leg. There was a screech as the blade sliced through the metal of his boots and came to a stop. As she yanked it free, she lost her footing and tumbled into the pool again. Taking advantage of this, the monster hurled his trident at her. Topaz ducked, and it thwacked into the thigh of a passing slave. The audience fell about laughing, but Topaz was distracted. Cetus advanced on her and lifted his sword for the kill. Everyone froze in anticipation.

Suddenly Jake shoved Nathan aside and ran out, unsheathing his dagger. He hurled himself into the pool and stabbed Cetus's thigh. Neither Topaz nor the crowd could identify this new masked participant at first; the guests assumed that he was the brave Perseus come to save her, and cheered with delight. Cetus gave a deep, rasping groan and tried to swing a punch at Jake, but then dropped to his knees, blood pumping from his wound.

Jake picked himself up and went over to Topaz. 'It's me,' he panted. 'The chain' – he took hold of it – 'how do I undo it?'

'Are you mad?' Topaz shook her head in fury. 'You must leave now! You risk everything.'

He paid no attention. 'How do I undo it?' he yelled again, yanking the metal links.

In the crowd, Charlie and Nathan stood frozen in horror, the latter holding Lucius back in case he was also tempted to join the fray.

'Charlie, what now?' Nathan whispered urgently.

'I don't know,' Charlie replied in despair, nodding towards Leopardo and Agata on the other side of the stage. 'Like everyone else, they think this is part of the show.'

He was right: they were both smirking, as yet unaware of what was really going on.

'Jake!' Topaz cried as Cetus suddenly lurched to his feet again. He swung Jake round, grabbed him by the neck and started to lift him off the ground. As his immense hands tightened their grip, Jake's mask fell off and his face – now a startling red – was revealed.

As Leopardo watched, his eyes began to widen in uncertainty. Then his smile gradually faded. He knew this boy: it was that inept agent from the opera house in Stockholm. Quickly he scanned the faces in the crowd and found another he recognized: Nathan Wylder. Leopardo's lips quivered and he clenched his white teeth.

Then everything happened at once.

The audience cheered as Jake was lifted higher and higher, his legs thrashing in midair. Topaz picked up a large rock and smashed it over the monster's head. His eyes bulged, then rolled up in his head. He let go of Jake, lost consciousness and fell back into the pool.

'*Periculum!* Danger!' Leopardo yelled at the top of his voice. 'Look to the emperor,' he ordered as he pushed through the mob and jumped down into the arena, unsheathing his sword as he did so.

Suddenly there was pandemonium. The screaming guests charged for the exits. Agata Zeldt slowly rose to her feet, her face incandescent with fury.

As Leopardo bore down on Jake, Nathan jumped into the ring, landing on Cetus's chest (the unfortunate soldier was just coming round when he was knocked out again) and intercepting Leopardo's blade.

'All the vermin are here, then!' The fair-haired youth swung round to face him. 'I knew that snake couldn't be trusted.'

Then swords were crashing, twisting, slicing; faces were set, fierce with concentration. In the midst of all the mayhem, Jake couldn't help appreciating what a sensational swordsman Nathan was. At times he was a peacock, but when he truly needed to fight, he was awe-inspiring – as swift and balletic as he was savage and strong. That said, Leopardo was more than a match for him, and on this occasion he was the luckier of the two. Nathan misjudged a cut by just an inch; it was enough for his opponent to knock him off balance, strike his hand and disarm him.

Leopardo was just preparing to finish him off when Topaz finally eased apart the weak link in the heavy chain, releasing it and hurling it into his face. There was a crack as the iron struck his teeth. Jake actually saw a chunk of white enamel fly out of his mouth and land in someone's pudding. The blow was decisive: Leopardo looked incredulous, insulted; then collapsed onto his knees and fell head first into the water.

Only now, almost paralysed with white-hot fury, did Agata act, uttering a murderous cry that made people's blood run cold. 'Stop them!' she cried, thrusting her way through the crowd towards the edge of the arena.

Without thinking, Jake rushed across to intercept her, jumping over the balustrade. 'You are a monster!' he yelled as he came face to face with her. He had no weapon, but picked up a goblet of wine from the nearest table and flung its contents into her face. There was a look of astonishment, before she lunged for Jake's neck. Now he took hold of the whole table and swung it towards her. It made contact with her jaw, and her head jolted back;

plates and glasses smashed onto the ground. Jake swung again, and this time Agata lost her footing and fell onto a pile of broken crockery and half-eaten food.

Jake was about to attack her with his bare hands when Nathan yanked him back, dragging him away. 'Enough!' he ordered. There were guards every-where, fighting their way through the frenzied crowd to come to Agata's aid. Charlie, Topaz and Lucius joined Nathan and Jake, and they forced their way back to the other side of the arena and through the archway leading into the villa.

'This way,' said Topaz, leading them along a labyrinth of slaves' corridors and back stairways until they reached the huge vaulted kitchen. Here, amidst clouds of steam and clanking metal, lackeys were busy cleaning up after the banquet. They were too tired to challenge the intruders. Charlie resisted the alluring, mouth-watering sights and smells as Topaz guided them through.

The back door was open, and just outside stood a cart, from which a hairy man in a leather apron was unloading carcasses of meat. As he disappeared inside with half a cow across his shoulder, Nathan wasted no time in leaping up onto the vehicle.

'All aboard,' he shouted as he took hold of the reins.

The others scrambled up, Charlie reeling as he came face to face with the dead eyes of a wild boar. '*Enchanté*,' he said drily as Lucius helped Topaz up and jumped on.

By the time the butcher re-emerged from the kitchen, his cart was gone.

Nathan flicked the reins, urging the horses round to the front of the villa and nearly colliding with another platoon of guards who were pouring out of the main entrance. One long-limbed soldier managed to pull himself up onto the back of the cart, sword drawn.

'Excuse me.' Charlie politely edged Topaz out of the way and launched the wild boar at their assailant. With a resounding crack, snout met face and the man was thrown off. 'There are times,' Charlie commented, dusting his hands, 'when cruelty to animals is acceptable.'

As they flew up the road, the soldiers jumped into their own wagon and set off in pursuit.

Nathan steered the rickety butcher's cart down the hill towards the Roman Forum, the ancient wheels shaking and rattling with the strain. Their pursuers rapidly picked up speed. Within moments, the guards were firing darts from their crossbows.

Nathan whipped the horses on, faster and faster. Too late he noticed a hole in the road ahead – there was a screech of metal and the cart took off for a moment. It landed with such a jolt that Lucius over-balanced. He reached out for Topaz, but it was too late – he was already flying off the back of the cart. Topaz gasped in horror as he rolled straight into the path of the wagon.

In unison the watching History Keepers covered their eyes as Lucius was trampled by the horses' hooves. One animal tripped over the human obstacle, and came crashing down, pulling the others with it. There was a melee of dust, of neigh-ing, of twisting necks and thrashing limbs, until finally the wagon came to a halt.

'We have to stop!' Jake shouted, peering round. He could just make out Lucius's body amidst the carnage.

'You don't get to say anything!' Nathan shouted at him. '*Never again*, do you understand?' Jake had never seen his friend so angry – he was livid with rage.

Nathan shook the reins harder and urged the

horses on down the hill. Topaz sat there, shaking with a whole range of emotions – shock, confusion, exhaustion . . . and loathing for Jake. She saw Lucius's body being dragged out of the wreckage, before the cart rounded a corner and she lost sight of him.

Jake was overcome with shame. The sense of his own disgrace was so unbearable that he felt physically sick. Once again – and more catastrophically than ever – he had ruined everything.

17 Lucius Down

'Sh-sh-should we go back for him?' Jake stammered in the gloom. They had just got back to the bureau and Charlie was lighting candles, with Mr Drake sitting stiffly on his shoulder.

Nathan turned on Jake. 'I told you to keep out of this!' he said. Half an hour had passed since they escaped Agata's villa, but he was still furious. 'Do you understand?'

Jake nodded obediently.

'Your weapon, please,' Nathan demanded, sounding like a cross teacher. Jake undid his belt, fumbling clumsily with the buckle before finally releasing it. Nathan snatched the belt and scabbard from him and placed it on the table. Receiving the special sword from Nathan himself on the pier at Point Zero had been one of Jake's proudest moments. Since then everything had turned sour. 'Now sit down over there and keep quiet!' the American ordered coldly, pointing to Jake's bunk.

He turned, headed across the room and sat down. At any moment, he knew, tears would start welling up, so he sank back into the shadows against the wall and used what little will power he had left to keep them at bay. Crying now would be the ultimate disgrace and he was determined not to let it happen.

The others did not even look at him. They went about their business: Nathan examining papers; Topaz attending to the cuts on her face in the mirror; Charlie lighting more candles. The air was thick with tension. Only Mr Drake briefly peeked over his master's shoulder to examine the malefactor in the corner. Jake looked up at him, hoping that he still had one friend, but the parrot fluffed up his feathers and turned away.

The taut silence was eventually broken by Nathan. 'The capture of Lucius Titus is regrettable,' he said matter-of-factly, 'but there will be no rescue mission. It is too dangerous and the chances are' – he bit his lip – 'the chances are he has not made it.'

Jake felt his stomach flip over. He looked at

Topaz in the mirror. She froze, her eyes flickering, but said nothing.

'Does everyone agree?' Nathan asked quietly.

It was a while before Topaz, without turning round, nodded back at him. Charlie, who had waited to hear her opinion, solemnly followed suit. Nathan bowed his head respectfully. 'As I said, it's regrettable. He was a good soldier.'

Jake had to clench his fists and take deep breaths to stop himself from leaping up and shouting that of course they should try and save Lucius; that he was sure to be alive! But he knew it was no good. The damage had been done and he was to blame for everything.

Nathan continued in a businesslike way, 'Regarding Agata Zeldt's *end of dominions* – what we know, or seem to know, is as follows. Something is going to happen during the games at the Circus Maximus tomorrow. Though the details are sketchy, it is likely to be an assassination attempt. We believe that the target is the fake Tiberius. It is possible that rebel slaves will then be blamed for his murder. Unrest will follow, and Agata will use the confusion and bloodshed as an opportunity to take control. Her master plan, her ultimate aim – and we have no idea how she is to accomplish it – is to assume command of the Roman army. Need I tell anyone what that could lead to?' Nathan didn't wait for an answer. 'The greatest military forces the world has ever known in the hands of one of history's most demented malefactors.'

'And what exactly is she planning to do with the army?' Charlie asked, uncertain of everything.

'I don't know.' Nathan shrugged. 'Re-draw the boundaries of the world in her own diabolical image? The end of dominions, remember?'

Charlie was still shaking his head. 'It still doesn't add up,' he said. 'As a plan, it's completely flawed.' He pushed his glasses up his nose as he started to explain. 'The emperor is without doubt the supreme head of state – in fact, never has one man, in all history, held so much power. And, yes, his assassination, in full public view, by supposed rebel factions, would be catastrophic. But even then Agata couldn't take command of the army without the full support of the Senate. And this is not forgetting that the *real* Tiberius will still exist.'

'I don't know about the real Tiberius,' Nathan replied. 'Maybe he's dead already. But regarding the senate, we can only assume that she *has* their support. Remember, she's richer than anyone in the empire . . .'

'Sure, and of course money talks, without a doubt, especially in this city,' Charlie reflected, 'but there's six hundred of them, Nathan, and the Romans are also famous for their sense of honour.'

'Then we must assume that somehow she has taken those facts into account as well,' Nathan said firmly. 'There seem be no limits to what she can do. Besides, what else do we have to go on? Our mission is clear: tomorrow morning we head for the Circus Maximus and stop this assassination from taking place.'

Although Charlie was still far from convinced, he had no option but to nod in agreement.

The mood didn't improve much after that. Jake remained sitting on his bed. Charlie rustled up a cheese board (he was ravenous, having eaten hardly anything at Agata's banquet), then the three of them sat around the table, examining a map of the Circus Maximus and discussing their plan of action. Jake watched them from the shadows, hearing only snippets of conversation: 'The emperor's enclosure is this structure here . . . The games always start with a procession . . .' None of them turned round or spoke to him. They didn't even offer him anything to eat. He wondered if they would ever talk to him again.

Eventually Nathan rolled up the map. He stood up and gave Topaz a big hug and Jake heard him whisper, 'I'm always here for you. Always.' He turned to Charlie and gave him a warm pat on the back. 'There is one silver lining to all this, old friend,' he said. 'As our cover has been blown, we'll need to go incognito. I trust you packed your special equipment?'

'Beards and moustaches?' the other replied eagerly, producing a small case from his belt. 'I never travel without them!'

Nathan headed, yawning, towards his bed. Charlie went to sit on his bunk, gave Mr Drake a goodnight peanut and a little peck on his head, then lay down.

Jake watched Topaz as she extinguished all the candles but one on the table. Finally she put the last of the food on a plate and brought it over to Jake.

'Here,' she said, handing it to him. There were a couple of slices of cheese and some bread and pickles.

'Thank you,' he said quietly, putting it down on

the bed. 'T-Topaz,' he stammered, 'I don't even know where to begin with saying sorry. And I understand I may never be forgiven . . .' He looked up at her, blinking his big brown eyes. Her expression was cold and unsmiling, but he soldiered on. 'But, you know, I think Lucius may have a chance. He is so brave and clever and I'm sure that—'

'*Tu comprends comme sa vie a été dûr?*' Topaz interrupted him, the words almost sticking in her throat. 'Do you know how hard his life has been? Do you know what pain he has suffered?'

Jake remembered that Lucius had told him something of his life, the night they spent together on the bridge. 'He said he hadn't seen his parents since he was ten.'

'And do you know why?'

Jake shook his head.

'Because when he was ten, pirates boarded his parents' ship and took them away. His family was not rich – his father had a small boat-repair yard – but they were happy. Lucius was loved,' she said pointedly. 'One day they were sailing to Dalmatia: they'd saved enough money to build a little house there, by the sea. But just three leagues away from the coast the pirates attacked. Lucius was brave even then and put up a fight' – a smile briefly flickered on Topaz's face – '*mais c'était inutile* – it was pointless. He was a child. He was bound, chained and separated from his father, his mother and his little brother. He never heard of them again.'

'Brother?' Jake said softly. 'He didn't tell me he had a brother.'

'They took Lucius to the nearest port and sold him in the market for two pieces of gold. He spent five years – *la reste de son enfance* – underground in a silver mine, haunted by the screams of his brother as he was carried away that day.'

Jake's insides froze with pity. He looked at Topaz and saw that her eyes were glistening. He stood up and took her hand. She did not react, but nor did she pull it away. She carried on with her story. 'Then, when I was imprisoned by my own mother, he helped me whenever he could, without a care for his own safety.' Tears streamed down her face now. 'He was a beautiful person,' she sobbed quietly. '*Un gars magnifique.*' Charlie peered over at the sorry scene, but said nothing.

Jake wanted to throw his arms around Topaz, but she quickly wiped away her tears and climbed onto her bunk. Jake watched as she pulled up the bed-clothes and, still sobbing, turned her back on him.

Helplessly, Jake stood staring at Topaz's back. He wanted to tell her that everything would be all right; but he couldn't. The truth was, things were far from all right. Lucius was gone. And, on top of that, Agata Zeldt, the most evil woman in history, was at large. The following day she was planning an atrocity that would herald the *end of dominions*; but none of them even understood what it was, let alone how they could stop it.

At length Jake sighed and lay down on his bed. Still fully dressed, he pulled the blanket over him and stared at the wall in shame.

18 THE SECRET ROOM

'She's definitely gone,' said Alan, his binoculars trained on the retreating boat. It was dawn on the Mont St Michel, and he and Miriam were on the blustery battlements, suppressing early morning yawns.

They had waited two days for Oceane to leave her suite long enough for them to investigate the book with the palm tree on its cover. Oceane had announced the night before that she was planning a trip to the mainland to look at fabrics for her wedding. Alan and Miriam had got up at four and waited patiently, sharing a flask of coffee and watching the sea birds, until she and her pet lioness finally boarded the ferry boat (the History Keepers usually sent one daily to the mainland to pick up provisions) and departed.

'Let's go,' Miriam announced, heading for the nearest staircase. 'My toes are frozen solid.'

They made their way to Oceane's luxurious suite, slipped inside and went straight over to the pink china pot on the mantelshelf, where Oceane had put the key to the secret compartment. They had wondered if she might take it with her, so it was a great relief when they heard it clinking in the bottom. They took it out and opened up the safe behind the painting. The book with the palm tree on it was there.

Miriam seized it and examined the cover, screwing up her face in bewilderment. '*Flora of the South China Seas, 700 to 1500,*' she read blankly. 'It doesn't sound very important.' She shrugged. 'Unless of course you happen to live in the South China Seas in that time. And you're in the gardening business.'

Alan took it from her, unclasped the latch and opened it. His face lit up. 'Well, that's a little more interesting,' he said. Inside, cut into the pages, was a cavity with *another* key – this one much larger, and gold. He carefully took it out and examined it. There were curious interlocking symbols inscribed on the bow. 'Looks like Chinese. Mean anything to you?' He passed it to Miriam.

She shrugged. 'As you know, eastern languages are not my strong suit, nor yours. Galliana would know, of course. But what on earth is the key for?' She took the book from Alan and peered at the spine. 'They have volumes just like this in the archives. There must be a connection – that's where Jake saw her.'

Without further discussion they took the book and the key and made their way up stairs and down corridors, through the stateroom, then doubling back down more steps until they finally reached the intelligence section. Two decoders were already working at Meslith terminals by the light of flickering candelabras. Miriam and Alan nodded good morning and went straight into the archive room. It was still gloomy, with just a glimmer of early morning light filtering through the windows.

'Now let's see . . .' said Miriam, squinting along the various section headings. '*Weather*, *Tides*, *Moonrises* . . . Here we are: *Flora and Fauna*.' She leaned down and started looking carefully at the sub-headings: '*Flora . . . Mediterranean*, *Northern European*, *American*, *South American*, *Australasian*, *Chinese . . . South China Seas*.' She was now on her knees, examining the spine of each volume on the bottom shelf. 'Interesting. This is where Oceane's book should be. You see – there's 700 AD, and then it goes straight to 1500 AD.' Excited now, she started pulling all the books off the shelf. Suddenly she stopped dead and gasped, 'There it is – look!'

Alan gingerly got down, peered under the shelf and saw a keyhole mounted within a golden frame. 'Shall I do the honours?' he said, producing the key and inserting it in the lock.

'This is thrilling, isn't it?' Miriam exclaimed, clutching her husband's shoulder. 'I love a secret keyhole!'

Alan turned the key easily. The lock clicked and a section of bookcase opened, revealing a low doorway that led down into a small dark space.

'A secret room!' Miriam exclaimed. 'Even better than a secret keyhole. Light – we need light. Hold on,' she said and, almost sliding along the parquet floor, dashed back to the communications room. She returned a moment later with a candelabra, taking care not to extinguish the candles. She held it up as they both stepped down into the chamber.

'Good heavens, what is all this?' Miriam gazed around in astonishment. It was a windowless cubicle, only just large enough to accommodate a small desk, a chair and a rickety book shelf with a globe on it. On the desk lay an old Meslith machine and bundles of files stuffed with documents. The walls were covered in maps and plans. 'That's China . . .' She peered at an ancient nautical chart.

'And this is old Canton,' said Alan, inspecting another.

'They're *all* Chinese . . .' Miriam shook her head in bafflement. 'The books too; even the globe has Chinese writing on it,' she said. 'Alan, what on earth does Oceane Noire have to do with the Chinese?'

'Not just Oceane,' he remarked, picking up one of the files from the desk. 'That's Jupitus's hand-writing, no question.' He showed Miriam the front of the file. In neat curling letters it was inscribed with the words:

Correspondence
Operation Black Lotus
Top Secret

He opened it up. It was full of slips of parchment – Meslith communications, all written in a distinctive Chinese alphabet. 'These are recent,' he said.

'Alan . . .' gasped Miriam, clutching her neck. 'The initials at the bottom . . .' Each of the messages was signed with the letters XIX.

'Xi Xiang?' said Alan. 'It can't be!'

They both knew the name. Just as the Zeldt dynasty terrorized the *western* world, so Xi Xiang was the History Keepers' most feared enemy in the *east*. A killer as eccentric as he was ruthless, he loved to perform, to assume disguises, sometimes dressing up as one of his slaves, sometimes wearing elaborate costumes to oversee his bloody atrocities. Of course, disguising himself was something of a joke, as Xi Xiang's face was unmistakable – he had three eyes; the third, misshapen and lazy, hung over his right temple.

'We'd better fetch Galliana,' said Miriam.

The commander came down to the archive room in her dressing gown, pale with anxiety. She inspected the secret cubicle, before removing the file and sitting down at one of the library desks. She put on her glasses and, after verifying that the handwriting on the front did indeed belong to Jupitus, opened up the file. She had barely started to scan the first line of writing before the colour leached from her face. She clasped her hands together in horror, then leafed through the pages, eyes darting backwards and forward, until finally she slammed the file shut. Her hands shook as she removed her glasses.

'Contact Rose Djones immediately,' Galliana muttered shakily. 'She must apprehend Jupitus Cole – chain him up, whatever it takes – until he can be brought back to Point Zero for questioning.' She looked up at Miriam and Alan. Neither of them could remember seeing her look so anxious. 'Lives are at risk. Do you understand? *All* our lives!'

Three hours after his talk with Topaz, Jake still hadn't managed to sleep. A host of dreadful images spiralled around in his head – the fight in Agata's villa, Lucius's capture, Nathan's anger, Topaz's despair.

He was haunted by thoughts of young Lucius and his poor family: pirates cruelly separating them; Lucius toiling in the silver mine; the cries of his little brother fading across the sea . . . 'His brother!' Jake murmured to himself. 'Why did he not tell me he had a brother?'

And finally, on top of all this, Jake was aware that this was his *second* disaster in as many weeks. He'd already been responsible for losing vital atomium supplies and putting the whole service in jeopardy.

He shook his head again and again, as if that might somehow banish his thoughts. It didn't work. He turned from side to side, from his front to his back; he tried to focus on the single flickering candle on the table; he took long deep breaths; he even tried counting sheep. Nothing worked: there was no peace to be found.

Finally a single idea started to emerge. It was a terrifying one – but once it had taken hold, Jake knew there was no way of getting away from it.

I will go back and find Lucius. I will find him and I will save him.

Again Jake shook his head. He turned onto his stomach and buried his head in his pillow. But he could not dispel the notion.

I can't make things worse than they already are, he nagged at himself. *Even if Lucius is already dead, at least I will have tried.* He sat up. *If anyone sees me, I will say I am going for a walk.* And before he knew it, he was on his feet and tiptoeing across the room. There were quills, ink and paper on the table. He wrote a note, folded it carefully and left it lying there. Then, gingerly, he picked up his sword and belt from the pile of weapons and crept towards the exit.

No one woke up. Nathan was wearing his silk eye mask, smiling and mumbling to himself as he dreamed of some adventure. Charlie and Topaz were completely still. Jake quietly unbolted the door and slipped out. As it closed behind him, the candle on the table flickered and went out.

Jake fastened his belt and ran up the dark spiral staircase, past the faded mosaics. At the top, he edged open the secret door into the Basilica Aemilia. A few people lay sleeping in shadowy corners, and a handful of tradesmen were setting off on their early morning business. A hazy dawn light filtered in through the high arches as Jake stepped down into the Forum Romanum.

This too was almost deserted. The last of the night was lifting, like a grey curtain, to reveal a soft golden glow beyond. Jake saw two men on their knees, scrubbing the steps of the Senate House; a supervisor watched them, rubbing the sleep from his eyes. A figure in a white toga – a lawyer, Jake fancied – dictated a letter to his assistant as he hurried across the square, his leather sandals clicking on the stone. Three ladies flitted under the arches of the basilica opposite. Other than that, there was not a soul to be seen.

Despite the heavy task that confronted him, Jake found himself stopping for a moment and gazing in wonder. Bathed in an otherworldly light, the place looked more splendid than ever, its colonnades of white marble even more striking. 'What a marvellous place . . . what a marvellous world,' Jake whispered to himself. Then he turned grimly in the direction of the Palatine – a steep hill covered in lavish villas interspersed with dark green cypresses. He stopped and drew a steadying breath. Although he could not see it from here, he knew that at the summit lay Agata's stronghold and his own date with destiny. He straightened his belt, squared his shoulders and set off.

He skirted around the temple of Vesta and started to weave his way up the winding slope. He was a third of the way to the top, cutting between the high walls of two immense villas, when he realized that someone was following him.

He could hear crunching footsteps; even heavy panting. His follower was not very subtle: when Jake stopped and glanced round, he threw himself clumsily behind a bush, stifling a yell on discovering that it was covered in thorns. Jake saw him tussling with the undergrowth.

He feigned ignorance and carried on up a flight of steps, before darting into the shadow of a doorway and drawing his sword. His pursuer soon came into view. Jake could see that it was definitely a man – or a short, tubby boy, at any rate – but his face was obscured by the hood of his cape. He was wheezing, turning this way and that, mystified by the disappearance of his prey. There was something oddly familiar about him, Jake thought.

He waited until the boy had drawn level, then reached out, grabbed him and yanked him back into his hiding place, holding his sword to the boy's throat.

'Don't kill me! Please don't kill me,' the boy exclaimed, pudgy hands flapping wildly. 'Jake, it's me.'

Jake recognized the voice, but still couldn't place it. He tugged off the hood and swung the boy round. His jaw dropped in disbelief. He was about Jake's age, as wide as he was short, with ruddy cheeks, a runny nose and crazy fair hair.

'It's me, Caspar Isaksen.' The boy smiled uncertainly, then sneezed – a high, whistling sneeze.

He held up his hand and sneezed again; and a third time, the noise echoing across the valley. Then he produced a well-used handkerchief from inside his toga and started blowing his nose like a foghorn. 'So sorry,' he excused himself. 'The pollen here is truly murderous – plays havoc with my sinuses.'

'Caspar Isaksen . . .' Jake repeated, dumbfounded. It was the boy he had met the night he had lost the atomium. In fact, Caspar had borne the brunt of the disaster – shot by Leopardo and nearly drowned in the freezing Baltic. Jake had not forgotten the boy's furious tirade.

Whatever your name is, he had said, *I neither remember nor care – feel bad . . . feel like a traitor – because that's what you are.*

And here he was again – Caspar Isaksen the Third, in ancient Rome, dressed in a toga, cape and sandals, with his unruly blond hair, his cheeks ruddier than ever.

'Wh-wh-what are you doing here?' Jake stammered.

'Good question.' Caspar nodded. 'Crazy, isn't it?' Then he leaned closer and whispered, 'I appear to be on an assignment – a top-secret mission.'

'A mission?' Jake whispered back. 'What mission?'

'Hold on a minute . . .' Caspar starting fishing around in a linen sack he had thrown over his shoulder. 'I just need to check that my sesame sponge cakes are still intact – that was quite a move you sprang on me.' He withdrew a small cake from his bag, examined it briefly, then stuffed it into his mouth. 'Mmm, delicious,' he spluttered. 'These could almost make it into my top ten pastries of all time.' He thought carefully as he swallowed the last mouthful. 'Well, certainly the top twenty. Care for one?' he added, offering the bag to Jake.

He shook his head. 'I'm dying to know what you're doing here. Did Point Zero send you?'

'Of course, of course.' The boy nodded. 'Commander Goethe signed the order herself. In fact, only she and my father know about it.'

Jake remembered that Caspar's father – Caspar *Jakob* Isaksen – was in charge of all atomium production in his secret laboratory in northern Sweden. He recollected also that the Isaksen family had been the sole producers of the precious liquid since the History Keepers were first founded centuries ago.

'But what is your mission?' Jake persisted.

'As I said, it's top secret – *stratospherically* so – but

I don't suppose there is any harm in telling you. I was told that I might bump into some of you here.' Caspar looked up and down the deserted street and ushered Jake deeper into the shadow of the doorway, before continuing, 'I've been sent to try and reclaim the atomium consignment that was lost in Stockholm. Obviously you, more than anyone, will remember that . . .' he added pointedly.

Jake nodded grimly. 'And, once again, I am so, so sorry,' he replied with the utmost sincerity, 'for putting you in danger; for putting *everyone* in danger.' He was painfully aware that, during these last two weeks, he had been called on to apologize more than ever before in his life.

'Oh, let's not worry about that now,' Caspar reassured him with a pat on the shoulder. 'It's all in the past. You just did what you thought was right. Anyway, back to my mission. It turned out that the stolen atomium was fitted with some kind of tracking device. You see, each batch gives off a specific magnetic aura or something – it's all quite scientific and complicated – and Papa eventually tracked it down to these time and place coordinates, and I was sent here. I was just strolling around the Forum Romanum, wondering where I should go next, when I saw you walking past. I didn't know if I should speak to you or not.'

Jake exclaimed excitedly, 'Well, I know where the atomium must be! I know exactly. The man who stole it from us – *the Leopard*, as he called himself then – is in a villa half a mile up this hill.'

'Really?'

'No doubt about it! We have been there already and I am on my way back.' Jake remembered the mission he had set himself, and added seriously, 'But if we are to search for the atomium, the others should certainly come with us. They are in the Roman bureau, beneath the Basilica Aemilia.'

'Where did you say it was?' Caspar asked.

'In the Forum Romanum' – Jake pointed back behind him – 'underneath the Basilica Aemilia. It's accessed through a secret door at the back of the building . . . Caspar, are you all right?'

His companion's expression had completely changed. His uncertain smile had been replaced by a sullen scowl. 'You can shut up now, Jake Djones,' he sneered.

'What?'

'You really are spectacularly idiotic. But of course, I knew that the first time I met you.' Jake gaped in astonishment. 'You actually thought it was a coincidence, us bumping into each other?' Caspar let out a high-pitched giggle. 'I have to laugh! I made you think that *you* were the traitor in Sweden. And all the time it was me. Although that fool Leopardo wasn't supposed to actually fire a shot.'

'What are you talking about?'

Smirking, Caspar produced a thick silver bracelet from his bag – the same poison bangle worn by the Hydra. Jake stepped back in confusion.

'Stupid, stupid, stupid!' Caspar teased, advancing towards him. 'As stupid as your brother.'

'My brother?! What do you know about my brother?'

Caspar twisted the cap of the container, releasing the noxious vapour.

Jake held his hand to his mouth but it was too late – he had already inhaled the acrid smoke. It burned the back of his throat. He prayed that the vinegar he had drunk last night would still be working – but it was too long ago. *It lasts maybe three hours* – that was what Lucius had said. Instantly his insides were churning, and sharp pain shot from his skull down the length of his spine. Numbness spread from his neck to his chest, to his arms and fingers, then to his legs and feet. He reached for his sword, but was too weak to even grasp it. As he fell forward onto his knees, Caspar put his fingers to his mouth and gave a piercing whistle. Immediately eight Hydra guards came marching towards them.

'Why?' was all Jake could say as he collapsed on the ground. He twisted onto his side, but the poison was now affecting his vision. He was vaguely aware of Caspar chuckling to himself, 'Stupid, stupid, stupid,' as he devoured another of his cakes. Then everything went black. Jake heard boots marching towards him and felt rough hands hauling him up.

And then he lost consciousness completely.

19 THE END OF DOMINIONS

'*Cruelty, cataclysm* . . . and *carnage* are my three favourite words,' a rich, throaty female voice announced.

'They are not just your favourite *words*, Mother,' another voice – a male one – responded. 'They are your favourite *things*.'

The first speaker acknowledged this with a laugh. 'You're quite right, my darling, as always.'

'I prefer the word *decapitation*,' a third, much younger voice added. 'It has a beautifully final ring to it.'

Jake heard this conversation as if in a dream; the voices seemed both distant and close by. He still couldn't see, but he could *feel* a number of things. His whole body throbbed with pain; his head in particular felt as if a vice were clamped around it.

He could tell from the echo of the voices that he was now in a large room; he smelled something rich and pungent. He was sitting in a chair, his hands manacled behind his back – he could feel cold hard metal digging into his wrists. He tried to move them, but this brought another wave of agonizing pain.

'Look – he's awake,' the third voice remarked. Jake now recognized it as Caspar's. 'Do we need to do anything?'

'Don't worry, he's not going anywhere,' the second speaker replied.

Jake identified him too – his slight accent was unmistakable. *Leopardo*, he said to himself . . . *Caspar*.

Jake searched for answers in the fog of his mind. His memories were all disjointed, but at length he recalled what had happened in the dark doorway on the Palatine. The young Swede had turned against him. *I made you think that you were the traitor in Sweden*, he had said, giggling, *and all the time it was me.* Jake now understood that Caspar had been working for Agata Zeldt all along; the fat, clumsy boy, from one of the most important and ancient families of the History Keepers' Secret Service – the last person anyone would have suspected . . . *he* had betrayed them all.

Caspar had also mentioned Jake's brother. Why? What did he know? Had he seen him?

Gradually Jake's sight started to return: a dim shifting light slowly coalesced into hazy shapes. These in turn shimmered into focus. He was sitting at a long table – a vast slab of white marble. At the far end sat Agata Zeldt, with a falcon on her shoulder, Leopardo and Caspar on either side. With their pink cheeks and fair hair, the boys looked like diabolical cherubs adorning their dread queen.

On Jake's right, large windows opened out onto a tropical garden filled with oversized plants. To his left stood a long console table, also in white marble; upon it lay a series of strange-looking objects.

Set out before Jake's captors was a steaming platter of food that accounted for the pungent smell – a pile of dark, plump shapes. As Leopardo reached over and took one, Jake realized that it had a head and a long tail that stuck out stiffly. It was a mouse – or, worse still, a rat. Leopardo opened his mouth to take a bite, and Jake saw that one of his front teeth was missing, knocked out by Nathan the night before. Having bitten off the head, the boy began to chew on the little bones. On Caspar's plate there were already four dismembered carcasses and he was devouring a fifth. Meanwhile Agata was delicately slicing a peach; her pet falcon sat perfectly still, claws gently flexing, eyes fixed on the plate of fried rodents. Agata was dressed simply in a black tunic that emphasized the pallor of her face and the red of her hair. She studied Jake for a long time before she spoke.

'The History Keepers are certainly letting things slide,' she whispered with a sneer, 'if *you're* the sort of agent they are producing these days. I've seen fiercer-looking sand-flies.'

This elicited a snigger from Leopardo and a high-pitched giggle from his partner in crime. Jake turned to Caspar in fury, but when he opened his mouth to curse him, he found that it was still numb. Incoherent sounds emerged, along with a spray of spittle, and Caspar once again fell about laughing.

A battle between Jake and his facial muscles finally resulted in words: 'Your f-father,' he stammered. 'He's a t-traitor too?' He was determined, first of all, to establish how deep the conspiracy went.

Immediately Caspar's smile soured. 'My father is stupid!' he hissed. 'A stupid old man who treats me like a child. Why do you think I am here?'

'You – you *are* a child,' Jake managed. 'A spoiled, good-for-nothing child.' Each word was agony – his throat felt like sandpaper – but he continued doggedly, 'Where is Lucius?'

It was Leopardo's turn to be amused. 'That brainless hunk? You'll find out soon enough.'

'That's right.' Caspar gulped down another mouthful and wiped his greasy mouth on his sleeve. 'In no time at all, you'll be dying together.'

Despite everything, Jake couldn't help feeling a pulse of relief on hearing that Lucius was still alive; it meant that the claim he had made to Topaz was at least partly true. 'I would rather *die* with him than *eat* with you,' he spat.

'Oh, don't worry,' Caspar retorted, sniggering. 'You won't be eating . . . you'll be *eaten*.'

Jake ignored him and turned his attention to Agata. 'And you are worse than your brother. Ten times worse.'

Leopardo turned to his mother to gauge her reaction, but she was smiling. 'Rare praise indeed,' she purred as she put a dripping slice of peach into her mouth. 'Of course, I always knew that Xander was just an amateur.'

'Worse than him,' Jake continued, 'because what you are doing is so completely pointless.'

Now Agata's smile faltered. In the same instant, her falcon quickly turned to Jake, its beak opening.

'Pointless!' Jake repeated firmly. Had he not been pushed to the limit in the last twenty-four hours, had he not been told that he was about to die, perhaps he would not have spoken in this way. But he wanted to get under Agata's skin – and knew he could do that by piquing her sense of rivalry with her brother. 'At least Xander had a vision. You have nothing.'

Now Agata's face turned to thunder. 'I have a vision' – she thumped the table – 'you ill-mannered upstart!' Her falcon shrieked and flapped its wings as she got to her feet, bringing her fist down on the marble again. 'I have more vision than *anyone*. Soon I will own the world.'

Leopardo stood up, trying to calm her, but Agata pushed him aside. Her bird took wing and circled the room, crying out as she swept down the table towards Jake. He looked up as she approached, trying to look defiant, but his blood ran cold and his hands were shaking. He could see the lattice of blue veins under the pale skin, the dangerous black eyes, the thin, bloodless lips.

'By this time tomorrow' – she leaned close, and from her mouth came the odour of decay – 'I will be the most powerful ruler the world has ever seen. A *woman* – not a man; not a vain, arrogant male . . . a *woman* will rule the world.'

Only now did Jake understand the hatred that consumed her; it was directed not just at her brother, but at all men. 'Bring him,' she hissed as she turned to the nearby table.

Leopardo came over and, grinning his gap-toothed smile, unlocked Jake's manacles, yanked him to his feet and dragged him towards Agata. Jake's legs were still numb from the poison and he could barely stand.

'Do you know what this is?' Agata asked, pointing to the first object on the table. Close up, Jake recognized it immediately: it was a replica of the Circus Maximus, larger than the miniature one he had seen in the campaign room, a beautifully rendered architect's maquette. He did not reply.

'It is the greatest stadium that the world has ever known.' Agata clasped her long fingers around the model. 'An exquisite construction, don't you think?' She pointed to the *pulvinar*, the royal box that Charlie had pointed out the night before. 'This is where I shall sit with the emperor to watch the *entertainment*.'

'Entertainment!' Caspar giggled at Agata's choice of word.

'I will watch the senators and generals taking their places,' she said, tapping her fingers along the *spina*, the stone island in the centre of the arena. 'I will watch them all, Rome's most eminent citizens – those six hundred *men* who rule the world. I will watch them as they gather for the big race. They, like everyone at the Circus Maximus, will expect excitement, drama . . . maybe some death . . .' Agata's voice sank to a whisper. 'They won't be disappointed.'

'No, they won't be disappointed at all,' Caspar agreed, panting with anticipation. Jake was sickened.

'And *this* is the device that will *guarantee* all this – all that excitement and drama and death.' Agata whistled through her teeth as she pointed to the next object on the table. Jake recognized this one too: a curious container made of thick glass, hexagonal in shape and filled with black powder. Jake had seen a number of identical receptacles in the laboratory in Vulcano, but this one was studded with a network of minute pipes and cogs.

'This is the spare, of course, the prototype,' Agata told him, 'which I shall keep for posterity. The rest were installed in the Circus Maximus last night. Look,' she said, amused by the expression on Jake's face, 'he doesn't even know what it is.' She pinched his chin between her bony fingers. 'It's gunpowder, stupid. That ingenious combination of sulphur, charcoal and potassium – though of course we have spiced it up with some of our own special ingredients. Naturally, if you know your history, we *should* have to wait a thousand years to see it: the first batch is due to explode in 1044 AD. But it is such a delicious invention, it seems a shame to make people wait.'

Caspar listened, agog, and stuffed another mouse into his mouth, crunching the bones.

'And what better place to unveil it,' Agata went on, 'what finer location to introduce *modern carnage* to the ancient world, than the greatest and largest stadium of all time' – her eyes sparkled with fire – 'with a hundred and fifty thousand people watching?'

Jake was beginning to put the pieces together. In Vulcano, they had also discovered sulphur mines and reserves of charcoal. Now he understood why. 'You're going to blow up the Circus Maximus?' he found himself asking.

'Don't be dull-witted,' Agata replied. 'That would be pointless. There would be no one left to enjoy it!' She shrieked with laughter, and Leopardo and Caspar joined in. 'No, no, no. We shall be obliterating only a *very* select few.' She returned to the model of the Circus Maximus and pointed to the *spina*. 'Just the people here . . .' Her eyes bored into Jake's. 'Here, at the climax of the race, as the seven turns . . .'

As the seven turns . . . Jake noted the expression, but still didn't understand it.

'As the seven turns, *a fireball*, the like of which the world has never seen, will herald the bloodiest revolution of all time.'

'The senators?' Jake gasped to himself.

'All massacred. The leaders of this stagnant empire burned to dust!'

'And those who are not burned,' Leopardo added, 'will fall into the animal pits below and be torn to pieces.'

'What. Spectacular. Entertainment!' Agata cried out loud. Caspar clapped his hands in delight.

Agata's tone became playful again. 'Everyone dies – except one. Our emperor will be saved – not the real one, of course; he will be slaughtered on Capri – I already control all lines of communication to him. And Sejanus too will meet an unpleasant end. No, my *puppet* emperor. Following this catastrophe, "Tiberius" will announce his *permanent* return to Rome, to his people. He alone will command the great Roman legions – the greatest army in the world – against the "rebel factions", the "slave uprising" responsible for the bloodshed.'

She reached out and clasped her son's hands. 'For their own safety, the people will be crushed, controlled, *dominated*.' Her expression soured again. 'Before they are eradicated.'

Now Caspar hurried over and held out his chubby hands to join the other two.

Agata continued, as if in a dream, 'I will lay waste to the empire. Destroy all its literature, its libraries of knowledge. Purge its scientists and architects and planners. Demolish the bricks of civilization piece by piece, until there is nothing left but crushed bones and forgotten ideals. Then I shall own the world, control all its riches – its gold, iron, copper, silver, salt, and the remains of its stinking masses. A woman will rule.'

Now Jake understood the extent of her master plan. Its sheer audacity was mind-blowing. Agata Zeldt did not mean to assassinate the emperor (or rather the *fake* emperor). She intended quite the opposite: to eradicate the entire government *around* him; the senators and generals who had been running the empire since Tiberius became a recluse. She then meant to use her puppet dictator, the actor Austerio – as well as her rich, greedy friends from the banquet last night – to take control. Furthermore, she would blame this act of supreme anarchy on a non-existent uprising of slaves and fan the flames of chaos even more. Gradually she would immobilize the world, steep it in fear. Then she would tear it to pieces. She would destroy, for all time, the legacy of Rome that Charlie had talked of the day they entered the city – the great systems of law and government; the education and communication; the common language, the written word, the art and architecture. These and a million other advances would all be destroyed and the world plunged into a dark age.

'Now,' Agata said, ruffling Jake's hair, 'the time has come for you to die. Bring him,' she ordered, and swept out of the room. Leopardo pushed Jake along in her wake.

She led the way up the corridor, her falcon on her shoulder. As usual, any passing slaves froze, trembling, and bowed their heads. Jake hobbled along behind her, repeatedly shoved in the back by Leopardo; the grinning Caspar brought up the rear.

A pair of ivory double doors swung open, and they entered a room that was even larger than the last. It was dominated by a giant aviary. Jake heard a deep cackle and saw, on the right-hand side of the cage, three massive, bloodthirsty vultures. Last night he had seen the room from above, as they were crossing the roofs. But he hadn't appreciated the sheer size of the birds.

As Agata approached them, cooing with delight, they flung themselves excitedly at the bars, flapping their wings and jabbing their claws at her. She let them nip at her hands, ignoring the pain and the dripping blood. Her pet falcon shrank away from them, digging its talons deeper into her shoulder.

'Put him in there!' Agata barked without turning round.

Before he knew what was happening, Jake was being dragged towards the cage. His heart thumped at double, then triple speed. He turned in desperation. 'What do you know about my brother?' he shouted at Caspar.

The boy merely sniggered as the iron grille was swung open and Jake tossed inside. He gasped as it slammed shut behind him, then turned to face the vultures, his hands raised protectively. Only when they flew up against the bars did Jake realize that he had been placed in a separate compartment – though this was no doubt a temporary reprieve. As he edged back, he tripped on something. He shuddered to find a pile of bones, stripped bare but for the odd shred of putrid flesh. He had seen this grisly cadaver from the skylight last night, but there was even less of it now. The stench made him retch and stagger back – setting Caspar off again, giggling and clapping his hands.

'Don't worry, your time will come too,' Agata said, approaching her prisoner, 'once we have returned from the Circus Maximus. By then my darlings' – she waved at the vultures – 'will be truly ravenous.'

'What do you know about my brother?' Jake persisted.

Agata ignored him and headed for the door.

He shouted after her: 'Your plan will fail. The others are ten steps ahead of you!'

Agata turned and whispered through bloodless lips, 'Caspar's right, you *are* simple. We knew the bureau was somewhere below the Forum Romanum, but had not pinpointed it. *You yourself gave us its precise location.* In about ten minutes' time your fellow agents will also be dead – those two inept boys, along with the ungrateful traitor who was once my daughter.'

Jake's fear was banished completely. 'She was never your daughter. She got close to spy on you, that's all.'

Agata bared her teeth in rage; her cheeks momentarily turned crimson. 'Prepare for death,' she warned him, then took Leopardo's arm and left the room.

'I can't wait,' Caspar jeered from the doorway. 'The lousier the agent, the tastier the lunch!' And he slammed the doors shut behind them.

Jake was alone – apart from the vultures, which stuck their necks through the bars. Their loud cries had now turned to furtive cackles, as if they were already plotting how to divide up the feast.

'You don't scare me,' Jake shouted at them. It was a lie of course – they terrified him – but it helped him a little. He rushed at them, shouting a war cry. They shot away from the bars in surprise, but returned moments later, eyeing him hungrily.

'You tell 'em, Yake,' croaked a voice from the back of the cage.

Jake's heart leaped. 'Lucius . . .?' he called into the gloom. Only now did he notice the hunched figure in the corner. As he approached, Lucius looked up and Jake did a double-take. The soldier was a shadow of his former self – caked in blood, his face covered in cuts and bruises, one eye so swollen it was almost invisible.

'What would Nathan say?' Lucius forced the glimmer of a smile as he gently touched his shiner. 'Not popping now, are they?'

Jake laughed, despite himself, knelt down and threw his arms around him.

'Ow!' Lucius cried. 'Broken rib.'

'Sorry, sorry.' Jake let go and sat down beside him. 'So great to see you . . . *almost* alive.'

Although it was clearly agony, Lucius started laughing too. Then the vultures began crashing against the bars again, reminding them both of the fate that awaited them.

'So, Yake,' Lucius said finally. 'Six hours I plan how to get out of here.'

'Really? And . . .?'

He shook his head. 'There is no way out. Unless you can walk through walls.'

'Oh, I see.'

Then, with a shrug, Lucius produced something from inside his tunic. 'I have this.' He passed Jake a battered silver bracelet, one of the Hydra's poisoning devices. 'I stole from a guard, but it is almost empty.'

'Well, that's a start!' said Jake, so enthusiastically that it took even him by surprise. It was a Djones family trait to be upbeat in the face of disaster. He examined the bracelet, a wrist band studded with a disc-like capsule that turned to release the gas. Very carefully, he put it to his ear and shook it. Lucius was right: there was just the tiniest amount of liquid inside.

'What about vinegar?' Jake asked. 'Do you have that?'

From the back of the device, Lucius pulled out a little vial and held it up. 'But even if we make the birds sleep,' he said gloomily, 'we are still in the cage.'

Jake glanced once again at the pile of human remains; but Lucius reached over and turned Jake's head the other way.

Jake leaned back against the wall and closed his eyes. They were as trapped as it was possible to be: locked in a cage, sealed in a room, encased within a fortress; completely unarmed, with three of the most savage creatures on earth watching over them. Jake knew that they didn't stand a chance.

20 The Claws of Death

Topaz woke and immediately sensed that something was wrong. Nathan and Charlie were still fast asleep. She peered over the side of her bunk and realized that Jake wasn't there. She scanned the room, but there was no other sign of life.

She let herself down to the floor. Mr Drake, who had also been snoozing, perched on the end of Charlie's bunk, opened one eye and watched as she headed across the room to the door. She found the bolts undone. Mystified, she opened it, went out onto the dark landing and peered up the staircase. A warm wind blew down into her face. She was about to close it again when she suddenly heard a tapping. Someone was trying to get in from the Basilica Aemilia.

Jake, Topaz thought. *He must have locked himself*

out. She quickly ascended the steps, her bare feet silent on the stone. From the walls, Julius Caesar – depicted in mosaic, speaking in the Senate House – seemed to observe her as she flitted past. She heard a loud thump from above. Then another.

'Jake?' she called. Silence greeted her. 'Is that you?' she said more tentatively, her hand reaching out for the handle. Still no one replied. Topaz looked back down the stairs; the only sound was the faint whistling of the wind.

Suddenly there was an almighty cry, a great splintering of wood; then the door flew open and two guards burst in. Topaz gasped, turned and ran, but a huge gauntleted hand grabbed her gown. She ripped it free, but overbalanced and tumbled down the steps, banging into the mosaic wall. Again, Julius Caesar watched as she quickly picked herself up. Out of the corner of her eye, she saw several more guards, all wearing grey breastplates and beaked helmets, rushing in, weapons clanking at their side. She flew down the steps and burst through the door into the bureau.

'Hydra – here!' she cried at the top of her voice.

Nathan and Charlie had already been woken by the noise, and now leaped to their feet. As the enemy thundered down onto the landing, Topaz slammed the door – but a metal gauntlet had managed to slide through the gap and stopped it from closing. In moments, Nathan and Charlie were at Topaz's side, pushing against the door with such force that the gauntlet began to buckle. Finally they heard a cry of pain and the arm withdrew. Nathan and Charlie quickly shot the bolts home.

Topaz took a slug from the bottle of vinegar and passed it to the others. Now the guards were pounding against the door. The two iron bolts were no match for them. Within moments, the housing of the top one was coming loose.

'We leave by the aqueduct,' Nathan shouted as he ran over to Jake's bunk. Only now did he realize that he was missing. 'Where's Jake?'

'He was gone when I woke up,' said Topaz.

'Gone?' Nathan barked. 'Where?'

'I don't know,' she snapped back, then nodded at the door. 'Shall we talk about this later?'

By now Mr Drake had flown up and was circling the room in panic. Nathan pushed the bunk to one side, clearing the area around the grille that led down into the Aqua Virgo. He took the key from its hiding place behind a loose brick in the wall, unlocked the grille and pulled it out of its casing. It was heavy and the veins on his neck bulged with the strain. 'You first!' he called to Topaz.

But she was running around grabbing things, and already had the Meslith machine tucked under her arm. She was just collecting the bundle of weapons from the table when she noticed Jake's note. She unfolded the paper and read the one-line inscription: *I've gone to sort it out.*

'Topaz! Let's go,' Nathan shouted.

She scrunched up the note in her hand, went over to the hole and chucked the swords through. Then Charlie helped her down until she was low enough to jump, splashing into two feet of fast-flowing and surprisingly cold water. A round borehole, about as high as she was tall, disappeared off in either direction – pale, clay-like rock smoothed by decades of flowing water. She knelt down and retrieved the weapons.

Above her, the pounding on the door grew louder. The top bolt gave way and sprang across the room past Mr Drake.

'Here, quickly!' Charlie called the parrot as he too began to lower himself into the water. Mr Drake swooped down, alighted on his master's shoulder and clung on tight.

Now the second bolt sheared off, the door crashed open and the guards burst in.

Nathan followed Charlie and pulled the hatch down behind him. He produced the key and was about to turn it in the padlock when a blade shot down through the grille, only just missing his eye. The key fell, splashing into the torrent. Meanwhile Topaz had grabbed a dagger and thrust it through the grille towards the soldier – who now released a cloud of poisonous gas. It made them choke, even though they held their breaths, but had no further ill effects.

Charlie had noted exactly where the key had fallen; he plunged his hand into the water until he had located it, then thrust it into the lock. He had managed to turn it only halfway when four blades appeared above his head. The three agents jumped back to avoid them. The guards pulled at the grille – but the pressure on the padlock forced the key round and it dropped out into the water again. The gate was locked.

'Let's go!' Nathan shouted.

'There'll be an exit at the baths of Agrippa . . .' Charlie waded through the water, his voice echoing around the tunnel. 'From there it's only a short walk to the Circus Maximus.'

* * *

Jake had been sitting in the corner of the cell for half an hour, his hands covering his ears to block out the increasingly high-pitched screeches, when he suddenly noticed the glinting buckle at his waist. He realized that it didn't belong to his own plain leather belt; it was Nathan's, with its distinctive lion's head. He had been in such a state of panic when he left the bureau that he had mistakenly picked up Nathan's weapon and belt. Of course, Agata's men had taken the sword and scabbard, but mercifully had left the belt.

'Nathan, you might have saved us!' he gasped, leaping to his feet, unfastening the belt and examining the golden lion's head. He remembered Dr Chatterju demonstrating the device in the armoury at Point Zero. It contained a miniature winching mechanism that could lift a person (well, Dr Chatterju's slight nephew Amrit, at any rate) into the air.

'What's going on?' Lucius asked, looking up.

Jake was too excited to reply. He turned, strode over to the bars and, ignoring the occupants of the other cage, scanned the ceiling above it – in particular the skylight through which he had peered the night before.

'Just as I thought . . .' He clenched his fists in delight. 'The skylight's not locked. That's our exit!'

Lucius craned his neck round to see what Jake was talking about, but was none the wiser.

'So, how do we get to it, you ask . . .' Jake continued breathlessly, pacing backwards and forward, muttering. Lucius stared at him, baffled, until Jake suddenly clapped his hands together. 'It might just work.'

'What might work, Yake?'

'One of us stays in here, armed with what's left of the Hydra's gas. Let's just pray we have enough. The other opens this gate, the birds fly in, we release the gas, they collapse' – Jake, who loved a bit of acting when the occasion demanded it, threw in a mime of anesthetized vultures sinking to the ground – 'we occupy *their* chamber, closing the gate behind us, and then use Dr Chatterju's magic belt to escape!'

Jake might as well have been talking in ancient Egyptian for all Lucius could make of it. It took many minutes of patient explanation, illustrated with diagrams drawn in the sand on the floor, before he began to grasp the plan; though even then, Chatterju's miniature pulley was beyond him, and Jake suggested that he would just have to trust him on that.

Partly because of Lucius's injuries, but mainly because Jake wanted to prove his bravery, he volunteered for the more dangerous job of vulture-bait.

They shared out the tiny flask of vinegar and took their positions – Lucius by the gate, Jake in the centre of the cell, primed with the silver bracelet. Sensing that something was afoot, the vultures started flinging themselves against the bars again.

'Remember' – Jake's firm voice masked his inner terror – 'hold your breath for at least a minute so you don't inhale the gas – I'm not sure if there was really enough vinegar to be effective.'

'And what if there is not enough gas to make them sleep?' Lucius asked.

In truth Jake was unsure about this as well: they were unarmed, and if the plan failed they would be eaten alive, the flesh ripped from their bones. But the alternative was far, far worse. 'Lucius, listen to me,' Jake said in a low voice. 'In an hour's time, in the Circus Maximus, a catastrophe is going to take place – a disaster to end all disasters. If we don't get out of here and find a way to stop it' – he took a deep breath – 'the world *as we know it* will end today.' He snapped his fingers. '*Boom!* All gone!' It sounded dramatic, like something Nathan would say, but it was also true. Only Jake knew the details of Agata's master plan. He *had* to escape and get to the Circus Maximus – or die trying. He held up the silver bracelet and took a deep breath. 'There'll be enough, I am sure of it. Now open the gate.'

He gritted his teeth as Lucius slid the grille across to allow the birds through.

For a moment they were confused; the cawing died down and they backed away from the opening suspiciously.

'Not hungry any more?' Jake jeered.

Lucius watched the vultures as they huddled together, as if discussing their course of action. Finally their hunger took over; they turned in unison and took off, soaring through the gap.

'Now!' Jake shouted to Lucius, taking a great gulp of air before turning the capsule on the silver bracelet to release its contents. The birds flew, missile-like, towards him, their huge wings making the cage dark.

The faint red vapour billowed up from Jake's wrist, and he fought to hold his breath as the first vulture swooped down, claws finding his neck, beak darting towards his eyes. He shielded his head with his hands as the second bird thumped down, then the third. For a moment there was a whirl of screeching and slashing, feathers and claws. Then, quite suddenly, it stopped. One vulture let out a guttural cry, and thumped to the floor. A second quickly followed. The last, the largest of the three, continued to swoop down towards Jake, staring at him defiantly, until it too was overcome and dropped onto the sand.

As Jake leaped over its sprawling body, the vulture twisted and momentarily raised its head, but collapsed onto the floor again. Jake tore through the opening into the birds' compartment. Lucius followed and they slid the gate across behind them.

It stuck halfway.

Lucius pushed with all his might, until the veins in his neck bulged, but the metal of the grille was now distorted and wouldn't slide across. He and Jake rattled it frantically, but it wouldn't budge. The opening was now maybe a foot wide. Perhaps it was enough to keep the vultures inside.

'We go back in,' Lucius suggested. 'Break their necks.'

Jake shook his head. The effects of the gas were already wearing off: he could see a wing twitching, then a leg. 'Let's go!' He stopped at a point directly below the skylight, then looked at Lucius and pointed towards a spade leaned inside the feeding bucket just outside the cage. 'Get that. We may need it.'

Lucius did as he was told, slipping his hands through the bars and retrieving the shovel. The coating of dried blood and entrails made it stick to the pail and he had to pull it loose.

Jake surveyed the barred skylight above him: it had a timber frame. In order to provide the strongest hold he would need to fire the dart deep into this. It was a small target and he only had one chance to get it right. Urgency made him bold. 'Lucius, stand in front of me,' he instructed.

Jake positioned himself behind his companion, using Lucius's shoulder to steady his hands. He held up the buckle, aimed the lion's mouth at the wooden frame, carefully pushed down on the green eye – and fired.

There was a sharp whistle, followed by a flash. Before Jake had registered it, the silver dart struck the wood with a solidly satisfying *twang*. Jake pulled the wire tight. Dr Chatterju had boasted: *It could take the weight of Henry the Eighth – even in his heavy period*. Jake would find out very soon if this was even half true. Lucius was certainly no lightweight, and the two of them together would test the claim.

'You put the belt on,' said Jake, 'and I'll hold on to you.'

Lucius obliged, fastening it tightly around his waist. Meanwhile Jake took hold of the spade.

Suddenly they heard a clanging of metal behind them. The largest vulture had woken up and was now flying towards the bars. Still groggy, it misjudged the narrow opening and crashed down to the floor. Furious, it let out an ear-splitting screech before launching itself into the air again. *Crash!* Once more it struck the sides of the gap, but this time one wing got stuck; it struggled helplessly, then freed itself, clattering down again, the wing flapping uselessly. Unable to fly, it spat its fury. It was enough to wake its two partners in crime. Their wings stirred, their necks convulsed and their murderous eyes shot open.

'I think that's our cue,' said Jake, holding onto Lucius while tightening his grip on the spade. 'Press the blue eye. Now!'

Lucius pushed the sapphire into the lion's eye socket.

Nothing happened.

The other two vultures were getting to their feet now. One took off and flew around its new compartment, clumsily at first but gradually picking up speed. Jake realized it would be a matter of moments before it angled its way through the gap.

'Again!' Jake shouted. 'Push it again!'

Lucius pressed the button firmly. Now the line tightened, cracking like a whip, and they were quickly pulled off their feet, slowing down as their weight began to tell. Then, with a stiff click, the line stopped completely. They were just over halfway to the skylight, hanging by a straining metal thread.

'Use your hands,' Jake hissed.

Lucius reached up, and as he took hold of the line, the pressure on the buckle eased and the machine continued to ratchet them up again. They climbed inch by inch towards the skylight, Jake's knuckles whitening as he held on, Lucius's hands straining on the cord. Above them the wooden frame creaked as the silver dart pulled down on it.

They were almost within touching distance when the circling vulture managed to get the angle right and swoop through the opening. Jake flinched as it flew up towards him. He tried to hit it with the spade, but he could only use one hand, and it was too crafty. There was a rush of air as it beat its wings, before lunging towards his neck. He felt a sharp pain, and blood started trickling down his back. Above him the metal dart shuddered. Lucius continued to pull on the wire, his hands now raw and bloody where the line had cut into them. The vulture flapped its gargantuan wings once more, this time coming in for the kill.

Jake's eyes made contact with the bird's as he swung back his weapon. The rough blade cracked into the vulture's head. For a second it seemed to freeze in midair, then it choked, its neck coiling, and spiralled lopsidedly to the ground, lurching drunkenly along the floor before shaking itself back to life.

The boys had inched upwards only a fraction before it took off again. Then the next monster, the leanest and swiftest of the three, flew in and joined its accomplice; both circled around them now.

As Lucius reached his bloodied hand up towards the bars of the skylight, the two birds launched their attack from either side. It was a terrible assault, like treading water in a sea of daggers and razor blades. And although Jake kept his head down and eyes closed, he could feel the thump of their muscular wings and the sharp piercing of their talons.

'Yake! I can't hold,' Lucius wailed desperately. Jake opened his eye just enough to see Lucius's bloody fingers still straining on the cord as he ignored the pecks of the vultures. Above them, the silver dart was creaking and straining alarmingly.

Then Jake had a sudden thought: the silver bracelet. He still had it round his wrist. Perhaps there was a drop left inside. Even if it stopped the onslaught for a second, it would be worth it! 'Lucius, hold your breath,' he yelled as he twisted the cap. Nothing happened – there was not even the faintest whiff of gas. As he felt a beak tearing at his back, he closed his eyes. He thought again of his mum and dad – of Philip.

Suddenly he heard a booming voice; a roar so deep and guttural, it did not sound human. It was Lucius. He bellowed at the vultures, his face turning crimson. It was effective. For just a second, the birds hesitated – allowing Lucius to seize one by its neck. It shrieked, choking, beating its wings wildly. Lucius squeezed harder, teeth clenched, forcing the life out of it, until finally it went limp and he let it fall to the floor.

The last bird attacked with renewed fury, claws raking Jake's face and seeking a purchase on his back. Jake smashed the bracelet against the ceiling to open it. As the casing fell away, a tiny crimson cloud escaped, before dissolving into the air. It was enough: the vulture breathed it in; then its claws loosened and it fell, unconscious, to the floor.

Jake looked up at Lucius, who nodded, the glimmer of a smile on his face.

Then *crack!*

The wood gave way above, the silver dart about to rip itself out. Jake felt his stomach lurch and instantly thrust the shovel up through the skylight, hooking the edge of the blade through the bars as the wire snapped free and spun away below them. Lucius, with any strength he had left, managed to grab hold of the frame, unlatch the bars, then haul himself through and pull Jake up behind him.

For a while they lay motionless on the roof, their chests heaving up and down, before Jake turned to his companion. 'We need to go. Now.'

Four hundred miles south of the city of Rome, in

the villa overlooking the port of Messina, Jupitus Cole was woken by the tip of a rusty harpoon softly digging into his cheek. He opened his eyes and peered up at Rose, who was standing over him with a face like thunder, brandishing the weapon.

'Rosalind, why are you pointing a fish hook at me?' he asked calmly.

'Because it was the first weapon I could find,' she snapped.

Jupitus examined her more carefully – her rigid stance and gritted teeth. 'I usually find a cup of tea is a better way to start the day,' he replied in his most velvety tones, moving the point away with his little finger.

'If you move so much as an inch,' she told him, 'I *will* kill you!' To make herself clear, she thrust the harpoon further into Jupitus's throat.

Jupitus made an elaborate show of freezing like a statue. 'Did I forget your birthday?' he purred.

'Operation Black Lotus – what is it?'

He chuckled. 'What?'

'Jupitus Cole, I am not joking – I will cut your throat if I have to. You are unable to walk, remember. You do not stand a chance. Operation Black Lotus,' she repeated. 'What is it?'

He stared at her and shrugged. 'I have no idea what you are talking about.'

'I just received an urgent Meslith from Galliana,' Rose continued, producing a parchment and waving it at him.

'Girl's talk?'

Rose suddenly brought the harpoon down with a thump onto the pillow, before pointing it at Jupitus's neck again. 'She's found your secret room. Yours and Oceane's little hideaway,' she spat.

Jupitus frowned, then stared up at Rose with flinty eyes. Finally he said in a quiet voice, 'It's nothing to do with Oceane. She was just picking up messages for me.'

Rose gasped, practically hyperventilating with the shock. 'So it's *true*? You are actually in cahoots with Xi Xiang?'

'It's a little more complicated than that—'

'Complicated?! There are more than a hundred communications between the two of you!' Rose was pushing the harpoon into his neck so hard, it pierced the skin. 'Xi Xiang is one of our most hated enemies. Do I need to remind you that he butchered Galliana's husband, along with her only child? That he tied weights to the boy's feet and threw him off his ship? And you are plotting with him? You are a monster, Jupitus!'

Jupitus watched her, showing neither fear, nor anger, nor even guilt, but only the profoundest pity. He waited for her to calm down and then spoke in a soothing voice. 'Rose, listen to me. You may not believe what I tell you now, but it is the truth.' He took a deep breath. 'Yes, I have a secret room at Point Zero, from where I have communicated with Xi Xiang.'

This brought only sobs from Rose. Jupitus carried on softly, 'As you remember, Rose, Xiang and I, years ago, used to be friends.'

'Of course I remember! How could I forget?'

'But for nearly two decades we did not speak. Two years ago, a chance encounter brought us together in Tibet, in a distant corner of the Zhou dynasty. It was an extraordinary coincidence, nothing else, but I saw an opportunity and I took it.'

'What opportunity?'

'I pretended that I was disillusioned with the History Keepers, that I wanted a new life.'

'You *pretended*?'

'I became, in effect, a double agent, a *spy*, passing on "secrets" from Point Zero. Nothing important, nothing that would affect anyone, but enough to make Xiang believe that I was on his side and take me into his confidence.'

'If you were really a double agent, why didn't you tell Galliana?'

'You know why. Galliana can think straight about everything but Xi Xiang. It is her Achilles' heel. She would have closed down the operation immediately.'

Rose shrugged, reluctantly agreeing.

'Finally my work started to pay off,' Jupitus continued. 'The Black Lotus is the name of a project Xiang has been working on for years. Even now, I have only the sketchiest details. He was about to pass on vital information when the trail suddenly went completely cold. I have heard nothing from him since I left for London months ago, and have no idea where he is or whether he is alive or dead. The day we set sail for Italy, I asked Oceane Noire to check my secret bureau twice a day, in case anything had come through.'

Rose did not take the harpoon away, but she let it drop slightly.

'And Rosalind,' Jupitus continued, looking at her very seriously, 'I have to say, it felt good to be doing something important again. To be back in the game. It's the young ones who have all the excitement. We're nothing more than pen pushers these days.'

The phrase struck a chord with Rose. She smiled sadly and mulled over everything he had said. 'So Oceane Noire is just working for you?' she asked.

'Do you know why I proposed to Oceane?'

'I haven't the slightest idea.' Rose put her nose in the air. 'I assumed she'd put a voodoo spell on you.'

'Because she told me that if I didn't ask her to marry me, she'd tell everyone I was spying for Xi Xiang – and prove it. I'd worked too hard on the operation to give it up then.'

Rose felt another rush of emotion and tears came to her eyes. 'You – you mean,' she stammered, 'you *don't* love Oceane Noire?'

It was something that rarely happened, but Jupitus's eyes twinkled and his mouth curled into the warmest, most beautiful smile. 'Rosalind, how could you think such a thing?'

21 Circus Maximus!

'There she is,' said Charlie, peering out from the shadows. 'Isn't she just breathtaking?'

Topaz and Nathan nodded in agreement, the latter, for once, struck dumb. They were huddled in a portico in a dark corner of a long square that was packed with people. The boys were already wearing Charlie's disguises; beards and moustaches that made them look much older – in particular Nathan's, which was thick and black. Topaz had pulled her hair back and half hidden her face under the hood of her cape.

The object of their attention was the vast building at the far end of the square, towards which the crowd was hurrying.

The Circus Maximus.

They were facing its immense rear end, its

northwestern facade, and up close for the first time they could see that, even by the standards of ancient Rome, the building was a monster. Each of the two giant towers was surmounted by a striking golden statue of galloping horses and god-like charioteers, at least five times life size. The towers were connected by a series of twelve enormous arches, through which Charlie and the others could just glimpse the interior of the arena – tier upon tier of white marble, gleaming in the morning sun as the population of Rome packed themselves in.

'Can you hear it?' Nathan asked, uncharacteristically spooked. He was referring to the unearthly roar that came from within the walls – like the sound of a great wave, crashing over and over.

'That'll be a hundred and fifty thousand people taking their seats,' Charlie explained with a twinkle in his eye.

It had taken them nearly an hour to get here from the Roman bureau and their clothes were now almost dry (it was barely nine in the morning but stifling already). They had waded through the tunnel before arriving, as Charlie had predicted, at the baths of Agrippa. Then, after being forced to swim underwater, they were deposited in a fountain at the end of the *frigidarium* – the large outdoor pool. Three young ladies walking on the grass nearby had nearly fainted at the sight of the youngsters arising from amongst the marble sea nymphs, shaking the water off and strolling towards the exit; but they were revived by one of Nathan's trademark winks.

From the baths, they had made their way watchfully down narrow streets towards the Tiber. They had paused briefly in a quiet cul-de-sac to get their breath back. Here Topaz told them about Jake's note and they had discussed what he might have meant by *I've gone to sort it out*. They had come to the painful conclusion that he had set off to Agata's villa to save Lucius. They had all felt a twinge of apprehension. Topaz, in particular, had felt sick with remorse; she wished she had not scolded him so sternly the night before. After all, it was clear that, while Jake sometimes didn't do the *right* thing, he always did the *brave* thing.

To lighten the mood and keep everyone focused, Charlie had produced his bag of tricks and, after a debate as to who would look better in a black beard (Topaz reluctantly had to concede that it suited her brother better), they prepared to set off again.

'I think Mr Drake may have to stay here...' Topaz had pointed out delicately. 'I mean, if we're to keep as low a profile as possible.'

Charlie had not been happy, but of course he saw the logic. He set him carefully on a branch of a nearby pine tree with a handful of peanuts – along with whispered promises to be back soon, which he dearly hoped to keep.

From here they had doubled back along the river, past the temple of Hercules, across the Forum Boarium to the Circus itself.

'Shall we...?' said Nathan, cautiously stepping out of the portico and around the perimeter of the square. The others followed, looking around, double checking that no one was following. Once again they joined the stream of people hurrying towards the side entrances.

'The first thing you need to know about the Circus Maximus,' Charlie explained in a low voice, 'is that it is, without question, the prime destination of the Roman world. All roads lead here. From the storm-tossed shores of Hispania in the west to the deserts of Assyria in the east, its fame is unparalleled. It's epic, heroic, *gargantuan*,' he added, emphasizing each word with a shake of his clenched fist. 'It is a dream factory. The quintessence of the empire.'

Nathan and Topaz exchanged a knowing glance, enjoying their friend's enthusiasm despite their predicament. Indeed, Charlie was so excited about his visit to the stadium that, for a moment, he forgot about their dire situation: completely in the dark, aware that a catastrophe that could *end dominions* was about to unfold, but knowing nothing of what it might be or when it would take place.

'And the reason it's the prime destination of the Roman world? Well, obviously there's the building itself,' he continued. 'The largest stadium the planet has ever seen, or indeed *will* ever see. Capacity – a hundred and fifty thousand; construction – two hundred thousand tonnes of marble; timber from half a million trees.' The building loomed closer. 'And that's just the current version; in its four-hundred-year history it has already – rather carelessly – been burned down three times. That's why Augustus built this version in marble.' Charlie shook his head. 'So the place itself is a big enough lure, but it's what goes on here that really pulls the crowds.'

'The chariot racing?' Topaz offered.

'That's right. The Romans are fanatically, ridiculously obsessed with it. Obviously loads of other stuff happens here: wild-beast hunts, gladiatorial combat – you know, of course, that the Colosseum won't be built until the end of the century – athletic competitions, even theatrical events and musical recitals. But those are just distractions. The main event, the really big draw, is the chariot racing.'

The hullaballoo coming from the stadium increased, and by the time they had reached the southeastern corner, the roar was deafening – exhilarating and unsettling in equal measure.

They could now see along the side of the building: a vast precipice of arches upon arches upon arches disappearing far into the hazy distance of the city. The people were flocking from all directions, pouring out of every street and passageway; white togas and brown tunics surged into the honeycomb of entrances, chattering excitedly. Some were chanting and singing; others swigging from clay bottles, all cheered on by locals watching from their windows. To add to the cacophony, hundreds of street vendors plied their trade: flower-merchants, incense-sellers, jugglers, fire-eaters, fortune tellers and astrologers.

'It's free, you see, and everyone is invited,' Charlie explained, raising his voice above the clamour. 'And there are games on at least a hundred days of the year. It must be a logistical nightmare!'

Briefly Topaz was separated from the others and had to push her way forward again. Charlie was right: it seemed as if all of Rome was there – men, women, young, old, rich and poor. Throngs of children darted through the crowds, while the old made their way more sedately.

At length the three agents were swept along through an arched entrance and bumped, shoved and elbowed up a winding stone staircase. In the chaos, Topaz couldn't stop thinking about Jake. She was tormented by visions of what Agata, the she-devil, her so-called mother, might do to him.

At the top of the stairs they were jostled forward, and finally squeezed out into the arena. As a wave of cheers echoed around them, Nathan's heart soared and he had to remind himself that the applause wasn't actually for him. He gazed from one end of the Circus to the other, a faint, incredulous smile on his face. Topaz blinked in disbelief, while Charlie stared in awe. In the course of their work for the History Keepers' Secret Service they had seen countless wonders, but this was perhaps the most astonishing of all.

The arena was almost half a mile long from end to end. A vast man-made basin stretched between the Palatine and the Aventine, whose slopes were also teeming with spectators. There were six levels of seating. The bottom tier, edged by a balustrade and separated from the track by a deep drainage gulley, was the widest and contained the largest quantity of white – the colour worn by the richest citizens. From here the levels rose up, the rake gentle at first, but steepening dramatically towards the top. The higher you went, the noisier and more tightly packed the tiers. Charlie calculated that the top one alone, which looked miles away, must have held more than fifty thousand people. Its colonnade, punctuated by column after column, would have been an incredible structure in its own right, let alone as a crowning afterthought to the rest.

Running down the centre of the arena was the *spina*, the stone island that divided the track in two. 'Grisly fact . . .' Charlie announced. 'According to legend, it was originally made of the crushed bones of Rome's enemies.'

The whole island was teeming with men in

white, purple-edged togas; more were climbing up onto it.

'The senators, I take it?' asked Nathan.

Charlie nodded. 'Whether they like it or not, they're expected to attend. It's considered bad form not to be seen supporting the games.'

'And a no-show would be kind of obvious,' Nathan commented. 'They are rather the centre of attention.' He was right: all eyes were on them, a distinct, bright band of white and purple rising out of the sand. Some of the senators waved at the crowd; others chatted in groups as slaves offered them drinks from silver jugs.

Amongst the throng of senators, the *spina* also sported a number of intriguing monuments: at each end stood clusters of golden spiked cones, three times the size of a human, and, in the centre, a giant Egyptian obelisk. 'Looted from the court of Rameses the Second and now considered one of the wonders of Rome,' Topaz informed the others.

'And the emperor sits there, I take it?' Nathan pointed to the terrace in front of the *pulvinar*, the distinctive temple that jutted out halfway along the track. An empty throne – an enormous seat of white alabaster – was set beneath a bright red awning. Golden statues of eagles guarded each corner of the terrace, and flames flickered from a host of bronze torches.

'That's right,' Charlie agreed. 'The royal terrace is accessed by its own special passageway, which leads directly from the villas on the Palatine.'

'So they don't have to mix with the riff-raff, I suppose,' Nathan said.

'Let's go then,' suggested Topaz. 'I take it our emperor will be arriving at any minute, so we should approach – with caution of course.' She set off in the direction of the *pulvinar*. Apart from anything else, she needed to get thoughts of Jake out of her head. She kept thinking about Alan and Miriam and how she was going to explain his disappearance. The other two followed, threading their way through the crowd.

Suddenly the three of them were cloaked in shadow; it crept along the tiers of seating, darkening a great swathe of the arena. They looked up to see a roof canopy – a series of long white sails – being drawn across the top of the stadium by a network of ropes. Charlie shook his head and muttered something about the 'stunning technical pizzazz' as the senators in the centre were enveloped in welcome shade.

At the same moment Topaz froze. 'Hydra!' she hissed, and swung the others round just as four soldiers in grey breastplates and bronze masks muscled their way through the crowd, knocking people flying. They marched past and took up positions – a brooding, eagle-eyed group – close to the edge of the emperor's terrace.

'They're everywhere . . .' Nathan nodded towards other soldiers filing towards the *pulvinar*. 'Let's just wait here for the time being,' he murmured, his jaw clenched with frustration.

Lucius's ankle cracked as he landed and he cried out in agony, stumbling down the remainder of the slope. He and Jake had crept across the roofs of Agata's villa, searching for a safe way down. They had chosen a windowless corner next to a cluster of tall pines. Jake had successfully leaped across onto a tree and lowered himself down. Lucius, who could only see out of one eye, and not well from that, had misjudged the jump and tumbled through the branches.

'Yake, I think it is broken,' he said, wincing as he clutched his ankle. They were both in a bad state, scratched and bruised, but Lucius was worse:

not only half blind but cut to ribbons all over.

Jake knelt down and carefully examined Lucius's foot. 'It's badly sprained, but I don't think it's broken,' he said.

'Just leave me – best to leave me, Yake,' Lucius groaned.

'*Ssh.*' Jake put his finger to his lips, aware that they were still in enemy territory. 'You're not getting away from me that easily,' he whispered, smiling. 'I'll help you up. Let's go.' He put his arm round Lucius and slowly hauled him to his feet. 'You see the road there, winding down the hill? We just need to follow it. It'll take us straight there. You don't want to miss the fun, do you?' he joked.

Jake hid his panic well. He knew it was vital to reach the Circus Maximus as soon as possible, but he was simply not prepared to abandon his friend. He had saved Lucius and was determined not to leave him where he might be recaptured. Constantly on the alert for signs of pursuit, Jake helped his companion down the slope towards the Circus.

'There she is,' hissed Nathan, spotting the distinctive figure of Agata Zeldt emerge onto the terrace of the *pulvinar*. Dressed in a plain white dress, she deliberately hung back in the shadows, watching the crowd through narrowed eyes. Topaz, invisible in the crowd, stared back, and saw a chubby boy with flowers in his fair hair appear behind her.

Nathan did a double-take when he saw him. 'Charlie, am I going insane' – he nudged his friend – 'or does that boy look exactly like that oaf Caspar Isaksen?'

Charlie followed his gaze. 'From Sweden? Don't be ridiculous.' For a moment a group of guards blocked his view. When they moved out of the way, he caught sight of a youth stuffing a cake into his mouth.

'Hell's bells and Bathsheba!' Charlie gasped, barely able to believe his eyes. 'What on earth . . .?' Caspar giggled as Agata whispered something in his ear. 'What *is* he doing here? And with her?'

'It would certainly explain our little mishap in Stockholm,' Nathan commented drily.

'But he's an Isaksen!' Charlie insisted. 'One of the oldest, most revered families of the History Keepers' Secret Service! They go back eight generations.'

'And I'm a Zeldt, theoretically,' Topaz reminded them. 'Loyalty is strange animal.'

On the track, ten men in golden tunics filed out and lined up, their backs to the royal box. As the audience realized that something was about to happen, a great cheer swelled around the stadium. Each man carried a trumpet – a horn curved in the shape of a six. As one, they lifted the mouthpieces to their lips and blew. The blare of sound cut across the clamour.

Nathan and Charlie looked around as the roars of the crowd seemed to suddenly double in volume. A hundred and fifty thousand people had got to their feet and a blizzard of white rained down – pale flowers cast from every corner of the stadium. At first Nathan and Charlie wondered at this, but Topaz nudged them and nodded towards the *pulvinar*. It was no longer empty. The distinctive figure of Tiberius had appeared.

The emperor of Rome – the most powerful man in the world, in his robes of gold and purple. Of course, it was not Tiberius at all, but a second-rate actor from Herculaneum called Austerio. Even from a distance, Topaz, Nathan and Charlie recognized his puffy face. But as he held up his bejewelled hand and gave a regal wave, the crowd let out a tumultuous roar.

Nathan gazed over at the senators' enclosure on the *spina* in front of them. Some of the men waved and bowed towards their leader, but for the most part their smiles were forced.

'Where is that viper Leopardo?' Topaz wondered, her eyes still fixed on the royal box.

But there was no sign of him.

'*Non possum*, Yake.' Lucius sank to the ground, half blocking the busy road and halting the stream of vehicles. Everyone started shouting for them to move out of the way, so Jake quickly scooped him up and dragged him over to the side. It had taken thirty gruelling minutes for them to struggle down the west side of the Palatine, ducking out of the way every time they caught sight of a soldier, but the stadium was now tantalizingly close.

'We're almost there,' Jake said cheerily. 'Can't you hear it?' He put his hand to his ear, listening to the thunderous roar floating across the rooftops.

'Leave me, I beg you,' Lucius insisted. '*Non possum*.'

Jake hesitated. He was beginning to see his friend's logic: they were now a safe distance from the villa and he would be much more effective on his own.

Nearby, a man was roasting meat at a *taberna*. 'Look, I can eat,' Lucius said, his face crinkling into a smile, 'while you save the world.'

Jake bit his lip uncertainly, but time was running out. 'All right, it's a deal,' he said decisively. He pulled Lucius to his feet and helped him over to a bench beside the bar, then scooped up some water from a fountain and offered it to him.

After he had drunk his fill, the soldier looked up at Jake. 'Thank you,' he said quietly.

Impulsively Jake hugged him. 'I'll be back for you, don't worry,' he promised, and tore off down the road, weaving in and out of the carts and litters. He had been so worried about Lucius's injuries that he had forgotten about his own. Now, his bruises throbbed, his cuts stung, he ached all over and felt sick and dizzy.

'I have to find the others,' he muttered to himself. 'They'll be safe, of course they will. I'll find them. We'll defuse the bombs somehow – we'll do it.'

22 SEVEN LAPS TO DOOM

As Austerio seated himself on his alabaster throne, there was another blast of horns. The trumpet players turned and strode around the track towards the grand archway at the southern end. As they did so, a group of figures began to emerge from the opening, as if drawn by the music. The trumpeters turned and marched back along the track, now at the head of a grand procession.

In front were the athletes – young men stripped to the waist, their oiled bodies shining in the sun, each with a crown of laurels in their hair. Next came the cavalry: armoured soldiers on prancing steeds, swords held rigidly in front of their faces. A phalanx of musicians followed: a score each of flute and lyre players. And then the incense carriers bearing fragrant smoking torches. Next a troupe of dancers appeared: girls and boys in flowing silk, some waving spears, others clattering cymbals. Behind came the *mimi* – performers dressed as Roman gods and heroes: Jupiter, Apollo, Hercules and Odysseus – leading an army of fauns, satyrs and all kinds of mythical creatures.

There was a brief hiatus, and then another surge of applause greeted the entrance of the wild beasts. A dozen plodding elephants preceded a menagerie of lions, tigers, leopards and giant bears. The creatures were tightly leashed and held in check by strapping men in full armour. The sight made Charlie seethe with anger. The beasts and trainers peeled off and headed for the holding pens, through a gate in the centre of the *spina* – except for four brown bears, which were led onto a low plinth in front of the emperor's box and chained up in pairs. An attendant brought a basket of bloody meat, which he prepared to throw to them. One of the huge creatures lifted its head and roared in anticipation – making the crowd cheer again. Austerio looked down and his regal smile tightened a little, as if he was wondering what on earth he had got himself into.

The most deafening hurrah of all was reserved for

the charioteers and their horses. They emerged from the shadow of the grand arch – four stallions pulling each of the eight two-wheeled chariots – and formed a perfect line. The shiny, muscular horses wore extravagant feathered headpieces that matched the clothes of their drivers. These stern-faced men wore coloured tunics and leather gauntlets, and carried a many-tailed whip.

'Each colour represents a different district of the city,' Nathan explained, 'and the competition between the teams is fierce. Disappointed fans have been known to throw themselves onto burning pyres when their teams lose. It's all very Italian.'

Nathan, Charlie and Topaz watched as the eight chariots rolled forward in unison. *Everyone* watched them: the emperor, the senators, and over a hundred thousand others. The charioteers' eyes were hard and determined, their fists clenched tight around their reins. Nathan felt a pang of jealousy. He couldn't imagine anything more exhilarating than a race around the most famous arena in history, cheered on by over a hundred thousand fans.

'Look!' Topaz gasped, nodding down towards the furthest team. Four massive black stallions pulled an ebony chariot, driven by a black-clad charioteer with a shock of perfectly straight blond hair: Leopardo. Topaz quivered when he postured towards the crowd, chin out, mouth curled in an arrogant snarl. Agata, his proud mother, gave a loud cheer when she saw him.

'What on earth are they up to?' Charlie shook his head in exasperation. 'Don't tell me she's going to have him assassinate the emperor mid race!'

Nathan shrugged. 'I wouldn't put it past them. It's just the sort of stagy melodrama they'd like,' he said – as if *he'd* never been melodramatic in his life.

At this moment Jake staggered, panting with exhaustion, into the half-deserted square behind the arena. Hearing the roars of the crowds, he'd felt a mixture of panic, fear, and strange excitement. He'd attended a handful of football matches in London – one at Wembley – but the sound coming from *this* place was like nothing he'd ever heard before.

Jake peered inside: between the front arches and the twelve that led onto the arena itself, stretching the width of the building, was a wide portico. Here a small army of staff, officials and stable hands were busily preparing for the race. On one side he glimpsed stalls of spare horses and all sorts of charioteering apparatus. Beyond the pillars of the arches, in the brilliant sunshine, he saw the procession advancing along the track. The bare-chested athletes were coming round the end of the *spina*, starting on their return journey. It was when his eyes followed the dancers, cymbals clashing and ribboned spears held aloft, that Jake suddenly noticed the row of identical objects suspended above the end of the central island.

He stopped breathing.

Eggs. Golden eggs, each the size of a hefty boulder, lined up on a thick bronze rail. *One, two, three* . . . Jake counted them. To be sure, he counted again, his eyes widening in amazement. 'Seven golden eggs,' he murmured in disbelief.

His mind started racing as he began to put the pieces of the puzzle together. He had seen the symbols on Vulcano, then again last night in Agata's war room; the word *Counters* had been written beneath them.

'Lap counters,' Jake said to himself. 'There are seven laps; each one is counted with an egg. They must be shifted along or turned over each time the chariots complete a lap of the circuit.'

He thought back to what Agata had said that

morning: *At the climax of the race, as the seven turns, a fireball, the like of which the world has never seen, will herald the bloodiest revolution of all time.*

Now Jake understood what she meant. 'The seven – the seventh egg . . .' He felt the hairs stand up on the back of his neck. 'It's a detonator! The race ends, and the fireball goes off.' He realized he had only one option. 'I have to stop the race.'

Suddenly, in the area between the arches, there was a commotion. As the chariots peeled away from the end of the procession and entered the arcade, the trainers, assistants and stable hands swept into action: seeing to the horses, adjusting the harnesses, checking the chariot wheels and providing water and refreshments for the drivers.

There was a grinding noise as iron starting gates were secured over each archway. The charioteers began to manoeuvre their vehicles towards their starting positions, one behind every gate, and the trainers gave whispered encouragement or instructions.

As Jake watched, he got another shock. The last in line was Leopardo. He stood in his ebony chariot and flicked his whip, not just at his horses, but at his slaves. Sensing that he was being watched, he turned, but Jake quickly retreated behind the pillar.

'How do I stop it?' Jake repeated in despair, barely able to think straight.

In the arena, 'Tiberius' stood up and slowly walked to the edge of the terrace. He took out a white handkerchief and held it high in the air, gazing in wonder at the expectant crowd. Austerio had never had such an audience, and he was going to enjoy every minute of it.

Under the portico, the chariots edged forward, the drivers tensely clutching their reins. Leopardo closed his eyes and muttered a prayer.

Finally the emperor lowered the white handkerchief.

The gates sprang open. The chariots took off through the arches in an explosion of dust, and one hundred and twenty-eight hooves thundered down the track. The thousands upon thousands of Romans shouted and waved at them.

Without thinking, Jake dashed through an archway and out onto the track. He felt the ground thumping under his feet. He stopped dead, a solitary figure in the great empty arc of the arena. A huddle of senators standing in front of the golden eggs squinted down at him in bemusement as he suddenly turned, ran back across the track and in under the portico again.

The trainers and stable hands watched as he marched over to the stall of horses. One was already saddled for a rider, and quietly munching hay when Jake sprang onto its back, grabbed a whip hanging on the wall, dug his heels into its flanks and took off. (Well before Jake had even met the History Keepers, he was a more than competent rider. Old friends of his parents had stables in Kent, and he used to go often with his brother.) There were angry shouts, and men ran forward, trying to block his path, but Jake burst through them, under an archway and out onto the track, following the cloud of dust. He crouched low, and urged his horse into a gallop. It leaped forward, and Jake had to cling on for dear life. In truth, he had no idea what he was doing. He had acted on impulse – some part of his brain telling him that in order to stop the race, he would first need to be *in* the race.

On he flew, his horse relishing the chance to gallop unencumbered by a chariot. The shouting Romans were no more than a roaring sea at the edge of Jake's vision.

Within seconds he was closing on the rear chariot. It was trailing behind, one wheel skewed. Suddenly there was a violent crack, and the wheel took off like a missile. Jake's horse veered aside to avoid it as it spun and bounced up into the screaming crowd.

The vehicle tipped onto its side, sending the charioteer flying into the air and then crashing to the ground. The broken chariot continued without him, the snapped axle gouging a deep trench in the sand. Jake overtook it on the inside, but the four stallions raced on regardless, eyes wild, hooves thumping, feathered headpieces streaming in the wind.

Jake was now approaching the other chariots. In the thick pall of dust, he could barely make out the pounding hooves, flailing limbs and flicking whips. They rounded the sharp bend at the end of the *spina*, bunching perilously close together. The wheel hub of the innermost chariot grated against the marble wall in a shower of sparks. For a moment Jake thought it might tip over, but the driver shifted his weight, and the chariot righted itself and carried on into the far straight.

On the emperor's side of the stadium, frenzied

cheers now went up. The seven remaining chariots sped back towards the twelve arches. As Jake rounded the end of the *spina*, he noticed, above him, another row of large golden counters – these ones shaped like dolphins rather than eggs. Two officials pulled a lever to turn the first on its head; it flashed in the sunlight as it spun round. Jake was aware of their astonished gaze as he passed. It reminded him that what he was doing was madness; he would surely be apprehended at any minute. What was more, the gap between him and the chariots was growing. He carried on regardless: he *had* to find a way to stop them.

Nathan, Charlie and Topaz were tense with anxiety. They had edged closer to the *pulvinar*, each with half an eye trained on its occupants. Caspar had carried on stuffing his face, while Agata Zeldt had sidled forward and positioned herself at the emperor's side – but that was all that had happened.

They had watched the race begin and had noticed a single horseman take off after the chariots. Charlie had been unable to explain who he was. 'Just some lunatic, I guess,' he had murmured. It wasn't until he had rounded the bend and started galloping in their direction that Topaz began to look more closely. There was something about him that seemed familiar, even from a distance. Slowly, realization dawned on her.

'*Mon dieu!*' she exclaimed. '*C'est lui.* Look' – she grabbed the arms of her companions – 'it's Jake. That's Jake on the horse!' Her initial sense of relief that he was still alive was replaced by utter incomprehension. '*Qu'est-ce qu'il fait ici?*'

'I think the sun must be getting to you,' Nathan drawled as he focused on the rider. All at once he saw that Topaz was right. 'What in God's name . . .?' He trailed off, his jaw hanging open.

'Clever boy,' Charlie stated, the edges of his mouth twitching into a smile. 'I haven't got a clue what he's doing, of course, but he's a clever boy.'

At this moment Jake flew past, far below. Charlie had to stop himself from jumping up and shouting out. Instead he clenched his fists in excitement and murmured to himself, 'He has a plan! Thundering unicorns, he has a plan!'

Nathan shook his head, cautiously peering over at Agata Zeldt and Caspar Isaksen in the *pulvinar*.

Caspar was standing, mouth open, frozen in confusion – he had also seen Jake. Clearly dreading her reaction, he leaned over and whispered in Agata's ear. As she listened, her sadistic smile turned to an acid scowl and she bared her teeth in fury.

At this moment Charlie and Topaz gasped in unison, their expressions freezing in horror . . .

Jake saw the crash unfold. The seven remaining chariots were bunched together, charging down the home straight, when Leopardo, who was in second place, swerved over and shunted his neighbour into the wall of the *spina*. There was a blaze of sparks as the chariot ricocheted off it. It wobbled, then righted itself. Once again Leopardo sent his chariot slamming into the other. This time his opponent's wheel sheared off and somersaulted into the air over the backs of the horses.

The beasts whinnied in panic as chariot and driver crashed down beside them. The two central ones stumbled, and dragged the others towards the *pulvinar*; then they fell, right in the path of the other teams. The oncoming horses tried to jump over the obstruction, only for their chariots to become entangled and overturn in a screeching chaotic pile, yanking the horses back.

As Jake approached the wreckage, his horse

slowed down and stopped dead, spooked, almost unseating his rider. For a moment Jake took stock, wondering if his mission to stop the race might have already been achieved.

But then he saw that Leopardo had avoided the pile of horses and vehicles and was forging on. A team of greys also managed to free themselves from the ruck and took off after him.

Once again, Jake did not think; he just acted. To his right, a team of bays had also got free, but were now pulling an empty chariot. He twisted round in his saddle and, choosing his moment carefully, threw himself off his horse and onto the chariot. He grabbed the reins and flicked them. The four horses took off, veering round the crash site and accelerating in pursuit of Leopardo and his opponent. The crowd roared in ecstasy, seemingly unaware that a new charioteer had joined the fray, while Agata Zeldt twisted her hands in vexation.

A small army of attendants emerged to remove the jumble of chariots and horses and clear the way for the remaining competitors.

As he urged his horses up the back straight, Jake saw, out of the corner of his eye, the second golden egg being turned on its axis. He held on for dear life:

the chariot was light and springy – made from nothing more than strips of wood and metal braces – and shook with every little bump in the sand. Its two eight-spoked wheels were also wooden, with bronze tyres; a central pole fixed underneath the vehicle connected it to the horses' harnesses.

Suddenly Jake hit a deep furrow and was thrown into the air, losing his footing. He clung onto the reins and managed to land on the very back of the platform, glimpsing the track rush alarmingly beneath his feet. He pulled himself forward, securing the reins around his wrists, and planted his legs firmly. He started to get a feel for it, and accelerated, the wind loud in his ears.

23 FIREBALL ROME

After four nail-biting laps, Jake had not managed to make up any ground at all. He had thought of turning round completely and charging towards the others head on; twice he had attempted this manoeuvre – but the horses had been trained to circle in one direction and did not understand his command. Once they had started galloping, he could barely manage to slow them down. And now the gap between him and the others had widened, and when he passed the end of the *spina* and saw the fifth golden egg being turned, he began to despair. Every part of his body was throbbing with pain; even breathing had become agonizing.

But just when he felt he could go on no longer, something appeared through the dust ahead of him – hazy at first, but gradually coming into focus. It was the spectre of a man, hovering in the air before him. The uproar around Jake faded away as the figure took shape. His bearing was noble, his smile warm, his eyes bright. It was his brother Philip – not as he was when he disappeared three years ago, but as he would be now: a young man of seventeen. Jake knew that this was simply a mirage, a product of his delirium, but now he felt sure that Philip was alive somewhere, that he was calling him from some dark corner of history. The apparition faded and finally vanished, the eyes lingering a moment longer than the rest.

Once again the thunderous roar of the crowd deafened him – the sound had returned, along with his resolve. If Philip was alive somewhere in this world – somewhere in this multiverse of time – *that* was a reason to go on.

Jake bent his knees and urged his horses on faster. The crowd, sensing his determination, leaped to their feet as he swung round the end of the *spina*, hurtling into the far straight.

Agata Zeldt, no longer keeping a low profile, rushed to the edge of the royal terrace (literally stepping on the toes of the emperor), gaping as Jake advanced. He saw her – a flash of red hair as he flew past.

The ground trembled as he began to catch up with the other two teams. Finally he drew level with the second charioteer, a huge, muscular man with a dark beard and a scarred face, who did not turn to look at Jake, but stared imperiously ahead, using his whip on his straining greys.

Just as Jake overtook on the inside, his opponent suddenly veered over, trying to force Jake against the wall of the *spina*. But he held his ground, and the chariots locked together. Now they went careering off in the other direction, towards the perimeter wall. Jake forced his opponent further and further over, so that his outer wheel dropped into the deep drainage gulley. It screeched along, forcing both chariots almost to a standstill. Suddenly Jake managed to disengage his wheel as his adversary tipped over and fell to the ground.

The roars of the crowd were now at fever pitch. Jake charged on in pursuit of Leopardo's black chariot. As he headed round the *spina* once more, he saw the *sixth* golden egg being turned on its end. One lap to go.

Leopardo finally glanced round and did a double-take when he realized who was behind him. He flicked his whip at Jake, who saw in horror that each of its tendrils ended in a razor-sharp claw. Jake ducked as it whistled past his head and pierced the flank of one of his stallions. The horse cried out in agony as the razor scoured out a tranche of flesh. Jake seethed with fury, determined to defeat this monster. When Leopardo brought his whip down a second time, Jake seized an end, wrapped it around his hand and yanked, almost dislodging his enemy. But Leopardo pulled back even harder, tightening the leather around Jake's hand.

The Leopard had further tricks up his sleeve: he kicked a lever on the floor of his vehicle, whereupon a series of knives shot out from the hubs of his wheels. He smiled maliciously as he pulled on the whip, dragging Jake's chariot in towards the rotating blades.

Jake was powerless to stop it: the spokes of his wheel splintered, the axle snapped, and the chariot went flying, taking Jake with it. He pressed down and launched himself, somersaulting through the air and landing with a jolt on the shaft of Leopardo's vehicle. He looked down and saw the ground thundering past inches below him.

The crowd was euphoric. Everyone leaped up out of their seats, shrieking with delight – everyone except Agata, whose nails were digging into her neck. Next to her, Caspar watched in blank confusion.

As Jake picked himself up, balancing precariously on the straining shaft, Leopardo, no longer smiling, drew his sword and slashed out at him. Jake dodged the blade, then lunged forward, taking hold of the boy's wrist and smashing it down on the front of the chariot. As the weapon clattered to the floor, Jake leaped over and head-butted Leopardo; but the savage managed to grab hold of Jake's face. As the black stallions galloped towards the finishing line, Leopardo squeezed tighter and tighter, his fingers digging into Jake's eyes.

Agata felt she could breathe again – but only for a second. Suddenly the horses stumbled over a piece of wreckage. The reins were pulled out of Leopardo's hand. Jake took his chance, and punched him on the chin, then on the cheek – before leaping out and rolling across the sand. For a moment Leopardo teetered drunkenly on. Then the chariot crashed into the wall, and he was hurled out, to land sprawled in the drainage gulley.

The seventh golden egg had still not been turned.

Agata's bloodless lips trembled. For a terrible

moment she thought her son was dead, but then he moved his head and tried to lift his arm. She turned, spitting, to two of her guards. 'Help him, you idiots!'

As they made their way down onto the track, Agata noticed three more figures leaping down into the arena: Nathan, Charlie and Topaz. 'Traitors! Witch!' she cried, rounding on the remaining soldiers. 'Kill them!' Her face was purple with fury. 'Kill them all! Hack them to pieces!' So piercing was her cry, Caspar and Austerio put their fingers in their ears and watched as the guards charged down onto the track.

The History Keepers dashed over to Jake. Topaz fell to her knees beside him. 'Jake!' she gasped, cradling his head in her hands. His face was almost unrecognizable, covered as it was with congealed blood, cuts and bruises.

His eyes flickered open, and when he saw the apparition above him, a hazy goddess framed in sunlight, he smiled.

'What were you doing?' she asked in amazement.

'F-fireball,' Jake stammered.

'Fireball?' Nathan asked. 'What fireball?'

Jake gathered his wits. 'Bomb,' he told them.

'Gunpowder. There.' He pointed a bloody finger towards the *spina*. 'The senators . . .' He mimed an explosion with his hands. '*The end of dominions.*'

'There are bombs underneath the *spina*?' Charlie clarified.

Jake nodded, pointing again. 'When the seventh egg is turned.'

A jolt of realization shook them all.

'The plan is to murder the senators,' Charlie exclaimed, 'not the emperor.'

'We have to get them off there . . .' Nathan's brain was already searching for a solution.

Jake reached out for Topaz, clutching her hand. For a second he lost himself in her eyes. They had been cold and hard for so long, but now they seemed to sparkle like they had the day he first met her. 'Lucius is safe,' he said.

Topaz leaned over and kissed him. 'You're astonishing,' she whispered.

'Topaz! Behind you!' Nathan shouted as the guards approached, swords drawn.

Topaz jumped up, drawing her own weapon as she swung round. She fought them off with ruthless precision, Charlie and Nathan quickly coming to her aid. All three were so ablaze with passion, so sharp with adrenalin, they dispatched the soldiers almost instantly.

Jake felt a warm thrill pulse through him. '*You're astonishing*,' he repeated to himself, and decided that, if he died now, he would die happy.

More soldiers jumped down into the deep gutter to help Leopardo. Though dazed, he had only one thing on his mind: the seventh golden egg. 'On your knees,' he ordered one of the men, who duly bent down. Leopardo used him as a step to clamber back onto the track. But when he emerged into the blazing sun, the whole stadium swam in front of his eyes and he collapsed onto the sand.

Once more the guards pulled him to his feet. He shoved them aside and doggedly limped off towards the golden eggs at the end of the *spina*. 'You will die,' he snarled at the senators. 'All of you will die.'

Agata's eyes widened in alarm as she watched him. 'Darling,' she murmured, 'what are you doing . . . ?'

Once again Leopardo's legs gave way; but once again he picked himself up and pressed on.

Nathan realized that he had to act fast. He spun round and tore over to the plinth where the bears were chained up. He picked out a huge joint of meat from the feeding basket and then unshackled the largest – a great beast covered in scars. Using the meat as bait, he lured the bear along the track towards the steps at the other end of the *spina*. A number of the senators watched in horror as the bear lumbered across the sand towards them, snarling and salivating. Some of them started to edge away and climb down the far side, running for cover.

Agata was not watching them. Her eyes were grimly focused on Leopardo, now climbing up the steps towards the golden eggs. 'Darling' – she shook her head in confusion – 'what are you doing?' She turned on Caspar. 'What is he doing?' He didn't need to answer. Leopardo meant to detonate the bomb himself.

The bear padded along, hypnotized by the smell of the bloody meat. Suddenly it lunged towards it – but, like a bullfighter, Nathan twisted it out of reach. The great beast reared up on its hind legs, growling in fury.

The watching crowd were once again on their feet, thrilled by this unexpected twist to the games.

Now Leopardo had reached the top of the steps and was staggering towards the row of eggs. His expression was so murderous that the counting officials fled into the throng. He stepped onto the plinth and reached up for the last egg. The metal, scorching hot from the sun, burned his hand as he touched it.

Realizing that there was no time left, Nathan swung round and hurled the joint of meat. It spiralled through the air, flicking a helix of blood in all directions, towards the heart of the *spina*. A group of senators watched in astonishment as it spun down towards them. They parted, and it landed with a crunch on the stone. The bear took off after it, bounding up the steps. In unison, six hundred senators sent up a howl of terror, and started throwing themselves over the parapet, a great sea of white and purple pouring down onto the track; it spread across the stadium like a giant flower suddenly opening its petals. The bear was big and clumsy, and struggled to climb the narrow stairs towards its prey.

Ignoring the intense heat, Leopardo reached again for the egg, but was now jostled backwards by the surge of senators. He hissed with rage as he pushed his way through them. He gritted his teeth and stretched out his hand. 'I do this for history!' he cried, and this time he swung the egg decisively on its axis.

'No!' Agata gasped, her eyes wide.

But there was no explosion. Leopardo had not turned the egg fully round. For a moment he stared at it in bafflement. All around him men were fleeing in panic as the bear went to collect its prize. Leopardo was oblivious, his mind fixed on one thing only. Once again he thrust up his hand and turned the egg.

This time the mechanism clicked into place.

Agata stopped breathing, her gaping mouth frozen.

Jake noticed a strange silence, as if everything was suddenly muffled. Then his ears popped, he heard the boom and felt the wave of intense heat. There was a flash, and Jake saw Leopardo take off into the air. He looked graceful, almost balletic, even as his head came away from his body.

'Noooooooo!' his mother wailed, her face lit up by the explosion.

There was a great *crack!* Then the end of the *spina* collapsed in on itself, the three black marble cones falling like skittles. Animals began to pour out of the wreckage: tigers, lions and leopards. The bear that had charged onto the platform had stopped in its tracks, the meat hanging from his mouth. It too leaped off the *spina*, crashing down into a cloud of dust. The whole auditorium stood frozen in bewilderment.

More explosions followed, one by one, across the central island, hurling volleys of rock into the air. The giant obelisk teetered back and forth, there was a grinding sound, and it too tumbled onto its side. The inferno was extraordinary, spectacular, the flames even brighter than the sun overhead. Wave after wave of heat rolled over Jake and his companions.

Screams rang out around the stadium as people rushed for the exits, the weak and old pushed aside and trampled in the frenzy. Thick smoke covered the track. The animals, some injured and howling with pain, emerged from it, along with choking, shell-shocked senators. One had lost his arm and was searching around for it, and several lay on the sand, lifeless. But most of them had survived the explosion and were climbing up into the auditorium.

'They're going,' Caspar mumbled to Agata, a piece of cake hanging out of his mouth. 'Should they be going?'

Agata wrung her hands, snarling like a wildcat as she glared down at the History Keepers.

Coughing in the smoke, Topaz was collecting the swords of the vanquished soldiers as Nathan and Charlie helped Jake to his feet.

'How many times do I have to ask?' Agata screeched at the last of her retinue. 'Kill them! Kill them all. Kill my daughter!'

The soldiers edged away from her: they were reluctant to go down onto the track and face the wild beasts. A lion was eating a severed hand, while a tiger was standing, roaring, over a still white bundle, the body of a senator.

Then Agata noticed Austerio, his face flushed with panic, mumbling to himself as he made to escape. She intercepted him and slapped his face.

'You belong to me, you toad,' she hissed, dragging him back to the throne by his ear. 'You do what I tell you!'

The poor actor cowered away from her, tears streaming down his cheeks. 'I can't work like this,' he blubbed. 'I have a very low tolerance to danger. I switch off at the merest hint of it.'

Agata set about him, venting the full force of her rage. He covered his head with his hands, begging for mercy, as she pummelled and punched him.

Seeing what was happening, Charlie immediately

spotted an opportunity. He jumped up onto the balustrade and, motioning towards the stricken Austerio, shouted at the top of his voice that the emperor was in danger: '*Imperator in periculo est! Imperator in periculo est.*'

The noise in the auditorium was such that only a handful of people heard him to begin with. But when they grasped what was taking place on the imperial terrace, they turned to their neighbours, pointing. First astonishment, then anger swept through the crowd. Already convinced that some deadly uprising was afoot, the mob surged towards their emperor.

Caspar gulped when he saw them, and tugged at Agata's gown. She stopped hitting Austerio, and turned to see a mass of people approaching, shaking their fists. She held up her hand and, in a thunderous voice, commanded them to stop, but they ignored her.

Agata realized that she had run out of time. She let go of Austerio, dropping him like a sack of rubbish; then turned and threw open the double doors of the *pulvinar*. For a second she looked back at the seething ocean of people; at the smoking ruin of the *spina*; at the broken, bloody pieces on the far side of the arena that had once been her son. Three tigers were circling them, licking their lips.

Agata snarled defiantly. 'Let ignorance kill you,' she shouted at the people, and disappeared into the building. Caspar and the remainder of the guards followed, slamming the doors behind them.

Nathan was the first to jump up onto the terrace. Charlie and Topaz helped Jake up after him.

Still trembling, Austerio peeked through his fingers. On recognizing the agents, he sat up, shaking his head in wonder. 'My fans,' he sobbed. 'Come to save Austerio!'

'That's right,' Nathan deadpanned, heading straight past him and throwing his weight against the doors. 'Just in time for the finale.'

Charlie went to help him, and eventually they broke through.

'Shall we?' Nathan asked, turning to the others.

Topaz looked at Jake. 'You stay here – it's safer.'

'You think I'm going to leave you now?' he cried.

The four young agents stepped through the doorway.

'Wait for me!' Austerio called, rushing after them. 'Don't leave me with this rabble.'

Inside was a square white chamber lined with

statues and lit by smoky braziers attached to the wall. At the back stood five soldiers, guarding the entrance to the long tunnel into the Palatine. As they spotted the intruders, they raised their weapons – but there was uncertainty in their eyes.

'Really, boys' – Nathan smirked – 'you have to know that the game's up now!'

One of the guards reached for his silver bracelet, but Nathan was ahead of him. He sent his dagger flying through the air towards a brazier. It sliced through the tether attaching it to the ceiling, and burning embers tipped out onto the man's head. The remaining soldiers rushed forward to help him, but tripped on the hot coals. In a breathtaking series of moves, Nathan disarmed the first man with a clean cut, paralysed the second with a crack of his elbow and flattened the third by toppling a marble bust of Augustus onto his head.

'Are *we* allowed to play?' Charlie asked wryly as all four agents closed in on the remaining soldier, who pointed his sword at each of them in turn, and cursed.

'Hot potato.' Charlie winked, scooping a coal up with the point of his sword and flicking it neatly into the folds of the guard's tunic.

As the man hopped around in panic, Austerio

stepped forward. 'What a drama,' he commented drily, shooting out his belly and sending the soldier crashing into the wall. 'You see?' he said, pouting. 'Not just a pretty face.'

'Let's go!' Nathan ordered, and the five of them rushed along the passage in pursuit of Agata, their footsteps echoing loudly. At the end, far in the distance, they saw a rectangle of light that blinked as two figures cut across it. The four agents quickened their pace, Austerio wheezing as he tried to keep up.

It seemed an age before they reached the light, but suddenly they saw a staircase lit by brilliant sunshine. Nathan peered up and signalled for the others to follow quietly. Weapons held at the ready, they cautiously ascended.

They emerged into a tropical garden filled with brightly coloured flowers. Jake recognized it from early that morning – he had seen it from the room where he had learned of Agata's diabolical plans. It was deserted, and Nathan led the way through the trees towards an archway.

They headed through into the arena where the party had taken place. It looked different in the daylight, empty and quiet but for the trickling of the fountains. Suddenly, from above, they heard a curious *whoomph*, and a huge shape rose high over the garden. Jake stared up in puzzlement, but Charlie recognized it immediately.

'The balloon!' he exclaimed. 'Agata must be escaping in it.'

He was right – it was swaying to and fro, nearly inflated.

They tore over to the door next to the statue of Saturn. Nathan still had the key, and he hurriedly unlocked it. They all dived through and charged up the spiralling steps – one flight, two, three . . . At the top, Nathan headed through another door.

At that very moment the balloon took off, Agata and Caspar ensconced in the basket, the former clutching a veneered wooden box, her pet falcon clinging to her shoulder. As the canopy filled to capacity, lifting them into the sky, all four History Keepers launched themselves towards it, each grabbing one of the ropes that hung down.

Under their weight, the balloon dropped back to earth. Agata reacted instantly: with a flick of her sword, she sliced through Charlie's rope, then Nathan's. The balloon took off again, Jake still hanging from one side, Topaz from the other.

Agata looked down at her daughter and their eyes

locked. There was so much history between them. Agata's sword hovered, its point an inch from Topaz's eye: she could run her through and never hear from her again. But she stopped herself. Just one word came from her lips: 'Ungrateful . . .' Then she hacked the rope in two. Topaz plunged down, her dress billowing in the wind. Nathan and Charlie rushed forward and managed to catch her.

'Jake!' Topaz called as the balloon suddenly surged up again.

Jake's stomach lurched as he saw the whole of Rome spread out at his feet. With grim determination, while Agata was distracted watching Topaz, he pulled himself up to the edge of the basket and grabbed hold of Caspar's toga. Jake felt his sweaty belly wobbling as he gave a high-pitched giggle.

'I've said it once, I'll say it again,' Caspar jeered. 'You and your family are the stupidest people in history.'

Jake clung on, his eyes fixed on the wooden box in Agata's hands.

'I'm going to enjoy your death . . .' Caspar produced a dagger with one hand and grabbed Jake by the neck with the other. Agata's falcon fluttered agitatedly about the basket.

Jake looked down again. He was so high above the terrace that Topaz and the others were now nothing more than moving dots.

'Goodbye, Jake,' said Caspar and brought the weapon down.

The blade flashed, but it never reached its target.

Everything seemed to happen in slow motion. The malicious glint in Caspar's eye froze, replaced by a look of confusion. He cried out as Agata leaned forward and, with one hand, tipped him over the edge of the basket, intending to rid herself of both boys at once. Caspar's dagger dropped from his grasp; but for a second he clung on, staring up at her in amazed horror.

'You're weighing me down,' she said, peeling his fat fingers off, one by one.

Suddenly there came a piercing squawk as the falcon accidentally singed its wing on the burner. It flapped crazily in Agata's face. As she swiped it away, she dropped the box onto the floor. Jake saw his chance, lunged over the edge and snatched it. At the same moment Caspar lost his grip on the basket. He fell, but grabbed onto Jake's clothes first, his weight pulling them both down. They plummeted, clothes flapping, locked in a tangle of limbs. The ground shot up to meet them. Caspar hit the terrace first, cracking the marble. Jake landed on top of him, his fall cushioned by the other boy's big belly.

For a moment Caspar stared up stupidly, watching the balloon soar away across the city, realizing that he had been abandoned.

Jake rolled off onto his knees and held out the box. Nathan grabbed it, opened it and smiled. Inside were two full vials of atomium – the same bottles that had been stolen in Stockholm.

They turned to look at Caspar. 'I can't feel anything,' he murmured, suddenly frightened. He tried to lift his hand. 'Why can't I feel anything?' A pool of blood was spreading out from beneath him across the white marble. He looked at them all in turn. Even in this state, his crafty mind was still working. 'Maybe I went a little too far . . .' He tried to smile. 'Agata Zeldt brainwashes you, you must realize . . .' He stopped. 'Why's it going dark?' he panted.

'Caspar,' said Jake, 'you have to tell me – have you seen my brother?'

'I don't have to do anything for you . . . It's as black as pitch!' he cried, his body shaking, his face pale.

'Answer me!' Jake persisted. 'Philip – did you see him? Tell me!'

'Yes, I've seen him,' Caspar sneered. 'I even tortured him. But I expect he's dead by now.' He tried to laugh. 'He thought you'd forgotten all about him . . . *The History Keepers*.' He spat out the words. 'You're all amateurs.'

Jake shook him. 'Where have you seen him?' he demanded desperately.

'Such terrible darkness,' Caspar sighed. Then his eyes froze and he was still.

'Where have you seen him?' Jake wailed again. But Caspar was gone – along with everything he knew. 'Where? Where?' Jake sobbed. Topaz threw her arms around him and held him tight. Nathan and Charlie looked at each other sombrely.

Agata's balloon floated off into the distance, climbing higher into the hot afternoon sky. In every street, the traffic stopped and the people looked up, struck dumb by the apparition floating noiselessly overhead. It drifted northwestwards over the Circus Maximus; over the Field of Mars, the Tiber Island and the watermills of Trastevere. It crested the great Gianicolo hill and vanished from sight.

24 A PLACE IN HISTORY

Nathan and Charlie solemnly covered up Caspar's body. He may have been a traitor but everyone was filled with remorse. He had, after all, once been one of them, a History Keeper, and from one of the noblest families of all.

Removing his corpse was not practical; but after they had crept down the stairs and evaded the remaining guards, they went straight to an undertaker's – a *libitinarius* – that Charlie had noticed in a row of shops at the foot of the Palatine. Here they spoke to a cheerless, gaunt man (Jake wondered why funeral directors invariably looked half-dead themselves), and left money and instructions for a full ceremony. They knew that at some stage they would have to meet Caspar's family; they wanted to reassure them that he had been buried with dignity.

The next stop was the *taberna* where Jake had left Lucius. As they made their way through the traffic, Topaz nervously quickened her pace. When she saw him sitting by the bar, she rushed forward, took his bloody face in her hands and kissed him. Jake stopped and looked at them both. He found that he was no longer jealous but proud, for in his own way he had brought them back together again.

Nathan and Charlie went off to collect Mr Drake from his hiding place (the parrot was so delighted that he hadn't been left behind after all, he completely forgot to be angry with his master), and then on to the Forum Boarium, hoping to find someone to take them back to Ostia, where the *Conqueror* was docked.

Their timing couldn't have been better: Gaius, the blind perfumier, had sold all his stock, and was inundated with orders from affluent housewives. In short, he needed to return to his home town urgently to make more. Charlie and Nathan were only too happy to help him out. They boarded the cart with the old man (it was much more spacious without the jars), went to pick up the others at the *taberna*, and the whole troupe, Austerio included, set off on the journey back to Ostia.

As they trundled up the Caelian, Jake looked back at the metropolis below, at the sun setting over the Circus Maximus. The stadium was empty of spectators, but an army of workmen was already clearing away the rubble of the *spina*, ready to reassemble it. 'It's not the first time it has been rebuilt,' Charlie said, 'nor will it be the last. They'll make it better, stronger, even more majestic than before.'

As they rounded the summit, Gaius started singing. Austerio joined in, and Lucius too. Although they didn't know the words, the others also started humming the tune; even Nathan – who usually hated sing-alongs – was unable to resist. Jake took one last look at Rome, now a mass of twinkling lights in the dusk below, before it vanished from sight.

He lay back, looked up at the ultramarine sky and thought back to the events of the day: the escape from Agata's aviary, the chariot race around the Circus Maximus, the bombs, the wild beasts, the hot-air balloon (he shuddered at the thought that he might have died five times over) and, finally, the sensational news that Philip had been seen alive.

Alive.

Yes, I've seen him, Caspar had sneered. Wonderful news – even though his later sentence seemed to banish that hope again: *But I expect he's dead by now* – and, worst of all: *He thought you'd forgotten all about him*. Never. Philip would *never* be forgotten.

Jake looked up as the first stars blinked in the heavens and decided that, for tonight at any rate, Philip *was* alive – that the apparition he had seen in the arena was somehow a guarantee that he existed somewhere in the world, at some time in history. With that, a strange peace came over Jake and he fell into a deep sleep.

He was awoken in the middle of the night by Topaz and Lucius talking in hushed whispers.

'I don't understand,' Lucius was saying. 'Why do you have to leave?'

Topaz searched for the right words. 'Lucius, I . . . I come from a different part of the world, far, far away from here. And I have to go back . . . It is my duty,' she added solemnly.

'Duty?' Jake could hear Lucius's voice crack with emotion. 'Is there someone else you love?'

'I suppose . . . there are many things. It is almost impossible to explain – it's a question of honour.'

There was a long silence before Lucius said, 'I wanted to build a house by the sea for you.'

Jake opened his eyes slightly and saw that Topaz was stroking his face, a tear rolling down her cheek.

'We'll make sure you're safe,' she said. 'That you have somewhere to go.'

They said no more. She held onto Lucius's arm tightly as the cart trundled along through the night.

It was when they were arriving in Ostia the following morning that Jake suddenly had a brainwave about Lucius. (The idea that the Roman had lost everything – not only his job, but Topaz too – was dreadful. In fact, the subject had been on everyone's minds.) Jake remembered the story that Nathan had told him on their way to Rome – about Gaius's unfortunate history.

He turned to his friend. 'You said that before Gaius lost his sight, he used to be a carpenter, didn't you?'

'What of it?' the American replied.

'Well, maybe the old man knows someone who can help Lucius find a job. He also comes from a family of carpenters. His father used to repair boats.'

Nathan pondered for a moment, then smiled

broadly. 'Jake Djones, you really are a genius. I'll broach the subject.'

When Nathan really wanted to be civil, there was no one more charming or helpful. He took Gaius and Lucius to one side and the plan was embraced with enthusiasm. Soon the pair were shaking hands while Gaius's dog barked and jumped around for joy. It turned out that Gaius knew lots of people who could employ Lucius; moreover, he still had his old workshop and would be delighted if his new friend could make use of it. He added with a twinkle that his town was full of beautiful young ladies.

On hearing this Topaz grimaced a little and looked down at her feet. And Lucius, always the gentleman, came and put his arm round her.

It was not easy to say goodbye. While Charlie went to buy some provisions for the journey and Nathan and Jake returned to ready the *Conqueror* for the voyage to Messina (via Herculaneum, to drop off Austerio), Topaz and Lucius wandered along the quay. They bought some fruit and sat on a low wall, watching the ships come and go. Lucius got down on one knee in a last vain attempt to persuade Topaz to stay with him. In the end, however, they both returned to the ship looking miserable.

Lucius gave everyone a hug – holding onto Jake for a full minute before whispering in his ear, 'I hope you find your brother, Yake.'

'I hope you find yours,' Jake replied earnestly.

'Look after yourself. I will never forget you. Not as long as I live.'

Lucius and Topaz shared a final sad embrace, then the four History Keepers – and Austerio – boarded the ship and cast off.

Jake and Topaz stood side by side at the stern, staring back at the dwindling figures of Lucius and Gaius. Jake remembered the story Rose had told him on their way there – how she had fallen in love with a farmer in Peru. *Of course, it's hopeless falling for a civilian*, she had sighed, *because they can't go back with you. It's hard enough explaining you live on the other side of the world, let alone the other end of history.* Jake said nothing to Topaz, but reached out and took her hand. It was warm, soft, trembling. She squeezed Jake's fingers and a lump went down her throat.

Austerio was tremendously excited by the speed at which the ship tore across the sea, and kept offering up theatrical blessings to Neptune. At Herculaneum, they accompanied him to the theatre and he bade them a dramatic farewell – before being reunited with his long-lost 'enemy', Fico the Fantastic. On seeing the two actors together for the first time, it was quite clear to everyone that in fact they were utterly devoted to one another.

When the youngsters reached the open sea again, Nathan appeared at Jake's side with the sword that he had confiscated. 'I believe this belongs to you,' he said. It was the weapon with the dragon hilt that Nathan had presented to him at Point Zero. Luckily Jake had left it in the Roman bureau, accidentally taking Nathan's, when he had rushed off on his crazy mission.

'Thank you,' he said, taking it gratefully. Then he added with a timid smile, 'I've learned a lesson or two.'

'The truth is, we all get carried away from time to time,' Nathan said. 'At a ball once in Habsburg, Vienna, I thought I could carry off skin-tight leopard print. I was the laughing stock of the city.' His tone became more serious. 'Every one of us is hot-headed from time to time – even Charlie has his moments.'

They headed south for Messina, and before long

sighted the hills of the large island. Just before they had set off, Nathan had sent a Meslith to Point Zero, informing the commander of their progress. They, in turn, had contacted Rose and Jupitus, who were standing very close together on the quay when the *Conqueror* arrived.

Jake jumped ashore before they had even docked, and gave his aunt a great hug. She pretended to be horrified by all his cuts and bruises but really felt quite proud. Jupitus waved at another ship along the quay, announcing that the *Hippocampus* was fully operational again and that they should all set sail immediately. Then he gathered up his crutches, limped over and struggled aboard alone.

'You two getting on all right?' Jake asked tentatively.

Rose grinned. 'Surprisingly well. Why don't you come with us and tell me all about your adventures?'

When Jake had first seen the *Hippocampus* at Point Zero, he'd felt sure that he'd seen it before. As he climbed aboard now, he had the same sensation: its sun-bleached timbers, its sails of cream and blue stripes were still familiar.

Both ships set off across the bay side by side. Within minutes they had rounded the lighthouse and were heading for the open sea.

Rose appeared from below with a tray of tea and biscuits. 'Refreshments . . .' She handed a cup to Jupitus. He took it, barely raising a smile; then Rose and Jake sat down cross-legged and started dunking their biscuits.

'Why do I recognize this ship?' Jake asked.

'What's that, darling?'

'I feel like I know it somehow – even the name . . .'

Rose was one of those people who could neither lie nor keep a secret without blushing or becoming twitchy. She was now doing both: fiddling with her teacup as her cheeks went red. Jake examined her suspiciously, making her even more self-conscious.

'You know something, don't you? There *is* a reason the ship's familiar . . . When I asked Mum and Dad about it before, they started behaving oddly too.'

'I'm not behaving oddly,' she insisted.

'Rose, you've gone pink.'

'Drat! I'll get into such trouble if I say anything. Your parents have sworn me to secrecy.'

'So there *is* a secret!'

Rose took a slurp of tea and munched a biscuit, wondering what to do. Finally she sighed. 'Well, I suppose you were going to find out soon enough.'

Jake felt a thrill of excitement, as if he were about to hear something momentous. He was not disappointed. Rose looked round and checked that Jupitus wasn't listening, then leaned in close. 'You *have* sailed on this ship before, a number of times . . . when you were a baby.'

'A baby?' gasped Jake. 'I don't understand.'

'When you were very young,' she whispered, 'your parents and I took some trips on it together, as a family. Alan, Miriam, me, you . . . Philip.' And now the bombshell: 'The last time was Persia, 1327—'

'Persia? 1327?' Jake stammered.

'I remember because your mother had terrible toothache,' Rose reflected.

Jake had to get up and go to the rail to take some calming breaths. 'So I've been to history before?'

'Just a couple of times – before we all gave it up. It seemed wrong to leave you at home. And you were no trouble at all. Spent most of the time sleeping.'

Jake laughed.

'I suppose you'll have to tell your mum and dad I let the secret slip. No doubt I'll be in the dog house.'

At length the passengers on both ships took their doses of atomium in preparation for the horizon point. After the appalling outward journey, Jake braced himself for more of the same. But, although it was as dramatic, with the same amazing out-of-body experience, he didn't suffer any horrific hallucinations. They vaulted all the way to the Atlantic, to an entry point in the Bay of Biscay, just west of La Rochelle. It was getting dark by the time that Jake spied the conical shape of the Mont St Michel in the distance.

Ever since Rose's confession, Jake's mind had been working overtime, mulling over the information that he had already travelled into deep history as a young child. He had asked her a number of other questions but, making sure that Jupitus wasn't within earshot, she insisted that his parents should fill him in on the rest. Now he clung to the rail at the prow of the *Hippocampus*, willing her on. He had so much to say to his parents – not just about Rose's revelation, but about Philip.

So when the ship docked just behind the

Conqueror, to an enthusiastic welcome, Jake was the first to disembark, running down the gangplank towards his parents.

'Heaven's above! What have they done to you?' asked Miriam. Like Rose, she was taken aback by the damage to his face.

'Miriam, that's no way to greet him.' Alan pinched Jake's cheek. 'This is what an adventurer looks like.'

Jake was about to blurt out his news, when Jupitus suddenly gave an urgent cry. 'Foreign craft approaching!' Everyone turned at once.

Another ship, its slanting sails silhouetted in the twilight, was cutting across the sea towards them. Instinctively the whole group huddled together as Galliana quickly produced a telescope from her belt and examined the vessel.

'It's Chinese,' she said, sounding equally alarmed.

'Should we arm ourselves?' asked Jupitus.

It was enough for Oceane to clutch at her pearls and retreat into the safety of the castle, pulling Josephine along behind her.

Galliana continued to stare through her telescope, examining the occupants of the craft. She could make out six silhouettes, standing at the prow. 'I've seen this ship before. It belongs to the Chinese bureau.' Then, as she identified one of the passengers, she relaxed. 'That is Madame Tieng, no question.'

There was a communal sigh of relief.

'Are you sure?' asked Jupitus.

Galliana nodded. 'She is smiling at me.'

'Who is Madame Tieng?' Jake asked.

'She's the commander's counterpart in Peking,' whispered Miriam. 'A formidable lady. But what on earth is she doing here?'

Eventually the ship docked, a gangplank was lowered and the travellers nervously filed down onto the pier; distinguished-looking men and women, all dressed in exquisite Chinese clothes. Jake noticed there were no youngsters amongst them – they were mostly Galliana's age. They shivered in the brisk Atlantic wind. The ladies looked like rare flowers imported from some exotic clime.

Madame Tieng, a striking white-haired woman with black eyes and rosebud lips, stepped forward and bowed to Galliana.

'We escaped in the dead of night,' she informed her. 'The Chinese bureau has been ransacked.'

'Ransacked?' Galliana asked, trying hard to hold onto her emotions. 'By whom?'

Madame Tieng looked up at her. She shook her head and closed her eyes. 'By Xi Xiang's men,' she said. 'I sent a young team in search of him, but I believe we are all now in danger.'

There was a horrified gasp. Jake had no idea who Xi Xiang was, but it was clear from the hurried, nervous conversations that another mission would soon be sanctioned, perhaps to the east – maybe to China itself. He already longed to be part of it. His father was right: he was an adventurer, it was in his blood. He was a History Keeper – surely he had proved that now. And, after all, he had travelled to history as a baby.

He turned round and locked eyes with Topaz; then both of them looked out to sea. Jake thought again of his brother Philip. The Atlantic breeze seemed to stir his heart.

'You're alive,' he murmured as it ruffled his hair. 'I know you are out there . . .'

ACKNOWLEDGEMENTS

Once again I would like to thank the five wise goddesses: Jo Unwin, Becky Stradwick, Sue Cook, Sophie Nelson and Lauren Bennett for all their incredible work and never-ending support. And, of course, Ali Lowry for being his fantastic self.

Finally I would like to dedicate this book to my brother Justin, and to Berne, Lukas and Zak – in memory of Justine, a wonderful and inspiring lady, who will never be forgotten.

COMING SOON

THE
HISTORY
KEEPERS
NIGHT SHIP TO CHINA